About the Author

Joan Westerman grew up in the post war era in Newcastle, Australia. Her earliest memories were forged by the seaside, and indeed the sea was in her blood. As a child in a large family, Joan felt isolated from her older siblings, who were all so different. As an adult, her teaching career took her to many rural and city locations, where she experienced friendship and a sense of belonging.

Joan has now retired to a small seaside community, where she resides happily with her partner.

Dedication
To my soulmate, Briar, and my children and
grandchildren.
Thank you for sharing the journey.

Joan Westerman

ARCHIE

AUSTIN MACAULEY
PUBLISHERS LTD.

A CIP catalogue record for this title is available from the British Library.

ISBN: 9781784553326 (paperback)
ISBN: 9781784553333 (eBook)

www.austinmacauley.com

First Published (2016)
Austin Macauley Publishers Ltd.
25 Canada Square
Canary Wharf
London
E14 5LB

Acknowledgments

To all those who have overcome hardship to lead a fruitful life.

Chapter One

The bubble was rising slowly within, and Archie could feel the hot anger pushing and shoving. It was almost as though it threatened to choke him, but he fought to gain control. He knew why the feelings of rage and despair were coming back, and he wanted to deal with them somehow, but now was not the time. He had other things to do. Other things to attend to. No, now would not do at all.

Outside he could hear the soft pad of feet coming nearer through the spinifex, and he called out a greeting.

"Hey Jesse, z'at youse out there, eh?"

There was silence for a short moment, then the rustling sound of legs brushing the dry grass nearby. Archie waited patiently, for he understood the importance of the elements of surprise and invitation that were necessary even now amongst his mates. Despite their so-called 'savvy', they were still ruled by the customs and culture of the elders, and chose to accept and recognise the links with the past. Otherwise, what did they have, now that most of the land and the stories and the patterns of life were all but fading from their lives?

"Yeh, watcha doin', man? We's bin waitin' fer ya down by th'ol creek bed, eh," called Jesse, the taller of the two approaching boys, "where ya bin?"

"Yeh, Arch, watcha doin' in here all by yerself? We's bin lookin' fer ya all over," chimed in Jackson, the scrawny and motley one.

Archie smiled and tried to shake off the anger that had been stalking him, not wanting it to spoil the afternoon that lay ahead. He knew that the three of them could suit themselves for the rest of the day, and there were lots of places they could go without restriction. That was one of the things he most enjoyed about community life; the freedom and independence.

He shook his head and smiled at his mates. He'd known them for as long as he could remember, ever since they were all born right here at the edge of the old cattle station. He looked around at the familiar landscape as they came towards him, and suddenly the clouds that had settled within his head were gone, just like that.

Archie laughed and hooted out with glee. "Wanna go down the river bed to th'ol' fishin' hol youse guys? There might be some ol' line we could chuck in. Might catch us a barra' fer tea, eh?"

"Dunno, mate," replied Jesse.

But Jackson was all for it, and started off along the path towards the river without looking back, knowing full well that the others would soon follow.

"Geez, wait up will ya?" wailed Jesse. "How come yer in such a godawful rush all of a sudden, eh, waddya doin' yer mad bastard Jacko?"

Archie clicked into gear and ran after Jacko, with Jesse suddenly spurting alongside. It felt good to be out here in the red dirt with his mates. Just the three of them, as it was so often. No adults, no school, no teachers, no little kids, no chores; nothing, just them and the bush. He hollered and yelled aloud, letting go of the ghosts that had haunted him when the bubbles of anger were stuck in his gut. It felt great to be alive suddenly, and he knew that the others felt it too.

Small clouds of red dust rose as they ran, and their tough feet kicked up pebbles and bits of grass from time to time. They ran and they ran, easily covering the long distance to the waterhole by mid-afternoon. They were fit and lean and hard, and their adolescent bodies glistened with tiny beads of sweat in the heat of the Kimberley sun, but it meant nothing to them as they ran.

It simply came naturally, it was their heritage. It was what defined them in this space of time, but the three boys were oblivious to life-issues as they stopped at the waterhole and fell to the ground.

They lay spread-eagled on the hot sand under the huge river-gums, panting from the long run. Their eyes were closed against the glare of the piercing Kimberley sun beating down on them. Their bodies rose and fell rhythmically with their breathing patterns, slowing gradually as they lay recovering. Their minds were almost empty, but not quite. Images of their people and their land formed a backdrop of unconscious patterns, but they didn't recognise the meanings just yet.

Suddenly Archie broke the silence.

"Eeeeeh! Hev youse waddya doin'? Lez go, eh?"

Jacko and Jesse rolled over and opened their eyes slowly, scanning around for a few seconds before leaping to their feet to follow Archie. They stood at the top of the sand hills that led to the water, watching and waiting, checking things out. They looked up at the sky and the trees and out over the long plain of spinifex that led to the rocky outcrops far away now in the distance.

This was their country, their peoples' country, the birthplace of their ancestors; and they belonged. They knew of the tracks of the animals and the smells of the bush and the local bush tucker and the songs and legends of their people since time had begun out here in the vast tract of Kimberley dirt and scrub. It was who they were and why they were, but now there was something else too.

Now there was another belonging. Another life. Another way. The three boys had all experienced it, all tasted it, all been absorbed by it; but they were still set apart.

Whitefella culture. Whitefella ways. Whitefella rules.

They were blackfella eh, and proud of it too, but somehow the collision of the two worlds was part of their life, and they were stuck with it forever.

"Come on youse two!" Jesse yelled, as he rolled down the sandy river bank and splashed into the water at the bottom. "Come on in, there ain't no crocs in this one!" he shrieked as he plunged deep into the cool clear water below.

"Aaaaagh!" screamed Archie, as he and Jacko followed Jesse don the long sandy hill to the water.

"Watch me youse!" shouted Jacko, as he danced and jumped and leaped down the sand and splashed noisily into the cool water with his mates. "Shit this is grouse, eh?" Water tossed and splashed and cascaded around the three boys in great shiny arcs, as they flung their arms round and round and round. Jacko was the most competitive of the three, and began showing off to his mates as usual. His antics made the others laugh, as they watched him try trick after trick in the water beside him. Handstands, leaps, dives, twists, kicks, splashes.

"Looka' me Jesse, watch me Archie, ain't that sumpin', ain't it eh?" Jacko cackled and spluttered at the others watching half-heartedly there in the cool water.

"Geez youse got tickets on yerself aincha, waddya reckon eh Archie?" said Jesse, turning away from the cavorting figure of Jacko. They were both tiring of his antics by now.

"Yeh, bloody mongrel showorf bastard!" replied Archie, feeling a bit left out.

"Wanna race to th'other side, youse?" called out Jacko suddenly, grinning from ear to ear. He knew that he was the strongest swimmer of the three, and he knew that the others knew too, but he reckoned that he could con them into one more race. Yeh, he reckoned he could.

"Nah, not me," answered Jesse, "why doncha jez race Archie this time, he's orright."

"Shit youse, both of yez, why me, eh?" snorted Archie indignantly, "buggered if I'm gunna lose ta that mongrel again!"

Jacko and Jesse both cracked up laughing at Archie's suddenly seriousness; it was only a friendly challenge after all.

They couldn't understand Archie's moodiness, and the look of annoyance on his shiny black face made them both laugh even more.

"Geez Arch, would ja just 'av a look at yer, fair dinkum yer's gawn all gaga on us, ain't 'e, eh Jacko?" screeched Jesse, laughing fit to burst by now.

"Christ Archie, get a hold of yerself will ya fer gawd's sake," chipped in Jacko, who was oblivious to Archie's earlier moods.

Ignoring Archie for the moment, the others turned away and started a splashing fight there in the middle of the river, hooting and laughing and shouting with glee. They were carefree and uncluttered, and Archie watched them carefully out of the corner of his eye, wishing that he could just lighten up a little and join in their antics.

"Aw come on will ya, Arch, let's all swim over th'other side, waddya say?" called out Jacko, trying to ease his friend back into the fun a little.

"Yeh, Arch, come in will ya, we ain't got all day 'av we? Sun'll be goin down in a cupl'a hours, an' wel'll 'av to head home," put in Jesse, attempting to end Archie's moodiness for the time being.

Archie looked over at his mates and made a quick decision; he would have to 'get over' it for now. They were out here together, and they were supposed to be having fun. It should have been a time to share laughter and to have a bit of a clown around and he was spoiling it for them. He knew that he needed to snap out of it and join in the skylarking with the others.

"Righto youse two, let's race to th'other side then, ready set go!" shouted Archie, as he dived clear of his mates and came up in the shiny translucent water a metre or so ahead of them, swimming flat out.

"Orright you bastard, orright!" shouted the others, as they splashed their way in hot pursuit across the water.

"Bastard mongrel Archie, yers cheatin' again!" they spluttered.

It was a good twenty metres to the other side of the river at this point, and the silence of the afternoon was now broken by the loud splashes and raucous laughter of the three boys as they endeavoured to win the race to the other side. They all thought that Jacko would win, but Archie and Jesse tried their hardest anyway. You never know what might happen, they reasoned.

The sun was still high in the sky and the heat haze shimmered in the bright azure blue above the riverbank as the boys drew near the other side. The trees and spinifex and the bush were all still. No animals could be seen in this hot part of the day, for it was too early for feeding time yet.

As they neared the other side, it was Archie who led the trio, with Jesse and Jacko close behind him.

"Yahoo, I did it!" screamed out Archie as he hit the sand first. "Yeh man, woohoo!"

"Shit, owdya do that, Arch mate, I was goin' flat out!" panted Jacko, as he flopped in the shallows beside Archie. "Bugger me!"

"Struth, Arch, waddya been eatin' lately, ya fair flew across that water mate!" gasped Jesse, as he splashed in beside them in the shallows.

"I reckon yers bin takin' them steroid thingies, Arch, ha!"

Archie rolled over and lay on the sandy bank at the edge of the river. He closed his eyes while he got his breath back. He smiled as he looked over at his mates; he was damned pleased with himself for winning the race. It was a good feeling, this small victory. They all knew that Jacko had been the strongest swimmer forever, and normally no one could beat him. Usually they didn't even get close; but today he had won. It felt good, real good!

The other two boys wanted to get over the race and let it go, but Archie was suddenly feeling strong and powerful and invincible, so he tried to string things out a bit longer there on the shore. He pushed their buttons and tried to gloat a little, knowing that Jacko would rise quickly to the bait. He knew that really he shouldn't tease, but it was such an ingrained trait, such a part of their lives, that he couldn't resist the urge this time; after all, it was now his turn to brag.

"Geez, Jacko, youse been on the grog or sumpin', mate, I beat ya hands down!" he boasted, puffing up his chest with pride.

"Bloody smart alec Archie, reckon yers funny do yers? We'll race back later an' see jez how good yers are, orright?" snapped back Jacko, none too pleased with the goading from his mate.

"OK, yers on!" grinned Archie, who was beginning to think that if he'd beaten Jacko once, then maybe he could do it again. He lay on his back gazing up at the harsh blue sky, and noticed that the sun was now moving towards the west. Archie knew what that meant, he had grown up with the sun and the stars and the moon and the earth as his backdrop, and he knew without conscious thought the time of day and the seasons and weather and animal habits in the bush that was his home. He knew how the earth changed in cycles, and the differences between the dry and the wet up here in the Kimberley. This was the gift of his people, his heritage, his tribe. This belonged to him and he to it; the people and the land were fused, and would always be so. Theirs was the dreaming.

Jesse sat up suddenly and prodded Jacko to get up. The two boys stood over Archie, demanding and insistent. They knew it was getting late, and they wanted to fish before they left the waterhole. Maybe they'd catch some barra' to take back to camp and cook over the open fire. Ah, that'd taste good!

"Come on youse, let's find some line an' go fishin' while there's still time. Git orf yer arses youse!" exclaimed Jesse, wanting to break the spell of the swimming race, and get back to reality once more. He knew that they had only about an hour left before they had to head back to camp, and he wanted to catch something for their tea. To show off a little. To make them worthy. To provide for the women and kids. To show the elders that they were fast growing into men who could hunt and kill.

"Spread out and see who can find some line first!" Jesse yelled to his companions, encouraging them to join in another kind of race. It was still a competition, after all, and maybe he could win this time.

They were all up and scrambling around the water's edge now, digging and flicking sand everywhere in their hunt for line to fish with. It was Jacko who found some first, and he hollered with success as he dragged some tangled fishing line, complete with hook, from the lower branch of a nearby tree.

"Yeehaa, I've got some line!" he yelled. "Just looka' that boys!"

Archie and Jessie glanced around at Jacko before scrambling over to where he sat, and began pulling at the line he had found. They wanted some for themselves, and reckoned that if they untangled enough, then maybe they could all have a piece each. But what would they do for hooks?

They continued the search now for anything they could fashion into fishing hooks, maybe an old nail or a bit of rusty wire. Meanwhile, Jacko had cast his line into the waterhole already carving the water cleanly with the invisible line, as though slicing a cake. Jesse and Archie watched enviously for a moment from their vantage point further along the sandy bank, before resuming their search.

"Got some mate!" called Jesse. "Here ya go, there's heap of ol' fence wire buried in the sand right here."

Archie turned to see Jesse smiling gleefully at his discovery, and suddenly the joy that he'd felt over the swimming victory was gone. It had disappeared, and in its place he could feel the dark clouds gathering once more. He was baffled and disappointed and angry and hurt, and he sensed that the whole afternoon was turning against him.

Turning competitive again. Shutting him out.

He wanted to just have fun, but he sensed that what the others thought was trivial was more serious for him. More meaningful. Deeper somehow. It wasn't really all about the three of them anymore; there was something much more than that just under the surface, and he wanted to scratch below and root it out. He wanted to identify what it was. Archie knew that he shouldn't let it get to him; but it did anyway, and that was the problem.

There were times when it didn't really matter if he felt alone or flat or angry, but now was not one of those times. Archie was only too aware that his mates wouldn't understand his current mood. He knew from past experience that they would tease him and taunt him and poke fun at him for being different, and he knew that would only make things worse. Far worse. And he didn't want that to happen right now.

He kicked the sand and sent a spray of coarse grains hurtling into the water. He watched as they dissolved into tiny bubbles below the surface, and though of the fish that must be lurking there somewhere. He turned back to the others and hollered out to them.

"Any've youse bastards caught a barra' yet, or what? Come on youse, we've gotta head back in a little while 'fore it gets dark. They'll skin us if we're late again!"

"Get over it, Arch, we're not leavin' till one ov us has gotta fish, orright, mate?" replied Jacko, casting his line out again over the edge of the waterhole then propping in the lower branch of a nearby gum tree.

"Geez, Arch, why doncha jez siddown an' catch yer own fish mate, a decent sized one too. Then we c'n chuck this stuff an' git back ta camp safe before dark, yer moody bastard!" joined in Jesse, not to be outdone by Jacko in the judgement stakes.

"Ah, screw both of yers, I don't care if we catch a fish or not, I'm gowin' back soon with or without yers both, so there!" cried Archie angrily, sulking off to a small sandbar out of sight of the others.

He could feel his temper rising and the hot bubbles returning. He felt strange and sticky and hot. His neck ached and his skin prickled, and his gut was twisting inside. It seemed like no one understood him at all, and he could feel a big knot somewhere within. He felt odd. Sick even. Weird. He knew that the others wanted to be his mates, and he thought that was enough; but it wasn't. And that made him sad.

Archie didn't really know what it was that set him apart from his mates. He knew that it had something to do with who he was, but apart from that, he couldn't really quantify or label what made him the way he was.

He tried not to think about the differences, but somehow they always crept into his life, and Archie didn't always handle things too well. He didn't have the tools or strategies yet to define and manage his thoughts and feelings, but he knew that they were there.

"Christ, willya look at that youse, a bloody bewdy, jez lookadim go, yeeha!" shrieked Jacko from the edge of the waterhole, watching rapt as a big barramundi took his hook.

They all stood and watched from the shady shore as the giant fish leaped and splashed in the hot afternoon sun, marvelling at the size of the thing, and at Jacko's luck.

"Now who's the best at fishin', eh?" grinned Jacko from the bank, as he struggled to hang onto the twisting line. The fish was heavy and cumbersome, and he desperately fought its

twists and turns, not wanting to lose the damned thing in front of his mates.

"Geez, Jacko, how'd do that, yer crazy bastard!" yelled the others, somewhat envious of their scrawny mate as he struggled with the fish. They had often caught fish themselves at the same waterhole, but nothing of this size yet. They were both a little excited and a little jealous of Jacko's catch. Archie secretly wished that it had been his line that had caught the fish, and almost hoped that Jacko would lost it or snag his line before landing the barra' on the riverbank.

But Jacko held on and played the fish for a while till it tired, and then he slowly and carefully dragged the brute to the shallow water at his feet, before swooping on it and grabbing it with both hands. He raised the prize above his head and jumped around in a small victory dance, bragging and boasting and showing off to his mates. Then he held it out to his friends for their inspection, knowing full well that they would be pretty envious and impressed.

"Ripper fish, Jacko," said Archie dejectedly.

"Yeh, so'orright s'pose," chimed in Jesse, "wish I'd caught the bloody thing, but!"

All three of them stood around and stared at the fish for a few moments, and then Archie broke the silence.

"C'arn youse, it's getting' late, we'd better get gowin' if we wanna git back to tha camp 'fore it's dark. C'arn youse, 'urry up!"

They set off at a trot along the dry dusty track back towards the camp, back towards their people. Jacko carried the barramundi in his old T-shirt slung over his shoulder, but even so it was heavy going. Pretty soon the pace and the heat and the dry spinifex got to him, and he started to lag behind the others.

"Aw wait up youse, this bloody barra' is heavy, 'ow about yers take turns at carryin' the bastard, eh?" he mumbled, sprinting to catch the others.

"Yer gotta be kiddin'," laughed Jesse, "it's your bloody fish, mate!"

But Archie reckoned they'd all get a share of the fish tonight once it was cooked over the coals of the hot fire back at the camp, so he relented and took the fish from Jacko for a while. He joined the others and kept up their stride, determined not to let them know what he was thinking. Determined to keep to himself tonight.

Jesse finally relented too, and called out, "Here, Arch, chuck the damn thing here willya, I'll 'av a go fer a while!"

Jacko grinned; he knew that his mates wouldn't let him down. Hadn't they always shared everything?

He watched as the sun began to sink lower and lower in the sky, knowing they would only just make it back to camp in time. But the barra' would help, it would get them off the hook this time. The women would cook it, watched by the envious eyes of the camp kids as they played nearby in the red dust by the firelight. The dogs would growl and snap at each other as they smelled the fish cooking, waiting for some spoils. And he reckoned the men might even be a little bit proud of his catch, but he knew they would never say so.

Chapter Two

The dusk was fast turning to dark as the three mates neared the outskirts of the camp, and they paused for a spell, hidden by the dry clumps of spinifex. They could hear the camp noises as they sat and regained their breath; kids wailing, adults shouting, dogs barking incessantly. Archie could hear other sounds too; sounds that he couldn't share with his mates, sounds from the past, sounds that choked him. But he didn't let on.

The wind was picking up a bit, and they could now hear the whoosh it made through the bush, and the clank clank of loose tin on old roofs. Somewhere a door banged back and forth in the wind, and old window shutters thumped against wood and steel in the rusty and neglected dongas at the edge of the camp. These were the sounds and images given to them by the whitefella world; but they were their sounds too. Whitefella steel, blackfella homes; it was all merged into one inextricably here in the dark Kimberley outback which had once oh-so-long ago been only blackfella country.

The three boys had grown up with the merger of black and white worlds for as long as they could remember; it was all that they knew. They accepted their world at face value. It was their life. (But Archie yearned for something deeper, something more tangible, something he couldn't explain; he just knew it was somehow *there*).

Archie had sensed it from his first defining moment; it was a part of what made him different, but he struggled to clarify it and label it. It was too early on the roadmap of his life for that, but he knew it was there all the same.

"Eh, Archie, reckon they'll be wonderin' where we are yet, mate? Better get gowin' 'fore they get cranky on us, eh mate?" whispered Jacko, anxious to present his catch to the mob.

He was pretty pleased with himself for catching the barramundi, and he knew that he'd be able to get a fair bit of mileage out of the fishing story up at the camp. He knew that the little kids would be envious, and the adults would be pleased with the additional food it provided. He might even impress a couple of the teenage girls, and that would be something, he reckoned!

But Archie had retreated into his dark mood once more, and was now oblivious to Jacko and his damned fish. He scowled a curt reply, and then loped off through the shrub into the darkness, not wanting to be with the others any more.

He wanted to be alone. He wanted to sit by himself. He wanted to try to figure it out; but he didn't really know how, only that he couldn't be around people at the moment. It was just too hard.

"Aw, stuff yer then, g'wan, bugger off!" exclaimed Jacko, tired of Archie's antics at this time of day. It was late, and he was tired and hungry after their trip to the waterhole. Jacko was in no mood to pander to anyone at the moment. All he wanted was to sit down and let the women cook his tea, while he chatted to the adults and the kids about the afternoon at the river. Bugger Archie, he thought, let him sulk.

So Jacko and Jesse sauntered up to the camp by themselves, and went to the spot where the men were tending the campfire. They had lots to say and the fish to show, and they both reckoned that it would be a great night now that they were safe back in the camp. They knew that Archie would soon be forgotten, and it wasn't their fault that he'd gone off alone again. Damned if they'd take the blame!

***

It was getting late, and as Archie sat alone and hungry under the low rocky outcrop to the east of the camp, he wondered what it was that had set him off this time. He tried to understand his current unease, but all that he managed to do was to feel more isolated and betrayed.

He reckoned it had something to do with the mob, *his* mob; but he didn't know what exactly.

Back at the camp, Archie knew that the others would wonder where he had gone, and he also realised that the elders would be angry with him again for being absent. But that didn't stop him, and it didn't give him enough of a reason to return. His mind was still clouded with strange thoughts that darted through him and around him like bolts of lightning. He was hardly aware of his surroundings and the ever-darkening skies.

Archie was pulled out of his reverie by the sudden shrieking of birds overhead, high up in the rocks and crags above him. They were cawing and squabbling and flapping their wings madly against tree and branch and foliage somewhere, and Archie was now sufficiently alert to be distracted.

The noise and the fluttering spectacle relieved his moodiness long enough for him to take stock of his surroundings. Gone was the dense blackness within, as though it had almost never existed. Lightness re-entered his world once more, and just as suddenly as the burden of pain had enveloped his heart, it was gone.

Archie stood up and flung his arms and filled his lungs with the crisp night air. He danced and stomped and whooped with glee. He felt fresh and new and invigorated again, no longer afraid or lonely.

He rushed headlong back down the well-worn track to the camp. Back to the glow of the firelight. Back to his friends and his people. Back to where he belonged.

"Where's yer bin eh?" asked Jesse hesitantly, as Archie emerged from the darkness into the light. "We's bin worryin' about ya, mate!"

Archie grinned slowly at Jacko and Jesse. "Jes up th' track, youse, she's right OK?"

His mates knew better than to pursue the subject any further. Archie would tell them when he was good and ready. After all, they didn't want to spoil the joy of the fishing trip, or the camp fire cook-up. Things like that were simply not worth worrying about at present, so they let it go. They knew that Archie would be OK for a while now anyway. Him and his damn moods!

"Geez yer c'n be a right bastard sometimes Arch, gowin' orf like that all by yerself n'all, fair dinkum yer can!" complained Jacko, a bit peeved that Archie's absence had stolen a bit of his own thunder.

Jesse shoved in this two bob's worth as well, "Too right yer mongrel bastard Archie, gawd yer c'n be a right li'l bugger yer can, can't 'e eh, Jacko?"

"Too right!"

But Archie didn't care. He knew his mates well enough to know that they had been worried about him, that they really cared about him.

"Orright youse, gid over it willya's?" he replied softly, wanting to put an end to any further questions this evening.

But now the fire was roaring and sparking and sending flames shooting high into the night sky. The three young men squatted on the soft dirt a bit back from the flames, and were drawn into a trance as they watched, each sensing and feeling the close affinity with the fire.

This was blackfella stuff, blackfella belongin'. They knew their place and kinship and connections here in the vast Kimberley space, with the sky and the earth and the rocks and the animals and the people that were part of who they were. They knew it without words. They knew it without conscious thought. It had always been so.

But Archie felt the other thing intruding; the restlessness, the uncertainty, the unknown fear. He knew it was tied to their land, their customs, their spirit; but he didn't understand why just yet. And that made him mournful.

He sensed that it was connected to his maturing, his coming of age, his near-manhood; but it was taking over him in such fits and starts that he was left wondering most of the time. It was weird how upset he often got by the slightest remark or look or gesture from the other boys; he should have been used to it by now. But he wasn't; and it often left him hot and bothered and annoyed with himself.

He tried to blame the others of course, and his people. He blamed his parents and aunties and uncles for their indifference. He blamed the weather. He blamed the winds. But above all he blamed himself, and cursed his changing mind and body and see-sawing emotions.

Archie didn't as yet have much in the way of formal education; leastways in the paths of the whitefella system. His was a more cultural education; one that was passed down by the elders. But the trouble with that was, that it happened now only by chance; and less and less by design as the years went on, for the old structures had been sorely eroded by whitefella ways. Whitefella habits. Grog, gambling, welfare, cars, rifles, television sets, computers, houses, gardens, consumer goods, rubbish, trendy clothes, etc. Yeh, Archie had seen it all, and reckoned it was part of his problem. A big part.

***

He stretched and stood up and bent towards the fire. He could feel the warmth and smell the smoke and was seeped in the magic of it all, if only momentarily. Part of him felt like the little kid he had been only yesterday, but another part of him was already grown-up and yearning for fresh challenges.

Archie felt his emotions mingling with the physical thrills of untested sexuality, but this only caused him further grief and confusion. He knew that it had something to do with the way he felt about his mates; and Jesse in particular, and it made him a little ashamed. A little scared. But it was exciting nonetheless.

He cast a furtive glance over to where Jesse sat bathed in the glow of the arcing orange flames, and felt a surge of pure adrenalin run through him as he watched his friend. God he looked terrific, sitting there like some dark and brooding statue.

Archie hurriedly put any thoughts of physical contact out of his head, dismissing them as pure fantasy. But he secretly recognised them for what they were; and he knew that spelled trouble.

"Geez youse two, willya jez look at yers gone all still an' quiet. Penny fer 'em, eh?" muttered Jacko, breaking the brief silence there by the campfire.

Jesse responded by leaping to his feet and whacking Jacko a beauty in the arm with his fist. It was a playful gesture, but Jacko was stung by the impact, and howled at Jesse; "Bugger orf yer bastard!"

Archie responded by giving Jesse a playful thump, and before long the three of them were rolling round in the dirt by the fire, hooting and screaming and laughing fit to burst. They were boys once more, carefree and having fun, and Archie felt good.

Their play fighting came to an abrupt end as soon as the adults began kicking and shouting at them. "Gid out ov it willyers fer gawd's sakes?" yelled Jesse's mum, none too pleased to have the boys rolling round near the fire. "Gawn, git!" she shrieked.

The three boys jumped up laughing and dusted themselves off quickly there by the campfire, none too pleased at having been chastised in front of the elders.

It belittled them and made them look small, and they were conscious of losing some of the ground that they'd gained from the fishing escapade. Still, they were over it quickly, and sauntered off to where the little kids were playing.

"Wotcha doin' youse?" they called out to Jesse's little brother and his mates. "Wanna come an' see the big barra' we caught down the river eh?"

A swag of kids arrived suddenly, and followed Jacko and his mates over to the spot near the campfire where the big fish lay. They all admired it, and envied Jacko for catching it, but gave him a fair bit of good-natured cheek about it too.

"Aw geez, Jacko, I coulda' got one that big!"

"My ol' man reckons it took the three of yers ta catch 'im!"

"Don' look like much to me, man!"

Jacko got annoyed by their comments and soon tired of them. He was pissed off that things weren't working out so well. He'd expected more. He'd expected a lot more. He wanted some sort of adult recognition and acceptance. But not all this criticism from the little kids. "Be buggered if I'm gonna take this crap from yers all!" he exclaimed, and stomped off away from the fish and the fire and the teasing.

"Aw don' be an idiot, Jacko mate, they're only pullin' ya chain!" called his mates after him, hoping to lure Jacko back to the fun and the fire. "C'arn Jacko, s'orright mate!"

Archie felt sorry for his mate; he knew what it felt like to be shut out. To be let down. To be disappointed with the way things often worked out.

He wanted to reach out to Jacko and let him know that he understood, but he wasn't sure if Jacko would accept his help tonight. He wasn't sure if he trusted himself. He just wasn't sure.

But Jesse didn't care; he was indifferent to both of them at the moment, for other reasons. Girls. Teenage girls. Down from the top camp. Down for the food and the fish and the cook-up. He had spotted them sitting across from him in the soft yellow firelight, and his pulse was racing as he averted his eyes in confusion.

Jesse tried to act cool and indifferent. He sat and he watched and he waited. He didn't know what to do next, and he damn sure didn't want to mess things up. He needed to act cool, to stay safe, but geez did he fancy those girls! They were so damned tempting.

Meanwhile Archie had managed to get Jacko back to the campfire, and the two of them sat and enjoyed the activity of the cook-up beginning. It was relaxing just sitting back and enjoying the familiarity of it all, and the two mates felt peaceful and connected. They were home. They belonged. It felt right, and they knew it deep down in their bones.

Somehow they knew it had always been this way, from way back before whitefella had come here. Before things had changed. Before they had known the difference. Back in the dreamin'.

But all that had changed somehow, and now they had two worlds. Two cultures. Two paths; and sometimes it didn't feel so good. No, it sure didn't. Sometimes they reckoned that the whitefella path was better, stronger, easier than their blackfella ways; but still they clung to both.

Chapter Three

Archie was mesmerised by the fire, and the inner turmoil was stilled for now. He focused on the present, knowing that he would have to deal with inner issues sometime; but not now. It was so good being here with his mob for now, and he didn't want anything else to spoil his night. He felt proud and strong and calm finally; as though the day's dilemmas and anxieties had not really happened at all.

He wanted to just sit back and be absorbed by it all there at the campfire, and he knew the patterns and rituals that were supposed to get him through the night. It was all ingrained; a part of whom he was. Archie knew without question that he belonged here, had always belonged here; but still there was the tiny niggle of doubt about his future.

"C'arn youse," called Jacko, "let's git outa here fer a bit, waddya reckon eh?"

"Geez yer mad bugger, leave us alone fer a bit willya," replied Archi, not wanting to break the spell of the moment just yet.

But Jacko was suddenly insistent, and he pushed and prodded at Archie there by the fire. He was restless and he wanted some company and a fresh challenge before the food was cooked for their tea, so he kept at the others to come with him.

"C'arn willyers we'll go up th'other camp fer a bit, an' see who's hangin' round up there! Might be somethin' gowin' on ter entertain us, eh?" laughed Jacko persuasively, knowing that he'd get at least one of his mates to take the bait.

"Gawd yer c'n be a fair mongrel, yer can!" replied Jessie half-heartedly. He was still ogling the camp girls, and wanted to stay by the campfire for a bit, but he couldn't let the others know, or they would tease him mercilessly.

Archie decided that the idea of a brief diversion would be OK for a bit, so he joined Jacko. He knew that it would probably be another wasted foray into the top camp, but he thought that at least it would give him another chance to be with Jesse. (He hadn't seen the way Jess was eyeing off the girls, or he might have changed his mind. Definitely).

The three young men scarpered off through the bush along the track to the top camp, keeping their eyes and ears open for approaching figures. It was only a short walk, and as they neared the outskirts of the camp they kept to the side of the track and hid in the shadows of the rickety fences that surrounded the tired and worn dongas. In the darkness they could still see keenly. Their senses were pretty sharp, for they had grown up with the ways of the old hunters, despite the modern world.

Still, they were curious tonight, and alert for any trouble up here in this camp, for they knew that some of the occupants were tough and mean and a little creepy at times. 'Specially after the grog. And the gunja, and sniffin'.

There was none of that stuff down at their camp; the elders wouldn't allow it, and they knew it was a lot safer down there. But up here it was different. Up here bad people had got in. Up here at top camp there was the worst of the whitefella ways; and it hurt.

Archie stopped dead in his tracks at the sound of a 4WD approaching. It was going fast; engine revving loud. He could hear the sounds of shouts and whoops and cursing above the scream of the clapped-out motor, and he knew better than to show himself right now. He knew the consequences. He knew his people. He knew what the grog did to them. Yeah; sure he knew, and he had the scars to prove it, didn't he?

He cautioned to the others as they stood there silently in the shadows, holding a finger up to his lips and beckoning them to be quiet.

They stood stock still and waited as the pick-up roared past, churning the red dirt road with worn tires, and kicking up choking clouds of dust. They could smell the mix of diesel fumes and body sweat and alcohol and fear and craziness as the vehicle crashed and banged its way past, broadsiding a large clump of spinifex, and laying it flat. They knew that it would be dangerous and foolhardy to come out of the shadows till the coast was clear, so they hunkered down flat where they were, not moving so much as a muscle.

The night had suddenly become scary, and even though none of the boys would admit it, they were pretty afraid up there at the edge of the top camp. Damn afraid!

Archie was the first one to break the silence. "C'arn youse, let's git outa here, quick!" he whispered insistently. "Let's go!"

The others didn't need any convincing, they were off like a shot down the winding, rough track back to their own camp, and the safety of the fire and their family. They had sensed the unrest and urgency and despair and destructiveness up at the other camp, and they were damned sure that they didn't want any part of it. Not tonight. Not now. (Not yet).

But Archie somehow knew that it would reach out and grab them sometime, and maybe not let them go. He didn't know when, and he didn't know how or why; he simply *knew*. And that left him unsettled, angry, hurt, anxious, rebellious, confused. He didn't understand the implications of what they had witnessed. And felt. To him it seemed all wrong, as though someone had taken away the very souls of those blackfellas up at the other camp. And he didn't know how that could be. Or why. He just knew that somehow it was really *wrong*.

"Geez youse, that was shit-scary, eh?" exclaimed Jacko, as they got closer to their own camp.

"Christ mate, yer reckon!" chimed in Jessie, relieved to be back within sight of their own camp and the welcoming flames of the campfire crackling in the night sky.

The three mates began to feel human once more, as they rounded the last bend within sight of their camp.

"Yeh youse, I'm sure glad we're back here orright!" chipped in Archie. "Struth I am!"

As they approached the warm fire once more, it was as though they'd never left; and it felt good. Real good. Their spirits soared once again as they joined the others now; kids, dogs, elders, aunties, uncles, cousins. Their mob. Their people. Their life.

Gone were the recent images of the other camp. The shouting and roaring and strangeness and desperation and threats. It had receded and faded into nothingness now that they were back where they belonged, and the three boys were happy that it was so.

Archie threw himself on the soft red dirt at the western end of the fire, catching the sparks and smoke from time to time. He was exhausted by the adventures of the day, and their foray up to the top camp had almost completely drained him. He felt flat and wrecked, and a little becalmed. He was almost too tired to stay awake. He wanted to just lie down and sleep, but he knew that he was expected to participate in the evening rituals: the cook-up, the stories, the feeding, the sharing. Yes, he knew that he must; but tonight it was hard.

He closed his eyes briefly and dreamed of other things. Other people. Other bodies. In his mind's eye he could see himself with another, and he knew who it was. But he didn't want to know. Not yet. (Or did he?)

Archie tried hard to tune out and turn off his thoughts, but he couldn't. They were too strong. They were too sharp. They were too beautiful; and he wanted to keep them.

Archie felt like he was going through some sort of metamorphosis, and he wasn't at all sure whether it was normal. He had such strong urges and dreams and desires; stuff he couldn't share with the others. Stuff that both transformed him and bothered him. Stuff that sometimes he could do without.

Even so, it made his life interesting if nothing else, and often Archie withdrew into his secret world to escape. (But often it drew him in too, and those were the times he dreaded).

For Archie, there was nothing better than being alone with his new-found emotions and desires, even though they sometimes terrified him. They were electrifying and scary. They were heart stopping. They were fraught with the unknown; and that was exactly what caught Archie in constant dilemma.

It was as though suddenly the dichotomy of his existence was spread out before him; tantalisingly within reach, yet at the same time untouchable. Archie couldn't pinpoint exactly when he had started to feel this way, and he didn't have the words or the education or the skills to explain just what it was that was going on, but he knew that it was *there*.

He had sensed for some time that it had more to do with internal than external influences in his life, but how and why it had begun was still a mystery to Archie. He knew that his body was changing, and he knew that was pretty normal; after all, he'd grown up with the mob and their ways out here in the vast Kimberley plains. But Archie felt that somehow he was different. Somehow his changes were not the same as his mates. Somehow, he was all mixed up; and he didn't know why.

He wished just for once that things could stay the same; that they didn't have to go through the changes. That *he* didn't have to go through the changes. But at the back of his mind he knew that wouldn't happen. That his life *was* changing. And in more ways than one.

Archie sighed and stirred and flicked some dirt casually at the fire, wondering yet again if his mates knew what he was thinking there by the campfire. He guessed not. He knew that they were far more pre-occupied with more mundane matters. More earthy things. Fire, food, talk, song, teasing, bragging, laughing, escaping. He knew that his mates were going through the body changes just like him; but Archie was sure that they couldn't even begin to know what things were on his mind these days. At least, he hoped not. Especially Jesse.

"Hey, Arch, waddya doin' mate?" called Jacko from the other end of the clearing. "How's about sharin' some fish with us, eh?"

But Archie stayed silent, for he was watching Jesse, who was prowling around the girls from the top camp by now. He realised that Jesse was keen on the girls, and he knew deep down that was normal. But he also knew the feelings *he* had for his mate; and he worried and sweated that it was *not* normal; and that was a big part of his problem.

He closed his eyes again until they were tiny slits, just open enough to watch Jesse through the smoke of the fire. He felt so strong and manly and powerful just looking at him; but so confused too. Almost ashamed. Guilty.

Archie didn't know why he should feel these things; he only knew that he did. And it left him feeling odd. Hurt. Shut out. He wanted to still be mates with the others. He wanted to resume their normal life. He wanted desperately to wake up and find that he was only dreaming; but he knew that was not going to happen. For Archie, the thing that he most desired was out of his reach; or that's how it seemed to him anyhow.

It wasn't only about Jesse; he knew that. But Jesse was part of it. A big part. And somehow that changed things for Archie, things that he didn't really want changed. Things that he'd rather stay the same. But he knew that they couldn't; not now.

Geez, Jesse looks great, he thought. Stirred his gut. Made Archie hide in confusion. Archie wanted so badly to reach out and trace his fingers along Jesse's arm. To feel the warmth of his skin. To touch and sizzle and burn with the flames, but he knew that he couldn't and wouldn't; at least not yet anyway. Not ever. Maybe.

He glanced over furtively to gaze one more time at his mate, breaking out into a sweat just at the sight of his smooth hard skin, and his rough textured profile. To Archie Jesse looked perfect, and he thought that if he held his breath and captured this moment in time he could never be happier. The secret of the knowing and the anticipation of the not knowing was pure bliss, and all Archie's senses were alert and receptive.

It wasn't as though these feelings had just suddenly snuck up on Archie, he knew that they had been simmering for some time. But still, the recognition and the acceptance were two different things, and Archie was confused and elated at the same time.

He wanted so badly to tell someone, to talk it through; but he didn't know anyone he could confide in amongst his mob. It was not something that was readily accepted, and he knew then well enough to keep things to himself. He knew that disclosure would bring ridicule and teasing and hurt and reprisal and recrimination. He knew that the mob could be cruel. Unaccepting. Intolerant of differences. And sometimes barbaric.

Archie figures that for now it was his problem. And his alone. He could see no alternative but to hide his new-found passion; it simply had to be that way for now. He didn't know how long he could keep the emotions at bay, but he knew that he must in order to survive here with his mob, his family, his people. It was their way, and he accepted that for now. Always had; but maybe not for good.

Maybe he would change some day. Maybe he would leave the mob. Maybe he would branch out and go away from here and find another belonging somewhere else. Maybe; just maybe.

But all this was far from Archie's thoughts as he sat still by the fire watching Jesse, and marvelling at the depth of his animal instinct. His emotions. His longing. It felt good despite his uncertainty, and Archie wanted it to stay this way for just a little bit longer tonight. He didn't want things to change. He didn't want other people to know. He knew that everything would alter in its own time, but for now it was enough simply to be here near his mates. Watching. Waiting. Dreaming. He needed some space and some time in between where he was now and where he wanted to be, but part of him reasoned that there was nothing he could do tonight.

For Archie, the patterns of his life were structured by blackfella-time, and he knew that there was no escaping that for now. It was how it had always been out here in the Kimberley with his tribe, and even though Archie had been resisting the pull of other forces for some time, he knew things would not change for his mob. Not yet, anyway.

It was different up at the top camp. Some of his tribe were up there too, and more of the young kids were drifting up there from time to time. Looking for action. Searching out trouble. Seeking a glimpse of another way. Another lifestyle. Whitefella ways. Yeah, whitefella ways.

Archie knew what they got up to at the top camp; he'd been up there a few times. Snuck out with his mates. Gone skylarking. Watched the antics of some of the mob up there. Seen the booze. Smelled the gunja. Heard the fights and hoots and screams.

Chapter Four

Yeah, he knew alright. And it bothered him. Bothered him heaps. Sometimes Archie dreamed that the bad stuff that went on up at the top camp would creep into his mob too. Take over. Change everything. But so far it hadn't. So far the elders had managed to keep it out. Yeah, so far they had. But Archie knew that really it was only a matter of time before things changed. He knew, yeah he knew.

Archie reckoned that without some of the whitefella ways, everything would stay just fine, but he was smart enough to accept and enjoy the benefits of the good stuff too. The trouble was that he had grown up so far with both systems bound together, and he was starting to question the boundaries. To feel the pressures of both systems. To test his own culture just a little. And to wonder more and more about the whitefella ways. But what sometimes bothered Archie these days was that a part of him really *wanted* to try out the stuff going round up at the top camp. Wanted to experiment. Needed to test the murky waters of grog and gunja and parties and sex. Sometimes Archie craved the unknown, and it seemed to him that maybe the answers were up there at the other camp; forbidden and elusive and out-of-bounds for now; but not for always. Not forever.

***

Archie leaned back against the old gnarled stump and sighed. He was feeling out of sorts. Alone. Misunderstood, rejected, impatient. He wanted to join his mates at the fishing hole and have some fun by the water, but something held him back again. Something stalled and sank within. Archie felt restless.

He knew that the others would wonder where he was, but that didn't change how he felt, and Archie didn't want to join them in his current state. He knew they would tease him. Taunt him. Goad him. Especially Jesse, and he just couldn't bear that this morning. Ah, Jesse!

Archie curled into the tough fibrous shell of the old stump and smiled secretly at the thought of Jesse. He pictured what he would be doing out at the waterhole. He envisaged his face. And body. Ah, if only!

He knew that his thoughts were frightening and scary and unsettling, but his heart was racing and he felt so alive! So thrilled. So captivated. Archie wasn't sure if anything would ever happen between him and Jesse, but he knew for certain that he wouldn't risk contact around here. It simply wouldn't be tolerated. He knew, yes he knew.

But still that didn't prevent Archie from dreaming. Or watching. Or hoping.

One day, he thought, yeah, one day!

In the meantime, Archie figured that he would just have to keep it all to himself, just pretend. Play it cool. What else could he do?

He reckoned that his thoughts were his alone, and no one else need know. Not his mates. Not his family. Not his mob, they wouldn't understand. Or accept. Or tolerate. And he needed to belong. Somewhere. For now. For despite the fact that Archie was already independent and fast reaching adulthood, a part of him still felt childhood dependencies and needs and wants. Still needed to share. Still needed caring.

***

Archie stretched and stood up. Suddenly he wanted to go. It had become too much. He needed company. To be around his mates. To have some normality back in his day. He headed back towards the camp, wondering if his mates would be back yet from the waterhole.

It was early afternoon, and he reckoned that Jacko and Jesse would soon return. Archie figured that they'd make their way home in time for some fun before the evening meal. He needed some time to unwind, to adjust, and to get back to normality. Yeah, he sure needed that.

He kicked up the dry red dust as he ambled along the track back towards camp. Archie was pretty well unaware of his surroundings. His mind was focused on other things. Other people. Outside he appeared calm and smiling, but inside there was a mass of confusion going round inside his head. He felt as though part of him wase strange and new and unknown; as though somehow he had suddenly become a stranger to himself. It was as though he was no longer in control, and Archie didn't really know *why*. He only knew that it was disturbing and unsettling.

He wondered if the others felt these things too, but he sure as hell wasn't going to mention it to them. No way! They'd laugh at him and freak him out again.

As he neared the outskirts of the camp, Archie heard voices and noises, and he recognised familiar sounds of his home. It would be OK for now, Archie felt sure of that suddenly. But still, there were doubts.

"Hey, Archie, is that you out there?" called his mum from the verandah as he approached. "Where have you been, boy?"

Archie was silent for a short space of time, not wanting to give himself away just yet. But the other voice was insistent.

"Come on over here boy and sit with your old mum for a bit, eh?" she called to him from the yard. "Come on!"

Archie knew there was no getting away from the house now, so he went in through the old ramshackle gate and loped around the back to where his mum sat waiting. She was there in the old wicker chair, sitting exactly where he knew she would be, calm and serene. As he approached she squinted at him through filmy-white eyes, trying hard to make out the shape and picture of her only son as he neared. Ah, those eyes!

She was old before her time, yet Archie could see her strength and determination and inner peace. She sat with her tough feet scraping the hard dirt, softly drawing small circle patterns with her toes. She was wearing one of her floral dresses, tied loosely round her waist in the hot afternoon sun. Her hands opened and closed steadily as she impatiently beckoned Archie now, calling to him to join her under the old tin roof. But it was her face that told her story, etched into every line. Archie never tired of gazing at his mum's face; it was as though the whole of his life and his dreaming was somehow curled up there within. Waiting. Connected. Belonging.

When Archie looked at his mum he could see himself, and sometimes that scared him. Sometimes he ran away. Sometimes he felt the fear coming on. And sometimes he wanted to reach out and be held in her arms once more and cradled and rocked like a baby; but he knew that it was already too late for that now.

She had been a fine looking young woman in her day, and even now Murra was what most of the mob called 'handsome'. She was dignified. She had respect. And to Archie, she could be an awesome ally at times.

He knew that he loved her deeply, and he always would; but somehow that wasn't enough anymore. He needed to stretch and grow. He needed to spread his wings. He needed to test the waters of adulthood a little, and to find out what it was that defined the world of grown-ups. For Archie, it was time to stretch the boundaries of his so-far isolated existence, and he felt deep down that the time was right.

What he didn't know was how. Or when. Just that it needed to happen *soon*.

Archie sometimes believed that his world was turning upside-down, and that he was spinning out of control. But although that often took his breath away, it was exciting too. Challenging. Irresistible. He wanted to run and soar and shout and leap and laugh out loud, but instead he quietly joined Murra where she sat. His mother. His rock. The one who he could depend on, no matter what.

She was gazing at him now with *that* look. The mother-thing. The nurturer. The carer, giver, provider, patient one. And Archie knew what it meant; felt it right through his bones. He was caught in the culture-bind forever, stuck there, glued inside it. Nothing would free him this side of death, and he knew it. Yeah, he sure did.

But still a part of him resisted. Shrank away. Turned aside from the lines and the dots and the patterns and the songs of his people. Even while he sat down next to Murra, his mind was wandering, trying to escape. But it wasn't easy.

"Eh you, boy," Murra chided him gently, "why don't you sit with me any more like the old days when you were small? Why?"

Archie stared straight ahead, not wanting to answer his mother. Not wanting to disappoint her. Not wanting to tell her the things that were on his mind more and more these days. How could he tell her that he was changing so quickly? How could he talk to this woman who was his mother and now looked so old? How?"

He shuffled his feet uncomfortably in the sand, casting his eyes downwards to avoid her steely gaze. He knew what she was thinking. He understood her silent dread. He sensed that she wanted to make sure that everything was alright with him, but he couldn't give her that reassurance. No, he sure could not. It was his business what went on in his head, and men's business at that. No, he couldn't share it with Murra, and that made him edgy and sorrowful, as though a big part of who he had once been was draining right out of him and dripping away forever. Archie felt lost.

Murra placed her old gnarled hand on his knee and looked at him in silence. He could feel her body heat transferring to him, and it felt as though she was giving him this last chance at childhood. But he knew it was too late, and he didn't know how to tell her. How to stop the clock of time. How to stem the inevitable.

His heart was almost breaking for her, but he sensed that she knew it too, and accepted it, and cherished him despite his withdrawal from her. He tried to avoid her gaze there on the old back verandah, but he could see her and feel her even without looking. Her sense of her space was so strong and so powerful that it left Archie struggling to come to terms with, but it had always been that way for him, hadn't it? He accepted her for who she was, and knew without question her place in the mob, but she was still his mother when all was said and done. And he would never forget it.

"What are you thinking these days, boy? Have you been chasing the girls with your mates, Arch?" she asked him quietly, smiling at him a little cheekily all the while.

Archie didn't know what to say, didn't trust himself to answer just yet, and didn't want to give the game away. Not now. Not here. Not with his own mother. Oh no, that would never do!

"Nah mum, not me," he replied, hoping that she'd change the subject quickly to avoid further embarrassment. Archie didn't like where this was heading, and he wanted to get up and go inside, but he knew better than to leave the conversation at this point.

"OK boy, talk to you mum. Tell me what you and your mates have been up to lately, eh?" she asked gently, trying to prise a little chatter from her son, and hoping that their time out here this afternoon would continue. At least for a little while. At least for long enough for her to get a sense of how things were panning out with Archie these days. It was difficult for her to connect with Archie now; either she was busy with her circle of friends and the painting sessions at the learning centre, or he was busy mucking round with his mates after school. On the weekends there were always plenty of trips with the men that took Archie away from her. Trips to the waterhole. Fishing. Hunting. Kangaroo shooting. Men's business. But at least they weren't drinking; not yet anyway. And not ever, if she could help it. No, that's for damn sure!

But Archie was withdrawn and slightly testy there at home with his mum this afternoon, and he fidgeted and squirmed like a naughty schoolboy. He didn't want to be questioned. He felt too unsure of himself. He didn't want to have his mother probing into stuff that was his alone, and he damned sure didn't want her to know about the Jesse-stuff. She'd hit the roof, he knew.

So he stammered some sort of excuse about being late at the river to meet Jacko and Jesse, and before his mum could stop him he was off out the gate and down the track that led away from the camp. Murra hollered out after him to come back, but it was no use. Archie heard her, but kept on running anyway. Kept on going. Away away away.

He didn't care much where he was headed, as long as he didn't have to explain his thoughts and his actions and his boiling emotions to anyone this afternoon. He knew that his mother would be disappointed that he had gone again, but still he kept on going. He knew that she had guessed he was troubled about something; she knew him too well *not* to have guessed. But he reckoned that she's soon forget about it and get on with her work back at the house, so he tried to push it away and forget about Murra. Forget about her questions. And her looks. After all, it wasn't as though she had really suspected his deeper thoughts, was it?

But try as he might to forget his mother's look, her face kept returning to him as he ran further and further down the track, and he wanted to shake it and get rid of it, but still it was there.

Archie figured it must have been his conscience, but he didn't have the knowledge or experience or wisdom yet to deal with it, so it sat in his skull and rankled him for a while as he ran. It somehow didn't seem fair or right that his mother should have questioned him this way. It made him feel small and belittled, and he was trying ever so hard to feel like an adult these days. To feel strong and powerful and worthy. To be independent and smart. But somehow it always backfired and Archie ended up once again retreating back to his childhood, as though that was the safest way.

He needed to belong as an adult, but he was still governed by the experiences and expectations of his childhood. Despite his changing body and mind. It seemed to Archie that he was stuck in a void, faced with the daily dilemmas of whom he once was and who he wanted to be. He knew that his hormones were racing. He knew that his emotions were all over the place. And he sure as hell knew that he was having feelings that he reckoned were most likely unnatural.

What Archie was trying to figure out, was how to sort it all out. How to bring it all together. How to unleash the fire within his belly that breathed and writhed and pushed at his soul. How in hell would he manage that? He wondered.

***

Meanwhile back at the house, Murra still sat on the old seat, gazing straight ahead. Her cloudy eyes were focused far away, not seeing. Her heart was tearing slowly, slowly; as though something inside of her was breaking away. Her mind was sharp and clear, but she knew that her body was failing. Felt it in her bones. Knew the signs. Recognised the symptoms deep in her gut.

Of course she would not tell Archie. No good complaining. Just keep on going and get through each day somehow. That's the way it was out here in the Kimberley with her mob. Her tribe. Her people.

Murra knew that she could have gone into town with the others in the community truck. She could have visited the doctor, or waited for the nurse to come. But she didn't see the point of it; she knew she was dying. And no one could fix it for her; it simply *was*. She knew there were others in the camp who accepted the whitefella ways and the whitefella medicine; but she was blackfella, wasn't she? Bush medicine would do.

And besides, Murra felt the call of the dreaming; and knew it was useless to interfere. To run away. To try to save herself this time; too late for that for sure.

The signs and totems of her people and the land and her spirituality were waiting for her. Beckoning her. Murra knew her time was close. Yeah, she knew alright.

But she was fearful for Archie, her only son. What would become of him when she was gone? How would he cope without her? Would the rest of the mob take him in and nurture and guide him? She hoped so; yes, she sure did hope so!

In her mind Murra drifted back to her own childhood, her early memories out here roaming in the hot Kimberley plains. It had been a good time growing up with her mob, despite the harsh environment. Despite the changing patterns of their world. Despite the intrusiveness of whitefella. Murra had learned both systems, both cultures, both ways; but was still blackfella in her heart.

She had grown up with the songs and stories and customs and laws used by her people for always, and she knew she *belonged*.

It was more than words and thoughts and feelings; it simply *was*. Murra knew her people and her place in her world. The people *were* her world, along with the land. Ah, the land! This land. Her land. It was Archie's land too, and Murra hoped with all of her being, that Archie recognised the importance of his own belonging. His tribe. His culture. His place.

Murra scratched at her itchy feet and bowed her head onto her chest, trying to focus on what she needed to do now. She wanted to call Archie back, but she knew it was far too late. He wouldn't be back till teatime now. And it was her fault. She blamed herself. She should have just left him alone. Let things be. Given him space, and time. But Murra knew that she didn't have a lot of time left to give; that was part of the dilemma she faced. If only she could reach him before it was too late. Ah, if only! She recognised that Archie was fast growing up, and accepted all the problems that would bring.

It should have been up to his father, but he was no longer here. And someone had to tell him. To teach him. To pass on the messages. Yes, someone sure had to; and it looked like it might be her. Murra didn't trust the others enough to hand over the important things. She knew that she should have, but something stopped her, and forced her to reassess. No, *she* would be the one this time. It was up to her.

Chapter Five

Archie flopped down in the shade of his favourite old gum tree at the other end of the camp. It was large and gnarled and twisted, and provided a safe haven away from prying eyes, it was also far enough away from his house to keep Murra at bay for now, and that was what he most wanted. To be alone. To feel safe. To have some time out by himself.

He knew that she wouldn't follow him; it was not her way. Hadn't he always had to go to her? And hadn't she always expected him to listen? (The trouble was that Archie felt that she was listening to him less and less these days).

Still, she was his mother, and he had to respect her; it was the accepted way. The only way. At least it always had been as he grew up here with the mob. But more and more he felt withdrawal, and he wasn't sure if it was his or hers; only that it *was*.

Archie scratched at the rough bark of the tree, and absently began humming softly to himself. He failed to recognise the significance of the song as it left his lips; it was one that Murra had sung to him as a child. A sleeping song. A story song. Blackfella chant. Archie hummed and drew patterns along the lines of the tree bark, pushing his fingers into the knots and grooves and crevices of the old gum, as though marking a journey of sorts. Maybe it was his journey, his life path, his destiny; but for now Archie was too caught up in the present to be aware of what lay ahead.

He wondered what it was that Murra had wanted to say to him there on their verandah back at the house, and shame began to scratch at the base of his skull. He should have been more patient with her. He should have stayed and let her talk. Yeah, he should have listened; she was his mother, after all.

But something about the way she spoke had upset him. He had felt unnerved by her. She had rattled him just a little, and touched on things that he didn't want to discuss. Private things. His thoughts and dream and feelings. His future. Archie knew that he should have been far more lenient; but he hadn't. He couldn't. He simply wasn't ready to share the private stuff; especially not with Murra.

His fingers began to tap the rhythm of his song on the rough tree bark. Boom ba-ba boom. Choo-choo-choo. Boom ba boom ba. Boom boom.

Archie closed his eyes and leaned back against the cold wood of the giant gum. He could feel his pulse slowing, but still his mind raced. He was confused yet calm. He no longer felt the fear of flight. He was OK.

In his mind danced the stories of the dreamtime, and he smiled as he pictured the images and patterns that had been given to him so long ago. They were part of who he was, but he didn't recognise the significance of the treasures Murra had given him as a child. He didn't know what it all meant. He didn't understand that the gifts she had bestowed were so ingrained now that he would have them till he died. No, Archie didn't understand at all.

Archie felt the pull of his people strongly at times; he knew that he was at one with them, and they with him. But he knew their ways too, and sometimes that strangled him and held him back. He felt like he was treading water, marking time; hanging on precariously. It was as though a small part of him accepted the way that things had to be, but a bigger part of him yearned for more. Dreamed it could be better. Dared to be different. But he didn't always like what was happening to him.

He felt like there was a tug-of-war going on inside him, and somehow he was stuck in the middle, being pulled this way and that. Archie wished it was different. He wished he could be more sure of himself. He wished he could be more like Jacko and Jesse, but he knew that he wasn't. To Archie, right now it seemed as though his life was on hold. He was stuck halfway between his past and his future, and he sure as hell wished that something would provide the kick-start needed to move him on.

Archie gazed up at the bright blue of the sky and the soft wispy clouds that raced overhead. He was itching to *do* something. Anything. Just to get away from himself and his thoughts and his worries for a while.

Maybe he'd go up to the top camp. Maybe he'd wait here till dark and sneak up there by himself. Maybe, just maybe.

But he knew that he wouldn't. He was too damned scared, and he remembered the last time. Yeah, maybe some other time. But that left him feeling isolated and bored and slightly disconnected once more, and Archie stood up suddenly and kicked at the ground.

Sometimes he hated his life. Sometimes he wanted to just run away and disappear. Archie was pretty pissed off and frustrated; he wanted to just *go*. But where? That was the problem.

This wasn't whitefella town. This wasn't the city. This was the camp, his camp, and there wasn't much of anything here for him to do that he could think of. And that was the trouble; he was growing *away*. (Ah, maybe that's what Murra had sensed after all). Archie started tapping his feet in the red dust beside the old tree. His feet formed the dance pattern of his people, but in his head was the beat of whitefella music. Archie was torn, stuck between the two worlds. He bent and turned and twisted with the slow deliberate steps of his forefathers, but still the metallic rhythm of drums and guitar echoed in his skull.

He wanted to shut it out. He wanted to focus on the dance. He wanted to feel the life-force of his heritage take over, so that he could purge the bad thoughts from his being there at the far edge of his camp. But something held him back. Something undefinable. Something that part of him wanted and accepted and recognised as a challenge. Archie was momentarily lost once more, and his body stilled.

He stood and stared inwards at this time, closing his eyes against the hot afternoon sun. He knew that this phase would not last, that everything would soon return to normal. But the trouble was that for Archie the definition of 'normal' was becoming more and more blurred each day. More unattainable. He felt that his body and mind and energy were totally out of sync these days, and he wanted things back the way they once were. He hated this feeling; this limbo-land. He needed to regain a sense of balance in his life, but he didn't quite know how. He wished that he *had* been able to talk with Murra back at the house. Really *talk* to her. Tell her the things he was feeling. And dreaming. But he knew that he could not, and there was no getting around it.

Archie clutched his hands into balls then spread out his long fingers. He stretched out his arms and raised them skywards, beginning the low humming again. It came from deep in his chest and spread slowly upwards, till it emerged as the cry of his people. Blackfella chant. Tell stories in song. Messages and dreamin' stuff. Explanations. Meanings. Reasons.

The chant grew louder and louder there beside the spinifex clumps, as Archie dipped and bent low to begin the rituals. He knew without words or conscious thought of what the context was. He understood the significance. He felt the patterns and the rhythm in his bones. He was kangaroo, wallaby, fish, bird, goanna, and snake. He was sky, water, earth, sun, and moon. He was tree, bush, grass, rock. He was part of his ancestry. He was Archie. The red dirt shifted and rose in small eddies of dust as his tough feet arched and rose and fell in the pre-set steps he'd learned from the elders as a child. He tossed off his clothes and danced naked under the Kimberley sun. He was young and beautiful and strong and full of hope there in the vast outback landscape. He was *home.*

His mind was powerful now as the ways of his people took over. He felt nothing except for the strength and courage of his culture. He was totally focused on the telling of the stories of his clan. The dance. The steps. The movement and the chanting. It was enough for now.

Chapter Six

Jacko was getting sick of fishing, and wondered what they could do for the rest of the day. He called out to Jesse, "Eh mate, waddya reckon we go back ta camp an' find Archie, eh?"

"Bugger off!" responded Jesse angrily. "I'm not leavin' here jez yet, orright?"

"Christ, mate, don' bite me head orf!" replied Jacko, none too pleased with the response from his mate.

They sat in silence for a while, till Jesse broke the air once more. He was feeling a bit sorry for himself, and he knew that he shouldn't have yelled at Jacko that way. The trouble was that he had been thinking about those girls a bit lately, and he couldn't figure out a way to get to see more of them. A lot more, if he had his way! He didn't much care what Archie was up to at the moment; in fact he was getting more than a little tired of Archie's recent mood swing and odd behaviour.

Damn Archie, he thought, who cares where he is today?

Jesse had begun to feel a little uncomfortable around Archie these days. Sometimes his skin itched a bit and he felt jumpy. Sometimes he felt like he was being watched. He guessed it was a lot to do with what he thought of as Archie's 'bug-moods', but still he didn't like it. No, not at all.

Usually Jesse chose to ignore Archie when he was contrary or withdrawn, but lately it felt like something else had crept in. Something beyond his experience. Something that was definitely out of his control. Archie had a habit lately of being pretty much 'out there' at times, and it left Jesse feeling a bit creepy. It seemed as though Archie was trying to sort out something pretty big going on in his head, and Jesse sure wasn't going to try and assist. No, he sure wasn't about to do that.

"Hey, Jesse!" hollered Jacko from the riverbank suddenly, "wanna go back to camp now and see what the mob are up to?"

Jesse was shaken from his thoughts by Jacko, and that was OK for now. He didn't like dwelling on anything for too long, and besides, he knew there was a fair chance that the girls would be hanging round again once they got back. And that would give him a chance to do some serious chick-watching again.

"OK, mate, let's go!" he called over to Jacko, and without waiting for a reply started along the track back towards camp. He had already forgotten about Archie and his black moods, and an eager smile spread across his face as he and Jacko ambled along through the spinifex back towards home.

"Hey, mate, reckon Arch likes them girls too?" asked Jacko.

"Aw, dunno mate, 'e jez might," replied Jesse slowly, not wanting really to get involved in a conversation about Archie again. He figured it was Archie's business who he fancied, as long as it wasn't the girl *he* had his eye on. Funny thing though, he somehow reckoned that Archie wasn't really all that keen on the girls yet. No, he reckoned he wasn't. But Jesse wasn't bothered by that fact; after all, it meant more girls for him and Jacko.

They ran in silence for a while, but as they neared the camp it was Jesse who spoke first. "Shit mate, there they are, them girls we've bin chasin'. Man, looka them, will ya? Jez 'av a look!"

The girls in question were up near the camp garden picking over some of the vegetables, and totally oblivious to the eyes of the two boys as they neared. They were giggling and chatting, and their smiling eyes were clear in their shiny faces. They were young and carefree and lovely.

Jesse stopped in his tracks. He couldn't take his eyes off them. Those girls, damn they were appealing! He tried not to look at them, to search out his favourite, but it was too hard. He was drawn to them like a magnet, and even though he knew he shouldn't be here watching, he just couldn't help himself right now.

"Hey, mate, you orright?!" whispered Jacko, watching Jesse carefully.

"Ah, will ya look over there!" Jesse replied, lowering his voice so the girls wouldn't hear. Least he hoped they wouldn't, not yet anyway.

Jesse and Jacko crouched down low in the bushes at the side of the track, giggling and shoving each other. They were not sure what to do next, and they sure as hell hoped that the girls wouldn't see them and run away. They both knew that they should really just saunter over and be casual and talk to the girls, but their hormones dictated their actions, and they were overcome with embarrassment and emotional energy.

Jesse broke the silence first, as he stood up to declare their presence.

"Hey youse, wotcha doin' down here, eh?" he called out to the girls in a brash tone that belied his quivering nervousness.

"Hiyez, waddya know?" chipped in Jacko, trying to declare himself as well.

But the two girls were caught off-guard and they ran off to the far side of the garden before halting briefly. They paused and turned towards the two boys, casting a glance each in their direction. They were a bit timid at first, but one gained some courage and called out.

"What's it to yers, eh? Youse bin followin' us or sumpin?"

Jacko and Jesse were gaining a bit of courage now, and chose to ignore the girl's question. They figured it would only get them in trouble if they responded straight away. The girls might even dob them in with the elders, and they didn't want to have to deal with that back at the camp.

The two girls shifted nervously from one foot to the other, giggling a little as they stood there at the vegetable patch. They kept their eyes downcast, but all the same they were keenly aware of the boys who stood opposite them now. They knew who the two boys were, of course; they had grown up together here at the camp. They were certainly not strangers to each other. They had played together as little ones. But none of the four were little kids any more. They were growing fast. They had started the journey towards adulthood. There was no going back, and they all felt the thrill of their first tentative steps towards acknowledging their own sexuality.

The taller of the two girls stepped forward, taking a tentative step towards Jesse.

God she was lovely, Jesse thought to himself.

She was lithe and angular and gorgeous, and Jesse was a bit nonplussed and suddenly lost for words as she neared.

"Wanna go fer a walk up the road youse?" she asked, hoping that she could be alone with Jesse at some stage. But not today. Not yet. Too soon, yeah, way too soon!

Jesse and Jacko tripped over each other in their eagerness to join the girls now, and the four of them laughed and nudged each other and teased and joked as the tension subsided. They were just innocent kids, after all; but were they?

"We've bin wotchin' yers now n' then, haven't we?" the tall girl said to her friend.

"Really?" replied Jacko, gaining a bit of confidence now that the initial meeting was over. He was a bit incredulous that they were actually sharing time with the girls this afternoon, but he didn't want to get too cocky in case they decided he was a bit of a dickhead. So he tried to stay cool and act tough. He didn't want the girls to think he was ignorant or stupid. He wanted to win them over somehow, and he figured that he and Jesse were off to a pretty good start. Yeah, this is going OK, he reckoned.

***

Murra was feeling the pain again, so she sat down once more in the old wicker chair. It came as a dull ache first, then changed to the familiar sharp jabs of pain radiating along her spine. Her back took the brunt of the attack as she hunched over to stem the pain, hoping that this time it would subside quickly. Sometimes it lingered for a while, and as she clutched the arms of her chair, she hoped that this wasn't one of those times.

Murra had things to do today, and she wanted some free time from her illness to be able to think. To be able to concentrate. To get things done.

She knew that there wasn't a lot of time left to her now, and she still had so much sorting to do. Important sorting. Tying up loose ends, finishing stuff she'd started in her life-journey.

And then there was the problem of Archie. (Maybe, just maybe, she should confide in him). But she knew that she couldn't. Wouldn't. Not yet; no, not yet.

Murra felt the pain ease and she slowly sat upright again, pushing her back straight against the chair. She had closed her eyes briefly to fight the latest onslaught, but she opened them now to survey her territory. Bushes, sheds, fence, trees, plains, distant hills.

Everything that lay spread before her was part of her world, her people's world; and it was precious. It was her life. It was her spirit.

Murra was consciously making mind-pictures in her head to take with her into the dreaming. She wanted to hold everything deep inside. She wanted to take it all in. She needed the peace of her land and her culture and her songs and her stories and her people; yes, she needed that alright.

But she needed to reconcile things with Archie, too, before her time was up, and that's where she got a little lost. A little frightened. It was hard; too damned hard.

Murra dropped her hands by her side and started to chant. "Eeeech, eeeeh. Ooooh!" she cried to the wind and the dust and the earth that surrounded her.

Nobody heard and nobody came, and Murra began to weep. Soft slow weeping, that broke her heart. Tears gently rolled down the grooves of her worn face, trickling down down down. Murra felt the salt of her tears wash over her, but she could do nothing to stop them.

Maybe they will cleanse my soul, she thought, as she sat there still in the old chair. Maybe, ah maybe.

But she knew that her tears could not really help her to fix up the problem of Archie. She knew she would have to figure it out for herself. And she was struggling to find a way. "Ah, what will I do with him? What?" she pleaded with the spirits.

But no answer came. There was total silence. Her world was on hold, and Murra felt yet another surge of pain run the length of her spine as she sat there patiently on the back verandah. Small fingers of fear traced upwards as she gripped the arms of the chair once more against this latest onslaught. Murra hoped it would soon pass, this present attack. But she knew they were becoming more frequent now, and she didn't know how much longer she could hide it from everyone. Especially Archie.

She had decided right from the start that she would not tell anyone until she really had to. She didn't want whitefella medicine. She didn't want to go into hospital. And she sure didn't want to die in some strange bed in the city far away from her land and her people and her rightful place. No; Murra sure didn't want that to happen.

But lately it seemed that things were getting a bit more out of control. The pain was becoming stronger and more frequent. She was finding it harder to cope. To get through each day. To complete all the tasks that she had set herself.

If it wasn't for Archie, Murra was sure she might have succumbed sooner; but she still had this last thing to resolve. She wanted to draw Archie close to her once more; to hold the last of his childhood firmly against her breast. But she knew it was not going to be easy. She knew he would flinch and turn away from her. And she sensed that her time was fast running out.

Murra sighed and drew in another long breath as the pain along her spine subsided. She was still anxious and unsettled. Still wondering how she could fix things before she died. But for now there was nothing she could do, and maybe that was the way it would be. Perhaps the opportunity to sort it all out with Archie would not come in time, despite her wanting. She just didn't know.

***

Archie had finished the dance steps. He was no longer chanting the words of his people. No longer dreaming.

He had decided to go and search for his mates down at the river. Despite feeling unsettled, he reckoned that he needed some company and some normality back in his day. Yeah, he sure did!

He set off along the track towards the river, this time knowing that he would be glad to enjoy the company of Jacko and Jesse. He figured that it wouldn't be too hard to find them now. He knew all their fishing spots, after all. And he knew they had left camp a few hours ago.

He wanted to reach them in time to have some fun this afternoon. He needed to shake out the bad stuff that had crept in after his brief time with Murra. Archie wanted to get rid of the blackfella stuff for now; it was too heavy. It weighed him down. It crept into his skull and his bones, and left him drained.

Archie knew deep down that he was only delaying the inevitable. That he was running away. That one day he would have to deal with his heritage. But not now. Not today. He was free for a little while.

He had sensed back at the house that Murra was calling him in, drawing him to her. Trying to pass on some important message that he only half-understood. He wished that he was a bit braver and a bit stronger and a *lot* more tolerant; but today he wasn't. Today it spooked him, and he needed some space. Some normal stuff back in his life. He needed his friends.

He had not figured on Murra's meeting today, and it had shaken him a little. Archie knew that he should have stayed with her and sat and listened, but he reckoned that since he was no longer a child, he could do as he pleased now. He didn't have to obey just because she had asked. But still, he felt bad. As though somehow he had cheated her out of something important. Something she had wanted to tell him. Something that was important to her and maybe to him as well.

Still, Archie guessed that it could wait. There would be plenty of time for that later. (But something in the way she had looked later made him a bit suspicious. And scared. And sad). It was almost as though somehow Murra was holding back a big secret, and Archie knew instinctively that it concerned *him*.

Why else would she seek him out? Why else would she beckon him so gravely? Why? It didn't make sense, but Archie knew without words that it was something pretty damn big; and he wanted to avoid it if he could.

Chapter Seven

Archie was about halfway along the track to the fishing hole when he heard voices; he stopped and stood still, listening. There were male and female voices, and he reckoned he knew who they belonged to.

He could clearly make out the brashness and cockiness of Jacko and Jesse up ahead somewhere, as he paused to identify the other two voices. Shrill laughing sounds came from beside the track that lay ahead, and Archie sank quietly into the bushes that surrounded him, wanting to hide for the moment.

Archie needed some cover while he figured out what to do. He guessed that his two mates were up ahead with a couple of the girls from the top camp. He knew that the boys had been eyeing off some girls for a while, hoping for a chance to get closer. *Much* closer. And he reckoned that finally they had.

But Archie was a little puzzled and hurt. He'd been left out of the fun, abandoned by the boys this afternoon of all times. And it was his fault. (Or maybe Murra's doing; he really didn't know.)

The sun was hot on his back as Archie squatted there motionless beside the track, watching and waiting. Listening. Breathing softly. He was starting to feel the familiar anger rising again, and he didn't like what he felt.

He had wanted to catch up with his mates at the river for some fun. He had desperately needed a diversion. And now Archie felt cheated and ashamed. It wasn't as though Jacko and Jesse were up to no good; simply that they had chosen the girls to be with, and not him. (He couldn't really blame them; after all, *he'd* been the one to leave them this morning and go off by himself, hadn't he?)

But that didn't help him to feel any better about things now; in fact, if anything it made it worse. Archie was stumped. His emotions were all over the place. He was tired of this roller coaster ride of inner turmoil, and he was hurting somewhere deep inside. He knew that it had a lot to do with Jesse, and he knew that he was jealous. But what he didn't know was how to fix it. How to take away the pain. Archie reckoned that he had to somehow put a stop to all this stuff, but he knew there were no simple answers. He was confused and hot and bothered, as he sat there surrounded by the sounds of laughter and light-hearted conversation up the track. Part of him wanted to join in. To connect with the others. To have some fun. But he sensed that he would be the odd one out, and therefore not entirely welcome this afternoon. It would have been different if they had all started out this morning together, but Archie knew he had stayed behind at the camp longer this morning. And he couldn't blame his mates for that. Hell no, he sure couldn't.

But still that didn't make it right, and in Archie's mind the dilemma he was now in was somehow not entirely his own fault; he blamed others as well. Jacko. Jesse. Murra. His people. His mob. Blackfella dreamin'; yeah that ol' blackfella stuff.

It was in his blood. It ran through his veins. It seeped into his gut and pulsed right through him. Archie knew it was there and he knew it would always be there; but that didn't mean that he had to like it all the same. No, he sure didn't have to.

The voices of the present suddenly overrode the voices of the past.

"Hey, youse, wanna come up to our camp fer a while, do yers?" called out the taller of the girls.

"Yeah, that'd be fun, waddya reckon, eh?" chipped in the other girl.

There was silence for a moment, then Archie heard Jesse respond. "OK, yers on!"

Archie could hear the sound of voices and laughter and nervousness, and feet tramping dirt, and bodies brushing spinifex as the four retreated up the track, away from where he sat. He wasn't sure what to do next. He wondered if it was too late to join them. To add to the group. To catch up with his mates and the girls. To go with them on up to top camp.

He wanted to go, to be included; but part of him sensed that he wouldn't really be welcome. Not now. Not this afternoon. He was smart enough to know that his mates had other things on their mind now, and it definitely didn't include *him*.

Once again Archie felt excluded, and he was annoyed with himself as much as the others. He knew that he should have joined his mates today at the fishing hole, then they would have shared the day together.

Archie blamed himself this time, accepting responsibility for his earlier actions. He was cross that he had left it too late now to join the group heading up to the other camp, and because of it that left him on the outer once more. He should have gone with Jacko and Jesse when they called round for him after breakfast. Yeah, he knew that now, but it was too late.

The voices of the others were slowly fading into the red dry dust as Archie decided to follow them at a distance. He didn't know why; just that he *would*. It seemed like a good idea, and would give him something to do for now. A chance maybe to salvage the rest of the afternoon, and perhaps even to announce that he was there and join in the fun with his mates.

He wasn't at all sure about the girls though, and was still stung by uncertainty about Jesse's involvement. He didn't want to accept it for what it was; he knew that much. For now he would just tail the group and see what they got up to; Archie could see no harm in that. After all, hadn't they always played and camped and fished and hunted and run together. Hadn't they, all this time?

But even as he tried to convince himself that this was no different to other times, Archie knew that it was. He knew he was getting out of his depth. He understood the implications. He wished it was different, just that the three of them were still together; but they weren't.

Archie sensed that Jesse and Jacko were happy to be without him today, happy to be with the girls; and he felt excluded and bitter. He didn't like it. No, not one bit. He knew that it wasn't normally like this, but it felt as though this was the start of changes in their lives. Big changes. Frightening changes. Unknown secret stuff that had suddenly snuck up and captured them during the night somehow. Mysterious hormonal-driven cravings. Men's business.

Up ahead the group stopped while one of the girls called out something to her friend.

"Hey Emma, waddya reckon we take the boys up to the ol' well at th' back of your house, eh?" asked Jodie in a faltering voice.

"Geez Em, dunno if that'll be OK or not," replied her friend nervously.

They had started off this exercise in meeting the two boys so casually and full of false bravado, but now that they were nearing their home camp, things seemed suddenly a lot different. They wondered if this was such a good idea after all.

"Geez you two, 'urry up an' make up yer minds, willyez?" asked Jacko impatiently. He was becoming fidgety and nervous, and not at all sure of what lay ahead this afternoon. His earlier cockiness had disappeared, and he was now beginning to wonder what the hell they were doing here at all. He knew they could get in big trouble. Serious trouble. Blackfella trouble; and that was pretty heavy stuff.

But Jesse was keen to keep going. To see what eventuated up here at the girl's camp.

"Aw come on youse, lez' go somewhere an' find some shade an' git outa this heat fer a while, waddya say?" he pleaded with the group laughingly.

For a moment the girls hesitated, then Emma responded. "Nah, it's getting' on a bit. Our aunties will be lookin' fer us soon. Youse boys better git back ta your camp, we'll see yers round sometime, eh?"

"Yeah, buzz off," added Jodie, relieved that things weren't going any further with the two boys today. She had begun to feel a bit reckless and a bit scared about what might happen later on, and she reckoned that they might have been heading for trouble. She knew there were taboos and rituals even up here at top camp, and she sure didn't want to get on the wrong side of her tribe at this stage. No sir, sure did not!

But Jesse and Jacko were suddenly on the offensive with the two girls. They were a bit taken aback at the sudden turnaround in proceedings, and reckoned that it was a case of being led by the nose. And they were none too happy about it. It seemed as though what had been a promising afternoon interlude had suddenly shifted to nothing. Any prospect of a bit of physical contact with the girls was clearly now out of the question, and the boys felt cheated and annoyed.

"Geez, what did we do, youse?" asked Jesse angrily. "How come yers changed yer mind all of a sudden, eh? Youse invited us up here, after all!"

But the girls remained silent where they stood at the edge of the camp, hands on hips now and facing the boys squarely in a show of defiance. They knew that nothing would happen to them, for they were within earshot of their mob now. They didn't believe that they owed the boys any explanation, so without another word they turned and trotted off up the track. The two girls covered the last remaining distance quickly, then turned a corner of the road and disappeared out of sight, leaving the boys speechless at the side of the road.

Jacko was the first to regain speech.

"Fuckin' cows!" he spat out.

"Yeah, reckon they's not worth it mate," responded Jesse loudly, swearing and cursing at the girls now and muttering under his breath. "Bloody shit deal, eh?"

There was nothing for it but to turn around and head back to their own camp, but both boys were pretty pissed off at the way the afternoon had turned out. They cursed to themselves for being so stupid and letting the girls lead them on, but still admitted that it had been a bit of fun after all. It hadn't been all bad, and they had crossed the first hurdle of being alone with the girls for a while anyway. Maybe the afternoon hadn't been totally wasted after all.

Archie heard them coming as they descended the hill, and decided to let them pass before greeting them, knowing that they might be annoyed with him as well. It wouldn't do to scare them or sneak up on them in their current mood, so he crouched deeper into the spinifex and hunched over low to avoid being seen by his mates. His mind raced with possibilities. He asked himself a heap of questions. He worried about joining his mates at this stage of the day. But still, he decided that he probably would. After all, he knew better than anyone how quickly their moods would swing back to normal. He knew that they would already be forgetting the girls' rebuttal. And he knew there was still time left this afternoon to get in some hunting or swimming or small adventure out in the bush somewhere. He might just join them, after all. Yeah, he just might.

***

Murra could hear the banging of hammers and the rough *skish* sound of saws on wood as she went back inside her house. She knew that the elders were directing some younger workers this morning, trying to teach them some carpentry skills. Trying to give them a better chance at some future employment. Hoping that the young ones would stay and help the community grow a little. Have pride. Be strong. (And stay away from the grog and some of the bad whitefella stuff!)

She opened the old rusty door to her donga and went through to the kitchen. The lino was faded and torn, and she scuffed her toes against the broken edges. But it didn't matter to Murra, it was only a house, after all, and she didn't own it. None of her people owned their dongas; they were just temporary residents. And that was just fine by them; they didn't see the need to actually *own* a house; the land was what mattered most.

Murra knew that she should sit and rest for a while, for the pains this morning had been particularly fierce, but she padded round the kitchen anxiously, trying to decide what to do about Archie. She knew that her time was short; and that was the trouble. He hadn't yet been through the initiation ceremony and she wasn't sure if there was enough time for the instruction and ritual before the spirits came. Before dreamin'.

Murra sat down suddenly at the old laminex table and buried her head in her arms. She sank into oblivion, not knowing what to do next. It was all too hard, too difficult. She needed help, but there was none. She needed her husband, but he had gone. Murra wept silently there at the table, as her old heart broke and the shattering of all that she was and all that she knew began.

Part of her sorrow came from the crumbling of the old ways of her mob. The trouble was that she just wasn't sure who to turn to now. Who to ask for guidance and help. Once it had been so straightforward. Once the women had all supported each other. Once there had been such strong rituals and beliefs and laws; but now they had almost gone. And that left Murra with no firm answers as to what to do.

She felt that it was up to her to see that Archie would be looked after once she had gone. She didn't just want him taken in by the mob. Roaming from one donga to another. Too independent. No, she sure didn't want that for Archie; he had too much to learn still. Blackfella stuff. Important rituals and stories and ceremonies. But Murra knew that there probably wouldn't be enough time left, and that made her weeping and lamenting even louder.

She felt like pieces of her were breaking off. Bits of her homeland and her stories and her dreamtime seemed to be spinning somewhere outside of her now; round and round in large circles. Something was drawing her in, but other things were leaving; and her soul was crying out for guidance and forgiveness and recognition and acceptance there in the small cluttered kitchen. The room was spinning and whirling like the dances of the old ones. Murra could feel the rhythm of the stamping feet as they danced in the patterns of times long ago. She felt her pulse racing with the blood of her ancestors; she was at one with her people and her land. She let out a piercing shriek in her own language, her native tongue; no need for the whitefella words now.

Murra tried to stand to perform the final dance, but the pain overtook her. The rhythm and the songs and the cries of her people were fading. The images of her land and the sacred trees and the waterhole where she had been born were coming into view. Coming to claim her. Nearer and nearer. She was almost there. EEEEEHH!

Chapter Eight

Archie was almost ready to stand up and declare himself to his mates out there by the camp track when a strange thing happened. An odd feeling overtook him. A heaviness that seemed to pin him down.

He squatted amongst the spinifex and took a deep breath, trying to calm himself. He felt touched by something eerie, and Archie didn't know what it was. He simply knew that it *was*. He closed his eyes to shut out the sun, and inside the darkness of his skull there were weird shapes emerging. Faces with big circle eyes. Patterns of goanna feet and snake-belly swirls.

Archie could hear someone moaning, and the swish swish swish of the acacia bushes as the women filed past in his head. The wind became the soft songs of his ancestors; and he could hear his mum's voice calling to him now above the din. Calling his name.

Archie! Archie! Over and over and over' till the noise was almost deafening. He covered his ears and his eyes as he crouched even lower in the grass, hoping that it would all go away. Hoping that it would vanish as quickly as it had appeared. But knowing somewhere deep down within that it wouldn't.

Archie paused and sucked in his breath, trying not to recognise the symbols that he saw. Trying to make some sense of it all. Trying desperately to understand. He knew that it must have something to do with his mother, but he was scared. It felt so final. So definite. And he didn't want to think about the significance of these patterns and songs and cries that echoed in his head. Didn't trust himself for the moment. No, he sure didn't.

But as he slowly opened his eyes, Archie felt something strange. A feeling of power overtook him. He felt a calmness take over. Peace. Acceptance. Love. He knew that something amazing had happened; that someone had left, and yet stayed. Within. Within *him*. He knew without question that it must be his mum, but he didn't yet know the full truth. He didn't yet feel the full sadness. And he didn't yet understand that his childhood had suddenly disappeared forever.

In his mind Archie could still see his mum, still hear her voice and feel her touch; but he knew that she was gone now from this world. He knew instinctively that she was on the journey back to her people. Back to her land. Back to the ways and the time of the dreaming. Yeah, he knew that much for sure.

Still, he could do nothing for now; the mob would take care of everything from here. Her mob. His mob too. They would do it all blackfella way, because that is what she would have wanted; Archie knew that much at least.

He stood after a short while and headed down the track back home. He wanted to call on the women. He knew that they would take care of his mother. Arrange things. Sit with her, prepare the rituals. But he knew that he just had to let things happen.

Archie knew without speaking that she was dead, and he knew that he could not speak her name. The taboos would soon be in place, and his people would arrange the rituals. Yeah, it would all be done in the old ways. Not quick like whitefella funerals. No need to hurry now. Plenty of time; yeah, plenty of time.

Archie sighed and shuffled back along the track, stopping finally in view of his house. He knew that he shouldn't go in. He knew the customs. He had to respect their law and their ways and let the old people and let the women take care of it all.

But a part of him wanted to see her one more time. To know that she was still here to tell her he loved her. Yeah, part of him really needed to do that, but couldn't. So he stopped at the gate and bowed his head silently. And wept. EEEEEHH!

Chapter Nine

It had been hours now since Archie learned of his mother's passing, and he had fled up the track to his favourite secret place in the craggy caves beyond the camp. He knew that there were certain rituals that would take place in the weeks to come, but for now he didn't want to be part of them. He didn't want to be around people at all.

Archie knew that he was supposed to feel sadness and pain; but he only felt numbness deep within. It was like being suddenly turned to stone. He felt heavy and odd and detached, as though he had suddenly become someone else. As though the spirit world had beckoned him too. As though his mother was still struggling to communicate something really important to him. But it was too late, too late, too late.

At the entrance of his small cave, Archie could see the shapes of the surrounding hills and small tufts of protruding bushes, but he was so lost in his own world that they held no meaning to him now. He lay prone on the rocky shelf, clinging to the cold damp floor as though it was some sort of lifeline. As though it was his base of reality. As though there was nothing else for now.

He knew that there would be many people back at the camp who would wonder where he was, but he sensed that they would understand his need to be alone for the time being. Archie wondered briefly if his mates were thinking of him. What would they do? Would they come and search for him, or let him be for a while? He knew that it was important to send his mother off in the right way, and that everyone had a place in her departure to the dreamtime; but *he* had a place too, didn't he?

Archie was confused and bewildered and overwhelmed by his mother's sudden departure. It was almost too much to bear. He felt guilty and ashamed and sad and angry and hurt and abandoned and betrayed. It was not his fault, he knew that, but still a part of him sensed the enormous loss and change to his life that had suddenly occurred. He needed comforting and solace, but he chose to remain alone. For Archie, to seek out others right now would simply be too much.

***

The sun was sinking slowly in the sky when Archie finally decided to take action. To seek out something that would ease the pain.

He left the cave and scrambled back down the overgrown track towards camp. But he didn't go towards his own camp, he wasn't ready for that yet. Instead he veered off the path and headed off in the direction of the top camp. The other camp. The bad one.

He was no longer worried or scared about what might happen up there; he needed something different to help him now. Something forbidden and unknown. Something elusive. Archie craved company that would not pry or demand or question; and he desperately needed something to take away his pain.

If his mum was still here, he knew that he would not have gone. Especially alone. Especially now. But she had gone. She had abandoned him; and he had to act alone. Had to sort things out his way, and for the time being he needed something to help him a little.

Grog. Booze. Alcohol. And maybe some gunja. Archie didn't think about the consequences too much as he approached the camp; he just *went*. He reckoned that there'd be someone up here who could give him what he wanted for now. A part of him felt apprehensive, but he was damned if he'd let that get in his way now. After all, there was no one here to tell him what he could and couldn't do, and Archie was tired of listening to inner voices of restraint.

As he neared the camp, Archie could hear voices. Loud voices. Angry voices. Somehow it didn't seem to matter at the moment, for that was how he felt inside anyway.

He rounded the last corner of the track and stood there silently, as though there was still some part of him that wanted to resist. To flee. To withdraw. But he knew suddenly that he would go into the camp. Seek out somebody. *Anybody*. Just for relief.

As he neared the row of squalid looking dongas on the outskirts, the voices grew louder. An argument was in full swing, and Archie could make out male and female voices now. Shouts and threats and teasing filled the void between him and the tin houses, and Archie approached cautiously but resolvedly. He went in the second gate, and walked up the dry dirt path towards the door. Old toys, bike parts, motors, dog chains, and rubbish lay strewn about the yard. An air of neglect and hopelessness pervaded the scene, as Archie slowly stepped onto the concrete verandah. It was like his camp, but it wasn't. There was a sense of abandonment and despair and frustration and isolation and anger here that didn't exist at his camp down the hill. At least, not yet anyway.

Archie rapped on the door and stood silently waiting; but there was no response. He knocked a bit louder the second time, hoping that someone would hear him, but secretly wishing as well that they wouldn't. There was still no reply, so Archie got bold and pushed the old wire door. Slowly, so slowly, it opened, and Archie could see into the kitchen of the donga.

There were pots and frying pans and dishes and food scraps all over the benches, and Archie could smell the greasy remnants of cooking. He stepped inside and called out to see if the occupants would hear him, but the arguing in the other room must have drowned out his voice.

Suddenly there was a loud thump and a bang from somewhere within the house, and Archie's bravado fled. He turned back towards the door, hoping to escape before being found out, but he had left it too late. A door to his left flew open, and Archie was confronted by a large man in the hallway, holding a bottle of beer in one hand and a shifting spanner in the other.

"Eh, youse, waddya doin' in 'ere, eh?" shouted the man, as he advanced towards Archie. "Geez, who said yer could come in, eh?"

He grinned leering at Archie, who by now was beginning to feel a bit terrified at the situation he had landed himself in. He knew the reputation of the guys up at this camp, and it wasn't too good. In fact, it was not good at all. Archie reckoned he had done some stupid stuff in his life, and got up to a few good pranks with his mates; but this time he was alone. And scared. And helpless.

He knew that he should never have come up here, but it had seemed the obvious choice tonight. He reckoned that it had been a stupid choice though, especially seeing that no one from his mob even knew he was up here. And *that* thought terrified him even more. But it was too late to get out of it now; he would have to try to bluff a little and buy some time.

"Hiyers, I reckon I must have got a bit lost. I was jez lookin' fer a mate of mine an' I thought he'd come up 'ere," fumbled Archie, not knowing what the response would be.

He wanted to run away, but he figured that he wouldn't get past the door before the other guy grabbed him, so he stood his ground. He tried to remain calm, with some degree of control, but it was difficult. *Very* difficult. His feet and legs felt like they were turning to jelly, and a strange dull ache of anticipation sat heavy in his belly.

Archie was frozen to that spot on the old worn lino in a stranger's house, and time seemed suddenly to vanish. He felt as though he had moved into another dimension, another existence; and it was strange. Weird. Freaky. There was a loud rushing sound in his ears and his feet and hands were curling and clawing at something, but he didn't know what. He felt cold all over and he had the shakes. From somewhere deep within he sensed a shifting, as waves of fear and nausea racked his body there in the hallway. From somewhere distant he could hear a soft moaning echoing through his skull but he was too distraught to understand its meaning.

Suddenly his body collapsed onto the floor as Archie's legs gave way. He pitched forward into the arms of the burly stranger, fading into darkness as unconsciousness briefly took over. There was nothing but the soft moan of desolation, but Archie didn't recognise the sounds as his.

He woke moments later to a strange sight; someone was gently calling out to him and trying to reach him. He thought it was his mum, but knew that it couldn't be. Archie closed and opened his eyes a few times, blinking at the person before him to gain some focus. His senses were all askew, and he tried hard to regain what he had lost. Where was he and what had happened to him? He wondered.

Suddenly the room cleared and everything came flooding back, as though time had reasserted itself for Archie. He saw snatches of who he was in his mind, and snatches of where he was with his eyes. He was overwrought with the events of the day, and suddenly all that had happened caved in on him, and Archie let out a long lonely wail of despair there in the stranger's lounge room. It had suddenly become too much for him to bear, and his body was overtaken by loud sobs as he lay there, hoping for anything to ease the pain.

"Geez, mate, what's happened to yer?" asked the stranger anxiously. "Don' cry man, there's a good fella, you'll be all right mate!"

But Archie was desolate, and he couldn't stop the sobbing and shaking that seemed to have totally taken over his body. He lay still, trying to get back a tiny bit of strength, but nothing happened. It was as though another force had possessed him, and he seemed to have no control over things any more. He was a bit embarrassed by it all, but knew that there was nothing he could do for now.

A large gnarled hand suddenly reached out and began stroking his arm, comforting him. Easing the pain a little. A voice uttered soothing sounds in a soft tone that melted in his ears. Words of a song began to fill his head, and Archie wasn't sure if he was dreaming or if it was real, but he closed his eyes and soaked it all in any way. It felt good. He began to relax. He was beginning to feel a little better. Somehow, things were returning to normal.

"Mum, Mum!" he called in his head. "Is that you?"

But there was no response, nothing but grey shadows and the quiet whisper of the wind in the spinifex of the plains.

"Where are you, Mum? Where?" Archie called softly.

"S'alright mate, s'alright," another voice replied, and Archie knew that she had gone. He opened his eyes and looked up to see the stranger sitting there trying to comfort him. Touching. Watching. Chanting. Archie felt the fear begin again, but something in the eyes of the stranger told him it would be OK. So he lay back on the worn couch and rested once more, trying to take in what had happened to him. He knew it had something to do with the loss and death of his mother, but the pieces wouldn't all fit together very well, and he was still confused. Still dazed. Still feeling faint and disorientated. And alone. So very alone.

But to Archie's surprise, the man who sat with him suddenly smiled and stood up. He walked over to the fridge that stood in one corner of the untidy kitchen and reached for a can of beer.

"Here ya go then, I reckon you could use this, mate. Get it down, an' yer'll feel orright," he grinned at Archie, passing him a cold can.

Archie was a bit shocked and more than a bit confused by everything, but he had his wits about him enough not to refuse the generous offer.

"Er, thanks," he muttered, taking the can from the smiling stranger. He decided that if he was ever going to try a beer, now was sure as good a time as any.

Archie ripped off the ring-top, and the sharp and bitter smell of beer assaulted his nostrils. It made him feel nauseous for a moment, but he figured that would go away once he drank some of the stuff.

He'd seen others react the same way the first time, and he'd smelt alcohol often enough on the breath and clothes of his father before he'd gone away. (But that had been a long time ago, and he wasn't so sure any more if the smell was the same as now.) Archie figured it wouldn't do any harm to have a drink with this guy; after all, that's why he'd come up here to top camp, wasn't it? (And he sensed that it would not do to refuse the hospitality either. No way!)

So he raised the cool can to his lips and took an uncertain swig of the liquid, hoping like hell that he didn't gag on the first mouthful. It felt smooth and pungent as it trickled down his gullet, and Archie was aware of something else as he took that first taste. Freedom. Adulthood. Independence. Mateship. It felt good; damned good.

For a moment Archie savoured the bitter-cool taste that had hit his throat and trickled down to the pit of his stomach. He knew that his life had changed, and he knew why. What he didn't know, was what would happen next. And right at this moment, he didn't *want* to know. No, he sure didn't! It was fine just to be here with some company for now, even if he didn't really know these people and he didn't know what would happen next. It didn't seem to matter to Archie; for now it was OK.

"Name's Roy," croaked the guy on the couch suddenly, grinning at Archie and extending his hand. "Roy the Roo."

"Hiyers," replied Archie, not too sure what to say in reply. He felt a bit threatened suddenly, and a bit scared of the situation he had landed himself in, but he was gaining a bit of himself back now. Maybe it was the grog. Maybe things had calmed down a bit. Maybe he was over the initial shock of his mother's death by now.

"Geez, mate, yer give us a bit of a scare back then, yer sure did!" exclaimed Roy the Roo, pleased to see the young man beginning to relax a bit now. "What's yer name then, an' where are yer from, eh?"

Archie hesitated for a brief moment before responding. He wasn't too sure about how much to give away at this stage, but he reckoned that he owed some sort of explanation to Roy for his behaviour.

"Jes up from lower camp. Got lost a bit wanderin' round, lookin; fer me mates."

"Bugger me mate, give us all a shock when yer collapsed, yer did! Fair dinkum, we thought yer was 'avin' a fit or sumpin', didn't we eh?" asked Roy to no one in particular. "We thought there must be somethin' pretty wrong fer yer ta do that!"

Archie scratched his chin and took another big swig of beer. It was starting to feel pretty good, and he was beginning to relax a little and enjoy Roy's company. Even if he didn't really know anything about the guy. He seemed OK, and he sure was concerned about how Archie had got there, and how he felt. And that was *something,* after all, wasn't it?

Archie grinned at no one in particular and took another long pull on his can. The cool beer trickled easily down this throat, and he was feeling fine. Not terrific, just fine. He sat upright a bit more there on the stranger's couch, wondering for just a moment how he'd got there. Then he remembered. His mum. Death. Running, running, running. Away through the spinifex. Up here to top camp. Stumbling and gasping and strange noises and people. Banging noises had echoed in his skull. Then darkness and nothing.

Something else came into his head. A name. Roy. Roy the Roo. (Where did that come from? he wondered) Archie looked up and surveyed the room. He had thought that he was alone, but there were others here in this house, and he guessed he should know them, but they looked odd. Not his mob −

different. He swivelled round and saw a vaguely familiar face grinning at him. (Who was that? he wondered.)

"G'day youse, 'ow are ya now then, orright?" asked the face.

"Yeah, guess so," responded Archie hesitantly, not quite sure where he was at the moment.

"I'm Roy, remember me, eh?"

Archie scratched at his brow and seemed a little puzzled at first, but suddenly he remembered waking up from his dream next to this guy on the couch.

"Yeah, I remember yez now, too right I do!" he chipped in, pleased to be able to enter the conversation once more.

Roy laughed and raised his can to Archie. "Cheers then, mate, git it inta ya!"

As Archie resumed his drinking, everything seemed to mellow, and the room where he sat took on a peaceful tone. He no longer felt threatened or anxious. He wasn't scared or angry or hurting any more. Archie felt relaxed and comfortable, as though being here now was where he was supposed to be. It didn't matter that he was not with his mates down at their camp for now. And it sure didn't matter that he was not with his people, his mob. There would be plenty of time for that later. For now he wanted some space, some time away, some time to chill out. Archie needed that, and it was OK.

"Want another can, mate?" called out Roy. "There's plenty here!"

Archie raised his can for another sip, and drained what was left of the liquid. "Sure, Roy, that'd be jez fine," he replied, not really sure if he should have another yet, but determined not to seem anti-social at the same time.

"Tha's it, get it down, eh?" grinned the Roo-man. "'S good fer ya!"

Archie took the new can of beer and flipped the top, listening to the zing as the bubbles frothed over the edge. He put it to his lips and tasted the cool, sour ale. Ah, that was great! The bubbles of beer tickled his nostrils and made him smile a little. Archie was beginning to enjoy himself. He felt as though this was right. He wasn't at all concerned about things that might be happening back at his camp, not at all. He didn't give a thought to Jesse and Jacko and his uncles and aunts and cousins and the elders. For Archie, they had ceased to exist for now, and he was happy just to drift with the drink. Yes, that would do him for now.

"Yer didn't tell us why yer came up here, Arch, did yer mate?" called out Roy.

Archie was a bit taken aback all of a sudden. He had been dreaming and quietly sipping his beer. He had forgotten where he was for a moment. And now he had better remember!

"Me mum jez died, 'n I can't go back down there jez yet; too soon," he replied, not sure if the others would believe him or not.

"Gawd, yer poor bugger!" exclaimed Roy the Roo. "No wonder yez was so upset when we found yer!"

Chapter Ten

Jesse was pissed off. Big time. He was bored. At a loose end. He needed something to divert him, and there was nothing that came to mind right now. Bugger Archie, he thought, how come he was never around when you needed him?

He wandered down towards Archie's place, but was stopped halfway there by some of the elders.

"Where you goin' boy?" they asked.

"Doncha know that Archie's mum jez passed on, eh?"

Jesse was horrified. He hadn't know; hadn't even suspected that anything was wrong. He guessed that he should have, but he knew Archie kept family stuff to himself most of the time. Geez, how had it happened he wondered. And what was he supposed to do now?

"Do you know where Archie is, boy?" asked one of the elders. "We need to talk to him."

"Nah, ain't seen 'im today, dunno," mumbled Jesse, not feeling too good about this death-thing.

It seemed to Jesse that everything was suddenly changing, that their lives were fast tracking to nowhere, and he didn't like it. No sir, he didn't like it! And what the hell was he supposed to do now to help Archie through this? How the hell could he do *anything* if Archie couldn't be found? Gawd, what a mess!

Jesse departed hurriedly and headed to Jacko's place, but then changed his mind. He didn't really want to see Jacko right now. He knew that he'd have to tell him about Archie's mum, and he really wasn't too sure about the reaction he might get. Nah, best leave that to the elders, they could do it, he reckoned.

He headed off instead down the track to the river. Away from the camp. Away from the elders. And away from Archie. Jesse needed to be alone right now, at least for a little while. He needed some space. Some time out. He needed to absorb what he'd just heard. Gawd, life sure was strange, wasn't it?

He wondered where Archie would have gone after he heard the news. Jesse knew that Archie had a few quiet places where he went to get away from things, and he knew where a couple of them were. He tried to figure out whether Archie should be alone, but he decided that maybe this was one time when Archie might need some company. Where would he go? Which of his secret spots would he hole up in today? Should he try to find him, or not? Jesse scratched his head and sighed. He had to think. Had to try and put himself in Archie's place right now, think what *he'd* want to do.

Jesse decided that Archie was most likely up at the caves. He knew that was his favourite place when times were rough. Archie had taken him up there once, and he'd promised to keep it a secret from the others. From Jacko. And his cousins. He ran down along the river track for a while, and then veered off in the direction of the hills. Jesse figured it would take him about half an hour to get to Archie's cave, so he stopped for a breather before beginning the slow climb up the dirt path. His head was spinning with the news of Archie's mum's death, and he wasn't at all sure how to react when he saw Archie. What was he supposed to do? And say? How would Archie be feeling right now?

Jesse knew that Archie's dad was long gone, and now that his mum was dead too he would have no one to care for him. Sure, there were lots of others in the camp who were 'family', but it wasn't quite the same, was it?

Jesse felt a huge sadness wash over him there on the track. He reckoned life sucked right now. God, it sure did suck! How come things like this happened totally out of the blue anyway? How come people had to die? What would happen to his best mate now?

He wasn't quite so sure how Archie would take his mum's death; hell, he didn't know what *he'd* do in the same circumstances. No, he sure didn't.

It seemed to Jesse right now that too much in life was fragile; all of a sudden his world was changing, and he seemed out of control. (Maybe that's how Archie had also been feeling? Maybe that was the reason behind his moodiness and anger?)

Jesse wasn't too sure about the way things had been going lately, what with raging hormones and dissatisfaction and growing away from old friends and arguments and disagreements with family. Not to mention his newfound interest in *girls*. Sometimes he was just sick of it all, and he wished that he was somewhere else. Wished he could be somewhere far away from the camp, away from his mob. And often, if the truth be known, away from Archie and Jacko.

It wasn't that his mates were annoying or intrusive, or even interfering. It was simply that he had the feeling lately that he had outgrown them, left them behind somehow. Jesse couldn't pinpoint exactly when or how or why it had happened; just that it *had*. He'd begun to wonder if the others felt the same pull away from their childhood and their people and their current existence, but he was never quite confident enough to ask. It didn't seem right, and he wasn't comfortable enough with his new mantle to test the waters of their friendship yet.

At this stage of his life, Jesse was just drifting, and that had worked OK for him till now. But lately other things had crept into his existence, and he was a bit confused. No, more than a bit. Big time. It wasn't as though he had simply changed overnight, but it often seemed that way. Jesse felt strung out, detached almost, and he didn't like it. No way man, he definitely did not!

And what about Archie; what would he say to him now? How did you share death with your mate? What were you supposed to say to them? Would anything make it right again?

He didn't think so; it was impossible. Archie was difficult at the best of times; and now this. Gawd, what a mess! Still, he should at least make the effort to find him, at least that's what Jesse told himself as he climbed the hill and drew near the caves.

"Archie, Archie, 'y there, mate?" he called out, hoping that Archie would respond. Silence. Nothing. Wind whistling and rattling the branches like ole dead scarecrows in a parched and barren field. Red dirt mixed with grey spinifex. Red dust dry against his cheeks. Storm clouds gathering within and without. Endless hushed howling of the unseen desert-dwellers. Old bony hands reaching out to claim him as he stood silent and still below the rocky crags. Waiting. Waiting.

"Yer there, mate? Archie?" Jesse hollered into the wind, hoping for a small sign or response. "Christ, mate, where are yer?" he called out feebly.

Desperation entered his soul. He wanted to go, but he knew that he needed to find Archie first, so he continued to climb to the cave entrance. His hands gripped and clawed at the rough shale of the hillside. His tough feet groped the track for footholds to help his ascent. His eyes were fixed on his goal, and he kept the upward push going with steely resolve. (But God, he hated to be here. Hated to have to confront Archie. Hated what had happened; the death. So sudden. So final.)

His head screamed *sorry, Archie, sorry*, as he scrambled up the last little bit of the incline. He reached the spot where the ground levelled out at the cave entrance, and flung himself down for a rest. God, he sure hoped that Archie was up here somewhere!

***

Archie slumped lower on the couch. His mind was slipping into another place. Somewhere he'd never been before. Somewhere new. And dangerous. His fingers lost their grip momentarily on the can of beer that he held, and it tilted sideways out of his grasp.

A tiny rivulet of liquid oozed along the seat beside Archie, forming a small pool of foam on the stained blue and yellow material. It felt wet and soggy against his leg, but Archie was too far gone with the booze to even notice it. His weary head nodded against his chest, and his breathing was coming and going in fits and starts. He felt wooden and cold; alienated from humanity. It all seemed to have gone so wrong, and he knew somewhere deep inside that something really important had come unstuck but he didn't know what.

He attempted to sit up and focus a little, but his body weight seemed to be held down by other forces stronger than him. Waves of nausea and demons of fire were whirring through him, but he felt powerless to hold them back. Circular dreamtime patterns and echoes of the spirit songs rose and fell within. He was consumed by them there on the couch, and he held his eye shut tight in case it was real. He didn't want to see them. He didn't want to acknowledge reality. He felt bad. Real bad.

From somewhere in the room a voice seemed to swim to him through thick glutinous waves.

"Archie! Archie! Maa-aa-ate!"

Drums echoed through his tortured skull as he tried once more to face the world.

"Hey, mate, what ya doin'?"

It sounded like, sounded like… what? Who?

"Wanna nothery, eh?"

Archie groaned and pushed himself up straight again on the couch. He needed to piss, and he wasn't quite sure whether his legs would hold him up. He opened his eyes and tried to figure out where he was. What was going on? How had he got to this state?

"Geez man, glad yer with us again!" a voice cried.

Shit, who is that? Archie tried to unscramble his brain a little. Without much success. He figured that if he tried to stand up then it would all go away, but he still wasn't too confident. Archie raised himself a little and pushed his feet firmly onto the floor, then he leaned forward and pushed himself off the couch.

So far so good.

He stood shakily and attempted to balance for a moment, grabbing the wall to steady himself. *Someone else is here. Who is that?*

"Shit yers look funny, mate!" a voice chuckled beside him. "Too right yer do."

Archie slowly turned towards the sound and attempted to make out the owner of the other voice. His vision was blurry, but he could see an outline, then a face. It was, it was... who?

Roo boy roo roo roo man Roy. Roy the Roo. Roy the Roo, that's it!

Archie smiled feebly at the Roo man. "Need ta piss mate!" he exclaimed.

"She's right over there," Roy nodded towards the bathroom. "Yez'll be jez fine!"

But Archie didn't *feel* just fine, no he sure didn't. He leaned heavily against the toilet wall, only just managing to stay on his feet long enough to relieve himself, before slumping to the floor. He wondered in his fuddled state how the hell he had got this way, and what was it all about?

Someone has gone, Arch, someone you know; someone very special.

He scratched his head and sighed heavily. He felt bereft. Desolate. Mournful. Something was shouting at him in his head; something important. But he couldn't make out what it was, and he felt sick and weary and heavy. It was as though the world as he knew it had ceased to exist, and he wasn't sure if anything at all had replaced it yet.

And why were the black circles spinning in concentric corroboree dances with muffled footfalls on the soft red dust in his skull? Whose was the voice calling out to him in slow sad songs? Was it... was it... who?

Chapter Eleven

Back at the camp, Jacko was bored. He'd been waiting round most of the morning. Hoping that Jesse or Archie would show up wanting to plan the day.

But so far nothing had happened, at least, not till now.

Suddenly he heard a low wailing sound; a sound so eerie and piercing that it made his skin crawl. Shit! What the hell was that? He instinctively covered his ears with his young hands, and crouched low beside the old gate outside his donga. Where was that sound coming from? He wondered. What had happened?

Jacko opened his eyes and swivelled his head towards where he thought the noise might be, and was met with a strange sight. The elders were coming. The women too. Slowly, slowly, they came. Up the road. Through the red dirt. Padding slowly on old tough feet. Nearer and nearer, but distant somehow.

Jacko was transfixed by the sight. He wanted to turn away, but he was held there crouching by the gate as though by other forces. The figures came closer, but he knew that they didn't see him at all. Their faces were closed in pain. Their eyes were shining, yet dulled. The women were moaning low and harsh now, as though controlled by primordial forces beyond their knowing. There was a strength and resilience about them; yet also such transient frailty.

Jacko felt himself sinking beside them. He knew that there had been a death, and he wanted to know more. But now was not the time. Soon. Soon. He would be told.

***

Archie regained some form of consciousness where he sat slumped on the floor by the toilet in Roy's house. *Shit, shit, shit! What the hell has happened to me?*

He sat up and looked around him, not quite sure of his surroundings. The floor and the walls of the bathroom were staring back at him; dull grey-green plaster and flaky paint. Vomit-brown lino, cracked and scuffed. Old stainless steel trough that had long since lost any hint of a shine. Wash bucket stuffed full of dirty clothes lying kicked over in the corner. A mop and broom askew in another corner.

Reaching up, Archie grabbed at the toilet bowl for support. He dragged himself to a kneeling position, and then took a deep breath to clear his head a little. A flicker of a smile crossed his face. *Geez yer must be a sorry sight, maa-aa-ate!*

***

Jesse was now sitting cross-legged on the floor of the big cave, scratching listlessly at the hard dirt floor. He wasn't too sure of what to do next, only that he had to find Archie somehow. And if he wasn't up here, then where the hell was he?

He tried to think of other places Archie might be. Down by the river? *No.* Back at camp? *No.* At Jacko's? *No.* Up at top camp? *Nah; but; maybe?*

Where would *he* go at a time like this? Would he stay or flee? Would he want company, or solitude? Think, Jesse, think! What would *you* do?

Jesse figured that maybe he'd want to get away and go somewhere different. Somewhere he wasn't known. Somewhere he could cut loose and not be himself. Somewhere like... somewhere like... top camp! Shit, why hadn't he thought about it earlier? Shit, shit, shit!

Jesse pushed himself over the ledge at the cave entrance and scrambled down through the low scrub towards the track.

His feet seemed to barely touch the ground, and he didn't feel the prickly branches poking at him as he ran. His legs were covered in scratches but he didn't care. He just wanted to find Archie. To make sure that he was OK. To help him if he could.

The track was steadier and more even now, and he soon found the section where the path up to the other camp veered off. Jesse paused briefly for a breath. His lungs were crying out for air, and his head felt a bit light, but he needed to get on. To find Arch. As he approached the camp, Jesse began to wonder how he would find Archie anyway; after all, this place was not exactly welcoming to strangers. Outsiders were not really encouraged to visit. And he'd only been up to the edge of the place before; never too far.

It had always been a game to them, hadn't it? *Let's go up to top camp an' see who's there; let's, let's, let's. Should be a bit of fun, eh? Might get some grog.*

But now it wasn't fun at all. Now he was here to find his mate, and Jesse felt a tremor of fear sweep through him like a cold dark wind. He stopped and took a gulp of air, trying to allay his fears and recover some nerve. He could see the houses on the outskirts now, and he was scared. Damn scared! But he knew that he had to go on. To do this for Archie. So he kept on going.

***

Archie was re-entering the real world, or that's how it seemed anyway. *Someone was coming. Nearer. Nearer. Feet running through spinifex. Hands reaching out for him. Panting. Wailing. Eyes shining amidst the swirling eddies of rising dust. Calling, calling. Archie! Archie, Aaa-ar-chie!*

The words were in his head, but he wasn't sure who it was. *Mum, Mum, is that you?* He closed his eyes briefly, then opened them again. No one was there. No one. Archie tried to focus.

He tried to remember what had happened to him. Why was he here in this strange house? And why did he feel so lousy?

Voices came through to him now from somewhere outside the bathroom, and he caught small snatches of conversation. It sounded slightly familiar, yet how could that be?

He rose to his feet and crossed to the mirror above the sink. *Shit, who is that? Surely that's not you Archie mate? Is it?*

Archie leaned there against the wall for a minute to regain himself. Bits and pieces of the day were returning to him now, like scraps of a jigsaw puzzle. Shreds. Fragments. Tatters of life. *Mother, mother, where are you? Mo-o-th-er!!*

The bathroom door suddenly flung open, and Roy was standing there. He looked over towards Archie.

"Y'orright, mate?" asked the Roo man.

Archie turned to reply. "Yeah, guess so, jez feelin' a bit crook."

The Roo man let a loud grunt and started to laugh.

Geez, it wasn't that funny.

"Christ, mate, yer should jez 'ave a look at yerself. Yer look godawful yer sure do!" he exclaimed.

Archie limped across the room and pushed past Roy. He went through the lounge and across to the kitchen. He was hungry, and he wondered if there was anything at all slightly palatable that would help him overcome the sick feeling in his guts. Man, he sure did feel lousy!

"Wadya want, Arch me mate?" called out Roy. "Want me ta fix yer some eggs an' bacon, eh?"

Arch stood there in the kitchen and stepped sideways to let Roy past. He shuffled from foot to foot, backwards and forwards, confused. He couldn't understand why Roy was being so kind. He didn't know what had happened this afternoon. He'd lost all perspective of time.

"Jes siddown, mate, I'll cook yer some stuff an' make yer feel better soon enough. She'll be right, mate, don't you worry about it!" Roy was fussing around the kitchen, trying to help.

Why is this stranger here with me and where is my mum and how did I get here?

Archie plodded over to the couch and lay down on the ruined fabric that was crusted with the remains of parties and fights and human contact. He was in no fit state to let it bother him. He didn't even notice. It was a haven, somewhere to lie and chill out. He curled his legs beneath him and scrunched his eyes tight against the light that was filtering low through the tatty curtains. He welcomed the darkness, and tried to relax. *But something was buzzing in his brain, coming nearer and nearer. Soft wings flapped at his cheeks and he could hear the soft distant songs of his tribe calling to him. Calling. Calling.*

"Hey, Arch, yer want yer eggs flipped, mate?" called a voice from the kitchen.

Archie groaned and slowly sat upright. (What had happened to the images in his head? What did they mean?) He scanned the room for faces, but there were none. The only sign of humanity was Roy. Roy the Roo. The Roo Man. (What was he doing here?)

"Well, will I toss them fer yer, Arch?" asked Roy.

"Sure, mate, that'd be jez fine!" replied Archie, not wanting to upset the Roo man. *But the voices were growing louder and the lines of his people were coming nearer and the time was almost there when he had to... had to... what?*

The smell of the frying eggs and meat filtered through from the kitchen, causing Archie to gag slightly with the greasiness of it all. He wanted something fresh and new to take away his nausea, but he knew that he would eat whatever Roy prepared for him.

"'S almost ready, mate, sit yerself down there at the table. D'ya wanna drink of somethin'?" called Roy from the kitchen, hoping that Archie would soon pull himself together a bit. He'd been a bit freaked out by him earlier. Arch'd been a bit weird.

"Thanks, Roy, water'll be jez fine by me," replied Archie, as he sat as the cluttered laminex table. "Smells good, mate," he lied, hoping to thank the Roo man for his efforts.

Roy plonked himself down at the table opposite Archie, smiling now that the cooking was done. "Geez, mate, yer sure can eat!" he laughed watching Archie chew.

Chapter Twelve

Jesse stopped still in front of the sprawling dongas at the edge of top camp. He was here now, and there was no way he would leave before finding out if Archie had come here too. He paused and kicked at the dry dusty road, trying to figure out what to do next. He felt alone and abandoned and a little scared. No, a *lot* scared.

It was already getting late in the afternoon, and he knew that he shouldn't really be here. Shouldn't be anywhere near the place. But he had set out to find his mate, and he knew there was a chance he might just be here.

Just as Jesse was deciding his next move, a door banged open in one of the dongas, and he could hear voices raised in argument. Curses and shouts filled the air briefly, followed by the sound of something being thrown or dropped. Jesse wasn't too sure what was going on, but he sure didn't want any part of it. No way!

He crouched down and hid behind a trailer parked haphazardly in the roadway, trying desperately not to be seen at this stage. His skin crawled a bit, and he felt prickly and hot. His nerves were on edge. He felt clammy and frightened. But he wasn't about to run away, not yet anyway.

The noises subsided as quickly as they had arisen, and Jesse looked across the street to see two figures emerge from the house. They were arguing still, and Jesse could easily make out what they were saying.

"'S not my fault the poor bugger got drunk!" shouted the man. "How was I ta know he'd never touched the grog before?"

"Geez yer think, Roy, he's only a kid," replied the woman beside him. "Yer shouldn't 'av givin' 'im so much!"

"Christ, I was only tryin' ta help the miserable kid!" shouted Roy angrily. He was pretty annoyed. He'd tried to help Archie, after all.

From where Jesse was stationed behind the old trailer, he tried to work out if it was Archie they could be talking about. Maybe it was, and maybe not. But he had to find out; somehow. (But could he just stand up and ask these total strangers about it?)

Taking courage, Jesse decided that he *would* show himself, and stood up to face Roy and his friend.

"Hey, youse, 'av you seen me mate, Archie?" he called out, hoping that he'd get a chance to talk some more. "He might have come up here lookin' fer grog."

At first there was no reaction from across the street, and Jesse waited nervously, watching for any sign of aggro. He was still ready to flee if he had to, but he stood his ground for now, hoping that the others would help him.

"Geez, another one. Where ya from, mate?" called out Roy. "Yer a mate of Archie then, are ya?"

"Yeah, I've bin lookin' fer 'im all arvo. His mum jez died yer know," replied Jesse, wishing that he could leave, get away from here. Go back to his mob, and safely.

Roy glanced across at Jesse, and suddenly a big smile lit up his face. He grinned and pushed open the gate. "What's yer name, kid? Come on over. Archie's inside. Had a bit too much ter drink, he did."

Jesse was still feeling nervous, and he wasn't at all sure whether Roy was genuine or not. But he knew it was worth a shot, and he had to check the place out to see if Archie was really inside. *Please be in there, Archie, cos I need to talk to ya and you've gotta come home with me cos your mum's died an' now there's stuff to be done an' the elders an' the women are all waitin' fer ya, so come on, come on, hurry up, Archie!*

Chapter Thirteen

It was time to go. Archie's mum's body had gone back to the land of her ancestors, and her spirit had returned to the dreamtime. Her people had come for her, and in the end all that was left were the songs.

Archie stood under the tin verandah of the house that had been their home. He had packed up his things, and had taken one last look through the place he had shared with his mother. It was sad and worn and stale. It smelt of death and failure and neglect. He needed to leave this place. He needed to get away. It was too hard and too close to stay. (And after his drinking session up at top camp, the elders had decided for him anyway. There was no going back now.)

He picked aimlessly at the peeling paintwork and surveyed the dreariness of it all. He didn't want to stay, now that his mum had gone. He knew things would never be the same again for him here, and he could see no sense in prolonging the inevitable.

But will part of you come with me, mother, and will you stay with me on my journey?

The battered community land cruiser pulled up outside in a cloud of red dust. Archie tossed his few belongings into the caged back, and settled in the front seat next to the driver. Jacko and Jesse had come down to say goodbye, and he felt pangs of sadness and lost memories wash over him there in the scuffed vinyl interior of the old vehicle. Visions from his childhood swam before him, glowing and pulsing and racing with time. Silver fish leaped in translucent arcs above the cool green of the river, and he saw the fishing lines zing as they stretched outward. The three of them, laughing and teasing, racing each other through water and red dirt. Hollering and hooting and cursing. Out over the spinifex their voices could be heard, hanging on the edge of the sun.

Archie felt like he was caught halfway between where he had once been and where he felt he should be. There was no closure, just a half-formed sense of something new reaching out to him. He should have felt some excitement at this new chance, but instead he felt dread and uncertainty.

Archie hated transitions; and he was right in the middle of one.

They pulled up outside the store, and Archie could see the usual bunch of people and dogs. Kids fought and scuffled in the dirt by the railing. Women waited for their turn to go inside and do the shopping. Men chatted idly, flicking occasionally at the flies that hung over them like Catholic veils of silence. Dogs mawed and bit and flashed their teeth. They cocked their legs and pissed against the hot corrugated tin, sniffing all the while for traces of other dogs. They were all snarls and brawn and balls.

"You gowin' ta town, eh?" called out one of the old timers, sidling up to the cabin of the 4WD. "We gotta go see the doc."

"Yeah mate, jump in," replied Ken, the driver, "we'll take yers in."

By the time they left shortly after, Archie was sharing his seat with three others plus Ken. He didn't care, he was used to it. Mob-way. Sharing. Help each other out, eh?

The trip to town was out along the old stock route, and despite the roughness of the track, they went pretty damned fast. Too fast for Archie's liking. It seemed to Archie that they were living on the edge all the way, but he knew better than to complain. Yeah, just sit tight and hold on, he told himself, that's the way.

Archie was alone inside his head for most of the trip into town. The red dirt flew by as the land cruiser sped along the track, bouncing and grinding and rattling its way through the ruts and grooves. Now and then he could hear snatches of conversation, but he drifted out of it into his own world.

Mum, mum, is that you I can feel soft against my skin cradling me and soothing my fears? Where are you, and why don't you come to me anymore? Why? Why?

Archie held tight with eyes closed, hoping for deliverance: he wished that he was anywhere but here. He needed to be alone. Above all, Archie wanted some space; but for now that was not to be.

He was jolted into reality by a sharp bend in the road, and fell heavily against the others as the vehicle slurred and fishtailed. Archie felt giddy and a bit sick. He opened his eyes to inspect the road as they managed to successfully negotiate the bend.

"Geez will ya slow down a bit?" he asked impatiently.

"Yahoo!" exclaimed the others in the front. "Wicked drivin', mate!"

Archie adjusted his position in the cab, and closed his eyes again. He could feel the hot body sweat and smell the rankness of heat and booze and grimy unwashed feet and hair and armpits beside him, but he chose to ignore it for now. There wasn't much else he could do; he was stuck here till they reached town, and he knew it. Still, he hated the fugginess and closeness and stench.

Where are the songs and the voices and the tribal feet beating patterns in the spinifex, and why have you left me all alone now, Mum? Why?

Archie smiled at the memories, but he knew it was way too early to regain them. He was too young and too lost and too afraid of what lay ahead. He needed some reassurance, but didn't know where to search. Archie knew that there was no going back to his mob for now; too late, too late. It shouldn't have been this way, but it was. It seemed to Archie that it was almost as though it had to happen, that it was preordained, but why?

Ah the voices were growing louder and the songs of his mother's people were drifting now like soft wispy tendrils of smoke, calling him, calling him… where?

"Hey, Arch mate, watch doin' tonight in town man, yer gonna camp with the mob, eh?" asked a voice beside him.

"Yeah, sure thing," replied Archie indifferently, not wanting to put the others off at this stage. After all, they had gone out of their way to arrange things for him. To try to help. To sort out the next step for him. And he knew that he should be grateful. But still, it was hard. Archie was alone. Deep down, that's where he was.

Back at the camp, Jacko and Jesse would be wondering how he was getting on. Wondering about his future. Thinking and planning about the next time they would see him. Talking and laughing and chatting as usual. Going down to the river to fish.

But for Archie, things were different now. *Quite* different. He had already left their mob, and was heading to a new camp on the other side of town.

He wondered what it would be like. There were a thousand questions spinning inside his head. He felt dizzy just thinking about tomorrow, much less any space of time beyond that. Would he find his dreams again?

Archie wanted desperately to *be* someone. To make a difference. To stand out a bit from the crowd. And maybe this new place would help him just a little. Get him started. Help him recognise his dream. He needed that. Needed to recognise the secret for what it was. But the trouble was, he didn't really *know* about the dream yet. It was too unformed still. Too nebulous. He wanted something far more concrete and positive and upfront than that, and he sure meant to find what it was.

Chapter Fourteen

Archie looked up as they came to a stop in town. They were here. He gazed out of the window of the land cruiser momentarily, then opened the old door and stepped down. Dust and flies and heat assailed him, and he could hear the conversation of the others from the cabin mixing in with the outside sounds of the town.

"Jez look at that, eh Arch," cried the driver, "over there!"

Archie followed his gaze over to the Roadhouse, wondering what he'd been pointing at. There were a few of his people wandering along the road, aimlessly kicking at the curb. Vehicles were pulling in for petrol and diesel. Station wagons, four-wheel drives, rigs towing boats and vans, trucks, small sedans. People were waiting and sitting around. Some at the pumps, others queuing and cursing. It was the only service station in town, and it was a long way from the nearest camp. The next fuel was over 300km away, and the constant stream of travellers knew they must fill up here. Fill the jerry cans too. Splash it in and pay the bill. Credit cards, cash; it was all the same.

"Hey, Arch, we're gowin' into the shops in town. Wanna come with us?" called out the driver after he'd filled up with diesel.

His name's Ken, Archie, why don't you just try to talk to him?

"Sure, yeah, I'll come with yers," replied Archie, hopping back into the 4WD.

They rolled out of the roadhouse, and Archie could already see a new line of vehicles slowing down along the road preparing to stop for fuel and food and the toilets.

Tyres crunched over gravel as they entered the car park at the shops. A line of blackfellas were stretched right along the entrance; sitting, talking, laughing, shouting, cursing, drinking, eating. Kids played and tumbled along the concrete walkway. Dogs snarled and cocked their legs against rusty steel posts. Everywhere was the litter and rubbish created by the whitefella: cans, wrappers, plastic bottles, cardboard, mesh, butts, broken glass. Disposable junk from a disposable world.

Archie got out as they pulled into a car space. White lines and black people. Painted signs hung over the row of shops: supermarket, post office, takeaway café, liquor, hardware store. All in a row of corrugated tin and gaudy peeling paint. And the people seemed at first glance to be merely slowly-moving parts of the whole tapestry. The place was littered with broken waste and broken dreams. Broken souls. Broken people. Humanity here seemed to Archie to be slipping silently over the edge, as though the concrete boundaries of the footpath formed the rim of the abyss. It all seemed tired and tatty and smudged; a human vacuum of misery and despair.

There was nothing that Archie could see at first glance to relieve the monotony of the scene. People talked and he couldn't hear their words. Different tongue. Different skin group. Different mob.

Archie spoke three languages, but the only snatches of conversation he understood here were creole words. Rough and rude. Commanding, invading. Pleading.

"Hey, Kennie me mate!" called out one of the blackfellas leaning in the supermarket entrance, as he recognised the driver. '"Waddya know, eh? Got any money fer grog, mate?"

Archie cringed and stood still where he was. He was trying to take it all in; assimilate the scene in his head. He wanted deep down to try to understand, but it was too much to take in so quickly. And part of him was scared. Blackfella fear. Whitefella fear too.

"Hey, youse, where ya from?" called out one of the teenage girls. "Ain't seen you before."

She looked directly at Archie, and he was immediately overcome with shyness. He didn't want to be here, much less begin a conversation with a stranger. He felt shy and awkward. He didn't know which way to look.

Ah, Mum, Mum, where are you now when I need you and why did you leave so soon?

She was staring directly at him now, and Archie knew there was no easy way out.

"I'm just in town fer the night, movin' on soon," he replied, hoping this would put an end to any further inquiries. He didn't fancy starting up any dialogue at this stage, and he hoped that she would simply ignore him and go away.

Archie just wanted to be left alone. Everything had been moving too fast lately. Things had got out of control, and it felt as though the past weeks since his mother's death had been one long tidal wave of emotion and change and uncertainty. He had hidden from most of it in his head, but he hadn't fooled himself. Maybe it had been time to leave his camp and maybe not; but he had gone anyway.

He felt abandoned and solitary. His head felt as though he belonged somewhere else. The trouble was that Archie was no longer in charge of his future. It had all been decided for him after his mum's death. And so here he was.

But something was lying half-formed in his head. And someone was guiding his heart with their hands. And somewhere beyond the plateaus of spinifex and coolibah, the mounds of red dirt were swirling upwards and spiralling and spinning with the sounds of the ancient ones calling to him. Calling his name. Aaa-r-chie!

Archie turned his gaze away from the girl. He decided to go into the supermarket and see what he could buy. He had a bit of money that his mum had hidden away for him in a jar in the kitchen, and he was anxious now to spend some. Perhaps he could buy some of his favourite sweets; he didn't get to have them back at camp very often after all.

Now that he was more or less his own boss, Archie decided that he could spend his money however he liked. He knew there was only one store at the new camp where he was going, and he also knew that it wouldn't sell sweets.

Inside the shop, he was assailed by rows and rows of different goods. In one half of the shop, there were clothes and hardware and camping gear. Archie walked up and down the different aisles, trying to take in the variety of items for sale. Camp ovens, mosquito coils, tin plates and mugs, frying pans, plastic water containers, sleeping bags, swags, fishing gear; it was all here. He wandered over to the racks of clothes, attracted by some brightly coloured shirts.

Archie flicked through the garments till he found one his size. Slipping it on over his worn singlet, he looked around to see if there was a mirror anywhere within sight.

"Geez, her fancy yerself then, doncha?" a voice from behind him exclaimed.

Archie wheeled round to see the teenage girl from outside standing behind him. She was laughing at him with arms crossed and feet planted solidly, her head cocked slightly to one side in amusement.

"Yer gonna buy it then?" she asked. "Looks good on yer, it does."

Archie was embarrassed. He hadn't expected anyone to be watching him. He felt as though he had been caught out, and it put him off his guard.

"Er, dunno," he stammered back.

"I reckon yer should," she smiled encouragingly. "My name's Kirra."

Archie wasn't sure if he had heard right.

Murra? Did she say Murra?

"Hi, I'm Archie. Just come up from my camp. Goin' to a new camp tomorrow."

He peered at the girl nervously, not knowing what else to say. It was a bit hard. He hadn't had a lot to do with strangers. Archie felt uncomfortable.

Archie took off the shirt and folded it under his arm. He wanted to be by himself, and not have to talk to this persistent stranger, so he made some lame excuse about having to meet people and turned to go. At the cash register, he glanced around to make sure that Kirra was not in sight. Good, she had gone!

He paid for the shirt, then wandered down to the Café. Archie went inside, and surveyed the menu. He wasn't really very hungry. More thirsty than anything. He scanned the price lists and available foods and beverages. Hamburgers, chips, peas, sandwiches, hot dogs, fried rice, beef casserole. Soft drinks in cans and bottles. Juices, tea, coffee, milk shakes. Ice creams, lollies, chocolate bars. Fruit. Too much to choose from. He was a bit confused.

"Hi ya, love, what'll it be then?" called out a cheery waitress. "You new around here then? Haven't seen you before."

Archie smiled hesitantly, now knowing how to respond. He still hadn't made up his mind about what he wanted to order, so he turned back to the menu board again.

"That's all right, love, take yer time. I'll be out back when yer ready, so give us a hoy!"

Archie was relieved momentarily to have some space once more. He wasn't used to shops and crowds and strangers. He had grown up with his mob away from here. This place was all so different.

"I'll have a hamburger and a chocolate milk shake, please," he called out to the space at the back of the counter, hoping that the cheery waitress would hear him. "How much will that be?" (Maths had never been his strong subject at school. When he'd gone, anyway, which wasn't that often.)

"Ah, there you are. Now, what was it you wanted, lovie?" asked the waitress as she re-emerged from behind the back of the shop.

Archie mumbled his order again, beginning to think that maybe this hadn't been such a good idea, after all. He'd really only wanted to get away from Kirra. A bit of breathing space and a change after the long ride up here to town with the others. Yes, that's what he'd needed.

"That'll be $7.50. Coming right up. You just sit yourself down at one of the tables, and it'll be here in a jiff," said the smiling waitress, "no time at all."

Despite his earlier nervousness, the woman's manner was infectious, and Archie began to relax. He looked around at the tables, and chose one away from the door and windows. There were lots of magazines strewn carelessly on a cheap laminex table in the corner, so he took one of these and began to flick through it. His reading was poor, but he enjoyed the pictures. There were lots of shots of beaches and sea life and cities and houses and famous people. It seemed to Archie that there was a whole world just hiding in between the covers of the magazine, and he began to wonder about things beyond his world. Beyond the camps. Beyond his people. A world which was strange and different and exotic and exciting. A world that perhaps he could be a part of one day. And maybe belong.

Archie was lost in the pictures now, feeling some sense of affinity with the lure of the unknown. He marvelled at the textures and patterns that were held in the images there before him and in the glossy pages. He flicked through the photos and was transformed beyond the present into somewhere that he wanted to be. Somewhere foreign to him. A thousand questions leapt into his head. Did people really live in houses like that? Were there really beaches of pure white sand? Were these tall buildings in cities all over the world? Where were the people he saw in the photo? Did people really wear all these strange outfits he saw in multi-coloured layouts? Why were the colours so different to those of his world?

Why is this page here?

Chapter Fifteen

Kira knew better than to hang around after Archie had gone. She'd been given a bum steer, and she was a little pissed off. He'd seemed pretty cute, and someone new around this place wasn't to be ignored. Kirra knew that it had been a bit more than just curiosity or boredom this time. Archie had seemed somehow different to the others, even though she couldn't really define why.

Perhaps it was because he'd been alone and strangely vulnerable. Aloof. Unsure of himself. Not like the cocky and swaggering kids around here that she was used to. Rough. Swearing. Dicks for brains, half of them.

Kirra knew the score; she'd grown up round here, after all. She was tough and street-wise, and pretty damned resilient. Had to be. Survival was the name of the game in this town. And god knows, there were plenty who didn't make it. Plenty who succumbed to the grog and the gunja and worse. Fights and brawls and violence were second-nature around here, where people could disappear without a trace. Here one day and gone the next. No questions asked. Just walked right off the face of the earth sometimes. Went bush. Got in trouble. Jail. Pfft! Gone, just like that.

Kirra's mob lived down by the river at the half-way camp. She wasn't sure why it was called that; something to do with the cattle runs of the old days. Water-stop for the drovers. Sorting place. Still, she reckoned now it was appropriate; it was half-way alright. Half way to nowhere. And that's exactly where most of her people were too. Lost halfway between worlds. Blackfella, whitefella; all the same to her. Lousy cheating bastards they were. Wouldn't give a toss for the whole darn lot of them.

She scratched at her shins and surveyed the bruises. She noticed that they were beginning to go purple. Last night she'd had to run away pretty quick after the old buggers at the camp got stoked up, and in her haste she tripped over the steel posts that held the dog chains. Damn, it sure had hurt!

Kirra was tired of wandering round the supermarket now by herself, and she figured that the stranger would now be back with his mates, so she decided to go to the café and buy an ice cream for herself. Be buggered if she'd share it with anyone today. Let them buy their own!

She sauntered over to the café and went in, trying to decide which cone she'd have this afternoon. Maybe chocolate chip or toffee. Strawberry swirl? Her concentration was suddenly broken by the sight of the teenager from the store. The shirt-boy. It was him. Kirra quickly decided to let it go and ignore him. Her pride had been dented as it was, and she knew better than to have a second go. But still, he *was* cute.

She glanced sideways at the table where he was sitting, and suddenly he looked up and met her gaze.

"Hi yer," he said, attempting a small smile to make peace with her. "Sorry about before, I just felt a bit awkward."

Kirra wasn't used to boys being honest. In fact, no one she knew would have admitted anything like their *real* feelings to her. She was a bit taken aback, but it was nice.

"Hullo again," she replied, "sorry if I upset you back there."

"That's OK. My name's Archie, by the way."

For a brief moment they just stared at each other, and then Kirra laughed and broke the silence. She felt as though she had just met someone pretty special; someone who would be an important part of her life. But she didn't know why. Just that it *was*.

Archie seemed to mirror the intensity she felt. He stopped eating and stared at her.

Is that you, Mum, I can feel tap tapping at me, is that really you?

"Would you like to sit down and share the table?" asked Archie, a little bit hopefully. The truth was, he liked this girl. There was something fresh and bold and slightly worldly about her despite her apparent roughness. She was brash but pleasant. Archie liked that.

Archie hadn't had much experience with people outside his mob so far, but it seemed to him that Kirra was OK. He felt relaxed with her, not awkward and shy like he usually was with strangers. There was something about her that reminded him of... reminded him... of... *who?*

"Yeah, alright, if yer don't mind," Kirra replied, joining Archie at the table as she spoke. "What ya reading then?"

Archie laughed and looked up from the glossy magazine he'd been leafing through. He felt as though he'd been caught out, and he was a little embarrassed. He quickly closed the pages and pushed the magazine away.

"Nothin', just fillin' in time," he replied hurriedly, not wanting her to know that he hadn't really been reading at all. Dreaming was more like it. Dreaming of places and people and happenings a long way from here. Dreaming of whitefella stuff and whitefella ways. Wondering if he'd ever get away to explore and see it all for himself.

But Kirra wasn't to be put off, and she flicked open the magazine he'd been scouring and scanned the glossy pages for herself. She settled for a double spread of fashion pages, and oohed and aahed over the images before her.

"Man, I would love to wear those!" she exclaimed, staring wide-eyed at the pictures before her. "Just look at those colours and patterns and the make-up, wow!"

Kirra was transformed in her mind to the world of fashion and models and catwalks and beauty, and her face glowed instantly with the excitement of it all. She sighed with contentment there at the shabby laminex table in the small café, momentarily lost in her own dreams. Ah, what she would give to leave this dump and get out into the big world!

She dreamed of cities and people; tall structures with glass and angles and controlled lines where smart people gathered. She dreamed of traffic and lights and cafés and clothes and trains and cars and brightness and change. The buzz of humanity.

Kirra closed her eyes tight, and briefly held the dream inside. Ah, that felt good. Then she opened her eyes and smiled at Archie, not wanting to let go her inner world, but knowing that she couldn't really share it yet. Not here. Not with this new friend. Not with anyone. Yet.

Archie smiled at her and looked a little puzzled. He sensed that she had been testing him a little with her silence, and he almost recognised her reticence. (Was it like his own dreaming?) He was a little puzzled, but decided to lighten things up once more with conversation. Try to find a common link. Something a bit easy that they could share for now.

"Where are yer from then?" he asked, hoping that would get things going a bit, and avoid topics that were still unknown to both of them.

Archie had a sense that there was more to Kirra than surface stuff; a lot more. But for now he didn't want to get into anything too deep. He was still feeling too raw. And he had lately had more changes than he really knew how to cope with anyway.

"Over at half-way camp, just up the road there," Kirra pointed.

"Oh, you always lived there then?" Archie asked.

"Nah, came here when me dad ran off from our camp up the river. Got some aunties an' cousins here though. How about you, where's you from?" replied Kirra, wanting to find out a bit about Archie in exchange.

Archie blushed a little then replied, "Over west a fair way, by the ol' cattle station. Been there most of me life. My ol' man buggered orf too, left when I was a li'l kid, dunno where he is, me mum jez died, that's why I'm goin' to a new camp."

Kirra was silent while she took all this in. She cocked her head sideways and snuck a glance at Archie. Then she looked down at the table while she absorbed his story. His place in life. His data bank. Maybe they had a fair bit in common after all, she thought. It seemed strange to Kirra that there were people out there with stories that somehow matched. Strangers that met suddenly and recognised a kindred spirit. People whose lives instantly connected for no apparent reason. Odd that, she thought.

"Dincha have family back at camp then?" she asked Archie, wondering why he had left so soon after his mother's death. Usually the mob took care of you. But still, there might be other reasons.

"Nah, not really," replied Archie, "anyways, me mum had told the elders before she died that she wanted me to get a bit of education away from the camp. Whitefella learning. New community. No grog."

He didn't tell her about the binge he'd had the night his mum had died. And he didn't tell her that he still craved drink now and then. Still remembered the night with the Roo-man. Still reckoned that the grog was what had got him through, and he hadn't minded that at all. No, he sure hadn't.

Archie reflected on the night he'd gone up to top camp. It was still so vivid and recent in his mind. Still so real to him. He could almost taste the bubbles of beer on his lips, and wondered if he'd get a chance to have some more alcohol soon.

Kirra broke his reverie with another question. "Hey, here's yer meal, Archie, d'ya want me to go now?"

"Nah, stick around for a while if yer've got nothin' else to do. We might go for a walk to the river this arvo if yer like. I'm in town till tomorrow anyway. Till Ken gets the transport organised to me new camp. Orright?" Archie looked at Kirra straight, hoping she'd say yes. Wanting some company now. Liking her enough to want to spend some time together.

He felt strangely at ease with Kirra, and sensed that she felt the same. There was an instant and easy affinity between them, and Archie knew that for his part it would not include any sexual overtones. He worried that maybe Kirra might see him differently, but dismissed those thoughts for now, concentrating on getting to know her as a friend. An ally perhaps; someone he could talk to and share time with. And maybe even trust, later on.

"Do yer wanna share my milkshake? I could get a yer a glass if yer like," Archie offered, smiling encouragingly at Kirra. He felt as though this would help ease them into something; a transition of sorts. He was trying to make an effort with Kirra, and he hoped that she wouldn't laugh at him and embarrass him there in the café. So far, things were going well, and Archie wanted to keep it that way. It was new territory for him, and there'd been so much change in his life recently, that he marvelled that he was talking to her at all.

"Nah, you have it, Archie, I've got me ice cream now," she replied, smiling at him with growing confidence. She liked Archie already, but not in the usual way. Not as a boyfriend. Just a friend. Confidante. Ally. She felt amazingly comfortable sitting here with Archie, and already sensed their affinity too. Strange that, she thought. Go figure! "Go on, you just enjoy yer hamburger," she said, looking across at Archie. "I'm not really that hungry anyway."

Archie grinned at her as he sank his teeth into the crisp meaty roll, savouring the taste.

Chapter Sixteen

Down by the river there was stillness and a slow sense of time suspended in the heat haze. Flies crawled over the food scraps dropped near the broken wooden table and seats. A large green wheelie bin lay on its side nearby, kicked over in the dust and waste of the picnic area. Rubbish spewed out of the open lid; broken bottles, cans, greasy wrappers, cardboard, soggy disposable nappies, plastic, newspapers. A blood-soaked bandage lay dirty and discarded nearby, tangled in the spinifex. It made Archie's skin crawl.

"Geez, will ya jez look at all this mess?" he cried out to Kirra, disgruntled. "Wouldn't yer think someone'd clean it up?"

But Kirra was oblivious to the detritus of human contact with the surrounds; she'd grown up with it, become immune to it, didn't even really notice it anymore. The land around the town was no-man's land, and what went on down by the river most nights was common knowledge to everyone from round here. Fights, cursing, boozing, sniffing petrol, drunkenness, squabbles, bashings, rape; she knew, yeah, she knew. Bad stuff. The worst.

The funny thing was that the next day it all seemed to unfold back to some sort of harmony, of acceptance. Somehow. Kirra didn't see how that could happen too often, except that it did. People forgot. And forgave. And smiled and got on with each new day, as though the dreadful occurrences of the night before had never happened. To Kirra, it seemed downright stupid, but that's the way it was. *Mostly.*

"Yeah, sure is a mess," she replied. "God knows, I've seen it all before."

Archie looked across at Kirra where they sat on the river bank, and wondered about her life. Was it as hard as he suspected? Had she been beaten, or worse? What had she been through already that he couldn't even begin to understand? How did she manage to stay so calm and seemingly unaffected by her surrounds? *Like top camp,* he thought.

"You wanna go fer a swim?" Kirra asked. "There's a good place just up the river a bit, round the bend."

"Nah, not today," replied Archie. It was getting late, and he knew that he would soon have to go and meet the others over at the town camp. He'd agreed to spend the night there with them, and he didn't want to get lost and miss out on his trip tomorrow. But still, he didn't want to leave Kirra just yet either.

He was enjoying her company more than he cared to admit. It had been a difficult time for Archie recently, and life-events had taken away his sense of freedom and innocence for now. His world had undergone a huge upheaval, and it felt good to be with someone he could relax with for a little while.

"Some other time, maybe we could go swimming," he offered as a sort of truce, not wanting to upset his new-found friend at this stage. "I have to meet some of the mob soon at the town camp, so I can't be too long."

He glanced across at Kirra to make sure that he hadn't offended her by declining the offer to go swimming. The last thing Archie wanted right now was to alienate her.

"It's OK. Yeah, we'll go some other time, maybe," she replied. In truth, Kirra was a bit deflated, but she sensed that there'd be lots of other times when Archie came to town that they could continue their friendship. So she let it go for now.

"Come on, race you up to the shops. The loser buys the ice creams up at the café," laughed Kirra, trying to change the mood back to something light once more.

"Okay, let's go!" shouted Archie, leaping to his feet as he headed off down the dusty road. "Yeehaah!" He was glad that

Kirra was smiling and laughing again. It made him feel warm inside, and he needed that now.

He had left the known behind, and was heading into the unknown, and it was scary.

Mum, Mum, will you come with me on the journey?

Archie felt a surge and a rush of wind as he streaked past Kirra, running running. His calloused feet kicked up small stones and sent them flying in the dust and heat by the river. He felt free and uncluttered once more, like the many times he had run and raced with Jesse and Jacko so often in their childhood. He puffed and he surged and he blew out the bad thoughts that had been threatening him, wanting to enjoy the last bit of time he would have with Kirra today.

But suddenly she was there right beside him, straining at his elbow. Her hair was brushing his shoulder as she drew level, and she smiled at him sideways as they raced the short distance to the footpath near the shops. As they reached the café door they were together still, and they pushed and shoved at each other till they fell together laughing on the doorstep. They were a mass of tangled arms and legs and shining eyes as they lay there briefly, panting and laughing and full of the excitement of the race.

"Geez, yer can run!" exclaimed Archie as he looked over at Kirra next to him. "Fair dinkum, yer's great fer a girl!"

"Huh!" snorted Kirra, as she untangled herself and scurried to her feet. "What make's yer think that boys are faster anyway?"

They both regained their feet and scrutinised each other outside the café. Archie might easily have been upset about the race if it had been Jesse or Jacko, but decided that it was OK to draw equal with Kirra. She was different. She was his new friend, and somehow it didn't matter if he hadn't won. Archie was fine with that, he felt good.

They were both laughing now, and Archie pushed the door open and led Kirra into the café for their ice creams.

"Guess we buy our own then, seeing neither of us won, eh?" he declared to Kirra. He really wanted to buy them both an ice cream, but he sensed that Kirra was pretty independent, and a deal was a deal, after all. Archie didn't want to risk offending her again, so he sauntered over to the counter to check out the range of flavours.

"Which one d'yer reckon I should have?" he asked Kirra. "What's your favourite?"

"Hokey pokey, I love it," answered Kirra, pointing to the big tub in the fridge at the counter. "It tastes yum!"

Archie had never heard of half of the ice creams on display here, so he scanned the colours to see which one he liked.

"I'll have the blue one," he said to the waitress behind the counter. "It looks cool."

Kirra and Archie paid for their cones and went over to the magazine table to sit and eat them. They watched each other as they slurped at the cool refreshments, and Archie couldn't help grinning at Kirra from time to time. He felt childish yet sort of grown up all at the same time. He felt happy. Archie was enjoying life right now, and he wasn't worried about the future for the time being. It felt good.

"When do you have to go?" he asked Kirra casually, as they finished their ice creams.

"Not yet, in a little while maybe," she replied. In truth, Kirra really was in no rush to get back to half way camp at all, especially now that she had met someone as friendly and interesting as Archie. No, she sure wasn't in any hurry this afternoon. Not now. But she knew that she would have to get back before evening. There were chores to be done, and she knew that her mum relied on her for most of them. All of them really.

Kirra would face the same routine tonight that she faced most nights. Prepare the tea, get the water, wash the little kids, feed the dogs, clean up the dishes, tidy things away, put the kids to bed, watch out for her mum, fetch the ciggies and grog, stay out of the way of men, try to hold it all together.

It seemed that half her life had been spent with a child on her hip and another few toddlers staggering along behind her. It was Kirra who did most of the caring and tending, while her mother mostly drank. Cask wine. Beer. Rotgut, whatever. Down down down. Liquid salvation. Fix-me-up. Warmth, *Ruin.*

Kirra didn't entirely blame her mum; she knew that many of the mob were the same. Not their fault really. Nothing better to do. No work, no jobs, no culture, no land. Gone. Their land and their dreamin'. Mostly gone. *And what were they supposed to do now with their lives and their future?*

They had the whitefella money, of course. Dole money. Free. And whitefella shops and liquor stores and clothes and food. Yeah, they had all that alright. But what else did they have besides? Kirra often wondered. What had happened to their pride and dignity and independence and self-worth? Their songs and dances and rituals? Their systems and laws? Where had they all gone?

Kirra could feel the anger and injustice of it all as it slowly crept inside her skull, and she kicked out at the chair as she finished her ice cream. It hurt. *She* hurt. And she wanted something more. Something better; for herself and her people. But she didn't know how to fix things, and that made everything in her life so much more frustrating.

"You OK?" asked Archie, noticing Kirra's dark looks suddenly. *I know how you feel!* "Do you want to go for a bit of a walk before your go back to camp?" he asked kindly, trying to bring things back to normality once more. "I'll have to go soon and meet Ken, but we could walk round the shops a bit if you like."

But Kirra was not so easily diverted. "I hate it!" she cried out to Archie. "All this drinkin' an' arguin', an' fightin'. Jez hate it, d'ya understand?"

Archie didn't know where to look. He was worried about Kirra, and he wished that he could do something to distract her just for a little while. Anything.

"Come on," he pulled at her hand, "let's go over to the supermarket and you can show me where the chocolates and soft drinks are," he said firmly. "I'll buy you something."

Kirra let Archie lead her out of the café and along the footpath to the supermarket. She decided that it wasn't fair on Archie to load him with all her problems. He would be gone tomorrow after all, and she didn't know when she would see him next. And why should he care about her woes, anyway?

She smiled at him and broke out of her darkness. Back into light. Reality.

"Nah, you don't have to buy me anything, I'm OK," she laughed at Archie. "Really, I'm fine."

Archie was relieved to see Kirra back in good spirits, and he grabbed her hand for a moment and squeezed it tight before letting go. It was a signal to Kirra that there was some sort of bond between them. A sharing. A sense of wholeness and belonging. It just felt right, despite everything. Archie knew that he would see Kirra again, and soon. There would be lots of shared times ahead when they could get to know each other better. He knew that they had forged a solid friendship already. And somehow he knew that Kirra felt it too.

Chapter Seventeen

Archie had been sitting on the hard ground at the town camp for a while now, waiting for the fire to be stoked up for tea. Ken had been shopping at the supermarket, and had a load of supplies in the back of the land cruiser. Plastic bags. Whitefella goods.

There were thick cuts of cheap meat to throw on the grate over the fire. Packet of bread and some margarine and sauce. A bag of potatoes to wrap in foil for the fire. And of course, lots of grog. Slabs of cans for the town camp. Had to be sociable, give the mob a bit of cheer. "Here, get that inter yers, do yer good!"

Where have I heard that before and why can I see Mum's face scowling at me now from somewhere... somewhere.

"Have a beer, Archie? One won't hurt you tonight, mate," insisted Ken, pushing a can into Archie's lap. "To toast your new life, eh?"

Archie wasn't so sure if he should drink at all, but he knew also that he couldn't offend Ken. Besides, he could suit himself now, and no one was here to tell him what to do, were they?

So he decided to join in, and he accepted the beer with a smile. "Geez thanks, Ken. Don't mind if I do," he replied as he opened the can.

Pfft! There it was again! That sound, he'd heard it before. Where?

Archie frowned as the familiar bubbles spilled over the edge, and he raised the cold can to his lips. The beer tasted bitter-sweet, and Archie recognised the joy he felt as it slid down his throat once more.

Ah, gedidinyer the Roo-man had said's good ferya.

The fire suddenly kicked into life, and Archie felt relaxed as he watched a couple of the elders throw some logs on. The flames roared and tossed against the night sky, and Archie was transfixed by the joy of the spectacle. His mind was at one with the flames, and in the fire was his world, and a small sense of security and belonging.

And the flames of the past were dancing. And the feet of the ancient ones were padding. And the stories of the dreaming were sung in lines and circles and patterns, rising and falling in the thin wispy smoke-swirls, echoing and ebbing in the night-breeze. And the darkness was thick... thick with... what?

Spirit-life seemed to surround Archie as he sat mesmerised there by the camp fire. It was as though the fire managed to bring out some part of him that he was trying to recognise. To learn, to accept. Archie knew that it had something to do with his mum and his people, but he wasn't sure how much of it he really knew. Or remembered.

You do, Archie, you do, I taught you... remember?

But the lines and connections were incomplete, and Archie could only recognise snatches of words and stories and songs and dances. He tried to piece them all together there by the firelight, but somehow he fell short. It was too hard. He felt like he only had threads and tatters of it all, and he wanted more. A lot more.

And sometimes he wanted a lot less, too. Sometimes he just wanted whitefella stuff. Sometimes the blackfella stuff got in his way and he felt stifled and choked and cheated. Yeah, sometimes he hated the dreaming.

Archie sipped on the beer and leaned back against a tree stump by the fire. He was feeling warm and mellow and OK. Time had become meaningless again.

He thought of Kirra suddenly, and wondered what she would be doing over at half way camp with her mob. Archie hoped that she'd be alright. It seemed to him that some of the stuff she'd talked about was pretty dangerous, and he wished that he'd been able to stay with her a bit longer. Help her out a bit more. Just be with her.

"Wanna nothery?" called a voice from the darkness, which Archie recognised as Ken's.

"Yeah, OK," he murmured back, reaching out to accept the fresh can of beer. A part of him warned that he shouldn't be drinking again. Not after last time. Not after the experience up at top camp. But to Archie, that was already ancient history, and besides, things were different for him now, weren't they? Yeah, he'd be just fine with another beer! Sure he would!

Ken smiled at him encouragingly as he handed Archie the familiar can. He reckoned that the young bloke deserved a night on the grog after all he'd been through lately, and besides, what harm could it do? He was with the mob tonight, and they'd keep an eye out for him, after all. At least, that's what Ken reckoned, as he sat across from Archie and opened another can for himself too. Ah, it tasted good, damned good.

A couple of the old ones were starting up a song. Guitars strummed. Laughter and music and singing filled the air. Feet stamped in the dirt by the firelight, and Archie marvelled at how easily some of the fellas round here could pick out a tune and make such sweet sounds. It brought a lump to his throat, and made him feel proud and strong and glad to be blackfella once more.

Maybe that's your calling too, Archie. The music. The music the rhythms and patterns of words and songs and stories of your people. Blackfella songs. Whitefella songs. Maybe...

The chords and the lyrics echoed through his skull as he rocked gently to the rhythm and the beat of the music. It felt *right* somehow, as though something there within him was stirring. An awakening of sorts. A beginning, however tentative. What was it he was trying to hold?

"Play that one again," called out Ken from somewhere in the dark, "sounds good mate."

Archie listened intently as the chords formed a background to the lyrics. He felt the music go through him again; it was almost as though the words held a meaning just for him. What was it that they were trying to tell him?

You know, you know, Archie. I told you in my songs and stories of the dreamtime. I drew the patterns in the sand for you, and showed you the meaning long ago when you were such a little boy. Didn't I?

Somewhere in the back of his head Archie was beginning to make the connections, but it was too soon yet for the meanings. He recognised parts of the puzzle spinning round, caught in the words of the song. The strum of the guitar seemed to be telling him something. But he couldn't quite make out what the message was. He knew it was something to do with... to do with... what?

"Hey, could yer play me favourite, mate, you know, The Pub with No Beer?" called out Ken, laughing over his beer. "I just love that Slim Dusty fella, mate."

Archie smiled and withdrew into the shadows once more. The beer was warmer now, but still tasted OK as it dribbled over his lips and ran down, down his gullet. Ah, the taste! Pretty damned good, eh?

When the music and the singing stopped, Archie leaned over and spoke to the guitarist. He wanted to know how he had learned to play. Who had taught him? Was it difficult to learn?

"Nah, not if you've got the rhythm, it's easy. Jez takes a bit of practice to learn all the chords. That's all," he replied. "Here, I'll show yer if yer like."

Archie was eager to try, but figured that now was not really the right time. He asked if he could have a try later on, after they'd eaten. He didn't want to embarrass himself now in front of all the others there by the campfire. No way.

***

Kirra was busy as usual. Tea was finished, and she was clearing the table and stacking the dishes. The little kids were getting restless and ratty, and Kirra sighed heavily as she thought of preparing them for bed.

Outside on the back verandah of the house, her mum was sitting in her usual old steel chair and drinking. Again. Cheap wine spilt over her lips as she crooned a tune to herself, mumbling and stuttering occasional words in harsh staccato fashion.

"Eh, Kirra, waddya doin' in there, love? Come out here an' sit with yer ol' mum fer a bit, woncha?" the old woman called out.

Kirra shuddered and went on with her tasks, knowing that her mum was already drunk enough not to insist on her presence tonight. It was the same almost every night, and Kirra was well-used to the vagaries of life here with her mum and the kids on the edge of the camp. She knew what was expected of her, and she kept her part of the bargain and kept the house going. Without her, what would happen to her mum and the younger ones? Who would look after them and take care of them?

But sometimes Kirra felt cheated by her lot. Angry with the world. Annoyed that things were always so one-sided, and that she had to take the responsibility for the family all the time. It just didn't seem fair.

She was a pretty smart kid, and very bright. Despite her irregular school attendance, she always got good reports from her teachers at the local school. They saw her potential, and recognised her ability to retain knowledge easily. She was encouraged and guided to higher aspirations, but they knew that her family's failing left her with few opportunities to achieve her goals. It was a common story, but one that the teachers tried to grapple with nonetheless.

For Kirra, part of the problem was the gap between her two worlds. She was like Archie. She felt stranded halfway between blackfella culture and whitefella ways. The demands of her mob were stronger than the demands of the mainstream system of the whitefella world, but she was subject to both on a daily basis. Torn this way and that by both systems. Both laws. Existing on the edge.

Ignoring the cries of her mother for a little while, she gathered up the kids and got them into her bed, all piled in with each other. She read them their favourite story, then tussled their hair and kissed them all goodnight. She spoke to them in their own language, the language of their people. Then she turned out the light and went out to the verandah to check on her mum.

It didn't really matter that she was drunk; Kirra was used to it. She thought it was normal; and it was in this place. Especially on pension day.

"Hiya, Mum. D'ya want something to eat now?" asked Kirra, hoping that at least she could encourage her to eat something tonight to soak up the grog a bit. "There's some meat and salad inside for yer," she added.

The woman turned and gazed at Kirra, then a tear trickled slowly down her cheek. She was old beyond her years, sad and lost. Her hair was matted and her face dulled by the years of neglect and pain and disillusion. Her eyes had lost their shine long ago. Her dress was filthy and tatty, covered by the stains of food and wine and sauce that she'd been unable or unwilling to prevent from spilling. She seemed tired and beaten, as though life had simply passed her by and kicked the stuffing out of her once too often.

She managed a feeble smile as she recognised her daughter there beside her. "How are yer, Kirra? Are the kiddies all in bed? D'yer wanna siddown an' 'av a drink with yer ol' mum then, eh?" she held out the cask for Kirra, but there was no response.

Geez d'yer seriously think I'd touch the stuff, Mum? God help me!

***

It was getting late at town camp. Archie had eaten some meat and spuds with a bit of salad and some bread and sauce. He was still drinking, but had slowed down since tea. It was good to be here with Ken and the mob from the town, but he had to admit that he'd been thinking about Kirra too. Wondering how she was getting on tonight. Hoping that things would be alright. He was probably a bit drunk already, but he didn't care. Maybe he'd go down to halfway camp later on and check that things were fine. Someone would show him how to get there surely.

Archie sipped at the can of beer and mulled over recent events. It had been a long day, and he sure was tired. Bone weary. Could do with a rest. But he was still too hyped up from the departure and the drive here. No, he figured that it would be a while yet before he would get any sleep tonight; and besides, they weren't leaving town till after lunch tomorrow. Ken had things to do and people to catch up with before he drove Archie to his new home. And he didn't intend to leave before he was ready.

Archie stood up and stretched. He wandered over to the other side of the dying fire to see if Ken was still around. He had decided to try to find Kirra before it got too late tonight, and he needed someone to give him some directions to her camp.

"Hey, Ken me mate, there you are," Archie exclaimed, "d'yer know the way over ta halfway camp on the other side of town?"

"Waddya wanna know that fer?" Ken replied, curious about Archie's sudden inquiry at this time of night. "Ain't no good you goin' there now, mate, too late," Ken stated.

But Archie had got it into his head now that he had to see Kirra tonight, so he persisted.

"Jez wanna see someone I met today, orright?" he asked.

Ken grinned and winked at Archie with a knowing look. "Oh, jez someone, or a girl yer met in town, eh?" Ken figured that Archie might have found someone to spend time with today, but hadn't reckoned he'd be this keen. "Orright, I'll drop yer over there, but don't be too long willyers?" said Ken, reaching in his trouser pocket for the keys to the 4WD. In truth he had been a bit worried about Archie since he'd driven him into town this morning, but he knew that it wasn't really his problem. He was only doing his job, and if Archie went astray, then he wasn't accountable, was he? He figured that Archie could look after himself. At least, he hoped so anyway.

"Come on, jump in then, Arch, me mate," called out Ken, revving the motor of the old land cruiser. "She'll be right. Jez make sure yer get back here tonight, orright?"

"Thanks, Ken, I won't be too long," replied Archie, secretly pleased that it was OK with Ken.

"D'yer want me to pick yer up later?" asked Ken, as he neared the other camp. "I could come back fer yer if ya like."

"Nah, I'll walk, she's right," replied Archie as he got out of the vehicle. "G'night."

Archie watched as the headlights faded up the road, then turned round and faced the new camp. He stood still for a while, listening, trying to get his bearings. He could hear voices and shouting and arguments and dogs barking. The sound and smell of a campfire up the road. Engines running. Something breaking. Laughter. Banging.

It reminded Archie of the day he had gone up to top camp and got drunk. But this was fresher, scarier, somehow. Perhaps it was because of the unknown.

Archie wanted to turn around and retrace the track back to the town camp, but he'd come here to find Kirra, so he stayed. After a short while, he headed up the road towards the firelight. He passed a few sheds and houses. Lights were on here and there. Looked just like the other camps he'd been in so far. Yeah, almost the same.

127

In truth, Archie knew that he shouldn't really be here. Shouldn't be messing around another camp. And perhaps he wouldn't have come at all except for the grog giving him a bit of false courage. Yeah, the booze had given him the edge.

Still, he faltered for a moment while surveying the scene, then decided to press on along the road leading to the spot where the campfire blazed against the night sky. His mind was preoccupied with Kirra, and he was worried that he might not be able to find out where she lived. He thought about the possible dangers of arriving unannounced, and then dismissed them as irrelevant. He'd be alright, wouldn't he?

But somewhere deep inside he could hear a voice whispering to him and warning him and calling out his name and beckoning to him to run to go now to get away from this place, and hands reached out for him to lead him somewhere... somewhere... away from here.

As he neared the end of the street, Archie was suddenly confronted by a group of men from the camp. His path was blocked, and he didn't have the time to turn and run.

"Eh, waddya think yer doin' here?" called out one of the men pushing at Archie as the others closed in. "Where d'ya think yer gowin', mate?"

Archie wanted to turn and flee, but it was too late. He would have to face the music now. There was no way out. He tried to speak, but fear had grabbed hold of him, and all that came out of his lips was a half-formed splutter. "I jez... I jez... wanna... see..." Archie gasped, knowing that he was not making any sense at all.

He was suddenly grabbed from behind and pushed to the ground. He could hear shouts and curses and swearing as they held him firm. His face was shoved hard into the dirt, and his arms were twisted up against his back. A strong knee landed on his shoulder as one of the men knelt down, pinning him to the ground.

"Yer can't jez come up here an' sneak around at night, mate. Who are ya? What mob you from, eh?" asked a rough gravelly voice. "We don' like strangers here, mate!"

There was no reply. Archie was unable to speak with his cheek and mouth pressed into the roadway. It was too late to try talking his way out of this anyway; way too late. Archie was scared. He wished to God he'd never come over here to half way camp tonight. He wished he hadn't been drinking the grog with Ken. He wished that his mum was here to protect him and that he'd never left his own mob. And he wished that somehow Kirra would appear to save him. Yeah, he sure wished that!

But it wasn't going to happen. He was in trouble, and he knew it. Serious trouble. Archie tried desperately to break free from the hold they had on him there in the roadway, but he couldn't. He tried to shout or scream, but nothing came out of his mouth except some thick globby spit that mixed with the dust of the road and dried on his chin in the heat. He couldn't move.

Suddenly Archie felt a sharp pain run down his back and along his spine. His captors were hitting him, kicking him, punching and scratching at him.

It's too late, too late... K...iiii... rr... aaaa!

Somewhere in his head Archie heard the sounds of drums and thunder and saw lightning flashes, and then there was nothing. Darkness invaded his world. Silence. Emptiness.

Mum, Mum, where are you? I'm falling falling and the stars are shining somewhere and I feel lost and it hurts... Mum!

Chapter Eighteen

White. Everything was white. And bright.

It hurt his eyes, even though they were closed. And the scraping sounds invaded his ears. Ssshh, sshh, ssshh! What was that? he wondered.

Scuffling and muffled voices. Buzzers echoed. Footsteps. Metallic gasping. Someone was shaking him, but who?

Is that you mother? Are you here with me now, are you? Motherrr!

A soft voice warm in his ear. Breath light on his cheek. Skin against skin.

Someone was calling him. *Aaa... rrr... chie!*

He opened one eye tentatively and then the other. It was difficult to see, and he struggled with definitions and images.

Where am I and what is this place and where are you mother and have I really entered the dreaming and it looks so strange and weird and not at all what I imagined it to be and where are all our people?

Archie lay very still, hoping that it would all go away. He was confused. He felt isolated and disorientated. He wanted to stay with the dreams a little longer and not face the reality of what he had just seen. He didn't like the whiteness or the sounds.

He was beginning to come back to himself, and he could feel the pain returning.

How did I get here and what has happened to me?

A voice at his cheek whispered his name once more, and he thought that he knew whose it was.

Is that you, Mum?

"Sshhh, Archie, it's alright now, you're safe here," the voice reassured him. "No one's going to hurt you again."

Archie felt someone squeeze his hand, and he opened his eyes once more to see who was there.

It's me, Kirra, don't you remember?

He looked up at the face hovering above him. It smiled. A tear slowly trickled towards the mouth. He tasted the saltiness as it dripped onto him. He remembered.

Kirra.

He wanted to talk, but his mouth didn't seem able to work. It felt dry and cracked and broken. He caught her gaze and held it there in the whiteness that surrounded them.

What happened to me and why am I here and what are you doing sitting here with me and why do I feel so sore all over... Kirra?

She seemed to understand without words, and spoke to him gently, trying to explain. She held his hand in hers and tried her best to help him, to soothe him. Just a little. It was all that she could do for now, but it was enough. Just to have her there meant everything to Archie for now; he needed that. Sure did!

As he slowly regained his senses, Archie looked around him and surveyed the scene. He had already figured out that he was in hospital, and snatches of memory were returning to him.

Darkness. Fire. Driving up the road with Ken. The booze. Strangers. Lights. Threats. Pushing and shoving and punching. Yeah, he was remembering it now.

"God you gave me one hulluva fright, Archie," wept Kirra beside him. "I thought yer was dead!"

Not yet, not yet as it is not my time. I have too much to learn and too much to say and too much to accomplish before the dreamtime.

Another voice suddenly invaded the room where Archie lay. It was harsh and shrill and worn. It came from the next bed, behind the curtain.

"What about Nanny Oden, is she going to the wedding? I'm not going, not even if they send for me. You know he was practicing in the church, don't you?"

Kirra smiled and started to giggle. She looked at Archie and laughed. Maybe this would help him to forget the pain.

"I had a square one, yes, I had a square one. I was trying to pop it up my bottom. That's where it goes. I can't get me pants down. I've only got two hands."

Even Archie was trying not to laugh now. It sounded so funny. A bodiless voice coming from what seemed like nowhere. Geez, what a hoot.

"Have they still got the horses out the front? Did I hear right that Cecil had passed away? He'd be buried by the back garage. They never married you know; him and whatsername. There were three kids and all. She had them you know."

Kirra and Archie gripped each other while they laughed aloud. They tried to keep fairly quiet, not wanting to disturb the old dear in the next bed. But it was too hard. Her voice was too loud. They could hear everything that she said.

"Have you got my case? Did you get my folder, it's in there? And what about the things in my dresser?"

"Christ I'm gunna burst soon if she don't shut up!" giggled Kirra. "Fair dinkum I am!"

"Susie's mother brought my Xmas lunch round for me. Beautiful homemade pasta it was. It was in Warimup. Is Alex my black-haired boy out there? He don't drink any more. Don't smoke either, he gave it up years ago. Is Henry there? Henry, Henry, come and see me. I tried to get the paper off that damn thing on my leg and it's real sore now. I tried to have a shower. I've met a lot of people that took on the cows. That, oh, what-do-you-call-it? I know Marty, he did. Then Arthur. He lives at the end of the street, near the mill, where we used to get the milk. You know, I can't think of it. Both Aunty Lil and Uncle Brad have died. You were here, weren't you? I remember seeing you at the doctor's, then a few weeks later I saw your death notice. Oh no, it wasn't you. You only had ulcers, didn't you? No, I forgot who it was. I know she had an ulcer on her leg anyway. We told her about the honey for healing, but she wouldn't want a sticky leg anyway."

A nurse came to the ward to check Archie's dressings. Both he and Kirra were relieved at the interruption. But the old lady in the next bed just kept right on talking, having a one-way conversation with no one.

"What are those spiders doing on the lawn? Never seen ones like them before. There's snakes in the house too. She was a gorgeous girl. Her grandfather better look after her. Anyway, you can have a cuppa. Don't take any tablets unless you open them yourself. Sharyn slept for two days, right through. Two days and two nights. Is there anyone there? I want a cuppa. Strong tea. Would you like to run down my back, please? Do you want to talk to me? I'm not a snob you know. God, I've never seen anything like it."

"That'll do for now, Annie," said the nurse sternly to the voice behind the curtain. "This young man needs his rest."

"Leah, are you there? I'll be gowin round there soon. Her mother's such a beauty. Sittin' home suckin' beers. She's a great cook. I'm not stuck up. I'll talk to ya. I won't even look at you if you don't want me to. Are you Geoffrey? Oh no, I only met him before Xmas. We had a cup of tea."

"That'll do now, Annie," commanded the nurse, who was busy enough on her rounds without the vagaries of the old woman. She knew well enough that nothing short of a tranquiliser would shut her up, but it was worth a rebuke anyway. "There's people here who are sick and injured you know, Annie," she added, hoping that might do the trick.

But the woman in the next bed was not so easily put off, and launched into a fresh monologue, ignoring all pleas to stop.

"It won't come out. Ya might have to milk me like a cow. Oh God, it's burning. It's gonna hurt me, I'll prob'ly never sit down again. People play about with things they know nothing about, you know. It's unbelievable. Everybody wants to have a look. He's going to light his cigarette so he can have a good look."

The pain was beginning to hit Archie now, and the old woman's ramblings were annoying and no longer very funny. Kirra had asked her to tone it down a few times, but she totally ignored any requests and kept right on going. Ploughing her way through the afternoon. No regard for anyone else on the ward. None at all.

"Did Dave tell ya what the spider was that was running on the lawn? Did he? Funny people. I can't go home yet. Have to shift all the furniture first. Are they little cows or horses? We had 'em over in our place once."

Archie clenched his bandaged hands and let out a long sigh. He wanted to know more about last night. At least, he *thought* that it had been last night. What had happened to him? How did he end up here in the hospital? Had someone attacked him, or had he been in a car crash? Why was he unable to move?

He looked across at Kirra and was reassured momentarily. Then Annie started up again from the next bed. Bloody Annie!

"They use that filthy language on telly now. Even little kids say it. Is David there having any tea? Well, where's he having his then, out in the car? I know his number if you've got a car. I can ring and get him to come down. I'll get in the car and go somewhere. I might stay in town for the night."

"Geez, does the old bag *ever* shut up?" moaned Kirra. "I'm sick of hearing it. She's a real fruitcake, that one."

"Merle cooks nice fruitcakes. Won a prize at the show with them she did. The Royal Show, not just local. I give her the ingredients. My good chook eggs too. And my best cow's milk. Said it tasted like pure champagne she did. Liquid gold. Yer see that ring she was wearing, well that belonged to my great Auntie Flo. Yeah, she give it to me on my twenty-first birthday. Lost it at cards I did. Merle won the game and the ring.

Wouldn't ever give it back to me, she wouldn't. Bloody cow, that's what she is."

Archie lay back against the pillows and drifted in and out of sleep. It was a strange and captive environment, this hospital. He felt as though he was cloistered. Stuck here against his will, which he was, in a way.

He knew that the staff was just doing their job, but being a hospital patient right now was not where he'd choose to be. If anyone had bothered to ask, which they didn't, of course.

He was only here by default, or that's how it seemed to his muddled mind. He didn't know the details of who had brought him here and when, only that he *was* here, and that's what mattered most for the time being.

Archie looked down at his bandaged leg, and winced as the memories suddenly began flooding back. Pictures formed in his mind. Sounds and bangs and thumps. Screeching tyres. Laughter. Screams.

Were they his screams he could hear echoing in his skull?

Archie winced as the pain from the gash in his leg jabbed at him once more. He looked around the hospital room. It was a strange feeling to be held here, captive-like. He tried to remember the events leading up to his present situation, but it was still a haze of sketchy recollections and pictures. Images flashed through his mind, but he couldn't piece them together well enough to fully explain things.

His brain was still fuzzy with the effects of the night before. Too much had been happening to him lately. His life seemed to be on a collision course between the past and the future, and the present wasn't great shakes at the moment either. What Archie really needed was some space, some time out to lick his wounds, and maybe this time in hospital was just the thing.

Suddenly Archie sat bolt upright. He had just remembered something. Something important.

"Ken! I think I was s'posed ta meet him at lunchtime for a ride to the new camp. Where is he, d'ya know? Has he bin here lookin' fer me?" he asked Kirra anxiously, wondering if it was too late to go now. Trying to remember if he'd dreamed the whole thing, or if it was real. What was he supposed to do now? What?

But before Kirra could answer, the old lady from the next bed interrupted. "Ken! Did someone say Ken? I knew Ken once. Ken. Kennie. Kennie Goldsmith. Aw, he was gorgeous, a right dandy he was. Me an' him used to go dancing, we did. All over. Even went to the big city dances, we did. Lor', he could dance, could Kennie. All the girls were after him you know, but he stuck with me, he did. Reckoned I was the best partner he ever had on the dance floor. I was too, I could turn a heel, I'll tell ya. Trouble with Kennie though, he weren't much of a partner off the dance floor. A right bastard he were when it came down to it. Just wasn't really up to it, an' that's a fact. Ah well, that's life, eh?"

But Archie was tired of Annie's stories, and had other worries of his own.

"Has Ken been in?" he asked Kirra. "I was supposed to go to me new camp today."

"Yeah, he knows. Said he'd be in later this arvo to check on yer an' see how long you'll be in here," replied Kirra, not really wanting to share her time with Archie at the moment. She figured that Archie had enough to worry about just getting better after his savage beating last night. The trip to his new home could wait. He needed to get his strength back first. And at least with him here in the hospital, she could visit him every day for a while. Yeah, she'd like that. It was the least she could do.

Kirra realised that Archie must have come down to half way camp to visit her last night. She felt guilty that he had been beaten up because of it. Maybe it was all her fault? She looked across at Archie lying there covered in bruises and bandages as a fresh pang of pain crossed his face and made him wince. Kirra tried not to hurt too.

"C'n I get yer anything from the kiosk?" she asked gently, hoping to ease the pain a bit for Archie. "Maybe a magazine or some chocolate or somethin'?"

"Nah, she's right, Kirra, but thanks anyway," replied Archie. He was getting tired once more, and he was trying hard to fight the pain and stay awake a bit longer. But what he really wanted was rest. Sleep. Darkness.

Mum, are you there? I'm in pain, Mum, and it hurts and I need you here to take care of me, Mum!

Archie closed his eyes and breathed more easily as the pain began to subside. He felt Kirra's hand close firmly round his as he drifted in and out of consciousness. He liked that, it was reassuring. It felt like... felt like... who?

"Nurse! Nurse! Where are ya? I need me cuppa and no one's been here to take me order. I like it strong yer know. Arthur was strong. He was me first, yeah he was. Such a gentleman too. Took good care of me, he did. Till that bloody war, then off he went, sailed away to fight for King and Country. Never did come back, the silly bugger. Jez disappeared outta me life. Gone, pfft! Jez like that. Typical, eh? Bloody men, what would they know about hard times? You tell me, I know all about it. Raised the kids all by meself I did. Worked hard all those years. Struggled I did, but it were worth it, doncha think? They turned out jez fine, them kids of mine. Jez fine."

Kirra sighed a long deep sigh and looked down at Archie. He had fallen asleep briefly, and she couldn't help but smile as she watched his face. The pain seemed to be absent for the time being, and Kirra hoped that he would rest for a while. She hoped that Annie would shut up too, and stop her rambling it was getting beyond a joke. She was sick of the old lady muttering and spluttering in the next cubicle. God, she could go on!

"Are those spiders still there on the front lawn, luvvie, can yer see them from the window? Geez that's odd, I never seen spiders like them before. Must be the cows, they always attract things yer know. Used ta be lots of them cows down the farm. Milking ones. Had the best milk in the country, them cows. Everyone said so."

Kirra let go of Archie's hand gently and stood up. He was still asleep, and she needed a break. Needed to get out and breathe some fresh air. She hated being closed in and the feeling of somehow being trapped in here. And she hated the smells of the hospital even more. Somehow, it reminded her of death.

"Did I ever tell yer about the day they told me about Kennie, dear? A telegram, it were. That's all, thank you very much! No by your leave or nothin'. Jez a lousy bloody scrap of paper. Course, I knew didn't I, the moment I opened the door. Jez knew he were gone, like. Still, it were a shock though, seeing that bit of paper."

The old woman's voice trailed off as Kirra left the room and went down the corridor. She pushed her way past all the hospital paraphernalia that cluttered her path. Basins, oxygen bottles, machinery of all descriptions. Trolleys stacked with half-empty food trays. Wheelchairs, mobile drip stands, stacks of stainless steel pans and jugs. Used linen bags and mops stood pushed against the far wall of the nurse's station as Kirra made her way outside. But the smell was what affronted her most.

She opened the doors at the far end of the corridor and exited near the visitors' car park. It felt so good to finally be outside once more. She had forgotten how fresh the air was, despite the heat and oppressive afternoon sun.

Kirra needed to shake off the troubles of the last twenty-four hours. She needed some space of her own for a while.

Chapter Nineteen

Archie was hauled from his sleep by someone tapping his shoulder firmly. His name was echoing in his head. Archie! Archie! He opened his eyes to find that he was staring straight into the face of the duty nurse. She leaned over him and clutched her clipboard to her ample chest. She spoke briskly to Archie, as though it was expected of her to assume this formal manner.

"Now, young man, when did you last use the bedpan, eh?" she asked.

Archie scratched his head and moaned. "How the hell would I know?"

She checked his stats then turned towards the doorway. Archie hoped that she'd leave him in peace for now, and was glad to see the back of her. But it wasn't to be. She marched back briskly with a bedpan wrapped in paper under her arm and pulled the curtains closed around his bed.

"Here you are now, do you need some help to use this? Here, let's get you sitting up a bit so's I can pop this under you. There, that's better."

The nurse from hell, he thought.

Help me, Mother, it's too awful in here and I hurt all over and now they want me to use a bedpan and I just can't, I can't, I can't, Mo-th-errr!

It wasn't supposed to be like this. He was supposed to be somewhere else. Archie was disgusted with the indignity of the task at hand and frustrated with the situation he had landed himself in. Why did it have to happen now, when he was on his way to his new home? It didn't seem fair, and he resented his situation.

Time popped along slowly in bubbles of teasing transparency. Archie was stuck in limbo once again. Caught in the middle of another transition. He reckoned that he'd been dealt another of life's injustices, and he hated himself for it. Yeah, he felt bad.

The only bright spot on the horizon as far as Archie was concerned was that Kirra had found him again, and surely that had to mean *something*, didn't it?

He leaned back against the hard white sheets, too tired and drained from the small effort he'd exerted in trying to force nature along. Hadn't worked anyway. Nothing to show for his troubles. He closed his eyes and thought of Kirra. Had he imagined she was here, or had she really been by his side this afternoon?

The ward nurse returned and removed the bedpan with a 'we are not amused' scowl on her face. Archie didn't care. He was too tired and too dispirited to bother right now. He just wanted to be left alone for a while.

"Nursie, oh, Nursie. Can you come over here, love? I need me bandage changed 'cause it's slipped down me leg dearie. You know we used to tie the cows that way, 'specially the lame ones. Yeah, lots of knots there were. But they still gave the good milk, right up to the end. Didn't they, love?"

Archie winced and screwed his eyes shut tight against the bright light of the room. He wished that he could shut his ears too. Maybe he'd ask Kirra to bring him a Walkman with earphones when she returned. If she had one, that is. Maybe not.

He wanted to sleep away the rest of the day and get rid of this pain, but he couldn't see how he could do that in here. Too many noises. Too many interruptions. And of course, there was bloody Annie always rabbiting on about god knows what!

"There's Arthur out there with the horses now. See him? Gawd, he's handsome, ain't he? Used to turn all the girls heads in his young days, did Arthur. But I was the one who stole his heart, aren't I the lucky one, eh? We used to go courtin' down by the creek, me an' Arthur. Cor, them were the days! Went skinny-dippin' once yer know, we did. Nearly got caught by me dad bringin' the cows in for milkin. Did we laugh! Laughed fit to burst, me and Arthur. We sure did. What a hoot!"

Someone came into the room and sat down heavily next to his bed. A cough. Chair scraped on lino. Feet shuffled.

Archie opened his eyes and turned his face towards the sounds.

Ken it was Ken and he hasn't forgotten me he has come to see me after all!

"He yer, Arch, how are yer, mate? Feelin' any better? I came in this mornin' an' stayed fer a bit, but you was out fer the count. Jeez, they give yer a good gowin' over last night, Archie me mate," spluttered Ken all in one jumble of words. He was trying to get it all out, let Archie know that he cared. Normally, Ken was the quiet type, but he had been shocked at Archie's appearance when he first saw him. And in truth, he blamed himself for being foolish enough to take him over to the other camp last night at all. Yeah, he should never have listened to Archie, should have just left well enough alone. That's what yer get fer helpin' out, he thought bitterly.

Archie smiled at him through sore and swollen lips. He was glad to see Ken, as he'd been worried about what to do about the trip to the new camp. What if Ken hadn't showed up? He had enough to worry about without being totally abandoned, and for now he was mighty relieved.

"She's right, Ken. I'll be good as new in a coupla days, you'll see. Dunno what really happened last night, don' remember much at all." Archie turned to Ken with a puzzled expression on his face. Hoping that he could fill in some of the gaps. Maybe Ken had been there after the fight? Maybe he had even been the one to bring him into the hospital? Had he come over to halfway camp after he'd dropped Archie off last night? Archie had a stack of questions that he wanted answers for, and he figured that Ken might just be the one to get the ball rolling in that direction. But he was too tired and felt too sore to pursue it for now, so he let it go and sank back against the hospital pillows once more.

Annie piped up again. "Is that you, Ken? I told them you'd come. Did you bring me folder from the suitcase, the one under me bed? It's got all the names in, you know, all the family and that. Nurse! Nurse! Bring us a cuppa willya? One fer Kennie too, he likes his black with no sugar. Black an' 'orrible I always says. That's one of our lil jokes, eh, Kennie? How's the horses, love? Did yer leave them out the front there? I saw them this mornin' yer know, all frisky they were, jez like you used ta be, Kennie. Cor we used ter have some times, you an' me, didn't we, love? Remember Maud? Maudie? Jack's little girl? She died yer know. Got tossed off the horse that day and tangled in the reins. Went down jez like that, broke her neck. So sad it were, poor Jack were never the same again after that. Never got over it. Broke his poor heart it did."

"Geez, who the hell is that? What's all that about?" asked Ken, as he stared over at the next bed. "Does she always ramble on like that?"

Archie turned to Ken and frowned. "Yeah, its bloody tiring listening to the old chook fer hours on end, I can tell yer, I'm sick of it."

"Arthur were sick too before he went off to the war. I told 'im not to go, jez see the doctor an' get a certificate, but he wouldn't hear of it. Gotta fight fer the lads, he said, wouldn't listen to his wife an' family. Nah, what a waste, bloody stupid it were. All them men, jez cannon fodder, that's what they were. Took the best of them. And their horses. All gone now, slaughtered. Fer what, that's what I'd like to know?"

"Geez, mate, yer gotta laugh at the old dear," said Ken, "she's a bit of entertainment in here, ain't she?"

But Archie found Annie depressing. He was sick of listening to her harsh whining voice as it droned on and on non-stop. He found it confusing and unsettling, and it did nothing to help his immediate comfort. Yeah, he just wished she's stop eavesdropping and shut up for a while. He wanted to talk to Ken in private, without the constant interruptions.

"What happened after you dropped me off last night, Ken? D'yer know who hit me?" he asked, hoping that Ken would be able to shed some light on his injuries.

"Nah, mate, they were long gone by the time I came ter pick yer up. It was Kirra who found yer at the camp. Yer was unconscious by then, an' she ran and phoned our camp. Soon as I heard I jumped in the 4WD and took off over there like a bat outta hell mate. Picked yer up an' brought yer here to the Emergency Department, an' the nurses took over an' looked after yer. I waited round fer a while till they cleaned yer up an' bandaged yer an' all, then took meself home fer a bit of sleep. Came back after brekkie, but you was sedated, mate, so I jez sat by the bed fer a while then went back to the camp. No use trying ter find out too much about them mongrels who bashed yer, Arch, jez have to let it go, mate. Too much bad blood over there. Could get yerself into more trouble. An' Kirra too, she has ta live there you know. Best ta jez leave it, Arch, an' get on with things, OK? You'll prob'ly be outta here in a coupla days anyway, mate, with a bit of luck."

"Don't talk to me about luck, that's what Kennie always said. Reckoned he had the luck of the Irish, that's what 'e reckoned. Bloody fool! Luck o' the devil more like. Couldn't hold himself straight if they tied him to a post, he couldn't. Nah, not him! Liked a tipple too much, he did. An' too bloody often too. Used ta be fun at first. Laughin' an' jokin' an' clownin' around. Yeah, he sure had a way with yer, he did. But then 'e'd get angry. And scary. Used ta give me goosebumps just bein' with him when he got drunk, yer know, fair dinkum it did. Made me do stuff I knew I shouldn't. Yeah, that Kennie could be a right bastard he could, I swear to God."

"Geez, luv, wilyer shut it fer a while, eh? Me mate's had a bad time lately as it is, and he don't need no more of that drivel from you," called out Ken indignantly, hoping to get Annie to be quiet finally, at least for a little while.

But Annie would have none of it, she just ignored him and kept right on talking. As though there was no one else in the room at all.

"Where's me cuppa? I like that better than me sherry these days yer know, used ter be that I'd always have me sherry. Every night with Arthur. Drank it fer years I did, even though I hated the stuff really. It were all fer Arthur, cos 'e used to buy it fer me. Thought I liked it. Thought that's what ladies drank, 'e did. Silly bugger, never did have the heart to tell him I'd rather jez have a cuppa tea I would. Used ta get up early in them days. Still do. Six o'clock. First light of day, that's me. Everything's so still an' peaceful then. The birds are just waking up, an' the sun's beginning to show itself in the sky. I'd put the kettle on first thing an' make meself a cuppa. Take it out the back to the garden, an' sit out there with me cat an' just relax an' think of nothing much at all. Best part of the day, yer know. Yer just can't beat it, all alone with nature I were. With him still snorin' in his bed too. Ah. It were grand. I still wake up at six yer know. Still, after all these years. Who woulda thought, eh? An' I'm still here!"

I wish you weren't, thought Archie, I need some peace too and I'm not getting any in here! I wish you'd go away or at least just stop interrupting and talking and reminiscing for a while. Aagh!

"D'yer want me ter get yer anything from the kiosk, or maybe something from town, Arch?" asked Ken, hoping to distract the old dear in the next bed for a bit. He suspected by now that he was wasting his time, but it was worth a try anyway. God, it seemed like *nothing* would ever shut her up.

"Yeah, a bit of chocolate would be great, an' maybe a can of coke," replied Archie, too tired from all the hospital routines now to get enthusiastic about much. He really just wanted to rest. He wished that everyone would go away for a while and leave him alone. Archie was dog-tired, and he was feeling the strain of it all. And his injuries seemed only a part of it.

The old woman just made it worse for Archie. A first it had been amusing, and he and Kirra had laughed and laughed. But now it was totally frustrating, and he wanted her gone. He'd had enough, and decided that next time she started prattling on about her strange life he'd press the buzzer and scream out for the nurse. It was simply too much to take any more.

Ken returned with his treats, and for a while Archie was happy just to enjoy the taste of some dark caramel chocolate and sip on his coke. Ken smiled at him and tried to cheer him up. He told him about his trip up north and his adventures with croc's. He described the bush up round the north country, his homeland. His spirit place. He told Archie about catching large barramundi and hunting kangaroo and goanna.

Archie leaned back against his pillows and closed his eyes. It was good to listen to Ken tell his stories. He enjoyed their simplicity and vividness. He could relate to them; not like the senseless ramblings of the old woman in the bed beside him. No, Ken's stories were real and meaningful.

They were like the stories someone had told him before when he was a small child crouched at his mother's knee by the campfire so many times and he almost recognised who it was but he couldn't quite bring it back now... could he?

"Penny fer 'em, Archie," laughed Ken, as he watched Archie's brow tighten with some unseen frustration. "Wotcha thinkin' about, mate?"

Archie opened his eyes a bit startled. He had been caught up in the dreamtime for a moment, back in his past somewhere. Someone had been holding his hand and telling him stories, but who?

"Nah, she's right, Ken, jez dreamin'," Archie replied, a little embarrassed.

"I used to dream all the time yer know! Yeah, when I was a small kid me mum reckoned I was the biggest day-dreamer she'd ever met on the face of this earth, and that's God's truth yer know. Reckoned I couldn't keep me mind on me chores for more than two seconds, she did. Said me head was always in the clouds. Away with the fairies, that's what she used ter say. God strike me dead, she'd say, yer'll be the death of me, yer will child. Get yer head back on yer shoulders an' get on with it! Used ta belt me if I didn't finish me chores on time too, the cow! Yeah, I'd get the cane handle of the feather duster round me legs I would, sure did sting sometimes. Bloody hell, you'd think a girl could have some time to dream, wouldn't yer? Nah, not if me ma had her way, I can tell yer. Not me, she'd be on me like a ton of bricks she would. The old battle-axe, God rest her soul," Annie finished.

Archie looked across at Ken and sighed. He'd had enough.

"Ken, willya buzz the nurse and ask if I can be moved to another ward away from the old bat, she's driving me crazy," he pleaded. "I can't stand much more of her talk!"

"OK, mate, hang on and I'll go find the ward nurse and see if I can fix it fer ya, orright?"

Archie lay back and waited patiently. He closed his eyes and his ears and his mind to the external world. He drifted into his dreaming, away, away.

Chapter Twenty

Kirra had been sitting outside the hospital when Ken arrived. She wanted to go back in to sit with Archie, but she didn't want to be there with Ken. He was a stranger. Not one of her mob. She knew it would be imposing.

There would be plenty of time later to visit Archie again, so for now, Kirra decided she'd better head home once more. Back to her camp. Back to help her mum. And the little ones. There would be chores waiting.

Kirra turned away from the hospital and headed back down the road out of town towards half way camp. It wasn't a long walk, but she knew that she'd better hurry now. She'd been gone for the best part of the morning after finding out about Archie's fight the night before. Kirra knew that she was needed back at home, so she hurried down the path that led there. Besides, she knew that Archie was in good hands now in the hospital.

As she neared home, Kirra heard the familiar sounds of her camp. It was early afternoon, and she felt guilty that she had not been home to prepare lunch for her family. It was a task that she usually did, because she could never rely on her mum to be sober enough after the night before.

Her brothers and sister came running up to her as she arrived home. They clung to her knee-length shorts and clutched at her hands. It was as though they depended on her strength for their survival, and usually they did. It was Kirra, after all, who kept things going in the household. They knew it, and her mum knew it. And Kirra knew it too, even at her age.

But it won't always be this way, and I won't always be here to care for you, fetch for you, bath you, cook for you, clean for you, help you through every day... will I? No, some day I'm going to get away to the big city and make something of myself in the outside world away from this camp and this town and this mob, who stifle me, cage me in, threaten me, restrict me, overburden me with limited expectations… yeah, someday!

Kirra sucked in her breath and clenched her fists to assuage the onslaught of guilt and anger and frustration she felt as she set about tending to the little ones there at the house. Her mother was nowhere in sight, and Kirra knew from past experience that she would still be sleeping off the excesses of the night before. Snoring away. Lost in the fug of drink and dreaming. A mother to no one.

"You gonna fix us some food, eh, Kira?" asked her sister. "We're pretty hungry and we've finished all the cereal an' milk for brekkie. Only some white bread left and a bit of butter."

Kirra stooped down and picked up the little girl. She balanced her on her hip and went into the kitchen to survey the mess. Cans and wrappers and half-empty bottles lay spilled on the bench, and a dribble of milk stained the floor. Two of the dogs were busy fighting over the remains of last night's tea, and Kirra booted them in the backside and pushed them outside. She put her sister down on the bench and filled the sink with some water, then reached for the dishcloth. The leftover food scraps and bottles and cans were placed in the rubbish, and then Kirra wiped down the bench tops and table. She went through to the laundry and got the old mop and some more hot water in a bucket, adding a dash of disinfectant. A quick mop of the floor in the kitchen completed the clean-up, and Kirra stepped outside and strode off towards the store. She hurried up the street to make sure she got to the shop before it closed for lunch. Kirra knew there'd be arguing and whingeing if she didn't get the family fed before teatime, and she knew that her mum needed to be woken up and fed soon.

She got to the store just in time, and filled her shopping basket with milk, bread, cheese, vegemite, cordial, fruit, and some sliced ham. Her goods were tallied and then the total entered in the store ledger. Kirra knew there was no need for cash, they just paid for things each welfare day.

She carried the shopping home, then set about making a large plate full of sandwiches for her mum and the kids. Vegemite, cheese, ham. An apple each. Big jug of cordial.

"Come an' get it!" she yelled out to the family. "Grub's up! Wash your hands first before yers come an' eat."

Kirra put the large plate of sandwiches in the middle of the kitchen table, and then went through to her mum's room. The large figure of her mum was prone on the bed, one arm flung carelessly over the edge, dangling near the floor. Her mouth was open, revealing a gappy row of poorly-filled teeth. They were stained with years of neglect and nicotine. Her hair was matted and unwashed, framing a soft but somewhat puffy face. Her large tough feet poked out of the covers, and Kirra could see that her mum had slept in the clothes she had on last night, as usual. Faded flowery day dress. Tatty clothes and tatty dreams, thought Kirra.

Her mum snuffled as Kirra shook her gently by the shoulder to wake her. A small trail of spit led from the corner of her mouth and traced a spider web path across the dirty pillow. She opened her eyes and grimaced at Kirra.

"Waddya want?" she barked at Kirra. "Jez leave me alone an' let me sleep fer a while, willya?"

Kirra looked up at the ceiling and sighed. It was the same routine every day. Without fail. Kirra knew the score by now.

"Mum, yer gotta get up now an' come and have somethin' to eat. Yer know what the doc said about yer diet. Come on, yer gotta get some tucker interya." Kirra sometimes despaired of ever making headway with her mum. Still, she had to try. "C'arn, I got yer favourite ham sandwiches out in the kitchen. Come an' have some lunch with us, Mum."

She helped her mum to sit up, then left her and went back to the kitchen to put the kettle on for a cup of tea. She knew that by the time the kettle had boiled, her mum would be in the bathroom tidying up a bit. Fixing herself up a little, ready to join them in the kitchen.

God, thought Kirra, the woman could fix herself up a bit each day on the outside, but what about the inside? What about her inner self? How would she fix up the lifestyle, the self-esteem, the dependency on a flawed system, the loss of her culture and her land and her identity − the broken dreams, how would she fix those things, eh?

Chapter Twenty-One

The heat was pressing down on Archie like a steam iron. He wiped his brow and shuffled sideways in his seat, trying to find a comfortable position. Sweat was beginning to run into his eyes, and the overhead fan did little to save him. The air hung heavy and oppressive in the classroom as Archie scanned the row of youths beside him. They were black like him, but different. They spoke different languages and had different skin groups. But they'd all ended up here with Archie at this school in Pantura, away from their families and mobs.

It had been two months since his fight in the town, and Archie's wounds had healed. He still had a small scar on his leg from the biggest cut, but apart from that, there were no visible signs of the beating he'd received. Outwardly, at least.

Ken had brought him to Pantura after he'd been released from the hospital. He had thought it better to get Archie away from any hint of trouble. Away from half way camp. A fresh start for the young lad, that's what it would be, after all that had recently happened in his life.

So Archie had said a brief farewell to Kirra in town the morning he'd left, then climbed into the land cruiser and headed off west to the new camp.

But I'll come back to town to see you when I can, Kirra, and I won't forget how kind you've been to me and we will have lots of times in town to share together and go to the café and for walks and swims at the river, won't we… Kirra?

They'd driven for about an hour along the highway west, and then turned off at the old cattle station into bush country for the final leg of the trip to Archie's new home. It was familiar country to Archie, yet somehow slightly different too. The red dirt road with its deep ruts and dry river bed crossings was almost the same, but there was a different *feel* to the land. Different dreaming and spirits here. Different stories.

They'd arrived in the late afternoon as the sun was beginning to sink in the west behind the rocky outcrops, and Archie had felt a sense of excitement tinged with apprehension too. He knew that there was going to be a new group of people to get used to, and he knew that there were other kids like him who'd come here to be away from family for a variety of reasons. Archie had no reason to think it would be easy, but hoped that things would turn out OK. He needed some stability in his world for now, there'd been enough change.

At the outskirts of the town a rusty sign hung from a fencepost which stated that this was an alcohol-free camp. Archie smiled, and wondered if it were true.

As they drove through the few streets they passed the usual row of tin dongas behind cyclone wire fences. Rubbish and junk lay around the yards, and dogs were roaming the streets in packs. They'd stopped at the store to get some food, and then headed up to the teachers' houses to get directions for Archie's accommodation.

Now here Archie was, stuck in a classroom with a bunch of teenagers, trying hard to learn English from an old text. They were all dispirited this afternoon. It was way too hot to retain anything. The book they were supposed to be studying was boring. They'd read it over and over till it had ceased to hold even the slightest shred of interest, but the teacher ploughed on regardless, ignoring their disinterest. They were totally disengaged from the learning process, but she didn't seem to care. Her soft voice droned on and on as the boys slumped in their chairs. They put their heads on the desks, and one by one they closed their eyes and drifted into an uneasy sleep.

Archie woke from his brief catnap to hear someone calling his name.

Who is that calling me calling me, is it you, Mum, why do you call me now and what do you want and where are you... mother?

"Archie, Archie, which word best describes the way the main character feels in this passage?" the teacher asked in her exasperated way.

Geez, how would I know, Miss, I'm not a bloody genius and the book is in English and I'd rather talk my language and we don't' have books to write down our history you know, Miss, we have songs and dance and dreamtime and corroboree and laws and spirits and stories told that go way back beyond anything you know or thought possible, Miss, and yet here you are trying to fill my head with whitefella stuff that means nothing to me, Miss, what are you doing?

Archie sniggered across at his mates and feigned an interest just to keep the peace for now. He knew the book they were discussing off by heart. He'd memorised it easily, and could recite it paragraph by paragraph, and the teacher took that for reading. That was just fine with Archie, it meant that she kept off his back during English. Well, mostly anyway.

But today she was tired and irritable, and there was still an hour to go till home time. She had been discussing and dissecting and reviewing this book for weeks now, and expected far more progress with the class than was evident at this stage of the term. She thought that her method of transmitting skills was pretty darned good, and she was constantly baffled and disappointed by the fits and starts of progress that seemed to occur in the classroom. She knew that with only a few weeks of term to go, the pressure was on to bring the group of senior students up to scratch. She would have to begin testing soon for their mid-year reports, and she felt the frustration of failure advancing relentlessly there in the outback classroom where she had elected to teach recently. It was not a feeling she was used to, and it left her more drained than the incessant heat and dust and humidity and isolation.

What the hell am I really doing here in this godforsaken outpost and why did I leave the safety of my ordered world back in the city and who was I kidding when I answered the ad in the national paper that seemed like the opportunity of a lifetime and a chance to work with these kids and get to know life from their perspective... why isn't it working out the way I planned, why?

She had uprooted herself and her partner and packed up her home down south to seize this chance, and now she was really not sure at all if she had done the right thing. No, not sure at all.

The initial excitement of the adventure had worn off, and she had to admit that working here in this small isolated community so far away from most creature comforts was a lot more trying that she had imagined it might be. It wasn't really the lack of facilities and amenities that got to her though; they didn't really mind roughing it, and could do without cafés and supermarket and picture theatres and pools and the sea and even their friends and family. They had the internet to keep them in touch with the outside world, after all, and weekend trips camping and visiting town.

What really got to her was the attitude of the boys in her class. She'd taught in some pretty tough schools in her time, but nothing she'd experienced before in her teaching career had really prepared her for this current work environment, and she was almost totally at a loss as to how to change things to a workable solution.

She felt hemmed in and totally unappreciated. She felt ignored and almost useless. For Shelly, this was a new experience in the world of teaching, and not one that she ever envisaged occurring at this later stage of her career.

But she'd had such high expectations and she'd always wanted to live and work in an indigenous community to learn about the issues with their culture and their way of life and how they adapted to today, and whether they thought mainstream education was the key to their future, but somehow it had all unravelled and gone wrong for her and she didn't know how to fix it or if she should even try, did she?

The boy next to Archie flicked his pen at his cousin in the chair in front and called out to the teacher in a gruff and intimidating manner. "Hey, Miss, I'm gonna go bounce on the trampoline, Miss, it's better out there than being stuck in here with these dumb books!"

The others laughed and joined in the chorus of protest.

"Yeah, Miss, we're gowin' home soon anyway. We've had this stupid book. It's a pretty weird story anyway, Miss."

Why do they laugh at me and ridicule me and hate me simply for trying to do my job and educate them? Why don't they try to see things from my perspective? Why do they shout and tease each other and kick and punch and disobey all the school rules? Why do they make it so difficult to teach them anything when I am trying so hard to understand? Why?

Shelly sat down heavily and let out a sigh of pure frustration. She knew that if she didn't do something quickly then the students would be out the door and she would not get them back inside for the rest of the school day. She racked her brain for yet another trick that might hold them a little while longer.

This isn't how it's supposed to be, I was told that the communities all wanted a mainstream education including English and Maths, but whenever I follow the guidelines set out, all I get is resistance and open defiance, and I don't get any support from the other teachers at the school, and I'm stuck between a rock and a hard place out here and where is the hand of friendship and encouragement and sharing that should be here for me, where?

"Archie, would you like to choose a story that I can read to you all over in the library corner? Go through and get one of my special books that I brought with me, OK? Who wants to hear a story before we go home?" pleaded Shelly in desperation, hoping that the class would respond in a positive manner and avoid yet another disaster today. She was tired of their antics, and just wanted some quiet time before the final bell of the day. Shelly hoped that they'd fall for it today. She knew they enjoyed lying on the carpet in the corner with their eyes closed and listening to stories she read. She was banking on the hope that it would work today too, otherwise they'd all just get up and go outside and fight over whose turn it was on the trampoline.

That was another bone of contention with the kids because they saw the thing as a diversion to play on whenever they liked and she saw it as a reward for work well done or something achieved and that's how it should have been, but it wasn't, was it? It didn't seem to matter to them whether she gave them permission or not, they would simply walk out during a lesson whenever they wanted to and start jumping on the damned thing, and she was powerless to stop them most of the time wasn't she?

But with only half an hour to go till the end of the school day, the boys decided that it would be good to hear a story read to them before they headed off home. Archie chose his favourite book, and they settled to hear the story, but it wasn't long before some of them became restless and fidgety. Teasing and slapping and shoving ensued, and Archie kicked out at one of the boys to make them stop but it only grew worse. The teacher was forced to abandon the story and try to regain some form of discipline there in the corner of the classroom.

Archie trudged home slowly after the school bell had sounded. Nothing seemed to be going right in his life at the moment, and he blamed the school for some of it. He'd been sent here to get an education and to stay out of trouble, like most of the other boys in the senior school. But it was hard, too hard at times. They were all lonely, and missed their mobs. Their own camps. Their people.

For Archie it was extra hard because he was still dealing with the loss of his mum, and he tried to pretend that it didn't really matter and that he could tough it out like the other boys, but the truth was that he was really hurting inside. Yeah, he sure was!

Mother, I feel lost and adrift somehow and they sent me away 'cause that's what you wanted for me and you told them it would be best to get right away somewhere and get a good education, so's I could make something of myself and I'm trying, Mum, but it's all so strange and so lonely, and I miss you, M... ooooo... ther!

"Hey, Arch, wanna come down the creek an' have a smoke with us, eh? Will's got some an' he don't mind sharin' do yer, Will?" asked Rett.

"Nah, course not!" exclaimed Will with a wide grin. "There's plenty ta go round. Got 'em up the store, I did."

The three boys headed off through the low scrub down the creek track. They laughed and joked and teased each other in creole, the common language they all shared. They were glad to be finished school for the day, and even more pleased to be away from the old bat of a teacher. God, did she go on! And everything had to be said in English, as though their languages didn't exist at all.

And what did she know of their language? And what did she know of their lives? And what did she know of the things that were important to them and meaningful for their future, what?

Back at the school Shelly collapsed into her chair as soon as the bell had gone and the last of the boys was outside the school door. She stretched out her legs and kicked off her shoes. She turned her face towards the ceiling fan, trying to eke out any tiny morsel of coolness the whirring blades might offer her. She felt totally depleted, as though something external had sucked out her life-force. She was drained.

Tears of tiredness and anger and unhappiness rolled down her face there in the silent classroom.

Why can't they see that I am only trying to help them, provide a springboard for their future, give them the knowledge they might need to survive and flourish and exist in the outside world, and why are they making it so hard for all of us, why? They don't appreciate anything I try to do for them – to make things easier and better and improve their chances in life. They don't even appreciate the fact that I stay behind and cook bread for their breakfast the next day and shop at the store for their food and get up at six each morning to be here by seven and get organised for the day ahead and set up the damn trampoline and put out their books and tidy the room and switch on the computers and... do they?

Chapter Twenty-Two

Kirra was excited. Archie had phoned last night and said that he'd be getting a lift to town this weekend. It gave her something promising to look forward to, and she was filled with anticipation.

She knew that they were only ever going to be friends, but that was enough for her and in a way gave her far more freedom to be herself. Kirra didn't need or want the hassles of a romantic relationship at this stage of her life. She was still so young, and she'd had enough near misses with drunken members of her mob so far to last a lifetime. She sure wasn't in any rush to repeat the experience. She'd already had to push away members of the opposite sex and escape their grovelling clutches on more than one occasion when the booze took hold of them, but so far she'd managed to escape with only her pride dinted and her clothing a little torn. The men and older boys had often tried to press her for sexual favours, but Kirra was too fast for them and had always managed to escape their clutches and hide out somewhere till morning. Still, their behaviour was enough to put her off anything more than friendship for now.

Her mother was no help either. She was usually out drinking or playing cards, and that left Kirra to fend for herself too often. Kirra had once confided in one of her aunties, but that had backfired when they'd told her mum, who only made fun of her and made things worse. So Kirra had learned to defend herself and rely on no one.

But with Archie it was different. Kirra had sensed a closeness right from the start. They seemed like kindred spirits and Kirra felt straight away that they were both cut off from real family and support systems and love. She realised that Archie wasn't interested in her as a sexual partner either, and that gave her the confidence she needed to begin a true friendship. Somehow, Kirra knew that Archie would be supportive no matter what happened in their lives. And she'd be his friend and would support him too.

But one day, Archie, I'm gonna get out of this dump. And one day, Archie, I'm gonna go to the city and I'm gonna get a decent education and study hard and make something of myself. One day you'll see… Archie.

Kirra finished washing the breakfast dishes and set about tidying the place before her mum woke up. She had decided to go to school today, and called out to her brother and sisters in the lounge room.

"Hurry up, youse, we're all gowin' ta school today an' I've made yer lunches, so turn the telly off an' git a move on willyers?" Kirra was impatient. She was fidgety and a bit unsettled now that she knew she would see Archie on the weekend. She wanted the time between then and now to speed up so she wouldn't have to wait, but she knew it was still two days away till he got to town.

Kirra knew that Archie would be staying with the mob up at town camp. He wouldn't come down here to half way camp again. Not after last time and the beating he'd got. No way, she'd told him straight, stay away. But Kirra could get away and they could meet in town. At the café or the shops. Or down by the river where they'd sat and talked before. Yeah, it'd be great to have Archie back in town for a couple of days to spend some time together. Kirra smiled at the thought of being with Archie once more.

"Come on, youse kids, let's go!" cried out Kirra impatiently, wanting to get to school now before the first bell. She felt some urgency now to get out of the house and away before her mum woke up. Usually she didn't mind, and stayed home to care for her, but this morning it was different somehow. Kirra needed some space today, and she knew that if she stayed home her mum would take up all of her time. No, not today.

Kirra and her siblings left the house together, and she smiled at them encouragingly as they trudged along the dirt road to school. It was already hot and sticky, and Kirra knew that the little ones would be tired by lunch break. Still, she was determined that they should stay at school today. She knew well enough that they had a habit of wanting to go home at lunchtime and sit in the house watching television. Kirra knew that her mum wouldn't make them stay at school. It was up to Kirra; she was the one who had most influence.

But sometimes she grew tired of the demands of her life. Sometimes Kirra just wanted to be left alone and enjoy life like her peers and simply have fun. Yeah, sometimes she resented the way things had turned out since her dad had left so long ago.

"Come on, youse, I'll buy yers all an ice cream after school if yers are good today, promise I will," Kirra coaxed, hoping that it would do the trick. She knew that it was hard for the little ones sometimes, but today they didn't seem to mind about school.

As they neared the school grounds, Kirra could see that already a few of her classmates were playing basketball on the dry grass near the toilet block. The boys were kicking a footy on the other side over near the junior classroom, and a few dogs were barking and snapping at each other by the door, fighting over some of the rubbish that had spilled from the open drum by the fence.

The older boys took care of the rubbish each day, dumping it in the row of 44 gallon drums that lined the side fence by the road. When the drums were filled, they set fire to them, leaving them to burn while they bounced on the trampoline or kicked the old leather footy around some more. Sometimes Kirra believed that the boys loved that footy more than anything else at the school, and maybe they did. Most of them played on weekends for the local team, and spent several nights a week down at the local oval training with the older guys in town. Football was their saviour, Kirra often thought, and good luck to them. There wasn't much else in their lives.

Kirra glanced across at the huddle of girls by the door as she entered the school yard. She knew them all. She'd grown up around here with most of them, and had spent her childhood sharing secrets and swimming and playing with them often enough. But she wasn't really close to any of them now, she felt like an outsider sometimes.

Kirra knew that they had grown apart as they got older. Maybe it had a lot to do with her role in her family. Kirra knew that she often didn't have time to spend with her friends, there was always too much to do around the house for that. Still, a part of her wished that it could be different in some way.

One day it will be different for me. One day I'll get away from here, and I won't have to look after my mum and take care of the little ones and clean and cook and shop and things will be a lot different, and I'll be living a better life away from here one day... won't I?

The bell rang and the teacher called them all into class. Kirra bent down and gave her sisters a pat on the back and a quick kiss goodbye. Her little brother had already run off and joined his mates in the yard.

"Be good and do what the teacher says today," she called out after them apprehensively, hoping that they would enjoy the lessons today.

Kirra turned and followed the others inside into the senior school. She put her lunch carefully in her locker space, then got out her pencil case and books and sat at her usual table by the far window. From here she could see the junior playground, and she watched for a moment as her sisters ran round excitedly with their friends. She hoped they'd have a good day, and that she wouldn't be called in again by their teacher today. Kirra sighed and turned to the front and waited for the teacher to call the roll.

Chapter Twenty-Three

Archie kicked at the soft mud by the river, dragging his toes in a circular line to form a pattern. The soft brown squelch oozed through the spaces between his toes, forming wiggly squirls. He laughed as he traced outlines of lizards and kangaroos in the soft earth beside the river.

"Hey, Archie, wanna drag on me fag?" called out Will from beside the river, breaking Archie's reverie for the moment.

"Yeah, come on over an' join us!" called out Rett, wanting to share some fun with his new mates now that school was over for the day. He liked Archie and Will, and the three of them had become good friends in the short time they had been at this camp.

But Archie was troubled by something; something he couldn't quite put his finger on. It was to do with the three of them, and another time, another river. But where?

Surely you remember your mates from back with your real mob, and surely you haven't forgotten your time with Jacko and Jesse, and Archie, how could you not realise that Will and Rett are just substitutes for all those times the three of you spent down by the river in your childhood, eh? Remember, Archie?

"Hey youse, wanna race in the water over ter the other side, eh?" hollered Rett to the others. "Bet yers can't beat me, eh?"

Where have I heard that before?

Archie and Will dived into the water at the deepest edge of the river and swam over to where Rett was clowning around.

"Yer on!" they shouted eagerly. "Ready set go!"

The three boys splashed their way noisily across to the other side, but it was Will who touched the bank first.

"Ha, I won!" he shouted at the others as they crawled up the bank out of the water. "I knew I could beat yers!"

Archie lay on his back on the river bank with his eyes closed. He tuned out and drifted with the slow steady pace of the running water beside him. He thought of the coming weekend when he would see Kirra again in town. He'd missed her more than he cared to admit. *Really* missed her. Archie didn't truly understand the importance of his friendship with Kirra yet, but he knew all the same that it was somehow special. And he sure as hell intended to keep it that way.

Archie knew that he didn't fancy Kirra the way his mates would. He wasn't interested in girls that way at all, he knew that much at least. He realised that Kirra was attractive and pretty damned smart and streetwise, but there was far more to her than that. She was someone he could trust. He could say things to her that mattered, and know that he wouldn't be laughed at or scorned. Yeah, she was a one-off that Kirra, and he was damned lucky to have bumped into her that first day in town.

"Hey, youse, what do yers wanna do now then? Will we go back to camp an' see what's happening?" called out Rett.

"Maybe we could find some girls eh, an' get up to a bit of no-good. Waddya reckon, Arch, me mate, sound alright or what?" asked Will tentatively trying to see if he could get a reaction from Archie now. He was teasing a bit because he'd noticed that Archie wasn't particularly interested in the girls back at the camp. Maybe he already had a girlfriend back with his mob? Yeah, that was probably it!

But Archie didn't want to go back to camp yet.

"Nah, youse two go. I'll catch yers later," he replied, hoping to be left alone.

After his mates had gone, Archie went back down to the river and splashed about in the shallows. It felt good to be alone again, and it gave him a chance to think about Kirra.

It was strange how he'd changed since meeting her. Changed for the better, he thought. He didn't have his dark moods so often these days, and maybe that was something to do with Kirra. Archie knew that whenever he had that inner anger now, more often than not he thought of how Kirra would handle it and what she'd do. He thought of her hardships and how she coped so well with things back at her home, and it made him stop and think about his own situation. Yeah, maybe he wasn't so unlucky after all!

Still, at times he felt hard done by, as though life had dished him out a pretty rough deal. Archie reckoned that most of his new friends at Pantura had been dealt a bad hand when you thought about it, but still, life was like that wasn't it?

He still missed his mum though, and felt guilty that he hadn't really been a good son to her, when she'd tried so hard to be a good mother. He knew that it was too late to tell her that he was always proud of her and that he had loved her as much as he could anyway.

It's alright, son, I knew that all along and I know that you loved me and you were a good son but I let you down and I ran out of time and I didn't tell you all of the things that I wanted to share with you and now it's too late too late... Aaa... rrr... chie! I wanted to tell you all the dreamtime stories. I wanted to share with you more of your ancestors ways. I wanted you to have the initiation. And I wanted you to accept that you are part of a rich culture and to be proud of who you are and where you come from. I wanted you to understand all these things, Archie, so that your path in life would somehow be more clearly defined, but I left it all too late.

Archie floated freely and let the river current take him slowly on its course. He looked up at the trees and the bright blue sky as he drifted. There were clouds forming overhead, and Archie could feel the changing atmosphere that preceded a storm. He knew that he should get back to camp. His aunty would wonder where he was, now that his mates would be back. But he stayed prone in the water, delaying the departure for as long as he could. His mind was relaxed. He felt renewed and invigorated and at one with the spirits of water and land. He *belonged*.

Chapter Twenty-Four

It was near dark when Archie entered the front door of his aunt's house. The first rain spots were splashing heavily against the donga as he went in. Ominous thunder rolls and spectacular lightning flashes were raging against the backdrop of the night sky, and Archie could feel the hotness build. The moist air strangled him.

"Where you bin, boy, we's bin worried about yer out there with all this storm stuff comin'?" called his aunt from the kitchen. "Come in 'ere an' say hullo to yer ol' aunty, boy!"

Archie padded through to the kitchen obediently, not wanting to upset his aunt. His mum's sister. She did the best she could with him after all, and had taken him in here at such short notice. Still, sometimes it was hard for both of them, and Archie often felt as though she wished he was different. Another girl, maybe, to add to her own two. Yeah, that would have been a lot easier, surely.

Still, she had accepted him as part of her family, and provided a roof over his head and his meals, despite the fact that Archie remained for the most part an outsider, aloof. It wasn't that he meant things to happen this way. But they had, and he had to accept it for now.

Ah, Archie, try not to be so hard on her and try to get along a bit better with everyone. They are your family, my family too. I trusted them with you, and now that I'm gone, I cannot do any more than that. Try, Archie, try.

As soon as he entered the kitchen Archie felt suffocated. He wanted to go to his room and have some time alone, but his aunty always insisted on this 'togetherness' thing. He hated it. It felt intrusive. He wished that he could spend more time just thinking and listening to music and trying to read the books that the teacher had given to him, but his aunt had other ideas.

Archie knew that he should be more grateful. He realised that without this opportunity he would have been stuck in the middle of nowhere, but still he was resentful. It wasn't as if anyone had asked *him*, after all, and that's what upset him the most.

"You bin out with Will an' Rett again down the river, eh, Arch?" asked his aunty as she stirred the stew in the large saucepan. "Waddyers all git up to these days, eh?"

Archie knew better than not to answer, so he stalled a little. "Nothin' much."

He sat at the table and picked at the bread that had already been placed there in readiness for tea. The crust came away in small chunks in his hand, and Archie chewed at it hungrily.

"Here, lay orf the bread willyer, Arch, or we won't have enough ta go round fer tea, there's a good fella," his aunt said, hoping to get a bit more conversation out of Archie yet. "Yer wanna finish settin' the table fer tea, please, Archie?"

"Orright, I'll jez go through an' wash me hands first," replied Archie, knowing that he would not get out of the chore at this late stage.

It wasn't that he had anything against his new family. They were cousins, after all. Family. Connected. It was more to do with the upheaval from his home at such a critical time of his development. Not that Archie could have identified the cause of his unrest. He just felt out of sorts most of the time, and he missed his mates and the mob back home. And he missed Jesse; *especially* Jesse.

And I miss you most of all, Mum, and I wish you were still here and I'm trying to be good and get an education and do the right thing by your sister's family but it's so hard and I'm so lost at times, and I need you still, Mother, why did you go?

In the bathroom Archie shut the door solidly behind him and turned on the cold tap at the sink. He let the cool water run over his hands and his arms, then splashed it over his face. Cool droplets ran down his neck and onto his chest. Trickles of sweat mixed with the tap water and formed patterns on his glistening body. Archie looked in the mirror and studied his reflection.

I am sun and moon and earth and sky. I am from the land of my ancestors. I am fish and snake and goanna and crocodile. I am part of the patterns and ways and laws of my people. I am owner of songs and dances and drawings. I am part of the rich culture of this country's custodians. I am proud. I am free. I am me.

Archie smiled at his reflection in the mirror and scanned his face. Could it really be changing from child to man? Was it so different from the face his mother had remembered when she died? Were the traces of his ancestors still recognisable?

"Hey, Arch," called a voice from somewhere in the house. "You gonna be long in there, mate?"

Reluctantly, Archie dried himself off and opened the bathroom door. His moment of privacy was over for the time being.

"That you, Aunty? I'm coming to help!" he responded as he made his way back to the kitchen. "Jez a tick."

Archie hurried to finish his chores now, not wanting to upset his aunt just before tea. She had enough to do looking after them all without him throwing a spanner in the works, and Archie chose to remain silent while he laid the rest of the plates and cutlery out.

It was hot in the kitchen despite the ceiling fan, and Archie was starting to sweat again. He wanted to go outside and stand on the verandah and watch the storm approach, but tea was being served. He put the plates on the table and sat down at his usual seat opposite his aunty. The steaming stew would be too hot to eat for a little while yet, so Archie poured himself some cordial from the big glass just at the centre of the table.

"C'n I have one too?" asked his cousin. "Sure is hot tonight, eh?"

Without looking up, Archie reached out for her glass and filled it with water, then took some bread from the board. He buttered it and spread it with his favourite honey.

"Geez yer c'n eat!" the girls exclaimed. "Fair dinkum yer can!"

Archie put the remains of his sandwich on his plate and looked down with embarrassment. It was more than just the oppressive night air that was upsetting him here in the kitchen, but he wasn't going to let on to his new family. Maybe they'd understand, and maybe not; but he wasn't going to take the risk tonight. He picked at the stew with his fork, trying to see if it was cool enough to eat yet.

It's just like the stew you used to make for me, Mum, and it tastes almost as good but not quite, and it reminds me of so many times we had together at the kitchen table in the brown donga, and I wish we could still have meals together sometimes... do you?

Archie silently devoured his meal. He didn't join in the conversation or try to speak. He didn't want to talk about the usual frivolous stuff his cousins did. No, Archie just wanted to finish the meal and seek sanctuary in his room as soon as he possibly could.

"Waddya doing after tea Arch? There's a good show on the telly if yer wanna watch it with us?" asked his aunt hopefully, trying to draw Archie out of himself as usual.

"No thanks, I've got some schoolwork to do tonight. Promised the teacher that I'd try to finish me new book before school tomorrow," Archie replied, hoping that his aunt would excuse him after the meal.

"Orright then, we'll do the dishes tonight an' let yer off this time, eh girls?" replied his aunt cheerfully as she rose to clear the table. "Orf yer go then."

Back in the safety of his room, Archie flung himself down on the unmade bed and stretched out full-length on the rumpled sheets. He lay on his back and gazed up at the ceiling. Shadows and darkness enveloped him, and the soft purple glow of distant storm clouds felt soothing. The low rumble of thunder seemed to be calling him, but he felt safe and secure for the moment here in his new home.

Archie was untouched as yet by the sense of family inclusiveness his aunt was trying to establish with him. He kept himself pretty much apart, and rejected the advances of friendship she made. It wasn't that he was intentionally trying to hurt her or exclude himself deliberately from the family; it was more to do with his pain at the loss of his mother. His rock. His lifeblood.

Somewhere deep inside, Archie knew that he had to accept the way things had turned out. Had to get over it, and move on. But still, it was way too early yet, and he was somehow caught in limbo-land. He should have been able to cry, to rage, to be angry; but there hadn't really been time. Things had just happened too quickly, and only now was Archie beginning to *feel* things again.

And the pain sits tight in my chest, and now that I'm here I don't know what to do with it and how to deal with it and who I can share it with, because you are gone, and I never really got the chance to say goodbye to you... Mother.

Archie was surprised to feel the anger rising once more. He was bewildered and ashamed. He wondered why it was coming back to him now and why he was feeling such strong emotions pushing at him. Pulling. Pulsing inside.

I don't want to do this, Mother, I didn't ask for any of this, I don't understand why you had to leave me and throw my world into chaos and let me go, Mother, why?

Lightning suddenly flashed at the window and weird crackly patterns spread across the room where he lay. His heart felt fragmented like the lightning forks as Archie succumbed to sleep.

Chapter Twenty-Five

Kirra jiggled from one foot to the other in her excitement. Archie's lift was due in soon, and she'd been here for an hour already waiting for him outside the café. It felt strange to realise that she and Archie would be able to meet again in person; so much better than the infrequent conversations on the phone. She looked around her at the usual scene of shoppers and kids and dogs and rubbish at the shops. The car park was already half full of Toyotas and trucks and trolleys left abandoned from last night's shopping. Empty cans and smashed glass littered the area beside the path.

A light wind played along the concrete, picking up rubbish and swirling it round and round before dumping it again. Kirra sighed and scanned the gravel road once more, hoping for a sign of Archie's arrival. She was nervous and flighty, wanting him to arrive so that they could share some more time together.

She had managed to escape the home duties this morning by making up a weak excuse about visiting a friend in town. Her mum had still been in bed when she left, and her sisters were lolling on the mattress watching cartoons on telly as usual. She'd plonked a bowl of cereal down for each of them, then dressed and left the house before her mum had the time to gather her wits and call her back. She felt as though she had earned some time for herself, and wasn't bothered by her early departure today.

A group of kids were squabbling nearby as she leant against the Post Office door, and Kirra turned to watch their antics half-heartedly. They reminded her of the kids back at her camp, and she wished she was somewhere else.

God I hate this place and I wish I could leave school and get away and go to the city where there are so many more opportunities and people and services and jobs and entertainment, and one day I'm just gonna walk out of here and hitch a ride down south, you just see if I don't!

A beat up land cruiser pulled up with a squeal of tyres on the gravel opposite where Kirra stood. Red dust coated the exterior and most of the panels and door were rusting. The driver swung into a car space, and the front doors were flung open as the occupants emerged. Before she even had time to collect her thoughts, Archie was standing there gawping at her.

"Kirra, Kirra, it's me, Archie," he called out to her as he approached. "Good ter see ya!"

Suddenly Kirra was shy and awkward, wondering if things between them would pick up where they had left off two months ago. She hoped so, she needed this friendship with Archie. Needed it badly. It had sustained her through many days and nights since they had last been together, and even though she couldn't quite put her finger on why, she knew that Archie was someone very special in her life.

"Hi yer's good ter see ya again," she mumbled, breaking into a smile at the sight of Archie once more. A huge sense of relief washed over her as she caught his smile back.

Kirra felt elated and free. She knew that everything would be OK for a while with Archie, and that they could simply enjoy each other's company for the afternoon.

"How are ya?" asked Archie, concerned about Kirra, and wanting to show that he cared. "Yer been orright since I last saw yer?"

"Yeah, jez fine," Kirra lied, not wanting to share the mundane boredom and frustration of her daily life at the camp. It didn't seem fair to unload all that on Archie right now, especially with him having only recently had such upheaval in his own life. So Kirra pretended that things were pretty much OK, and hoped that she could steer the conversation back to Archie for now.

"D'yer wanna go the café an' have somethin' to eat?" asked Archie. "I'm starving after that ride into town!"

173

"Yeah, good idea," replied Kirra, feeling that it would be a blessing to get inside and away from the public gaze for now. Some of these people here were from her camp, and she didn't want them going back and telling her mum or aunties that she was hanging round with boys. There would be questions and accusations and teasing if they knew, and Kirra had enough against her back home without that. No, she didn't need any more on her plate now!

Archie followed her into the café and they sat down at the familiar laminex table where they had first shared a drink. It felt a bit odd at first after so long away, but Archie soon settled at the table and started to relax a bit.

I've really missed you, Kirra, it's not the same taking to you on the phone with others always eavesdropping and trying to listen to every word you say and asking you who you're talking to and interfering when all I want is just to be alone and share some of my thoughts and dreams and worries with you, know what I mean, Kirra? Have you missed me at all, too?

"Watcha wanna eat and drink, Kirra?" Archie asked, hoping that they could enjoy some time in here out of the heat and away from the prying eyes of others for a while. "D'yer wanna hamburger an' milkshake?"

Kirra thought for a moment before replying. She was pretty darned hungry now that she was here. She'd been too preoccupied back at home to even give breakfast a thought, and she had waited quite a while for Archie to arrive this morning. "Yeah, orright, that'd be nice, Archie, I'll have caramel, ta. And a hamburger jez with meat an' tomato."

Archie went over to the counter to order their food. The waitress recognised Archie and smiled at him. She was friendly and maternal. Archie liked her, she reminded him of...

Mother, Mother, is that you there watching me and smiling at me and listening to me here in the café and can you see the change in me? I'm growing up, Mother, and I'm trying to fit in more with people but sometimes I still need you and wish that you were here for me and sometimes I just want to curl up into a tiny ball so that you can cradle me in your arms like you used to and it's still so hard... Mo... ooo... ther!

"How are yer, love? Yer been lookin' after yerself then?" the waitress asked Archie. She remembered that he'd had a bad fight down at half way camp last time he'd been in town. It was a regular happening round here, especially on welfare nights. She was well used to it by now, after twenty years in this godforsaken place, but still it sometimes left her shaken when she saw them the next time they came to town. After all this time, she couldn't for the life of her figure out why they had to brutalise themselves so often, and over so little, it seemed to her. But that's the way it was round here, and there was precious little she could do to stop it.

"Yeah, I'm jez fine," Archie replied, not wanting to say anything that might give away how he really felt. "I'm livin' out west a bit now, over at Pantura. With me aunty an' her kids,"

"That's nice, best out of here anyways," the waitress replied. "My name's Nora, hi yers again."

"I'm Archie, an' I guess yer know Kirra from out the camp anyways," Archie responded, trying to be pleasant and sociable this morning. He liked this place and guessed that he and Kirra would be meeting here whenever he could get a lift to town. He wanted to keep things friendly and cordial. He wanted to show he cared.

And I cared for you too, Mum, and I know that I should have talked to you more and told you things that I cared about and shared some of my fears and worries and dreams with you, but it was hard with dad gone and mainly aunties around, and lots of it was men's business and I couldn't really tell you. I was too embarrassed and I didn't even tell my best mates 'cause they would have teased me so I've kept it to myself all this time and just tried to get through each day and work it all out by myself, but maybe I should have told you and maybe you guessed anyway and knew far more than you let on, did you, Mum?

"Here you are then, love, yer order's ready," called out Nora from behind the counter. "Yer's payin' together or separate?"

"I'll get it," said Archie as he got up to get their food. "She's right, Kirra, my shout, eh?"

Kirra protested briefly, then realised that she didn't have enough money to pay for the food anyway. Still, she didn't like being looked after. She wasn't used to it. It seemed as though some of her independence was slipping away, and Kirra wasn't too sure about that. She was too used to being her own boss.

"My shout next time then," she put in grudgingly. "I always pay me own way, Archie, yer know."

Archie took the tray with the food and drinks over to the table and put them down. He carefully placed them at their places, and then went back to the counter for the two serviettes.

"Geez yer a dag!" exclaimed Kirra smiling. "Jez look at yer willyer? Yer could get a job waiting on tables, fair dinkum yer could, Arch!"

They both laughed, and Archie felt the tension disappear there at the table in the café. It was great to be with Kirra again, and he could tell that she had looked forward to seeing him again as much as he had. They smiled at each other across the table as they munched on the hamburgers. They both relaxed finally as they ate.

"Waddya wanna do after this?" asked Archie, not wanting to waste any time this afternoon. He knew that he would have to stay over at town camp with Ken's family tonight; after last time in town they'd made him promise he would not go near half way camp again.

"We could go over to the big hardware an' clothes store and browse for a while if yer like," replied Kirra as she slurped at the last dregs of her milkshake. "There might be some new clothes in that we could look at."

"Orright, I might see if there's any shorts, I need some new ones," replied Archie half-heartedly, not wanting to offend

Kirra again. He would much rather go down to the river and have a swim and spend more time alone with Kirra so they could just be themselves, but he knew that she didn't come up to town much herself except to do grocery shopping occasionally, so he agreed.

"Would yer like an ice cream before we go, Kirra?" he asked, hoping to stall for a little while longer. "I liked those ones we had last time, remember?"

But Kirra was too full from the hamburger and milkshake, and she would rather just get over to the store now and have a look as the fashions there, such as they were.

"Nah, later maybe, but thanks all the same, Arch. Let's go, eh?"

Nora leaned over the counter and handed Archie his change. "See yers later then," she called out as they left the café. "Have a good afternoon, wonchas?"

Chapter Twenty-Six

Kirra and Archie had been down at the river for hours. The sun was high and the day was hot. They were floating in the shallows, happy and carefree. Drifting.

"Watcha thinkin' about now, Archie?" asked Kirra as she turned towards the bank.

If only I could tell you all of my dreams and all of my worries and fears and insecurities, Kirra, but I'm still not sure, not sure yet.

"Hey, Arch, d'yer ever fancy the girls at your camp?" Kirra laughed, hoping to get a reaction of some sort now from Archie.

Ah, Kirra, if only I could really talk to you and let you into my heart and tell you how confused I am about my sexuality and how much I still miss Jesse and think about him all the time and how afraid I am of ever finding someone who understands and accepts and shares my feelings and feels the same as me, but I know, I know it shouldn't be like this but it is, I can't help it, Kirra!

Archie squeezed his eyes tight against the sun and his inner torment. He tried to shove his thoughts away and focus on something light. Something easy and uncluttered. Something he could share with Kirra. But the thoughts and visions of Jesse kept coming back to him, and Archie struggled with his internal battles.

He opened his eyes and released his pent-up emotions in a flood of rambling words. He told Kirra everything. All of his frustration and pain poured out like a raging torrent that he couldn't stop.

"Kirra, Kirra, I don't know what to do sometimes. At night I dream of so many things and think about my mother and all of the things she was trying to teach me and I didn't understand

and lots of it is only half-finished in my head because she never got the time to say it all before she died and now I have to find out for myself and I feel such guilt because I should have paid more attention to her while I had the time but I didn't know that she would so soon be gone from my life, I truly didn't, Kirra. I wish that I'd been able to talk to her about so many things but it was too hard, and now I still feel ashamed at how things have worked out for both of us, and sometimes I just feel so alone and so afraid and so lost Kirra. And no, I don't like girls that way, Kirra. I know that I should but I don't, I like Jesse instead, and it's pretty hard being different but I can't help it, Kirra."

Archie had been drifting with the slow pace of the river. His eyes were focused on the overhanging tree branches, and he tried to avoid looking at Kirra now. He felt embarrassed and totally depleted, as though all of his energy had disappeared.

"I'm sorry, Kirra," he stammered. "I didn't mean to say all that stuff, but somehow it all just came out."

Kirra watched him as he floated nearby, and then stood up in the river. Tears glistened at the corner of her eyes as she gazed at Archie. She was silent for a while, taking it all in.

Oh, Archie, Archie you poor thing, I understand and I really care and I know how hard life can be and I don't think any less of you for being that way and I'm glad you told me all about your mum and I know you feel bad about it but I'm your friend and I won't laugh at you, I'll help you, Archie, it'll be alright.

She leaned over to where Archie lay in the water and touched his hand. "It's OK, Archie, I won't laugh at you. I'm glad you told me those things. It's fine by me, true."

Archie opened his eyes and sat up in the shallows next to Kirra. He felt drained and tired, but a huge sense of relief spread through him as he saw Kirra's smile.

"Yer sure yer don't mind?" he asked her, hoping that it really was OK.

Kirra grinned at Archie reassuringly and told him that it was fine. She wasn't going to say anything to anyone about Archie's outpouring, and she knew better than most the difficulties faced by adolescents in the camps. Kirra had grown up fast, and although she was far more worldly and streetwise than Archie, she still felt some of the same emotions and sense of isolation. Kirra understood the impact of being different, or not belonging, and how it felt to be alone.

"I'm glad yer told me that stuff, Archie, truly I am. It must have been hard keepin' all that to yerself, especially now with yer mum gone an' all. You can tell me anything, you know. I don't mind, that's what friends are for yer know, Arch," Kirra urged him gently, hoping that Archie felt that they were *really* friends.

She realised how difficult it must have been for Archie to finally confide in someone, and a part of her was proud and pleased that it had been her. She didn't take that sort of sharing lightly, and despite her youth, Kirra understood the importance of trust and secrecy. She'd kept lots of things secret herself over the years for her own preservation, and it was easy to accept that Archie had done the same. Yes, she understood.

"Archie, yer don't have ta ever feel ashamed or guilty in front of me yer know. We haven't know each other that long, but I reckon we trust each other enough already, don't you? I'd never betray yer, Arch," Kirra stated emphatically, hoping that Archie would hear the passion of acceptance and understanding in her response.

Kirra didn't want Archie to feel awkward now that he had shared some of his innermost thoughts with her, so she tried to reassure him there by the edge of the river. Maybe she could tell him about some of her life too. Yeah, maybe *that* would help.

"Me uncle grabbed me once when we was walkin' home from a cook-up yer know. We was jez comin' in the gate of my house an' suddenly the ol' bastard jez set on me an' put his arms round me an' breathed his hot stinkin' beer breath all down me neck. God, was I scared! I kicked him in the shins an' let out such a holler that the kids an' the neighbours woke up an' he ran orf, jez like that. The mongrel, never did say sorry! Jez pretended nothin' had happened at all the next time he came round to see me mum, an' maybe he didn't remember 'e was so drunk. Ol' *bastard*!" Kirra cried vehemently, anger swirling to the surface again at the memory.

Archie looked up and was astonished to see that Kirra was crying now as she sat in the shallow water next to him. She lashed out with her hands and sent angry arcs of water spinning upwards, as though her actions would somehow assuage the injustice her uncle had caused. Her shattered emotions clung to the droplets of river-spray as they rose and fell. She breathed in the hot afternoon heat and snorted with rage though flared nostrils. Tears of salt drained into the corner of her mouth as she sat there moaning softly. Her pain was achingly tangible, and it was Archie's turn to provide some solace now.

"S'alright, Kirra, there there, don' upset yerself," he murmured, trying to ease her hurt. "I'm here ta help you, Kirra."

He reached out and took her hand in his, then led her out of the river and up the bank. Archie sat her down in the shade of a large river gum, and kept hold of her hand for reassurance. He let her tears flow and gave her some time to let out her fears and frustration, just as she had let him. He knew that she had been mistreated, but he didn't know how to help or what to say right now to make things right for her. He just wanted her to feel good again, to get back the laughter and fun. But he knew that she needed to get things out of her system, just like he had to. Funny that, how alike they were, bottling up all the stuff that really mattered.

Archie glanced over at Kirra to see how she was. He could feel her hand still shaking a little as he held it, and he tried to reassure her with soothing words.

"It's going to be alright, Kirra, I'm here with yer now, so don't worry any more, OK?" he whispered softly beside her. "Gawd we're a couple of fools, you an' me, ain't we?"

Kirra turned her head and smiled a thin smile. She looked into Archie's eyes to see if he was genuine, and decided that he was. She was beginning to feel a bit better now that she had begun to open up about some of her past.

But there was still so much inside and there were other times that her uncles had come to her when she had been alone and she still had nightmares from time to time and felt those tough knobbly hands reaching out for her and clawing at her and touching her in places that she knew were wrong, and groping and grabbing her and pressing her young body down, down till she was sinking and drowning and suffocating in the hot beery tension of the still dark nights, and who would save her, who, who, who?

Kirra looked up at Archie with eyes so sad that he wanted to cry. He wanted to fold her in his arms and protect her from the world. He wanted to inflict pain on the people who had hurt her. Above all, he wanted to make them suffer as she had suffered.

They sat for what seemed like forever, side by side at the edge of the river. They were still and silent, lost in their own worlds. Time rolled by with the slow-moving water, but Kirra and Archie were oblivious to its passage. The sun began to sink lower in the shimmering blue sky. In the distance the night-noises of the town began building.

"Where are yer stayin' tonight, Arch? Up at town camp with Ken?" asked Kirra quietly.

"Yeah, I'd better be gowin' soon too, and you'll have to get back home before yer mum 'n sisters miss yer fer too long, eh?" he replied reluctantly, not really wanting to break the spell of peaceful acceptance that they both felt right now. It had been a difficult time this afternoon down by the river, but somehow Archie knew that an important bridge had been crossed for both of them. He sensed that Kirra felt it too, without the acknowledgement. Yeah, somehow things would be a bit better for both of them now, he was sure of it.

Chapter Twenty-Seven

It was dark when Archie walked back into town camp where he was supposed to meet Ken and his mob. He was feeling lighter now than he had for a while, after his revelations to Kirra. Just getting some of the load off his mind had lifted his spirits and he swaggered up the road towards Ken's house feeling better by the minute.

Ken emerged from the front as Archie arrived. "There yer are, mate, how was your afternoon in town, eh?" asked Ken jovially. "What did yer git up to then?"

Archie smiled at Ken as he replied. "Aw, nothin' much, mate, jez hung round the shops an' went down the river fer a bit, you know."

He didn't want to tell Ken yet about his friendship with Kirra. He knew that it would be misunderstood and taken for something that it wasn't. Archie didn't want to get himself or Kirra into any trouble, he figured they had enough to deal with in their lives without adding anything else for now. So he kept it to himself, hoping that would be the end of it.

"Yer sure yer didn't go chasin' any girls while yer was in town, eh?" asked Ken cheekily, teasing Archie as they stood by the front porch. "There's plenty of available girls round here mate that'd take a fancy to the likes of you. Jez watch yer step though mate, could get yerself in trouble again yer know an' we don't want that, do we? Don't want you getting' yerself beat up again!"

Archie grimaced slightly at the memory of his first visit to town and the night at half way camp. He knew it had been foolish of him to go down there unannounced, and he sure had paid the price for his stupidity. No, he wouldn't make that mistake again!

"She's right, Ken, I won't be lookin' fer any trouble this time," Archie replied, "yer can bet on it!"

"Ready fer tea then are yer, Arch, there's some cold cans out the back if yer wanna beer, an' I've got the fire roarin' ready to cook the roo tails I got at the store. Help yerself, mate, I'll be back in a tick," said Ken, as he set off out the gate and headed up the road to see a few mates of his.

Archie knew it would be a while before Ken returned, so he went round the back of the house and over to the car fridge stacked with grog. He reached in and took out a cool can, then sat on the ground by the fire as he ripped off the ring top. Sssssss! Beer foamed over the edge of the can and trickled down the sides to form ice-cold rivulets that dripped onto Archie's shorts. He put the can to his lips and felt the familiar bitter-sweet taste in his throat once more. Ah, it was great!

He was mesmerised by the dance of the flames and the taste of beer and the quiet peace of his temporary solitude here in Ken's backyard. He felt strong and secure and uninhibited. Archie seemed right at this moment to be back on an even keel, as though his life had somehow balanced suddenly and unexpectedly today in town with Kirra. He felt as though he was ready to move forward again and not be afraid. He was gaining confidence and hope.

It's going to be alright, Mum, I just know it is and I won't forget you, no I won't, but I've got a new life now and I'm making new friends and I need to work hard at school and get an education so's I can maybe have a career of some sort and try and get ahead and make something of myself and prove to you that I can do it, Mum, it's going to be OK.

Ken arrived back as Archie was opening his second can of beer. He had invited a few of the mob back for the cook-up, and Archie knew they would stay till all the grog was gone and the food eaten and the yarns told. There'll be no more quiet time tonight.

Halfway through the meal one of Ken's mates got out his guitar. Archie tried to remember if it was the same person who'd played on his first visit to town, but he'd been too nervous and shy back then to take much in. Nah, he wasn't sure.

"Archie, you've met Flynn? He's from out bush, up north. Plays a mean tune or two he does. An' sings pretty good too after a few grogs," said Ken.

"Hi yers," mumbled Flynn, looking down at the ground as he strummed the guitar, "nice to meet yer."

Archie listened as the guitar chords echoed round his head. Something pulsed inside him. A recognition, a belonging. An urge to dance and sing and tap his hands and feet. The music seemed to be talking to him, calling him, urging something inside him to wake up, wake up! Archie felt electrified and dizzy, as though he had just made an amazing discovery. Some force he'd never felt before took over and captured him as he sat there enveloped by the music. He was transfixed.

And the sounds of the music that hung in the night air seemed like the call of his people and perhaps this is the sign I've been waiting for and the start of something that I've needed all along and the chance to somehow meld both worlds together here for me and give me the tools I need to be creative and express my inner self.

For Archie suddenly there was only the sound of the guitar there by the fire. He could no longer hear the backdrop of men's voices and cans opening and food sizzling and laughter and talking and dogs barking; all that he heard was Flynn strumming away and crooning some tunes to the night sky.

"Hey, mate, c'n yer play another fer us? I jez love those songs!" called out Ken from the back porch.

Flynn was silhouetted by firelight as he started up another song, his head bent slightly over the instrument as he concentrated on the chords. Archie thought it was an awesome sight, and something else pulled at his emotions. Something he didn't recognise at first. Something like what he'd felt watching Jesse all those times. He pulled his eyes away sharply and looked at the ground, embarrassed now by the sudden realisation.

"Hey, Arch, waddyer reckon, 'e plays pretty darn good, eh?" called out Ken from across the other side of the campfire. "'E could teach yer if yer like, couldn't yer, Flynn? I reckon you'd probably be good at music an' singin', Archie, I do mate."

Flynn looked up and stared at Archie as he played, not missing a beat. His eyes bore into Archie and seemed to devour his soul there in the firelight. Archie was held captive by this elusive stranger; mesmerised, unable to look away. His breath seemed to come in fits and starts, and his skin was alive with tingling sensations. Archie sat stock still and stared straight ahead while the music still floated through his body and the flames danced beside him. All the cockiness and self-assurance he'd felt earlier in the evening had suddenly drained away to nothing, leaving Archie exposed and raw and scratchy. He picked at the dirt by his feet, knowing there was nothing he could do or say right now to fix things.

Time drifted on with the music, and Archie had nothing left to signify its passing. He didn't know whether the evening was at its' beginning or end; just that it *was*. The beer and the food had all been consumed, and the fire was dying now too. Conversations were quieter. It must have been late.

But this new stranger is still here playing the guitar and his fingers are still strumming the chords and the sound of his voice is still echoing softly, softly in the damp night and his face is still quietly staring at nothing, nothing, as I watch and am held in his gaze and feel him draw me in and comfort me, comfort me.

***

Kirra was pacing around the kitchen restlessly this evening. She was unsettled and nervy. Her mind was entertaining a thousand fleeting thoughts, and she couldn't pin down any of them. She felt like a bag of sawdust held together with staples. God she was hopeless! What was all this about anyway?

You know, you know, Kirra, because you prised open the lid of the box and you started to let out your life and share it with Archie and all of the secrets you've kept hidden are now lining up in the corridors of your mind to be recognised and they now have a voice and won't be silenced and what did you expect when you threw away the key to the padlocked doors?

Kirra was nonplussed nonetheless. Part of her felt relieved that finally someone understood her problems and still accepted her, but part of her was scared. She worried about Archie. Maybe he'd say something to someone without thinking.

She finished peeling the spuds for tea and sliced them into chips. The hot fat was sizzling on the stove, and the fry pan was ready for the sausages and bacon. She'd do the eggs in another pan, and then toss in the chips when everything else was cooking.

Her mum waddled through and sat down at the half-cleared table. She lit a cigarette and gasped at Kirra through the thick smoke. "Wanna hand luv, anything I c'n do ter help?"

God, when did you ever help me, Mum?

Kirra was disgusted with the dishevelled state of her mother and the cigarette hanging from her mouth polluting the kitchen. She tried her best to keep the house in order, and almost single-handedly kept everything in place, but from time to time her mum would mess it all up again in Kirra's absence.

"Nah, she's right, dinner won't be long now, Mum," Kirra replied with sarcasm. "Why doncha go an' watch the telly while I set the table an' finish cookin' in here, eh, Mum?"

Kirra's edginess and tone were lost on the old woman, who continued to sit and smoke at the kitchen table. Kirra ignored her and continued with the preparation of the meal. She didn't have time for her mum's vagaries tonight. She was preoccupied with other more important issues than her mum's daily journey through struggle-town. Bugger it, thought Kirra, let her stew in her own juices for a while, I don't care.

But her mum had other ideas tonight. She was lonely, and wanted to chat to her eldest daughter. "Whatcher do in town today with yer friends eh, Kirra? Did yer meet any boys? I'll bet some of them townies fancy a pretty girl like you, eh, Kirra?" her mum smiled at her through stained and broken teeth. "Cor, when I was a girl we used ter git up ter all sorts of bother on a Sat'dy arvo in town, we sure did," she giggled as she glanced over at her daughter. "Used ta be lots of fun it did."

Kirra shrunk inside herself and cringed with embarrassment. The last thing she needed right now was to hear her mother going on about the things she'd gotten up to as a teenager.

And did you get raped by your uncle? And was your mother a drunk, too? And did your father leave after too many fights and too much bashing and too many drunken arrests in the town? And when did you lose your pride and dignity, when? When? When?

Kirra was boiling with anger and overwhelmed by the injustices of life. She was hurting and vulnerable inside, but tough and indifferent on the outside. Right at that moment as she stood at the stove turning the sausages over, she hated her mother. Hated what she'd become. Hated how she had let herself go. Hated her for letting things get so bad. Hated her for always hitting the booze and copping out.

Kirra felt like she was on fire. She was struggling to hold herself together. She felt like throwing the pan at her mother and shouting at her and hitting her and telling her how god-damned miserable her life had become. She gripped the spatula and screamed.

"I hate you, Mum! Just look at you, sitting there day in day out with yer booze an' yer fags an' the place like a pig-sty! Go an' have a look at yerself in the mirror, Mum, yer a goddamned disgrace, yer are! An' don't talk to me about boys, I'm just not interested, OK?" Kirra hurled at her mother amid tears of frustration and rage.

But Beryl just sat there, seemingly oblivious to Kirra's outburst. Her grimy face showed no emotion as she took another long hard pull on the cigarette. Her life was a wall of misery and acceptance, as though she had become immune to the very essence of existence. Time stopped for what seemed like forever as the two women collected their thoughts.

But then a strange thing happened. The wall of silence and tension collapsed and crumbled. Somewhere inside Beryl a dam suddenly burst. Pent up emotions that she'd suppressed for oh-so-long began forcing their way out, trickling and tumbling, carried along by the tide of a life spent in the shadow of what might have been. She let out a long slow moan as she sat there hunched at the kitchen table, and Kirra was overcome with awe at the sight of her mother's intensity and pain.

Do you feel it too, Mum, I know how it must hurt, I feel the same loss and pain and injustice at what our lives have become, but it's not too late to change things and make things better, and we can help each other if we try to overcome the obstacles can't we, Mum?

Mother and daughter were caught and held together in a timeless bond despite their differences. Despite the age gap, Kirra could feel her mother's pain. She reached out to the old woman seated at the table and gently held her hand, wanting somehow to take away her anguish. Make it better. Start the healing.

But her mother was inconsolable and couldn't respond to Kirra's gesture, there was too much grief present. She had built up too many barriers over too many years.

Beryl's eyes held her daughter's briefly, and for a moment there was a flicker of recognition and acceptance, but then they shut tight once more. She screwed up her fists and beat the table slowly and rhythmically, trying to drive out the demons. Her soft moaning became louder, and her body rocked backwards and forwards in the hot kitchen air.

"It'll be OK, Mum," cried out Kirra, disturbed and frightened how at the sight of her mum's agony. "I'll help yer ta sort things out a bit, Mum, don't cry now, there, there."

But Beryl kept on rocking and chanting. She beat at her chest and stamped the floor with her feet. She sang in her native tongue, words that had no meaning to her daughter. Then she caved in suddenly to silence and lowered her head into her arms as she sank dejectedly onto the kitchen table that was still only half-set for tea.

Kirra left her mother alone now and went out the back door. She badly needed an escape. She needed to breathe deeply and get some air back into her lungs and clear her head. She felt like she'd been hit by a truck, and it wasn't something she needed right now. There was enough going on in her life to contend with, and she wasn't sure whether she wanted to sort out her mother's problems as well.

Mother, Mother, when did it all go wrong for you? And what has happened in your past to make you like this? And why did you let your life fail you so miserably? And when did you start relying on the grog to get you through each day and help you escape from the harsh reality of your existence, when? When? When?

Kirra leaned against the verandah post and sucked in huge gulps of night air. She felt deflated, exhausted. She wished that she could talk to Archie and share some of her loneliness, but it wasn't possible to call him tonight. She closed her eyes for a moment and tried to focus on something bright to get her through the evening.

Chapter Twenty-Eight

Archie sat hunched in the shadows watching the embers of the dying fire back at town camp. Flynn was still strumming the guitar slowly, crooning a song in his language, staring at some far-off space beyond the darkness. Archie was awestruck.

"We're gowin' in ter bed now, Arch, yer comin', mate?" called Ken from over near the empty car fridge as he noisily scraped the remains of the food and the empty cans into a haphazard pile beside the fire.

"Nah, might jez stay here a while longer till the fire's out," replied Archie, not wanting to leave while Flynn was still here. He didn't know whether Flynn was even aware of his presence, but it made him feel good just being here watching and listening. He was soothed by the music. Archie felt great, and it wasn't just the effect of the grog tonight.

"Orright, see yer soon then, mate, don' be too long hey, yer gotta get back up ter Pantura tomorra, remember," added Ken as he left.

That left Archie and Flynn alone now here in the backyard. Darkness swallowed them up as they squatted by the flickering remains of the fire. Two strangers, closing in on each other. Close yet worlds apart. The unknown territory between them left Archie feeling breathless and excited. He was unsure and vulnerable, but he felt as though there was a connection between them. More than their race. More than their culture. Something he couldn't quite put his finger on right now. He just *felt* it somehow.

Flynn finished playing and glanced over at Archie. "Yer wanna learn how to play?" he asked cautiously, unsure about Archie at this stage. "I could show yer a few chords an' how ter hold the guitar if yer like. Come over here an' watch me, it's easy."

Archie felt something constricting his throat. His skin was alive and his senses cried out for contact, but he crept over cautiously to where Flynn sat. It was too early yet too late. He avoided skin contact, and plopped down in the dirt next to Flynn. He could feel the heat and the warmth and the strength in the silence between them. Words were left unspoken. Dreams were building, rising and falling in waves of anticipation. Archie could feel the excitement of the future weighing heavily against the dread of the past. He wanted to tell Flynn how he felt and see if there was a reaction, but the fear of failure overtook him there by the low flames. So he sat and watched and waited.

"Here, jez hold the guitar in yer hands first an' get used to the feel of the wood. It's not as difficult as yer'd think. If yer like music an' yer gotta bit o' soul, you'll take ter it in no time with a bit o' practice." Flynn leaned over and passed the guitar to Archie. His hands brushed Archie's arms lightly as he bent over the guitar. Archie was electrified. He felt a surge of power and adrenalin run through his body. He was overcome with sudden coyness. It was difficult to focus on what Flynn was telling him, but he didn't want to spoil things tonight. No, he sure didn't want to give anything away right now.

"Feels good," Archie whispered as he held the guitar. "I watched yer play an' I reckon I could learn if I had a guitar ter practice on. I'll have to ask Ken if he knows anyone who's got one they could lend me fer a bit while I learn. C'n yer show me how ter play some of the chords, Flynn?"

They sat by the fire for a while, both concentrating on the guitar. Archie was a good learner, and picked up the skills quickly. He forgot about his feelings for Flynn and became lost in the music. Something was taking over, something deep and powerful and significant.

Something to do with the songs that his mum had taught him so long ago.

Archie had a strong sense of another presence as he strummed the guitar and tried to make music.

Was it the pull of the ancestors and the songs and chants and rhythms and animal-howls calling him from somewhere way beyond time?

"That's pretty good fer yer first time," said Flynn quietly. "It's in yer blood I can tell, yer a natural, like me."

Archie looked up and smiled. Flynn's encouragement gave him the incentive to continue, and he bent over the guitar once more and played the chords he had just learned. He wanted to improvise, to make up a song of his own, to play what was in his heart. But he didn't want Flynn to listen, and he didn't want to be embarrassed at this early stage, so he asked Flynn if he could maybe teach him some more tomorrow before he went back to Pantura.

"Sure, no problems, mate. I'm hangin' round till lunch time tomorrow anyway. I c'n meet yer in the morning over at the café an' we can practice a bit more if yer like. Maybe go down the river fer a bit where it's quieter, eh?"

"Sure, that'd be great," replied Archie, forgetting all about Kirra now. They'd arranged to meet in the morning for a short while before he had to go, and he knew that it was important for both of them. But being here with Flynn tonight had totally consumed him, and his memory was clouded by his current euphoria.

Flynn stood up as the last of the flames subsided. It was late, and the heat had subsided. It would soon be getting cold as the night advanced. It was time to turn in.

"I'd better get up the road now an' find a bed fer the night, Arch. It's been real nice meetin' yer an' havin' someone appreciate me music yer know. I reckon yer'll be playin' like me real soon if yer keep up the practice, an' I'll see what I can do in the morning about getting' yer a guitar of yer own ter play, orright?" Flynn stretched out his hand to say farewell to Archie for the night.

"Hang on, Flynn, I'll walk up the road with yer a bit. Mind if I join yer, eh?" asked Archie tentatively, hoping to delay the end of the evening for just a little while longer.

They set off up the road in silence, each with their own thoughts and dreams held tight within. Archie knew that he would see Flynn tomorrow, and he was elated at the prospect of possible future meetings in town whenever he could get a lift in.

"You come into town much then, Flynn?" he asked as they neared Ken's house. "It'd be mighty good ter see yer now an' then ter catch up with music an' all, d'yer reckon?"

In truth, Archie was beginning to feel nervous. He wasn't sure if his friendship with Flynn was going anywhere at all. He didn't even know if he would see him again; after all, Ken said that he didn't come to town very often. And his people were a long way from here. Bush people. Kept to themselves for the most part. Didn't need company or trips to town or whitefella stuff. Nah, maybe he wouldn't see much of Flynn at all after tomorrow.

But Flynn was keen to catch up with Archie again too.

"Yeah, that'd be good mate. I'll be in town a few times ter get supplies an' play me music with this mob an' see a few of me mates at town camp yer know. We'll catch up regular, orright?" said Flynn as he turned into the gate of the nearest donga. "See yer in the mornin', g'night."

Archie muttered his goodnight to Flynn and danced up the road. He was definitely on a high. He wanted to sing to shout to whirl to stamp his feet and wave his arms and shout aloud there in the deserted street near Ken's house. He laughed out loud and let out his breath in long blows. Whoosh! Whooosh! Whooosh!

Chapter Twenty-Nine

Kirra was exhausted. She hadn't slept very well last night because of her mum. She was emotionally drained. Worn out. She had woken late as the hot sun cast a fogginess across her bed. Her eyes were shut tight against the glare, and Kirra wished that she could go back to sleep. But the room was too hot and she could tell that it was already later than she usually woke on a Sunday.

She threw back the twisted sheet and pushed her legs over the edge of the rumpled bed. She felt hot and clammy and dishevelled, as though something had come unstuck during the night. Kirra was at a loss to know what to do today.

She was supposed to meet Archie up at the café, but despite that, she didn't really feel like going into town this morning. Something had shifted overnight after seeing her mum's anguish, and Kirra felt that she should stay at home this morning just in case. She was worried about her and the kids. She needed to be here for them, to stay strong. Archie would have to wait. She didn't have the energy or time to devote to things outside the house this morning, it was too much.

But something inside her felt sad and something was tugging at her young heart, and bits of her were breaking away and drifting upwards slowly, slowly there in the hot still room where she still had the shroud of sleep hanging over her ever so slightly, and she didn't want to be here in this role today. She felt trapped by the spider web of duty and it was too much, too much...

Kirra rubbed her eyes and stood up. She had to shake off the inertness for now and get going. There were things she had to do, and she could no longer ignore them. She reached down and stripped off her bed hurriedly, wrapping the sheets into a ball at the end of her bed. Then she dragged all her worn clothes over and added them to the pile on the bed. Next she went over to her wardrobe and got out some fresh clothes, before padding down the hallway to the bathroom.

After her shower Kirra felt much better, and she dressed quickly before going out the back to the laundry with her pile of clothes. "Bring out yer washin'!" she called out to the family as she filled the washing machine. "It's washing time this morning."

Her mum appeared and stood framed in the doorway. The sun caught her freshly washed hair and clean dress. Kirra knew that she was ready for church this morning, so she hurried now to get the washing under way.

"How are yer this morning; Mum? Yer feelin' a bit better, eh?" she asked softly, concern and care in her voice. "I was worried about yer after last night yer know."

Beryl smiled at her daughter as she shifted out of the doorway and watched Kirra start the machine. "Yeah, I'm OK, love, don't you worry about yer ol' mum this mornin', I'm fine."

Kirra smiled at the old woman as she came out and stood beside her in the sunshine. She gave her hand a squeeze to let her know that everything would be alright. That somehow they'd get through this and work it out. That Kirra was there for her, despite everything.

She looked at her mum, and was surprised to see a tear silently rolling down her cheek.

"It's OK, Mum, don't cry," Kirra reassured her, "there, there."

Beryl wiped her eyes and smoothed down her hair. She blinked in the sunlight and brushed her hand over the clean cotton dress. She smiled a thin smile at her daughter, then turned and went back into the house. Kirra was left with the image of a different mother than the one she had seen last night. A stronger and softer image. A woman with some dignity returned. A real mother, or at least a glimpse of one.

It was dark inside the small country church as Beryl stepped across the threshold. Even at this relatively early hour, it felt soothing to be out of the heat. She crossed to her usual Sunday seat and bent down to pray. It wasn't much, just a tiny token of hope in the shattered existence that had become her life. But for Beryl, it was at least *something*. A gesture, an offering, a truce of some sort.

But where is the land of my people and where are the elders who once held us together and why have we strayed so far from our laws and our culture and where will we go now that we have adopted the ways of the settlers and given ourselves up to other laws and other ways and other signs and spirits, what do we believe in now dear Lord, what?

Beryl sat heavily on the old wooden chair and rested her head on her folded arms. She felt tired and old and used. Worn down by time and ancient memories. Obsolete.

Ah, but once it had all be so different and once she had been young and agile and full of life and hope and love, and once she had sung the songs of her people and gathered bush tucker and learned the ways of her tribe, hadn't she?

In her head Beryl could hear the chant of the elders, but she was thrown into confusion once more by the external sounds of the organ and the hymns. It made for a harsh contrast of jangling rhythms going on around her, and somehow Beryl couldn't unite the two sources of sound. It seemed that the contrast represented the source of her life's ambivalence, and for Beryl it became almost too much there in the tiny building that was supposed to be the house of God.

Whose God is this and why am I here listening to this music and is that my voice I can hear joining in the chorus and lifting and tilting in time with the crescendo of organ-music, is it? Is it? Where is the voice of my people?

A ray of sunlight filtered through the stained glass window in front of her, and Beryl saw this as a sign. She didn't know what it represented, but at least she felt *something*.

And it's not the booze this time and it's not the anger and the shouts and the threats up at the camp and it's not Kirra chastising me for being drunk again and it's not the littlies asking me a thousand times when are we going to do this and when are we going to do that and whinging that we never go to town together any more or down to the river to swim; it's not any of those things this time.

Beryl raised her eyes to study the window that the community had struggled to save for. It was bright and large and colourful, with a picture of Our Lord surrounded by motives of her people. They had at least insisted on that, as a way of compromise. If the community were going to pay for it, then at least it should have something of their story and their dreamtime in it too.

It had been made in the city and transported up carefully by road train, and when it arrived there had been a big party in town to celebrate. Beryl had attended, of course, with most of her mob from half way camp. It had been a reasonably quiet and sober affair, with the new minister insisting that the ban on alcohol for church functions be strictly adhered to.

But he didn't see what they got up to later down by the river bed and he didn't know that they had a few dozen slabs down there ready with some kangaroo tails and spuds for the cook up after dark when he'd gone back to the manse and safely ensconced himself in his air-conditioned world.

Beryl shrugged her shoulders and smiled briefly at the memory of that night. It was one of many in her life when she'd gotten plastered again. Smashed. Unable to stand at the end of the night. Lying drunk and asleep in the dirt by the fire, a blanket thrown haphazardly over her in the cold of the night by some kind stranger.

Fragments of her life paraded before her there in the church. She remembered childhood days of innocence and independence and simple pleasures with her family before they'd been forcibly removed from it all. Sent away suddenly, the family told to leave the station where she'd been born.

She remembered her grandma's stories of being ripped from the arms of *her* mother, scared and terrified of the strangers on horseback who'd come to claim her. As though her life till then had meant nothing.

And her gran still had the smell of fear in her nostrils and the sound of the horses hooves galloping, galloping still hung in the night air and the screams and clawing of the youngsters as they were taken away, and the wailing of the mothers and fathers and the shouting of the mob was still with her after all these years..

Beryl knew that was the start of her nightmares.

Why did you tell me those stories, Gran, and frighten me so much when I was still so young and vulnerable?

Her gran had never seen her own mother again. She'd never gone back to the land where she belonged. Her life had become someone else's from that day, and she had struggled with the transition for a while, and then given up. Accepted her new world. Got on with life in the Home the best way she could, and tried to forget about her origins.

But still it had stayed there all of those years and still her gran could bring it back from time to time, and still in the deep cold dread of the night she could see her mother crying and pleading and feel the soft splash of salt tears against her face and the shrill wailing would wash over her as the agony of the parting was re-lived.

"Jesus is the Lord, let us pray." Beryl could hear coming from somewhere in the room where she sat. "Our Father, who…"

And where is my grandfather dear Lord, and why did you take him away from me? He didn't understand about government policy and what it had to do with our lives and even now I'm still so bitter and angry that it had to happen that way.

Beryl looked up as the sun shone higher through the strained glass window. She watched as the colours spread dappled across the seats in front. Her mind was seeking peace and acceptance. She wanted some tranquillity back in her life. There had been enough frustration and blaming and denial. It was time for a fresh start, a new beginning. Beryl decided that Kirra had been right last night. It was up to her now.

Chapter Thirty

Archie was tired and bored. They were supposed to be learning maths rules and the board was filled with sums. Division and multiplication. Addition and subtraction. Solve the problems. He couldn't see the point of it all.

Why not just use a calculator, Miss, it's a lot faster.

Add up the money sums. How much change to you get from ten dollars? What can you buy with fifty dollars? Who can tell me the answers?

Geez, Miss, why would we need this stuff? We all know that you don't use money at the store, they just put it all down on your tab and off you go, sweet eh?

"Archie, can you tell me what you can buy with fifty dollars?" the teacher asked out of the blue.

Two slabs at least, Miss, with a bit left over for some chips at the café in town, Miss.

Archie remained silent and defiant. He didn't want to answer this morning. He didn't want to play her games. He sniggered at the boys beside him and spoke to them in creole. They laughed at each other and at the teacher. *Stupid cow.*

"Would you boys please speak in English? I've told you that before," the teacher responded huffily.

Will began to tease Rett in creole, and before long they were all involved. Teasing was one of their favourite pastimes, and it annoyed the hell out of the teacher. That, and not speaking English. Speaking their own languages.

"Stop that at once you boys, it's maths time now, and I won't tolerate any more fuss this morning," the teacher blurted out angrily, already sensing that it was far too late to regain control. That she had lost their attention yet again this morning.

That she was fighting a losing battle here in this outback classroom.

I wish I wish I was back in my own school in the city and I wish that I'd never come here and tried to help these kids and I wish that there was some way I could get through to them and find out what it is that makes them tick and what it is they really want from their education apart from wasting my time anyway.

Despite her efforts, the boys continued with their needling, and a fight soon ensued. Will and Rett and a few other boys began pushing and shoving at each other. Chairs were overturned and belongings scattered across the floor. The teacher went to the office door and called for the principal to intervene. *Again.*

God, I hate this place and I hate the way they totally ignore me and waste so much valuable learning time and turn all my efforts into nothing and simply ignore all my hard work and preparation and attempts to provide them with an education. Why do they constantly behave this way and act like two year olds when they really they are adolescents on the brink of manhood and should know better, shouldn't they?

As soon as the principal had settled them down and got them back to work he demanded another *word* with the teacher.

God here we go again and the old bugger will say it's all my fault and I should have tried harder and am I sure that the lessons were planned thoroughly enough and did I read all the background literature he gave me when I started here, and how come it's always my fault anyway?

Shelley felt deflated and switched off. The bell went for lunch, and she knew that she would have to gulp down her sandwich then do some yard duty outside.

And that meant trying to break up more fights and being laughed at and ridiculed and sniggered at and right now she simply didn't need all this shit, did she?

Shelly unwrapped her sandwich and pulled out her drink bottle. Normally she would have gone through to the office and boiled the kettle for a cup of much needed coffee, but the last thing she wanted right now was another face-to-face with the old bastard of a principal. She'd get another lecture about how to treat 'the boys' properly and about their needs and operating styles and learning patterns and she's had it up to the back teeth with all that shit. She had already worked out it made no difference at all.

Let's face it, buddy, you've been up here way too long and you wouldn't have a clue about life in the real world and I'd like to see you try and teach this group of kids you old bastard and when was the last time you got off your arse and off the god-damned phone and away from your precious bloody community meetings that are such a friggin' waste of time and actually tried to improve the educational opportunities of these kids, when? You think that dragging them to school each morning and sitting them at a row of benches and treating them like morons is an excuse for education?

Shelley rubbed her weary eyes and stretched her back muscles. She could feel a knot of tension forming in her neck, and stood up to ease her muscles. She paced around the classroom and surveyed the changes she'd made in the short time she'd been here.

The room was far more interesting and colourful and appealing now.

And did anyone thank her for her efforts? And did anyone understand the trouble she'd gone to back in the city before she came here? And did anyone acknowledge her efforts to bring up all the football gear and sports posters and bright coloured texts and fun games and interesting books that she'd brought here with her for these kids? Did they?

Shelly sighed and finished her sandwich. She gulped down a mouthful of tepid water and went over to the door. Her hand stopped as she went to unlock it, knowing that outside it would be hot and clammy and the boys would all be restless.

And I'd much rather stay in here under the whirling fan and try to regain my composure a bit before this afternoon's session. Why should I have to go out there and face their continued hostility and abuse? It shouldn't be this way and I should be entitled to a decent lunch break like my colleagues down south and how did this principal ever get this job and stay here so long ruling like some goddamn autocrat from the last century, tell me that!

Shelley unlocked the door and was faced with a blast of humidity that nearly knocked her sideways as she went outside. She carefully locked the door behind her, and wandered over to where the boys were listening to music. Archie was strumming an old guitar, and the others were listening.

He sounds good, I wonder if he's had any formal lessons — probably not, where would he get them out here and perhaps some of the young men here have been teaching him. I heard that they used to have a band and some of them were pretty good.

"Hi ya, Archie. Sounds good, I like it. What tune is that, and who taught you?" she asked as she approached the group.

Questions bloody questions as if I'm gonna tell you, Miss, I don't want you to comment on my playin' 'cause I'm jez learnin' aren't I, an' I don't want the other kids to tease me so do me a favour, Miss, an' bugger orf!

Archie put down the guitar and glared at the teacher there by the office door. He didn't like her, yet there was something about her that made him feel a bit sorry for her. He knew that she tried hard to get the kids on side. It wasn't her fault that none of the teachers ever stayed out here for long, that's just the way it was. The kids didn't make it easy to teach them, and they didn't trust outsiders anyway. Not by a long shot.

But Shelley was persistent. "Go on, play something, Archie, do you know any other songs?"

Yeah, Miss, three blind bloody mice and baa baa black sheep that's a laugh considerin' ain't it, Miss, hahaha.

The other boys wandered away and joined in a game of footy at the other side of the grass, leaving Archie alone with Shelley out the front of the school.

"Do you like music, Archie? You seem to have a good ear for a tune," she encouraged. "My son plays by ear, and he could pick up an instrument and listen to a song and play it just like that," she said proudly.

Archie was a bit intrigued, but his natural shyness around teachers prevented him from responding. He felt a bit sorry for this teacher who tried so hard to like the boys and plan lessons for them that were interesting and fun.

Not like the other teacher in the classroom or the principal who set down rules of iron and expected them to obey no matter what and didn't understand how much they felt like fish out of water here in this camp away from their own mobs.

"Yeah, I like music, Miss. I'm jez learnin' the guitar, an' a mate in town got me this one ta practice on. Next time I go ter town he's gonna show me some more chords," Archie replied with enthusiasm. He didn't know why he was telling her about his music, except that she seemed to be genuinely interested. That made him feel pretty good. Lifted his self-esteem. Gave him a bit more hope than usual.

"We could try to set up a music room if you like. Get a few instruments with a grant. Do some fundraising and see what happens. Would you like that, Archie? What do you think? Would the others be interested too?" asked Shelly with a hint of enthusiasm. She wanted to believe in these kids, encourage their talents. Make them feel good about themselves and find something that would give them a link to the outside world. A purpose in life. It was a hard slog out here, but she wasn't ready to give up just yet, despite everything.

Archie sat and looked down at the ground. He suddenly felt shy and awkward again in front of the teacher, although for a brief moment he had felt that she understood. Now he wasn't so sure.

"Dunno, Miss, maybe the others aren't that interested. I could find out though, if yer like," he replied cautiously.

"Hey, Arch, you comin' over here ter play footy with us or what? We need yer for the game, orright? 'Urry up, the bell'll be gowin' soon, mate!" called out Will from the far side of the grass play area, anxious to eke out the last bit of lunch break before lessons resumed for the afternoon session.

"Orright, mate, comin'!" called out Archie, carefully leaning his guitar against the office door. "Don't get yer knickers in a knot!"

Shelley remained on the seat where she had been talking to Archie. She was thinking about the possibility of a music programme for the boys, and planning her strategies for an approach to the principal. She knew he would instantly reject any idea that was not his own, so she had to figure out a way to get round him. To make him see the advantages to the students and the community as a whole. If her idea was going to work at all, she knew that he had to support her thinking, otherwise it was doomed before it even got off the ground. She needed to plan an attack that would make the music idea seem invaluable to the place, and she needed to get the old bugger on side somehow. *That* would be the real challenge.

Shelley closed her eyes against the harsh glare of the midday sun and stretched out her legs to east the ache in her back. She leaned back against the river gum and dreamed.

Chapter Thirty-One

Beryl left the church and went out into the sunshine. It was past midday, and she wanted to get home to Kirra and the girls. She'd had enough of God today, and had only half-listened to the sermon.

And did he say to live and let live and was he talking about me when he said suffer unto the Lord and why did he raise his hands and ask the almighty for answers to life's questions and redemption for all the sinners then look directly at me so's my skin crawled with guilt and shame? Doesn't he know that there are reasons for everything and life's not always what it seems to be, is it?

She straightened her rumpled dress and began the long walk home. For Beryl, this time was hers alone, uncluttered with the demands of her friend – the bottle. It was one of the few times she was sober during the week, and she saw it as a way to expiate her sins for the time past and the time that lay ahead. She tried to steer a straight and steady course through each Sunday, almost as though it might be her last.

And maybe if I don't give up the boozin' it might well be and then how would Kirra and the littlies cope without me? An' what would become of them? An' would Kirra be able to keep them all together and take care of everything and get on with her life as well, would she oh Lord?

Halfway home Beryl stopped by the river for a breather. She was still only just in her forties, but already the ravages of time and mistreatment and neglect had taken a huge toll on her body and mind. Most of her friends back at the camp were the same, worn down by neglect and sadness. She wished it was different, but struggled to accept that it could be. Somehow it seemed too late for drastic changes in her life, despite the pleading of Kirra and the obvious evidence of decay.

Still I guess I could try and what would be the harm of cutting back on the grog for a bit and you never know till you try something do yer? Maybe I could enrol in one of them courses they have here in town at the centre an' learn somethin' useful ter fill the time in, eh?

The river snaked past slowly as she sat there thinking. Beryl padded to the edge and soaked her feet in the cool water, feeling instant relief from the heat. She waded in further until she was waist deep in the swirling wetness. Her dress flowed out before her, so she peeled it off over her head and stood naked in the soothing water. She raised her arms and spread out her hands above her, as if praying. Her eyes shone with a fierceness and strength that was usually alien to her. She reverted to the child that once she had been, and the memories of times so long ago were hers once more to hold.

But my people are no longer here with me and my parents are long gone and the land of my birth is laid waste and the dreaming has faded into nothing and I have lost my way and why is every day so difficult to face without my friendly booze to get me through?

Beryl padded round a bit and drank in some of the river water. She made bubbles and splashed her hands and feet. She floated on her back and let the river take her slowly downstream. She felt light and airy and uncluttered. She felt free.

It didn't matter that the others would be waiting for her to have the Sunday roast that Kirra always cooked. Beryl had forgotten all about her family for now; she was stuck in the time of her childhood. Back at the old cattle station. Back with her mum and her dad and her mob. Back in the row of workers houses that she had called home.

She could smell the stew cooking in the camp oven over the old hot plate, and she could hear the voices of her parents calling out to her from the past. Bits and pieces of who she had been were dangling in front of her as she lay in the cool water, and in her mind's eye, Beryl was immersed in her childhood once more.

And I'm still here, Mama, without you and I still feel your touch from the old days and I still remember some of the stories you told and the lullabies you sang and the dances and animals and bushcraft and dreamtime, yeah, I still remember, Mama.

A bird call shrill overhead woke Beryl from her reverie with a start.

Shit, what time is it and what am I doin' driftin' along here in the river when I should be getting' back home before Kirra an' the girls get cross with me again an' think that I'm out drinkin' after church with them no-good honkies down the sheds. Get a move on girl, come on, hurry up!

Beryl splashed to the shore and retrieved her crumpled and sodden dress from the dirt where she'd pitched it. Never mind, it would have to do. She hurriedly pulled it over her head and began the last of the homeward journey at a trot. Her tough old feet barely seemed to touch the track as she shuffled along best she could, hoping that she wasn't too late for lunch.

Dear God, as if Kirra hasn't got enough to do on a Sunday with all the chores an' cookin' an' lookin' after her sisters without her useless ol' mum adding to the problems as usual. God, what will she think of me? Dunno what's got inter me today, fair dinkum I don't!

She raced in the front gate and collapsed through the doorway that led into the kitchen. The girls were all seated at the table waiting for her. A look of resignation and contempt spread across Kirra's face as she glared at her mother.

"Christ, Mum, d'yer reckon yer could be on time jez fer once, do yer? We's been waitin' over half an hour fer yer ta start lunch, an' now some of it's gone cold. I hope yer satisfied, yer cow!" blurted out Kirra angrily, pushing past her now and racing through to her bedroom. She'd had just about enough today, what with not hearing from Archie, and the fight with her mum last night, and now this! It was almost too much to bear, and Kirra was livid! Tears of rage and self-pity splashed onto her pillow as she flung herself face down on the freshly-made bed. Kirra felt like life was passing her by, like she was a total loser. God how she hated this place!

Some days Kirra just felt suffocated by the burden of family responsibilities that she had somehow inherited. It was overwhelming, and she was angry. It shouldn't be this way, and she got tired of the whole damn thing! Other kids her age didn't' have to put up with all this shit, surely?

A small hesitant voice interrupted her thought. "Kirra, yer wanna come an' eat now, we've saved yer the best bit an' your favourite bone with the marrow in it," said her sister gently, trying to help Kirra a bit. She didn't like seeing her big sister this way. Kirra was supposed to be the strong one, the dependable one, the mother figure in their lives. It confused her and scared her to see Kirra so upset and hurt.

Kirra wiped away her tears and sat up on the bed. She gave her sister a reassuring hug and tousled her hair. Kirra smiled and stood up, taking her little sister with her back to the kitchen for lunch.

"'S'alright, kiddo," she assured her. "Jez wash yer hands again an' we'll all eat, OK?"

Beryl was silent and contrite at the other end of the table, and Kirra avoided her gaze for most of the meal. She still felt angry and hard done by. She didn't trust herself yet to meet her mother's eyes; something hard and cold inside her felt like it would burst.

Chapter Thirty-Two

Inside the classroom it was hot and fuggy. Archie was stuck to the seat with sweat. He could feel the humidity rising, and knew that another storm was on the way.

Some of the boys were already asleep at their tables, and Will was over at the computer trying to type a story for the teacher about the book they had been working on all term. He was making slow work of it, and trying hard to stay awake in the oppressive afternoon atmosphere.

Archie was restless and bored. He'd heard the story so many times that it had long since ceased to hold any meaning for him. He wished that the teacher would just quit for the afternoon and let them go home early. But she just kept on and on in her monotonous voice, trying to teach them things that they couldn't understand. He closed his ears and his eyes and his mind, and dreamed of Flynn and his guitar.

Something landed on his neck with a sharp sting and Archie sat up abruptly. A rubber band fell onto the table, and he heard a snigger behind him.

Bloody fool, Rett, what was he up to now?

"Hey, Arch, mate, waddya doin' eh?" whispered Rett from the seat behind. "Teacher's pet!"

Bloody hell I'm not the teacher's pet and I don't want to be here right now and I didn't do anything to Rett to start this so lay off willya. I'd much rather be down the river playin' my guitar and I'm getting sick of this shit!

"Go on, genius, tell the teacher all the answers you suck!" spat out Rett. "We know yer think yer so smart, don't we boys?"

Christ, what did I do to deserve this and I feel like shit and I don't want to stay in here and take this right now, I don't!

Another missile suddenly glanced off Archie's ear as he sat there perplexed, wondering why Rett was attacking him today. It wasn't as if he had done anything to upset him, or at least nothing that came to mind. Archie was beginning to get annoyed. He didn't want to be stuck in the classroom this afternoon anyway. He had other things to do.

"Waddyer doin', man?" he confronted Rett, swinging round in his chair to face him. "I didn't do nothin' to yers, so cool it willyer?"

But Rett was cranky and irritable and looking for a diversion. He wasn't going to give up that easily. He leaned forward in his seat and kicked out at Archie's legs.

"Shit, Rett, jez stop it willyers?" cried Archie. "I've had enough, orright?" Archie was getting mad. He turned to face Rett and grabbed his shirt, yanking him half out of his seat. "Yer mad bastard, why are yer pickin' on me, eh?" Archie shouted at him. "I ain't done nothin' to you!"

But Rett was just spoiling for a fight by now, and had decided that Archie would do. He stood up hurriedly, knocking his chair flying as he did. His books and pencils rolled onto the floor with a clatter. The teacher rushed over to try and separate the boys, but it was no use.

Rett wouldn't give up. He grabbed Archie too, and they began wrestling on the floor.

"Fight! Fight!" shouted the others excitedly. They knew that this would put an end to the day's work, and they were more than happy with the diversion it created.

"Git 'im, Arch! G'wan, lay inter 'im mate, 'e deserves it, the cranky bastard!" they shouted as the fight progressed.

But the teacher had other ideas. "Stop this at once, you two, that's enough!" she commanded, in what she assumed was her best authoritarian voice. "I will not have this mess going on in my class!"

She knew that the principal was out for the afternoon, so she would have to try to sort this out by herself. It wasn't a thought that she enjoyed; she knew how rough these kids could be! They'd already threatened her on a number of occasions, and she was under no illusions that they respected her in the slightest. Still, she had to at least *try*.

"Archie! Rett! Stop that at once you two, I will not have you causing such an outburst in here this afternoon. Stop it! Now!" she bellowed at them, hoping that it would have *some* influence on their current irrational behaviour.

But the fight ensued regardless, so Shelley decided to remove the rest of the class from harm's way for the time being. She instructed the others to follow her outside, then left them to resume her efforts with the fighting boys back in the classroom, who by now appeared to have slowed down at least a little.

"Get up both of you and stop this nonsense at once!" she yelled at them again, trying to restore some sense of order in the room.

Rett and Archie stopped still and looked at Shelley with surprise. They had never heard her sounding so loud and strong. She sounded like she meant business, and it was enough for now to break the spell. They untangled themselves and sat up, wary not to touch each other or start up the fight again.

They were both still angry and unsettled as the teacher continued.

"Straighten up and go through to my office. Now!" she told them in no uncertain terms. "I will be there to deal with you both shortly, as soon as I get the others back to work!"

Shelley turned away from the boys as she strode to the door. She did not want to look back. She already figured that Archie and Rett would be sniggering behind her back, and she knew from bitter experience that her small victory would be short-lived. Still, at least she had the upper hand briefly for now, and she intended to keep it that way for the remainder of the school day.

"Come in and get on with your English worksheets boys, and no more funny business either! Is that clear?" she stated firmly to the other students, opening the door to let them back into the classroom. "We've had quite enough disturbance for one day!"

When they had settled, she went through to her office, a crammed and cluttered space she shared with two of the other teachers at the school.

God it wouldn't be like this back in the city and I wouldn't have to deal with such serious issues daily without the support of a welfare rep and I sure as hell would have staff support and a decent behaviour management programme and the kids would all understand that at school there were consequences and effective discipline procedures that were maintained but not here, oh no, not here!

Shelley found Rett and Archie sprawled on the floor flicking through some picture story books. They were looking at pictures of dinosaurs and snakes. They were smiling and laughing together, as though nothing had even happened between them in the classroom.

Ah, give me strength!

"Stand up and pay attention!" she barked at them. "Put those books down at once!" Shelly was still hopping mad and quite agitated from the recent events in the classroom. She had put a lot of work into her lesson preparation, and was annoyed that it had all gone out the window due to the fight.

Shelley recognised that her lesson plans here at the outback school were totally different to what she would have planned back in the city, but she was doing what the course outlines demanded, and she was trying her best. She had read all the appropriate 'background' material with which she had been provided, and discussed teaching strategies with the other teachers at the school.

Shelley had already held discussions with the principal on her arrival at the school about teaching styles for the students in her care, and though she hadn't agreed with his philosophies, had decided to accept his advice. After all, she reasoned, he *had* been here for some years.

But as the term wore on and the students continued to resist her daily forays into their education and block every attempt she made at engaging them in the learning process, Shelley was fast approaching the time when she would have to decide for her own sake whether 'enough was enough'.

It wasn't supposed to be like this and I thought I could really achieve something here with these kids and I know that my expectations were unrealistic now but I had good intentions when I answered the ad in the paper for a teacher up here and I put so much effort into getting here and I have put my life on hold and sacrificed so much for these kids and now it's all going down the drain and they don't really give a damn one way or the other really... do they?

Shelley heaved a huge sigh of failure as she stood there surveying the two perpetrators of the recent ruckus in the classroom.

You would think butter wouldn't melt in their mouths to look at them, but what are they really thinking behind those sweet innocent grins and those large brown eyes, and why do I feel so totally outclassed and isolated with these kids? I'll bet they hate me really and I'll bet they call me all sorts of derogatory names in their own language and have lots of laughs at my expense! What am I doing here?

But she had to deal with things now, and she had to do it quickly, before the other kids decided to cause another stir and upset the rest of the day. Shelley tried to adopt her 'don't mess with me' pose before talking to the two boys who slouched before her there in the poky office.

"You both know that fighting is against the school rules," she admonished them, "and you both know that I am tired of your constant attempts to interrupt my lessons," Shelley added, knowing full well that her rebuke would be wasted yet again. Still, she had to be *seen* to be trying. Had to try to chastise them and ensure that there would not be a repeat of their aggression today. (Although secretly she held little hope of either.)

"You will both remain behind after school to do some jobs for punishment, do you understand?" Shelley added, dismissing them curtly as they glared at her defiantly. "Back to work now, we still have some time left till the bell goes today."

Archie and Rett turned and went back through the adjoining door to the classroom, laughing out loud as they went.

The old bat, what would she know about anything? Who cares what she says, we ain't stayin' back after school, no way! She can go ta hell's far as we care!

Shelley brushed some chalk dust off her shirt and soothed down her hair. She felt old and worn down with the heat and dampness, and the continued battles that piled up each day left her drained. Her crumpled clothes mirrored her mind. She missed her friends and colleagues in the city. She missed the greenness and the beaches and the cafés. She missed the daily papers. She even missed the chaotic city traffic!

Well, dear, you wanted to try this and you wanted to come up here to the outback and wasn't it you who always said that if the opportunity ever arose you'd grab it with both hands, didn't you?

Back in the classroom there was quiet for a while. Shelley sat rigid at her desk, hoping that the boys would work till the bell went to signal the end of the school day. (She guessed that it was like praying for a miracle of sorts, and figured that it wasn't going to happen!)

"Miss, c'n I go to the toilet, Miss?" called out Rett, clutching at himself under the table.

The other kids all laughed and turned to watch her reaction.

Damn, we almost made it to the bell! Damn Rett, he's deliberately setting me up again, I know he is! As if he couldn't wait till home time!

"Alright, Rett, but make sure you come straight back in, won't you? There's only a few minutes left, and I want to get this English work finished today so that I can correct it tonight, OK?" Shelley relented, not wanting to give Rett the chance to rebel again for today. She had learned the hard way this term that often it was better just to let them go, to cut them some slack. But she knew underneath it all that they were taking the mickey, just playing with her. And they knew there was really nothing she could do about it, not a god damn thing!

Rett ambled outside and wandered up to the toilet block. He didn't go in, but ducked around the back to get a ciggie from his secret stash. He knew that the toilets were out of sight form the main classroom, so he lit up and leaned against the brick wall, hidden by the long spinifex that grew at the edge of the school yard. Bloody teacher! Bloody Archie, teacher's pet! He'd get him after school, yeah man, he sure would!

He was just considering whether to go back inside when he spotted Archie's guitar leaning up against the office door. Rett sucked in his breath and his eyes narrowed to a thin slit.

That'll show the brainy bastard, I'll fix his guitar for him! Woo hoo!

He slunk over to the office door and silently grabbed the guitar. Stealthily he returned to the back of the toilets and squatted down in the grass once more. Rett knew that there wasn't much time to act; the bell would soon go for the end of the school day. He drew away a short distance, clutching the guitar. Behind the school was an old shed full of car bits and motors and abandoned tools and benches and rubbish.

Gov'mint money's pretty good hey, we got heaps of stuff here in our workshop.

Rett crept inside and selected an old wrench lying on the bench.

A couple of blows with this an' Archie's guitar won't play no more, eh?

He muffled the sound with an old rag, and then laid into the guitar with a couple of quick whacks. Smash! There, that should do it! Rett looked mighty pleased with himself as he crept out of the workshop and ran the short distance back to school.

Bloody Archie, serves the mongrel right!

He wasn't bothered at all by the consequences as he placed the battered guitar back outside the office, and then sauntered to the classroom once more.

"There you are, Rett, hurry up now and finish your work. The bell will be going soon, and I want those sheets completed before you go home. Remember you and Archie have chores to do as punishment after school too," chipped in Shelley, anxious now that the short time that remained be fruitful.

Pig's arse, lady, yer've gotter be jokin' if yer think I'm hangin' round this joint after school today, 'specially after what I done ter Archie's guitar, I'm outta here right on the buzzer today, Miss, lickety split! You c'n shove yer jobs where the sun don' shine, Miss, an' see if I bloody care!

Chapter Thirty-Three

Archie had spotted the guitar at the end of the school day. He'd gone round the front of the building to collect a bucket and mop to do his jobs for detention. At first he didn't register what he was seeing. Then it had hit him; hit him hard.

He had reached down and picked up the remains of his first guitar. It had been reduced to a twisted mess of splintered wood and broken strings. Archie had been shattered. Something had twisted inside him too as he sat and started at the guitar. He had felt the rage building once more. White rage. Hot anger. He wanted revenge.

Bloody Rett the bastard, I know he did this to me 'cos of the fight today and he knows how much I love this guitar an' how important me music is to me an' trust him to wreck this instrument that links me with Flynn if only he knew how much it meant ter me, if only...

Archie had run with the guitar clutched under his arm. He'd been blind with rage and a sense of injustice. He'd felt prickly all over; hot and bothered.

I'll get yer Rett, yer bastard, jez see if I don't!

At the end of the street where Rett was staying he'd stopped and hunkered down in the tall spinifex by the side of the road. It was at the edge of town, and wide open beyond the boundary fence. Archie had taken a lighter from his pocket and flicked it to check the flame.

He'd leaned over and set the flame onto the spinifex; whoosh! The dry grass ignited quickly, and before long the flames had leapt skywards, dancing and crackling in the hot afternoon sun.

Yeehah! Take that yer bastard Rett! How do yer like it when someone hurts you, eh?

Archie had turned away from the flames and run and run. Up to the other end of the camp. Away from the evidence. Away from Rett's place. Away.

Before long a few people gathered around the fire to watch. No one seemed too concerned, it was only a grass fire and they knew it would soon die down. The only people who tried in vain to douse the flames were the school teachers. The others just sat back and watched; fire was second nature to the mob.

"Them bloody kids probly bin smoking agin." Archie had heard from up the road.

"Yeah, too right!" added another voice.

"Geez, those kids can be careless sometimes, eh?"

As the flames subsided and the fuss died down, Archie had crept back to his place and packed a small bag with a few of his belongings. He'd grabbed the bag and some money and his wrecked guitar and headed out the road to hitch a lift into town.

I'm not waitin' here ter find out what happens after the fire an' I don't want ter run inter Rett or Will or the teacher either, I'm outta here! They c'n all git stuffed!

Just before sundown a truck had come grinding along the track, heading for the main road. Archie had jumped in as it came to a stop on the red dirt road.

"Where yer goin', mate?" asked the driver. "Inter town?"

"Yeah, that's right," replied Archie. "C'n yer drop me off at town camp?"

"No worries, mate, gotta go there meself an' deliver some stuff ter one of me cousins," the driver replied.

They continued on in silence for a while as it got slowly darker outside. The dust flew as the old truck ground its way jarringly along the unmade road towards town.

Archie rang Kirra from the phone box at the roadhouse opposite the camp as soon as he got to town. It was so good to speak to her again, and she seemed genuinely pleased that he'd finally rung.

"C'n we meet up tonight somewhere, Kirra? C'n yer get away fer a bit?" Archie asked hopefully. He desperately needed to see her and talk to someone and calm down a bit. The guitar incident had left him pretty shaken, and that, added to his madness in lighting the fire, had really got him jumping. He knew that only Kirra would be able to talk some sense into him tonight.

"Gawd, Arch, it's getting late, but I'll see what I can do," Kirra spoke in whispers down the phone. "I think mum's gone ter bed with a bottle anyways, so I'll probly jez sneak out the back after I tuck me sisters up safe fer the night. Should be able ter meet yer soon over at the café, orright?" With that the line went dead, and Archie sat down on the grass outside the roadhouse and lit up a cigarette to try to settle his frayed nerves a bit. It had been a long few hours since he'd found the broken guitar, and he suddenly realised that he was hungry and thirsty now.

Archie left his bag near a large tree and strode into the roadhouse still clutching the guitar. Somehow he couldn't let it go just yet.

"Geez, mate, what happened to that?" asked the service attendant. "Bin in a bit of a fight with a truck, eh?" he roared laughing at his own joke.

Archie froze him out with a cold stare, and then went over to the food counter to order a hamburger and coke.

Shutupaboutmeguitarmate,orright.   *I'm still feeling bloody angry about it bein' wrecked an' all so jez can it! Bloody bastard Rett, I hope he gits it back at the camp, I sure do! I'm sure not gowin' back there in a hurry, no way!*

After he paid for his meal, Archie sat at one of the tables in the dining area and scoffed it down. He thumbed through a magazine as he ate, scanning the pictures of cars and computers and houses and cities and trains and planes, things he'd only ever seen in print and posters and on the telly.

Maybe it's time I headed out of here and went down south an' finished with school an' tried ter git a job an' go down to the city an' see all these things fer real, maybe...

Archie suddenly realised that he had to get down to the café to meet Kirra, so he threw his rubbish in the plastic bin and went out to collect his bag. It was dark now, and the headlights of the trucks and cars danced and flashed as they approached the roadhouse.

Weary travellers unloaded themselves amid the dust and glare of neon lights at the bowsers. Tired kids and pets emerged to stretch and relieve their aching muscles. Families that were travel- sick headed for the single toilet out the back in an old shed, while dogs cocked legs and pissed against the first available post or petrol pump. Cars and trucks and four-wheel drives towing vans and boats and bikes rolled in a non-ending parade across the bitumen and gravel. The slow moving mass of human cargo was drawn inexorably toward the doors of the restaurant where they could rest their weary bodies for a while and fill up on greasy food and the worst coffee you could possibly drink. It was still heaven for a short time, and no one complained.

Archie leaned down and retrieved his bag from under the tree, then slinging it over his shoulder he headed off down the road towards the café and shops. He was beginning to settle a bit now, and the food and drink had taken away some of his edginess. He felt unwashed and dirty, but he figured that wouldn't really worry Kirra too much. It was a hot night, perhaps they could go for a swim in the river to cool off. That'd be good for both of them. Archie was feeling a little bit guilty about dragging Kirra out here tonight, but he knew that she was only coming because she wanted to see him.

Archie reached the café just as Kirra arrived. They flung their arms around each other in joy. It felt so good to be back together for now.

"How are yer?" Archie asked Kirra excitedly. "Waddyer bin up to since last time I saw yer then?"

"Nothin' much, you know me, eh?" Kirra replied sheepishly, glad to simply be around Archie once more. She'd really missed him these past weeks, it wasn't the same just talking on the phone. But she was curious about his sudden trip to town. Then Kirra noticed the mangled guitar, which Archie was holding. "Geez, Archie, what happened to yer guitar? Who done that to it?" she asked softly, drawing in her breath.

"That bastard Rett smashed it back at the school 'cos we had a fight in class an' the teacher broke it up an' gave us the rounds of the kitchen an' made us stay in after school, but Rett wasn't gonna, so he snuck out ter the dunny an' smashed up me guitar jez fer a sick joke, the bastard!" responded Archie all in a rush, his voice thick with the anger and frustration and humility of it all. "I'll tell yer the rest of it later, lez get a drink at the café first," Archie finished, as he steered Kirra inside the door and hopefully away from further questioning for now. He wasn't quite ready to tell her about starting the fire and packing his bag yet, it still felt too rushed and too recent.

And some new plans are forming in my head, and I think I'll discuss them with Kirra tonight, and see if she wants to come to the city with me and get out of this place too.

It wasn't long before Nora the friendly waitress had spotted the pair of them inside the café. She had become like a surrogate mother to Archie since meeting him, and he was genuinely pleased to see her again.

"Well, if it isn't my favourite customers, how are yer, lovies?" she called out to them from the back of the shop. "Here, come over and say hullo to Auntie Nora both of yers! Well I never, here yer both are again then, what'll it be tonight, dearies?" she asked them as she reached out to give them an affectionate hug.

They both liked Nora, she always made them welcome in the café and gave them extra serves of chips and ice cream when they ordered. They liked the fact that she fussed over them and made them feel special for a while. She was large and round and caring and honest, and she treated both of them with respect, which is more than could be said for a lot of the people around here.

"Hi yer Nora,'s good ter see yer again, we've missed yer, haven't we, Archie," said Kirra, as she returned Nora's hug. "Archie's come to town fer a couple of days and I decided to come up fer a bit to meet him."

Nora grinned and looked from one to the other. She wasn't fooled one bit by these two, and she suspected that there was more to it than that, especially as she had already seen the look in Archie's eyes and the shattered guitar he was carrying. But they would tell her about it in due course if they needed someone to listen.

"Where yer stayin' then, Archie, up at town camp again?" she enquired, worrying that he had nowhere to stay tonight on account of arriving late. And she also guessed correctly that he had left his camp in a hurry and hadn't had time to arrange things with Ken before arriving in town unexpected.

"Yer c'n stay with me an' me sister over the other side of town if yer like, Arch. There's always a spare bed fer ya, an' we've got lots of yummy food an' drink in the fridge for the likes of you any time, yer know that, Arch, alright?" Nora said genuinely, hoping that if Archie *was* in any sort of trouble that it wasn't the sort to have immediate repercussions. Nora didn't like trouble of any sort, no she didn't.

"Geez, Nora, that's real nice of yer, that'd be great if I could jez stay tonight till I sort meself out with Ken tomorrow. I don't want to go over to town camp and disturb him at this hour. Ta," replied Archie humbly, feeling a huge sense of relief at having been 'rescued' by Nora tonight. Tomorrow he would have to go and see Ken, but tonight he was pretty exhausted and emotionally drained, and he could sure do with somewhere quiet to stay. Nora's place sounded just what he needed, and he sure was grateful to her for offering.

"You sure your sister won't mind if I stay?" he asked suddenly, wanting to reassure himself that it would be OK.

"Nah, she'll be fine, Archie, promise yer!" laughed Nora in response, giggling at Archie's sudden seriousness there in the café. "Now, what do yers both want ter eat eh, we'll be closin' in half an hour, so best get yer orders in, eh."

Archie and Kirra finally relaxed and placed their orders, then went over to their usual table in the corner. Kirra looked into Archie's eyes and considered whether to say something about his sudden trip to town. She was anxious to get to the bottom of things, to discover what had prompted Archie's unscheduled arrival tonight, but at the same time she wanted to give him the chance to unwind and chill out.

Archie read her thoughts. "Spose you're wondering what I'm doin' in town ternight?" he asked Kirra, breaking into a hesitant smile as he sat opposite her at the laminex table.

"Yeah, the thought had crossed my mind yer know," she replied cheekily, glad that Archie had broached the subject with her. Kirra knew that *something* must have happened back at the camp for Archie to hitch to town this late. "And what the hell happened to yer guitar, Archie? Who done that to yer favourite possession?"

Archie told Kirra the whole story about the fight in school and the teasing from Rett and how Rett had snuck out on a toilet break at the end of the school day and smashed his guitar in spite. He told her about setting fire to the spinifex near Rett's house and running away with a few of his belongings and hitching a ride to town.

Archie was still clutching his guitar as he finished, "An' I hope that bastard Rett gets what's comin' to him, Kirra, struth I do!" he spat out in conclusion.

They sat in silence for a few minutes as Kirra let Archie's anger subside. She watched as his tense muscles flinched then began to relax. She knew how much that guitar had meant to

Archie, and she knew how much he must be hurting now that it was useless.

"Never mind, Arch, we'll get yer another guitar somehow, jez you see if we don't!" she offered with conviction, hoping to lighten things up a bit while they waited for their food to arrive.

Nora came up to the table at this stage and told them their meals were almost ready. She'd overheard enough of the conversation about Archie's fight to be pretty concerned. When she'd seen his guitar earlier, she figured that something must have happened back at the camp.

"That's a crying shame, Archie mate," Nora said. "I know how much yer love yer music."

"Ah well, I'll jez have ter chuck this ol' thing away now I s'pose, but I can't bring meself to do it just yet," Archie exclaimed dejectedly, still not quite believing the sight of the mess he held that had once been his pride and joy.

"Never mind, lovie, here's yer drink n' banana split n' chips, and it's on the house tonight, so don't you worry about a thing, ol' Nora will take care of yer tonight, Arch," she boomed with a smile, giving Archie another quick hug there in the café. "Jez enjoy yer food fer now!"

Chapter Thirty-Four

Beryl woke up with a start in the sweat-drenched and rumpled bed. It must have been later than she realised, but the porch light was still on. She fumbled around in the dark, searching for the bedroom light switch. Her breath stank of cheap grog and cigarettes. She felt washed out.

I'm gonna give up the booze so help me, God, I will, I will...

She tripped over a pile of clothes near the bed, falling heavily on the floor. As she lay there sprawled unceremoniously between the bed and the wardrobe, Beryl for a moment saw her life scurry by in a dizzy kaleidoscope of dismay. She stretched out her arms and covered her face with two grimy hands. She rolled onto her back and suddenly began to sob as she lay there defenceless in the dark. She was overcome with grief and uncertainty and failure. Her life seemed to have come full circle to nowhere.

Dear, God, help me now for I have sinned and I'm begging you to get me up and guide me on the path of righteousness and lead me not into temptation for thine is the power and the glory...

Beryl was nearly choking with the dust and the taste of the grog and the startling effect of her overwrought emotions there on the bedroom floor. She half pushed herself up onto her elbows and screwed her body round to get leverage. Finally, she managed to get up on her feet and wobble across to the doorway.

"Kirra!" she called out in a frightened voice. "Where are yer, love, I need some help!"

But the only response was silence, and Beryl was even more frightened by the lack of a reply from her oldest daughter. "Kirra, where are yer, love?" she called out again, hoping that this time Kirra would wake up and come to the rescue. But all Beryl heard were the night noises surrounding her as she leaned heavily against the wall in the hall.

Silence. The soft whoosh of the wind. Creaking shed doors and rattling tin on the roof. Night birds rustling in the branches beyond the house. Spinifex grating against the fence. Snuffling and snorting of animals scratching in the dirt. The rise and fall of breathing in the other bedroom.

Where are you, Kirra? I need yer I'm scared of me own shadow tonight and I need someone ter help me, God's truth I do, and I know I don't deserve yer pity but I need it anyway, Ki...rrr...aaa!

Beryl shuffled down the hallway to the open door of Kirra's room. She peeked inside and gasped when she saw the bed was empty. A moment's panic set in before she crossed the floor to pull back the covers for validation. Perhaps Kirra was sitting in the dark at her desk. Perhaps she was out on the back porch. Beryl went out through the kitchen and swung open the back door.

Please let her be out here I need someone to talk to and I know I've been a bad mum and I know that I've let Kirra do all the work and look after the house and me and the little ones, but I'll try to make it up to her as long as she's OK dear Lord, please don't let anything happen to her like it happened to me – not that, no, not that, dear Lord!

Beryl went out onto the verandah and stood under the glare of the porch light, trying to adjust her eyes to the range of the night world beyond the house. She didn't understand why Kirra wasn't here tonight. Beryl thought at first that perhaps she may have just gone to visit one of her friends down the road without telling her. It was a hot night, and maybe Kirra couldn't get to sleep. She tried to calm herself and tell herself that everything would be alright. That Kirra would soon be home. That everything would be just fine.

But somehow it didn't feel that way and somehow things felt wrong, didn't they?

***

Back at the café Kirra was getting nervous and fidgety. It was getting late, and soon the café would be closing. Kirra knew that she would have to go soon. She sensed that something was not quite right, that her mum needed her.

"C'arn, Arch, hurry up an' finish yer drink willyer? I've gotta git back home soon, it's too late already an' I shouldn'a come up here tonight," she pleaded anxiously.

Archie saw the look of concern on Kirra's face and slurped down the remains of his drink. He pushed his chair back from the table with a scraping sound as he turned towards the door.

"C'arn then, I'll walk yer back to the edge of yer camp, Kirra. Sorry I dragged yer out tonight, I jez needed company an' I knew you'd help settle me down," he mumbled feebly hoping that Kirra wouldn't get into any trouble back home tonight. It was his fault, after all, he knew that she wouldn't normally come into town at this hour, and he sure didn't want to be the reason Kirra got into another argument with her mum. It had been his idea, and it wasn't fair that she should be the one to suffer any consequences.

"Don't be too long, Archie!" called out Nora from the back of the shop. "I'm jez gonna clean up a bit then I'm closing up and going home, so you see that you're back here in half an hour an' ready, orright?" she added hastily, busying herself now with mop and bucket.

"OK, Nora, won't be long!" called out Archie from beyond the fly screen door. "Back soon."

Archie and Kirra wandered past the row of shops and out along the footpath that led to half way camp. As they left the shops behind, the night grew darker and the concrete gave way to a dry dusty path. Town rubbish was scattered along the track, blown there by the winds and abandoned. The street lights had long ago ceased working, smashed for fun by the local kids on

Saturday nights after the footy. It was useless and costly to replace them, so no one bothered any more. The plastic covers swung in the breeze and slapped against tall steel poles that were bent at weird angles after repeated bangs and bumps and kicks from bored teenagers looking for brief diversions on their forays into town.

"Sorry I dragged yer out tonight, Kirra," Archie offered as a half-apology as they hurried towards her camp. "I hope yer mum's still asleep an' yer don' git inter trouble on my account."

"S'alright, Archie, she'll be fine," Kirra replied, not entirely convinced that this would be the case once she got home, but hoping that things would be just as she left them.

They were almost there now, and Archie gave Kirra's hand a tight squeeze and held her briefly in a hug. He didn't really want to go, but he knew that she was feeling apprehensive enough without any of his fears tonight, so he put on a brave face for their farewell tonight.

"Yer'd better go now, Kirra, an' thanks a million fer comin' in ter see me, I really appreciate it yer know," Archie said as he hugged Kirra. "C'n I see yer tomorrow up at the café after school?"

"Yeah orright, I'll see how things are at home first. I should be able to get to town by about four o'clock, alright, Arch?" Kirra answered impatiently. "Gotta go now, see yer, Arch."

With that she hurried away down the road towards her place, and Archie was left standing alone at the edge of the camp. He began to feel the fear of desolation and abandonment descend, but he fought it off and turned back towards town. Back towards the light of the shops. Back to the café.

Archie shoved his hands in the pockets of his knee-length shorts as he ambled back to the café. He was beginning to feel unsettled and frayed once more, as though things were closing in on him that he couldn't control. It wasn't a feeling he particularly liked, and he wanted to get rid of it fast. He tried singing a few lines of one of the songs he'd learned, but that only reminded him of the mess he was in all because of the stupid fight and his smashed- up guitar. He should never have left the camp without telling his aunty what had happened, and Archie realised now that she would be worried about him. Maybe he'd talk to Nora about it tonight, and she would sort something out. Yeah, he hoped so.

But she can't sort out all the fears in your head and she can't fix the future for you and she sure can't help with the dreams that you have and the nights that you lay awake thinking about Flynn and the images of your mother that hover around you like an aura reminding you of the ghosts of your ancestors... can she?

As Archie strode along the row of near-deserted shops now towards the café, he began to think for the first time of not going back. Ever.

And what will Nora say when you tell her your plans? And what will your aunty say if you don't go back there? And what will the teachers and school principal say about your failed education and lack of academic progress and any chance of a future without finishing school?

For the moment Archie didn't care about all of that; for the first time in his life he felt completely sure about *something*, and it felt damned good. He was determined to see it through, no matter what others might say. It felt *right*. He smiled to himself as he arrived at the front door of the café and waited for Nora to finish up inside. The more he thought about leaving school and not going back to his last camp, the better and more reassured he felt. Yeah, he felt great. *Free.*

"There you are, Arch!" exclaimed Nora as she drew outside the café, slamming the door noisily behind her. "Glad ter see ya back in time, let's go, eh?"

They walked silently along the dim-lit street towards Nora's place, each lost temporarily in their own thoughts for the time being. Nora's head was full of the day's trade and takings and orders and rosters for the week, and she didn't spare Archie a thought just yet.

I wonder what she'll say when I tell her my plans tonight and I wonder if she'll get cranky on it and lose patience with me and tell me not to be so bloody stupid and ask how I could even consider leavin' school at this stage of me life?

"Hey, Arch, wotcha thinkin' about, mate, yer's gone awful quiet on the ol' girl?" asked Nora out of the blue.

"Aw, nothin' much Nora, maybe we c'n have a chat back at your place with a cuppa, orright? Have we got far to go?" asked Archie, trying to sound non-committal as they walked along side by side up the road.

"Yeah, alright then, I'll put the kettle on as soon as we get in and we'll have some biscuits an' a good ol' cuppa, eh? Always does the trick, that's what I reckon, a good ol' fashioned cuppa!" Nora put in, hoping that Archie would download a few of his worries back at the house. She reckoned that he'd had it pretty tough so far, what with his mum dying and no dad in the picture and being sent away to another community far from his friends and all. Yeah, she reckoned he'd done it tough all right, and now this fight and his poor old smashed guitar, life sure could be pretty unfair!

"Here we are then," added Nora, as they turned into the driveway of a neat and ordered yard. "Here's me little nest where I rest me weary bones each night, Archie. Welcome to me humble abode, mate!"

Chapter Thirty-Five

Kirra snuck stealthily around the back of the house, hoping to find things just as they had been when she left a couple of hours ago. As she approached the verandah through the spinifex clumps, she suddenly noticed the figure of her mother hunched down in the old lounge chair, a cigarette dangling from her lips.

Damn I don't want an argument or a confrontation at this time of night I've had enough what with all Archie's worries and having to sneak out of here as it is and I wish that mum had stayed asleep and I guess I'll just have to try and make up some excuse about where I've been without mentioning Archie or town!

"Hi yer, Mum, what are you doin' up at this hour?" asked Kirra with a slight tone of impatience, hoping that her mum wasn't waiting out here for an argument or explanation. "I thought you'd still be sound asleep in bed!"

Beryl opened her eye and turned towards her daughter. She stared at Kirra and opened her mouth as though about to speak, then closed it again firmly. Something was bothering her, but she chose to not raise it with Kirra for the time being. In truth, she was mighty relieved to have Kirra home safely tonight, and the last thing she wanted to do was to upset her.

"Nah, I've jez bin sittin' here thinkin'," replied Beryl slowly, her words quietly drifting on the night breeze. "An' I've bin a bit worried about yer too, love. I haven't bin a very good mum, have I?"

Kirra glanced across at her mum and was surprised to see a few tears beginning to roll down her cheeks. She knew that her mum really cared about her, but most of the time she was either too drunk or too tired or frustrated to deal with life issues, and

Kirra had hardened early in life to her mother's rare emotional offerings.

Where were you, Mum, when I needed you and why have you hidden behind the haze of grog for all these years and what were you like when you were my age and why has it turned out this way for you and for me?

"S'orright, Mum, I know yer've done the best yer could, but sometimes it's jez too hard holdin' things together at home an' I get tired of havin' ta do it all by meself!" Kirra blurted out in reply, feeling the years of pent-up anger and resentment beginning to boil over. "I jez wish you'd give up the grog fer a while an' start takin' me an' the littlies more seriously, Mum! We deserve that much, don't we?"

Beryl looked across at Kirra then looked down again in shame. She was overcome with such sadness at the loss of wasted years that she was struggling to breathe. She felt herself gagging and gasping for air there on the back verandah, and Beryl wanted to escape into oblivion once more. She badly wanted a drink, anything to ease her pain. But she knew that it was now up to her to begin facing the demons, so she stayed put.

"I'm so sorry, love," she whispered to Kirra, "jez so, so sorry, you'll never know how much."

Kirra glanced over to see the expression on her mother's face change from one of total sadness to some sort of acceptance, and she knew right then that things would be different from now on. She knew that Beryl was waging some sort of internal war. She *felt* it right down in her bones.

Perhaps this time she'd get it right. Perhaps things would *really change round here and their lives might begin to improve. And perhaps Beryl would really try to stay off the grog this time and channel her energies into something more positive and talk about her past and regain some of her self-confidence and pride and self-esteem.*

Chapter Thirty-Six

Archie and Nora were sitting on the old settee in Nora's lounge room sipping tea. It was getting late, but neither wanted to retire to bed just yet. Nora was enjoying Archie's company, and Archie felt far too comfortable and relaxed to consider ending the conversation. He was surprised how easy it was to talk to Nora, and he found himself sharing things that he'd only trusted to Kirra up till now.

I wonder if you were still here, Mother, whether I'd be talking to you instead and I wonder what it would be like back at home again with you?

"D'yer want another cookie and cuppa, Arch?" asked Nora casually mid-sentence, "there's plenty more in the pot."

Archie grinned and accepted Nora's generosity. He was beginning to tire again though, and wished that Kirra was here, too, enjoying things with Nora.

Poor Kirra, I sure hope she doesn't get into any trouble tonight because of me and I wish that I could help her more and make her life a bit easier than it is.

"You're very kind ter take me in like this, Nora, and I'll try ter make it up ter ya somehow," said Archie as he finished off his last cup of tea and another biscuit. "Think I'll get ready fer bed now though, it's sorta bin a long day. Thanks again, Nora."

Nora laughed off Archie's thanks and stood up to remove the tray. She shuffled through to the kitchen and placed the cups in the sink.

"Here, I'll show yer where everything is, Arch, then yer c'n git off to bed, orright?" she hollered out to him. "Won't be a tick."

Archie sank back in his seat and closed his eyes in weariness. He was feeling the effects of the trip to town and the emotional roller-coaster that had preceded his flight from the camp.

Bugger that bastard Rett an' his stupid fight an' I hope he gits what's coming' ter him, I sure as hell do!

Nora had wisely placed his guitar out of sight when they had come home from the café, and she had no intention of giving it back to Archie yet. It would only add to his current dilemma and remind him of what he'd lost. Besides, Nora had a plan, and it involved replacing Archie's guitar as soon as she could get one sent up by road from the city. But for now, that was her secret, and she sure intended to keep it that way.

"Come on then an' I'll show yer the bathroom and yer bedroom. Yer c'n have a shower before yer go to bed if yer want, an' there should be some spare pyjamas on yer bed left over from when me nephew visited last holidays, so use them if yer like, Archie."

Nora fussed around and patted down the pillows and straightened the bed a bit before leaving Archie alone and closing the bedroom door behind her. It felt good to have a young one in the house again, and she didn't mind at all that Archie was sharing her home. It was a welcome break from her normal routine, and one that she welcomed right now.

"Night, Archie!" she called from the other end of the house as she switched out the lights and went through to her own room. "Sleep tight."

I hope yer don't do too much tossin' an' turnin' tonight, Archie, me mate, an' I hope that the day's events don't catch up with yer an' I hope that my little bit of comfort will help yer to feel wanted again and make yer realise that there are still nice people in the world who don't go round takin' advantage of yer an' wreckin' the things that yer hold dear.

Archie was feeling tired and wrecked after such an eventful day. He had a quick shower and put on the clean pyjamas that Nora had left out for him, and then clambered thankfully into bed. He was buggered. He stretched out his lean frame in the cool sheets and shut his eyes tight, waiting for sleep to overtake him. It felt good to be finally relaxed and safe, and Archie knew that for tonight at least there would be no further adventures. He drifted off to sleep.

Nora padded about the house for a while, waiting for her sister to come home from the cards night. She should have gone to bed herself, but the habit of waiting up for Jane was far too ingrained now after all these years to let go, so she put the kettle on for another cup of tea and sat down at the kitchen table with the newspaper. It was last week's edition, but that didn't bother Nora; she was only skimming the pages anyway. It was always the same news; war, death, accidents, politics, dramas, sport. Blah blah blah. Normally she took a keen interest in what was happening around the globe, but tonight after dealing with Archie's needs, she was a bit skittery and needed a simple diversion till Jane got home.

The kettle boiled and Nora got up to fill the teapot again. Then she took down the biscuit jar and placed a handful of cream wafers onto a small plate. She reached into the cupboard and got out two mugs, knowing that Jane would soon be home to share with her. The tea ready, she sat down at the table once more and pondered about Archie's dilemma. The guitar was easy to replace, but his future was the real problem. Nora liked Archie, she had right from the first time they'd met in her café. She'd seen enough kids come and go through the town, and she knew how different their lives often were. There wasn't much chance of a future for most of them around these parts with high unemployment and low school attendance and family violence and substance abuse. She'd seen it all over the years, and tried in her own small way to help whenever she could. And now was one of those times when she reckoned that maybe she could make a difference and give Archie a bit of a kick-start towards a better future. Not much, but at least a chance.

Nora figured that Archie would not go back to his aunty's now that he'd had the fight with Rett and his guitar smashed up. She knew that he needed an education, but guessed rightly that it would not be back at the last camp. Somehow she had to steer him in the right direction without seeming to be too overbearing.

The sound of an approaching car interrupted her thoughts. Tyres crunched on loose gravel in the driveway, and Nora heard the engine of Jane's car switched off as the car came to a halt. A car door slammed and footsteps advanced towards the front door.

Nora heard Jane call out to her as she came in. "Hi, Nora, it that you still up?"

"Yeah, in the kitchen, love, come 'n have a cuppa with ne an' tell me how yer went at the cards tonight," replied Nora, anxious to tell her about Archie and discuss her plans.

Jane entered the kitchen and brushed her long hair out of her eyes. She was younger and taller than Nora, yet somehow far more vulnerable. Nora was the practical sister who managed the café and took care of everything. Jane was the younger and prettier sister who was shy and fragile and unreliable. But Nora loved her and cared for her like a mother, and always would.

"D'ja win tonight then, eh?" asked Nora in a light-hearted manner, hoping not to precipitate one of Jane's 'moods'.

"Yes, I did," replied Jane in her more formal manner. "I played really well tonight, Nora, and I thoroughly enjoyed myself."

Nora smiled with relief. It was good to see Jane happy tonight; Lord knows there'd been enough times when she wasn't!

"That's great, Janie, I'm real pleased that yer had such a good night. Were all yer usual friends there then?" asked Nora with interest. She knew only too well that Jane's happy times needed lots of encouragement and affirmation, so she tried to sound as interested as she could at this late hour. Besides, she had an ulterior motive tonight, she wanted to gain support for her plans with Archie. And she needed Jane's approval to do that.

"Sit down an' have a cuppa with yer sister then, I've got yer favourite biscuits ready fer yer, Janie," Nora encouraged, hoping that Jane would accept and not go straight off to bed. She still hadn't told her that Archie was staying the night, and she didn't want to upset Jane if she could help it.

"Thanks, Nora, don't mind if I do," replied Jane as she joined Nora readily at the kitchen table. "I'd rather fancy a couple of biscuits and a cup of tea before I go to bed tonight."

The two sisters sat and drank in silence for a little while before Nora broke the silence. "Gawd I had a funny day today, Sis, struth I did. Yer know that kid I told yer about who lost his mum not long ago? Well he turns up at me café tonight all upset like an' clutchin' his wrecked guitar, an' I knew straightaway from the look of him that there'd bin some sort of bother. So I feeds him and ask him what's happened, an' before I know it I'd invited him ter stay the night with us. Yer don't mind do yer, love?" Nora gabbled all in one breath, wanting to get the whole story out quickly before Jane could say no. She looked across the table to gauge Jane's reaction, hoping that she would be OK with the whole Archie-thing till morning, when they could discuss things a bit more.

To her surprise, Jane just smiled back at her as she sipped on the hot tea. "That's fine for now, Sis, what do you think he'll do tomorrow, Archie I mean?"

"Well, I've thought about offering him a job helping me in the café. I'm a bit short- staffed at the moment and if it was alright with you he could stay with us fer a bit, just till he sorts himself out and figures out what he wants to do next. He's had a real rough trot the poor kid, an' I reckon he deserves a bit of a helpin' hand, know what I mean?" replied Nora. She hadn't meant to tell it so suddenly like this, but it was out now and all she could do was wait for Jane's response. Nora hoped that it'll be OK.

The neon light cast weird shadows on the kitchen walls as the two sisters sat quietly and contemplated this announcement. Nora felt uncomfortable, as though she had just cast a burden on them both. She shifted in her seat and gazed across at Jane.

"Waddyer reckon then, Sis, d'yer think it'll be aright if we ask him to stay fer a bit? He wouldn't be much trouble an' I'm sure he'll pull his weight around the house. What do you say, Jane?" asked Nora, hoping that her plans would not be rejected outright tonight.

But Jane had gone suddenly quiet. Her face had whitened somewhat and she looked a little peaky, as though the mere mention of having another boarder in their house had set off some sort of trigger in her memory that was altogether too unpalatable to consider.

"I don't know, Nora, do you really think we'd be doing the right thing for Archie? After all, it's not as if he hasn't got family to look after him. Didn't you say he was living with an aunt down at the camp? Why can't they take care of him, Nora? Why should we step in?" Jane asked with a worried scowl on her face. She didn't like change much, her life was routine and sheltered and pampered. Nora had always taken care of things since their folks had died, and that's the way Jane intended it to stay. No, it was simply too much of Nora to expect her to take Archie in now.

Chapter Thirty-Seven

Archie woke up in strange surroundings and immediately closed his eyes against the world. Where was he? He clung to the sheets and tried to think. Camp, school, fight, Rett, guitar, smoke, flames, running, running, running; had he been dreaming it all or had these things really happened?

He opened his eyes once more as images from yesterday melded together to form a clear picture. He *had* been in a fight yesterday and he knew that he was now in town, but where? Truck, dust, driving, guitar, café, Kirra, Nora, Nora... Nora!

Think, Archie, think, you know what happened and you know where you are, don't you?

Archie gazed straight up at the ceiling which was painted a clean and dazzling white. A fan hovered above him, still for now in the morning light. But already he could feel the heat building, and he knew from experience that it would soon be unbearably hot in the room where he lay. He sat up and placed his feet firmly on the floor, feeling the cool touch of lino. *Now* he remembered, he was at Nora's place!

He looked around him at the bedroom where he had slept, taking in the pleasant and tidy atmosphere. He felt calm and safe and reassured now, no longer afraid and apprehensive as he had been yesterday on his flight from the camp.

But what about school and aunty and my guitar and the fight and the fire I lit near Rett's place and running away to town? And what about Kirra, when will I catch up with her again?

It was no good worrying, Archie had to take things one step at a time. He decided to get up and go to the bathroom, then through to the kitchen to see if Nora was up and about yet. He didn't know what time it was, but it must have been still early.

Archie wondered what time Nora usually arose. He wondered if her sister would be here. He still hadn't met her, despite knowing Nora pretty well after all the visits to the café in town with Kirra.

"Ah there yer are, Archie," he heard as soon as he pushed open his bedroom door, "how'd yer sleep, mate, orright?" asked Nora in her cheerful voice.

Archie turned to see Nora lean her head round the kitchen door to greet him. He was glad that he'd spotted her first, and not the stranger who was her sister.

"Hi yer, Nora, yeah I slept jez fine. Be through in a minute after I've bin ter the bathroom," he replied as he turned the bathroom door handle and went in.

Nora smiled in response and went back to the kitchen to prepare some food for Archie's breakfast. She was glad to see him up and about, and figured that he must be hungry. Nora would have to leave in an hour to open up the café and get things ready for the day, and she wanted to have a chat with Archie first about his immediate future here in town.

Last night she had phoned his aunt from the café before she'd left to let her know that Archie was in town and would be staying with her for the night. She'd promised that she'd talk to him and get him to phone in a day or two. She'd also reassured his aunt that she would keep an eye on Archie for the time being.

"G'mornin', lovie, what'll it be then, sausages an' eggs fer brekkie an' a nice cuppa?" Nora asked as Archie padded into the kitchen and sat at the table, "bet yer hungry, eh?"

"Yeah, Nora, I could eat a horse!" replied Archie with a grin. "Thanks fer puttin' me up last night, I really mean it, Nora," he added.

"S'alright, mate, no problem," Nora said as she flipped the eggs and put some bread in the toaster. "I phoned yer auntie an' spoke to her too, so she wouldn't worry about yer. Maybe yer c'n talk to her soon, orright?"

Archie frowned and glanced across the table at Nora.

Why didn't she tell me that last night before I went to bed, he wondered.

"I meant to tell yer last night but there was so much happening what with one thing and another that it completely slipped me mind, lovie, sorry," Nora mumbled as she placed the eggs onto a plate beside the stove. "Anyways, no harm done, eh, Archie?"

Archie was relieved. He knew that Nora was genuine.

"S'orright, Nora, she's jez fine, thanks," he replied quickly, not wanting Nora to feel upset by her omission. "I'll phone aunty today from up the shops."

Nora served Archie his breakfast then poured them both a cuppa. She took the mugs of tea over to the table and sat down opposite Archie, watching him carefully as he ate. "Eggs orright fer yer then?" she asked Archie.

"Yeah, Nora, this's terrific, thanks," he replied as he munched happily on the cooked breakfast. "Yer's bin real nice ter me, Nora, an' I sure appreciate it."

Nora knew that now was as good a time as any to broach the subject of her plan for Archie, so she launched straight into it while he ate.

"I've bin thinkin', Archie, an' I was wondering if yer'd like ter stay here in town an' work for me for a while, I'm short staffed at the moment and I'm sure you'd learn the ropes pretty quick. What do you think?" she blurted out in a hurry, hoping that Archie would accept her offer. "I don't expect you to make up yer mind straight away, but would yer think about it, Archie?" she added as she sipped her hot tea.

Archie was a bit dumbfounded. He sure hadn't thought too much about what to do next, only that after yesterday he knew that going back to the camp was *not* what he wanted to do. But he hadn't even contemplated working at this stage, it just hadn't entered his head.

Still, yer could do a lot worse than stay here in town an' work for Nora at the café an' yer'd be able ter see lots of Kirra an' maybe save up fer a new guitar an' even see Flynn on his occasional trips ter town, couldn't yer, Archie boy?

Archie finished his sausages and took a gulp of tea from the blue mug with the picture of boomerangs adorning the rim. He looked across at Nora and slowly considered her proposal. He began to warm to the idea, and knew that it would be a perfect way to solve his immediate problems of where to live and how to fill in his days now that he was sure he was not going back to the school or the camp where his aunty lived. It sure was a very tempting and generous offer, and Archie felt relieved that for the first time in a while things were finally going his way.

"I don't know what to say, Nora. That's real nice of yer ter offer me some work and a chance to stay in town. Are you sure it's OK? An' what about yer sister, does she mind?" asked Archie, pleased that Nora was giving him this chance.

"Ah, don't you worry about Janie, I'll talk her round, you'll see. It'll all work out jez fine, I know it will, an' yer'll be able to see Kirra a bit more too, won't you?" Nora grinned across at Archie with a wink.

Yeah I will, Nora, but it's not what you think and we're just good friends and I don't think of her that way she's not my girlfriend at all.

"Nora, I'd love ter stay an' work at the cafe fer ya as long as yer think I could learn what ter do an'l I'll help yer around the house too an' pull me weight, honest I will," said Archie all in a rush, feeling that he wanted Nora to know how much he appreciated her generous offer. "An' maybe I can save up fer a new guitar after that bastard Rett smashed up me other one," he added, scowling at the memory of yesterday's discovery back at the camp.

"Don't you worry about that just yet," Nora said with a grin. "I'll fix things, OK?"

Archie chewed silently for a bit as he finished the delicious food that Nora had prepared for his breakfast. He was tired from the events of yesterday, and a little strung out. Too much had happened in the last twenty-four hours, and Archie needed to chill out for a while but he was grateful to Nora for all that she had done.

"Gee thanks, Nora, fer helpin' me, it means a lot yer know," he offered as a token of his appreciation there at the kitchen table. "I jez dunno what ter say, it's all so sudden like."

"That's OK, lovie, jez you finish yer brekkie an' have a bit of a think about it, there's no rush. I'm heading off ter work soon down at the café, so you just take yer time an' come down an' have a chat when yer good an' ready. Janie's here an' she'll see that yer looked after while I'm gone, orright, Archie?" said Nora in a rush, wanting to get the kitchen cleared and tidied now before she got ready for the café. She sensed that things would work out just fine with Archie. She knew that he hadn't been happy living in the new camp with his aunty's mob, and he was old enough to make a few decisions by himself now. Poor blighter, he'd had enough of the hard times and deserved a break for a change, and Nora sure intended to give him a chance at a fresh start.

Archie smiled at her as she patted him affectionately on the head. His life seemed to be suddenly taking a turn for the better, and he knew that he had Nora to thank for it. And Kirra. But Archie had grown a little suspicious of people since his mum's death, and he still wasn't too sure whether to take things on face value.

"Yer sure it'll be OK if I come an' work fer yer Nora? I mean, I wouldn't want to put yer out any more than I have already," he muttered apprehensively, hoping that his doubts were groundless.

Nora turned back to the table and gave Archie a big hug for reassurance, sensing that he was a bit overcome by the whole plan. "Sure, lovie, It'll be just fine, Aunty Nora will see that it all works out, so you jez stop worrying, orright?" she grinned warmly at him. "Now finish up yer brekkie an' go have a nice hot shower, then yer c'n decide what yer want to do. I'll see yer later at the café."

Archie finished eating in silence and took his plate over to the sink, where he rinsed it and stacked it with the other breakfast dishes. He went out to the verandah and sat down on the back step, trying to sort out the range of emotions that had overtaken him suddenly.

What should I do, Mother, do you think that I should stay here with Nora and work in the café and help out around the house – it means that I'll have a home again and I'll be earning some money and I can save a bit for the city and get a new guitar and see lots more of Kirra and maybe make some new friends and visit Ken over at town camp a bit more, what do you think I should do… Mother?

Chapter Thirty-Eight

Kirra was feeling listless today, and the teacher seemed to be talking to someone on another planet. His voice droned on and on through the stifling afternoon heat and his words were meaningless echoes spinning slowly in the fuggy atmosphere above her head. *Perimeter length measurement metric centimetre formula. Rules rules rules.*

What did she care? It meant absolutely nothing to her today.

Kirra's mind was elsewhere. She was thinking about Archie, and meeting him later in town at the café. She glanced up at the clock to see how much longer she was going to be stuck inside this clammy prison with her classmates. Half past two, only half an hour to go. Yippee!

Normally Kirra was one of the more attentive students in the senior school, but today she was restless and unsettled. She didn't want to be there, much less try to focus on the maths lesson. She didn't want to measure perimeters of imaginary fences and boundaries, and she couldn't care less right now whether she finished the task or not. All she cared about was hearing the home bell that would signal release and freedom and escape from this monotony.

A stern voice suddenly cut through the air waves. It was addressing her, calling out her name.

But why?

"Kirra, what is the answer to number seven on page forty-two, please?"

Huh, who is that and what are they talking about for God's sake?

"Kirra, did you hear me?" the voice cut in once more. "Answer me, please."

What, what, what, are you talking to me?

Kirra shook herself and turned towards the voice. It was the teacher asking her about the maths sum, and she'd better concentrate and try to get it right or she might be stuck here after school doing jobs. And today she sure didn't feel like detention, no way.

"Er, number seven, Sir, the answer is four metres and seventy-five centimetres, Sir," Kirra replied half-heartedly, unsure of herself this time. She knew that her mind had been elsewhere, and she wasn't at all sure if this was the correct answer, but she had to try anyway. She looked up at the teacher and sucked her breath in, hoping that her answer had been correct. Kirra knew that she was the smartest in the class, and usually the one to be relied on for the correct answer. But today it wasn't to be.

"Kirra, I'm surprised at you," the teacher commented, "that is the answer for number ten, the answer to seven if forty-two centimetres. Check your book again will you, please, and tell me if you had it correct after all."

Kirra reddened and looked down at her maths book. She was embarrassed and upset at her own foolishness, and she didn't feel like any more annoyance today. She just wanted to finish the set of sums and get out of here.

"Yes, Sir, I got the correct answer after all, sorry," she mumbled under her breath, hoping that was enough to shift the attention elsewhere for now. She didn't like being belittled in front of her friends, and for Kirra it was something that didn't happen very often. Normally she was the one who was first finished and could be relied on to get things right. But today she was inattentive and scatty, and she realised why.

Too much is happening right now in my life − what with mum and her worries and taking care of the house and the littlies all the time, and now this thing with Archie, who I thought I could depend on instead of having to take care of him too and sometimes it feels like I'm never going to have time left over for me... am I?

It seemed to Kirra that her world was shrinking instead of expanding, and sometimes she felt choked by grey walls. Like now, waiting for the bell to go. Sitting under the slowly-rotating fan staring at her maths book. Feeling isolated and hemmed in.

Kirra coughed to ease the boredom and oppressiveness, hoping that time would suddenly speed up and release her. Her feet tapped the floor impatiently as her mind drifted far away from where she sat.

God, will the bell ever go today?

Something was pressing in on her and she wanted to shake it off, but her mind felt like lead. Heavy fingers poked at her skull and waves of nausea seemed to suddenly come from nowhere.

Brring Brring! B-rr-ing!

The bell! Finally!

Kirra leapt up from her seat and was at her locker stacking her books away before the teacher had time to say anything to her about her inattentiveness. Grabbing her backpack, she was off out the door and away through the spinifex before the other kids today, not even waiting as usual for her sisters.

Just for once they can go home by themselves and get there safely, I'm sick and tired of the burden of always having to take care of them and today mum can do it, can't she?

Her footsteps were impatient and hurried as she sped along the familiar track to town, not waiting to see if any of the others were heading her way. She shifted the weight of the pack to her other shoulder as she ran, feeling the headiness of freedom overtake her now as she put distance between herself and the school.

Kirra reached the outskirts of her camp before she slowed and took a deep breath. She paused just long enough to stash her school stuff in some bushes, and then ran on towards town. She hoped that Archie had remembered and would be waiting for her at the café. Kirra was feeling happy yet slightly apprehensive, as though she didn't quite want to trust herself or let her emotions have free rein this afternoon. Maybe it was about Archie as well, but Kirra didn't want to worry about him right now, she had enough on her plate as it was.

***

Back in town, Archie was waiting at the café with Nora. He'd been there since lunch time, when he'd come in to talk things over with her. Archie had decided that he would accept Nora's generous offer of work, and he had been mulling over it all morning back at the house. Now that he'd made the decision though, he felt pretty good about things. Yeah, damned good really!

Nora had been genuinely pleased when he'd told her, and she'd jumped up and down then enveloped him in a bear hug right there in the kitchen of the café. She'd never had children of her own, and had tried to help out disadvantaged kids over the years whenever she could. It seemed natural to her that she should do so, despite constant protests from Janie about being taken for granted by some of them. Nora didn't mind, she knew the ropes. And she was a natural mother when it came right down to it. Yes, she was only too willing to help out when it came to Archie, and she simply ignored her sister in matters that were close to her heart.

"So, lovie, waddya gonna do for the rest of the day now that you've decided to come and work for your Aunty Nora, eh, Archie?" she asked with a big grin on her face, feeling blessed that once again she could care for another human being who'd had it tough. "Want some lunch while yer here?"

"Yeah, that'd be good, Nora, thanks," replied Archie, realising that he was getting hungry now. He knew that Nora was spoiling him a bit, and he wanted to be able to give something back in return. "How about you show me how the café works after lunch, then I can start helpin' you a bit. Yer don't have ter pay me though, not yet, I jez wanna help yer, orright?"

Nora grinned across at Archie and broke out into a big smile. She really liked the kid, and hoped that things would work out for him here for a while. Nora was not foolish enough to think that it would last forever, she'd seen enough round here to know that soon enough Archie would need bigger and better opportunities. And Lord knows she didn't want him staying in the town for too long, there were too many temptations. Nora knew it would only be a matter of time before Archie got mixed up in trouble of some sort. She knew that he'd already got drunk on at least one occasion and there'd been that fight down at Kirra's camp that had landed him in the local hospital for a short spell a while back. No, this was not the place for Archie if he wanted to make a decent go of things, but for now it would have to do. Besides, what other choices did the poor kid have right now? Not many, she reckoned.

"Hey, Arch, would yer like some curry an' rice for lunch? I've just made a new batch fer the café, an' it's one of my specials you know," Nora called out from the kitchen "It's only a mild one, not too hot."

Archie hadn't yet developed a taste for a wide range of foods, and wasn't too sure about the curry. His diet so far had mainly been plain foods and lots of meats, often cooked over an open fire. His mum had tried to make ends meets all her life, and Archie knew there had been no spare welfare money for extras. He decided to try the curry anyway. He didn't want to offend Nora at this stage. She'd already been more than generous with him.

"Yeah orright, Nora, sounds great," Archie replied tentatively.

"Right oh then, one serve o' curry comin' right up," Nora said cheerfully, ladling two large scoops from the pot onto a plate for Archie. "Here you go then, cheers!"

Nora sat at the table with Archie for a short while, thinking about food. She tried to cook a variety of nutritious foods here in the café to overcome the poor diet of many of the locals. She knew that many of them survived on junk food from the local supermarket, and the resulting health problems and obesity were taking their toll. It was a small gesture, and Nora knew that it did little to help the plight of the indigenous population, but she made the effort anyway, preparing salads and rice dishes and stocking lots of fruit. The trouble was that the years of poor diet and substance abuse and other health issues were way beyond her control, and Nora often felt guilty that she wasn't doing enough to improve things in the town.

"How's the curry, Arch, are you enjoying it?" she asked, knowing that she needed to get back to work. The lunch time crowd would be starting to filter in soon, and there were still lots of rolls and sandwiches to finish. "You finish up, love, then bring yer plate out to the kitchen an' yer c'n help ol' Aunty Nora with a few sandwiches if yer like," Nora added as she got up and went through to the back of the shop.

Archie smiled at the disappearing figure, glad to be here now. He felt as though a big weight had somehow shifted overnight, and he knew that he had Nora to thank for that. Somehow he knew that things would work out here for a while. Archie had hope and a chance of a solid future for now, and that was something, wasn't it?

***

Kirra had nearly reached the outskirts of the town now, and she slowed down to a fast walk to get her breath back. She was hot and thirsty, but that was nothing new. It didn't really bother her. Somehow she knew that once she was with Archie at the café, everything would be just fine.

Still the bad mood she'd developed at school persisted; try as she might to shake it off. Kirra knew that it was based on the session she'd had last night with her mother, and she realised that something had shifted in their relationship. The trouble was though, *what?*

Do you seriously think she's going to change this time and that things might just begin to improve... do you?

Kirra stopped and sucked in her breath long enough to regain control. She didn't want to feel like this when she met Archie. Kirra was looking forward to seeing him at the café again, and hoped that he'd worked things out a bit since last night. She had enough to deal with today as it was.

Yeah and what I need is a bit of fun and some relief from the constant pressure of life at half way camp and I hope mum does try hard this time to give up the booze and get her life back on track, I sure do!

Her footsteps made a pattern in the dust as Kirra wandered slowly now towards the shops. Despite the urgency of seeing Archie, Kirra held back a bit now, not wanting to get there too early. She didn't like hanging round the shops in case she ran into some of her mum's mob, and she didn't want to spend too long by herself right now. Kirra was still feeling a bit vulnerable and a bit spooked, and she didn't like it. She was not used to being like this, and it was shaking her up.

Geez, Kirra, will yer jez have a look at yerself girl, what are yer doin' bein' so worried today, chill babe, jez chill!

Kirra looked around for a place to sit down. She drew in her breath and forced herself to calm down. She was close to the river, so she found a log to sit on.

This is the spot where Archie and I first spent some time together an' we talked an' talked an' laughed an' had such fun, didn't we?

She found herself reminiscing about that first afternoon when she and Archie had met at the store. Kirra had known almost straight away that Archie wanted only to be her friend, that he didn't fancy her as a girlfriend, and that was fine with her. She'd actually been attracted to him because he was different to the boys she knew, the kids from the school and half way camp. And she sensed from the start that Archie felt the same, had just wanted someone to confide in, to spend time with, and to share his world.

Kirra knew that others would not understand her friendship with Archie and would tease her if they saw them together, so right from the start she'd been very protective of their privacy, always meeting at the café when no one from her camp was around. And Nora had befriended them too, and guarded their friendship. Yes, good old Nora!

But now that Archie has run away and landed himself in a spot of bother and had a fight again and had his guitar all smashed up, what's going to happen next?

Kirra was worried. She wanted some time to think before she went over to the café to meet Archie. She wasn't at all sure if she trusted herself not to get upset this afternoon, and didn't want to put that on Archie right now.

There you go again, girl, being protective of everyone else and caring about others and always putting their needs first. What about Kirra, for a change? Who's going to care for her? Do you think that Beryl or Nora or Archie are going to take the time to ask how you are going and what you are up to and how you are feeling and is there anything they can to do to help you, do you Kirra?

Chapter Thirty-Nine

Ken had heard that Archie was in town, but as yet he didn't know why. One of the mob at town camp had mumbled something about seeing him over at the café late last night, but Ken had dismissed it as booze talk. He knew that most of the mob were pissed last night, and he figured that if Archie *had* been coming to town he'd know about it. Yeah, must have been the grog talkin'!

Or at least he hoped it was, 'cause he was sort of temporary guardian along with his aunty back at the camp, and he was supposed to watch out for Archie, wasn't he?

He'd decided to let it go last night, but this morning was another matter. Ken woke up wondering about young Archie, and reckoned that he just might wander over to the café after breakfast and check things out. He knew Nora well enough after all these years in town, and he was right in assuming that she was straight up with everyone. Honest as the day is long. Yeah, one thing you could be sure of with ol' Nora is that she'd never hold back on the truth, unlike most of the other bastards around this place.

Ken shuffled through to his modest kitchen and turned on the gas under the battered kettle, then went over to the back door and hoiked a large glob of spit at the back fence. He coughed and spluttered for a bit, clearing his damaged lungs with noisy intensity in the morning stillness at the edge of the camp.

Back in the kitchen, Ken opened the fridge and gathered some eggs and bacon. He surveyed the usual mess that was his domain, scratching the stubble on his chin with gnarled worn hands. Yeah, it was a mess alright in here, but it was *his* mess, and he sure as hell didn't mind that.

The smell of frying bacon and greasy eggs made Ken feel right at home, and his face lit up with a smile of familiarity as he bent over the fry pan there at the old green cooker. His needs were pretty simple, after all, and he knew better than most that each day was a blessing. And he sure intended to keep it that way.

There's enough of us who've gone an' filled up the cemeteries an' died too young too young... ain't there dear Lord, and' that's the truth. I'm not ready to go jez yet so help me God!

The kettle boiled noisily and screeched at Ken, breaking his reverie. He poured the water into the chipped brown teapot and left it to stand while he flipped over the eggs and turned the sizzling bacon. Then he dropped a couple of slices of white bread into the spattered toaster that stood on the bench next to his fags.

Ah, life sure is grand, ain't it?

Ken poured himself a strong mug of tea and served the bacon and eggs onto some buttered toast. He grabbed his enamel mug of tea in one hand and the plate of food in the other, and crossed over to the door leading to the back verandah.

Outside Ken propped himself up on his usual seat at the old wooden table, then began eating. Fat dripped down his shirtfront from time to time and oozed out the side of his lips, running into his scruffy beard, but Ken didn't care. He didn't even notice, just munched away happily and slurped at the strong hot tea.

Finishing the food, Ken wiped his mouth carefully with his sleeve, and then pulled a cigarette from his pocket. He lit it with his lighter then drew in a large gulp of smoke, savouring the taste of it as the poison worked its way further through his system.

Damn, life sure is good, eh?

He stretched out his legs and closed his eyes and went into dreaming, not hearing or seeing anything or anyone in this world.

Ah, but the other world was different, wasn't it, Ken?

In his mind he saw the old people dancing and singing the songs of their world. Ken was part of that world, a world so different to the one he now occupied. Different rules, different lifestyle.

And the faces of his tribe glowed in the firelight as the voices echoed in soft murmurs above the crackle of the flames and rose upwards in a rhythmic chant that hung there still on the whisps of smoke above him.

Ken looked down to see his feet tapping the silent beat of his ancestors. He knew it was just foolish old man stuff, but it was what mattered most to him sometimes. It was the memories and the connections that gave him his pride in who he was, and he wasn't about to sacrifice that on the altar of whitefella creation, no way!

Ung-ung-aaarh! It's me, little Kennie, you remember doncha mama?

Ken smiled as he drew in the last smoke from his ciggie, sucking it all the way down to the filter. Normally he'd smoke roll-your-owns, but his cousin had bought him some packets of Winfields in town, so he treated himself to the luxury this morning. Damn, it tasted good!

Ken stood and stretched and gathered up his plate and mug before heading back inside to the kitchen. He surveyed the mess and the jumble of food scraps and dishes, wondering if he should tidy it all up before the day got too hot. But he had other things to attend to this morning, and the dishes could wait.

He filled the sink with hot water and pushed all the dishes higgledy-piggledy in, then turned towards the door leading to the lounge room. He was about to go in when he remembered about Archie, and decided instead to go straight into town this morning to check things out for himself. But perhaps he'd have another smoke and cup of tea first, just to take the edge off the morning haze.

Out on the verandah, Ken folded his arms and rested them on his ample stomach. He gazed out over the scrub that bordered his backyard, feeling wistful and melancholy and a little lost. His life seemed to be at a standstill, indeed it was almost as though it had passed him by without notice.

How did that happen, Ken, my ol' mate, and when did you suddenly develop arthritis and a limp and grey whiskers and start to feel old?

He paused and smiled to himself, not wanting the realities of today to remove the dreams of yesterday. Ken knew that in terms of his life journey he was well-advanced along the road, but still the memories of his yester-youth were fresh and stark before his eyes.

He thought suddenly of Archie and his problems.

And what is it about Archie that seems so familiar?

Ken knew that there was *something* there that tied them together somehow, but he couldn't figure out what it was right now. It had been lurking at the back of his head ever since Archie's mum had died and he'd been contacted by the elders, but still it was way too deep to elicit now. He was frustrated and tantalised by something hidden deep in his sub-conscious that he should have been able to recognise and could not.

He sighed and took a last puff of the tobacco as he stood up to go inside. He needed to get ready for town, and Ken knew that he was stalling this morning, not wanting to leave just yet.

And why are the bone people circling?

He shivered as if to shake it all off. He didn't want to accept the other stuff in his head this morning, too much was at stake. But somehow the shadows stayed with him and the whispers of the ancient ones still hovered, and Ken padded through the house feeling a little fearful and apprehensive and surrounded by demons.

Chapter Forty

Nora waved the breadknife around in emphatic gestures as she demonstrated some of the food preparation techniques for Archie in the kitchen at the café. The lunch rush had passed, and Archie had helped out a bit with the constant flow of customers. Nora was pleased with his progress so far, and she'd been surprised at how easily he seemed to take on the few tasks she'd given him.

"Here yer are, Arch, here's a milkshake for ya. Come an' sit down an' rest yer feet for a while and talk to Aunty Nora for a bit," she said wearily, as she produced a chocolate milkshake and went through to the tables. "Come an' sit over here an' we'll have a chat, orright?"

Archie complied, and joined Nora at one of the laminex tables covered with a white plastic cloth. In the centre of each table was a small coloured ceramic vase containing plastic flowers. On either side were salt and pepper shakers and a small silver serviette holder, an unlikely reminder of the civilised world that lay in other places beyond this one. Still, Nora was always one to make an effort, even if no one appreciated it most of the time.

"How'd yer like yer first session behind the counter, Archie?" Nora asked as she sipped on one of her many daily cups of tea. "D'yer reckon you'll be OK working here for ol' Aunty Nora then?"

Archie sucked at this milkshake through a plastic straw and grinned up at Nora. He felt pretty good right now, and knew that he'd get the hang of working here quickly. He'd enjoyed it despite his first misgivings.

Wait till Kirra sees me behind the counter serving customers, won't she be impressed?

"Yeah, I think I'll be alright working here Aunty Nora, I enjoyed it so far. Do you think I went OK?" he asked a little nervously, hoping that Nora would say something to overcome any doubts he still had. It was all a bit new to Archie right now, but his confidence had grown slightly even in this short space of time.

Nora smiled across at him reassuringly. "Yeah, you were just fine today, Arch. Pretty good for your first try anyways. I reckon we'll have you shipshape before too long, don't you worry about that," she added with an encouraging pat on the back to Archie. "What do you want to do for the rest of the afternoon, Archie? D'yer have any plans?"

Archie looked up from his milkshake and grinned. "Yeah, I'm meeting Kirra here later, I might jez wander round an' look at the shops for a while then come back to the café in a bit, OK?"

"Fine by me, lovie, it'll be good to see Kirra again yer know, I like her a lot, Arch," replied Nora, leaving the table now to go and tidy up a bit out the back. "Do you mind waiting about ten minutes in the shop for me while I clear up the dishes, Arch? Won't be a jiff. Help yerself to an ice cream if yer like," Nora called out from the back.

"Thanks, Nora, if yer need a hand jez yell out," Archie responded from where he sat. He stayed at the table for a while watching the passing traffic through the front window. Archie wondered if Rett and Will would be in town this weekend at all, but he knew that they didn't get away from the camp very much. He sure as hell didn't want to see them, especially not after the episode with the guitar and the fire he'd lit. Nah, Archie felt pretty safe now here with Nora at the café, as though for the first time since his mum had died he was being taken care of. It made him feel comfortable and secure once more, even though this was not his mob.

Archie knew that Nora had gone out on a bit of a limb to trust him and take him in, and he was going to do all he could to see that her faith in him wasn't misguided.

"Go on then, Arch, off yer go, mate. I'll be right here now," exclaimed Nora as she reappeared behind the counter of the café. "See yer in a little while then. What time are yer expecting Kirra, Archie?"

"Dunno, Nora, probably as soon as school's out fer the day. It'll take her about half an hour ter get in here though," Archie replied.

He hurriedly left the café and strolled along the row of shops outside. Archie didn't feel like exploring the supermarket or Post Office today, he wanted to go over to the general store and check out the clothes. He still had some of his mum's money left, and he wanted to see if they had any new shorts or tops in that he could try on. For Archie, the novelty of being able to go shopping alone had still not worn off, so he crossed the road and wandered up the dry dirt path to the big store with the welcoming yellow and blue façade.

Archie entered the shop and walked over to the racks of clothes. He browsed for a while, in no hurry to select anything to buy. There were clothes of all different shapes and sizes, but Archie was only interested in the range of shorts and tops and baseball caps.

A bright red T-shirt caught his eye, and Archie flicked through the rack to pull it out. It was about his size, and had a pretty cool logo on the back, so he held it up against his chest for size and stood back to look in the mirror. Archie thought it looked great, so he decided to buy it.

Holding the new shirt in his hand, Archie went over and started looking at some of the other gear for sale. There were shoes and socks, coats, baseball caps and wide-brimmed hats. Archie found a cap that matched his new shirt, so he tried it on in front of the mirror.

Lookin' cool, man!

He paid for his clothes and changed into the T-shirt right there in the store, then added his new cap.

Tryin' to impress someone are we, Arch, me mate?

By now Archie was feeling relaxed and increasingly confident, so he strolled over to the other side of the large store to check out the range of electrical goods they sold.

Man those CD players are cool, would yer jez look at them, Archie?

One of the players was on special, and Archie was sorely tempted to see if he had enough left for a deposit, but then he remembered the guitar which he'd have to replace soon. Nah, he could do without the player for now.

Bus jeez it looks nice and I'd love ter buy it an' start getting' some CDs of me own ter play, that'd be cool, eh?

There were too many goods to scan, and Archie was growing tired of shopping by now, so he turned towards the doorway and hurried out. Besides, he reckoned that Kirra would be in town soon, and he wanted to get back to the café and see what Nora was up to before Kirra arrived.

An' won't she be surprised with my news an' my new clothes an' everything?

Archie suddenly thought about his mum as he wandered back up the dusty road towards the main shops. He could almost feel her presence, and he knew that she hadn't left his world yet. In truth, he still thought about her most days, and wondered why she had died so soon. It still didn't seem fair to Archie, but he knew that he had to get on with his life anyway. That's just the way it was.

But deep down inside it still hurt. And somewhere within she still held him. And still there were times when the hot anger bubbled and rose to the surface and threatened to push him over the edge into chaos once more. Where are you? Mo...th...err!

***

Ken had been about to leave for town when he was overcome with a weird sensation. It was as though the ancient ones were speaking to him in his native tongue. Calling to him. Reeling him in.

He wanted to go, but he dared not. Ken knew that there was something important going on, but he couldn't decipher any of the symbols or messages or chants. All that he knew was that it had something to do with... what?

And the feet of the elders were stamping in the dust as they danced and made patterns and played their music and performed their rituals... but who was it for? Ken wondered.

He shuffled his old feet and crossed to the boundary, where he squatted heavily among the clumps of spinifex, observing the patterns of animal tracks in the red dirt. His eyes followed the fence line along the edge of the property, but Ken knew that he wasn't really searching for anything in particular. He felt like he was being given instructions, but he wasn't too sure from where.

Still the voices rose and fell in his head as he squatted there silently by the tangled wire with his eyes downcast and his hands clutching the old gnarled posts, but he couldn't figure out what the messages were.

Ken stood and stretched his tired back muscles. He tried to regain momentum, to get back in the swing of his reality, but the ancient ones were not quite ready yet to be done with him this morning.

What are they trying to tell me, is it about Archie?

Back on the verandah, Ken decided to delay the trip to town for a bit. He was feeling a bit out of sorts, and he needed a smoke and a cuppa to calm himself down again. He didn't like this feeling, and he wanted to just get on with the day. Besides, there were things that he had to attend to in town, so he'd better get a bit of a move on.

What's the rush, Ken me mate, the thing with Archie can wait just a bit, can't it?

Ken went back into the kitchen and filled the kettle once more. He lit the gas and looked around at the mess, then decided to clean it all up while he waited for the kettle to boil.

Yeah, might as well get the ol' place lookin' shipshape before I head into town an' look for Archie, eh?

The whistle of the kettle rang out across the kitchen just as Ken finished putting away the last of the dishes, so he crossed back to the stove once more. He poured the water into the old teapot and grabbed his favourite mug from the bench top. Ah, nothing like a good cuppa!

Back outside squatting on the step, Ken lit another cigarette. He breathed the smoke deep into his damaged lungs. Ah, that felt good! He was starting to relax again and just enjoy the simple pleasure of being here alone and watching the birds and the bush. Alone with his thoughts and his smokes and his cup of tea. Yeah, bugger Archie, that business could wait. He needed some time to himself for a while. He needed his space. He needed to settle down.

Somewhere deep inside though, there was a small niggle of doubt about Archie. What was it that played in his head from time to time about the lad, and why did it concern him? Ken didn't understand why it was there, he just knew that it *was*.

And the sounds of the ancient ones were calling. And the animal tracks of his youth were around him. And the shouts of the elders were warning him trying to tell him something, but what was it and why did they come to him now and what did it all mean?

Chapter Forty-One

Shelley was bone-weary. Everything in her life seemed to be unravelling, and she didn't know how to stop the flow of discontent that had overtaken her. It was too damned hard, and she wanted to get the hell out of here and away from these kids. She had taken up this position in the outback with such enthusiasm, and now it seemed all wrong for her. Shelley slumped on the desk in the sweltering heat and let out a long and desperate sigh.

What am I doing here and why on earth did I leave my friends and family and what difference will I really make to these students who don't seem to want an education at all anyway? Who is this all for?

The heavy fan spun round slowly above her head as she succumbed to self-pity there in the abandoned classroom. Too much had happened in here today, and none of it was what she had envisaged before she came here. It was all getting just too hard, and Shelly had had enough. She was not normally a quitter, but this time there didn't seem to be much choice. There was no way she was going to risk her health or her partner for this experience. If there was one thing life had taught her, it was to look after the people who mattered, yourself included. She'd tried damn hard to reach these kids and tailor things to their needs, God knows she had. But it wasn't working. If anything, things seemed to Shelley to be getting worse. She just couldn't take their indifference and defiance and rebellion any more.

It would be a failure of sorts to resign after such a short time, but there didn't seem to be any other way. The problems she faced were simply insurmountable, and she couldn't tackle them alone. It wasn't only the system, Shelley decided, but the other issues as well: homelessness, culture, language, values, dependence, expectations, health, welfare, education, employment.

There were simply too many obstacles to success up here, and Shelley knew that if she stayed for a lifetime it would be nowhere nearly enough time to scratch the surface. No, it was all simply way too hard.

I am only one person and I know that I should probably try a bit harder to reach these kids and make a difference in their lives but I don't really think that's what they want and maybe people should be asking them *more often about their dreams and aspirations!*

Shelley raised her weary head from the cluttered desk and gazed around the room. She could see all the work that she'd achieved in a short space of time, but it wasn't enough. There were still such huge gaps in the educational outcomes, and Shelley understood the significance in real terms. The problems were huge, and she was just one person. No, she couldn't do this anymore. She would tell the principal tomorrow that she'd finish up at the end of term.

The final straw for Shelley had been that damn fight between Archie and Rett. She'd known in a way that it had been coming. They'd been teasing and niggling at each other all afternoon, and the weather had been particularly sultry as well. Still, she hadn't anticipated the violent outburst from Archie when it had come, and when she'd seen his smashed guitar Shelly had understood why.

But it doesn't change the frustration I feel and it only adds to my sense of isolation up here and I wish that there were some proper support systems in place and some friendly faces to talk to after school and a decent coffee shop and somewhere cool and quiet and relaxing to retreat to at the end of each gruelling day.

The side door banged as a wind blew up. Papers and rubbish were swept along in small eddies around the building, and from her desk Shelley could see a willy-willy forming down the road. It gathered momentum and advanced towards the school, scattering dust and clumps of spinifex in its path. The pack dogs howled and ran into the bush, spooked by the sudden invasion of their territory.

As Shelley watched the wind gust sweep past the school building it seemed to suddenly clear the air around her. She saw it as a sign. A change of direction, an indication from somewhere to start again.

She knew now that she would leave and go back to her other world. Her real world. Her treasured existence back down south.

Shelley felt re-vitalised and refreshed, despite the heat. It was as though something major had shifted within, freeing her one more from the grip of hopelessness. She was no longer stuck.

As she rose to leave her classroom the principal popped his head round the doorway to see if Shelley was still at school. She looked away, and walked deliberately towards the exit door that led to her freedom. No, she would not acknowledge him today and stay here wasting time planning useless lessons that meant nothing to her charges. It was too much, and she would no longer play his game.

She hurried out of the school gate and up the red dirt road that led to her temporary home here in the outback. Shelley kept her head down and her eyes half-closed against the swirling dust that trailed behind her as she walked.

She was almost there when she heard voices up ahead. Shelley looked up as she approached the house and saw the usual gang of smaller children from the camp waiting on her concrete verandah. Her dog bounced happily among them, wagging its tail and barking. At least *he* enjoyed their company today.

Damn, I do not want visitors today and I don't feel like entertaining these chattering children and watching their amusing antics as they laugh and giggle and jabber on in their tongue. Not today. I want some peace and some time to myself to simply stretch out with a cold drink and reminisce.

"Hi, you lot," Shelley called out in greeting as she neared the house, "want an icy pole each?"

The smallest of the kids jumped up and down, while the others smiled shyly and nodded approval at the offer. Shelley knew that she shouldn't really spoil them, but they were camp kids after all, and quite independent even at this young age. She knew their folks didn't mind.

"Here you are then," Shelley said as she handed out the cold treats. "I have work to do now so you'd best get home today, alright?"

She felt a bit of a fraud, but the last thing she needed right now was a reminder of school. She'd had quite enough of that, and the truth was that there was no escape in a place like this. It was simply too isolated and too small and way too restricting in its location and lifestyle. Shelley knew that leaving was the only option now. She'd tried her best to no avail, and was not prepared to stay a moment longer than the end of term which was coming up in a few weeks.

Revitalised and alone once more, Shelley began planning her departure in her head. She would have to discuss it with her partner tonight, but felt sure there would be no opposition to her plans. Still, they were in this adventure together, and both had equal say in making decisions.

In her head Shelley began making a list of all the things they would need to do to get away from here. Her teacher's brain went into overdrive as she prepared mental checklists of all the details involved. Information overload kicked in: flights, packing, correction, notifying friends and family, changing addresses again, etc, etc. Shelley smiled and heaved a huge sigh of relief as she sipped on the long cold glass of cola there on the verandah by the beautiful ghost gum. She felt in full control of her life once more. It felt good. *Damn* good.

As she relaxed, the pictures of her life back in the other world began floating into her consciousness and she was overcome with longing.

Ah the ecstasy of wriggling my toes in the white squeaky sands of my favourite beach and watching the tide run out as the sun sinks lower on the horizon of the ocean. The taste of the salt spray. The harsh cold slap of the sea against the rocks as I bend over and examine the rock pool worlds. And the joy of the wild southern seas.

Shelley was so lost in her thoughts that she didn't hear the 4WD approaching up the windy road. A cloud of dust and tyres crunched against the concrete as the vehicle came to a stop not two metres from where she sat. A door creaked open and the figure of the school principal came round to her side, as Shelley tried to switch back to now.

"I missed you up at the school and we are supposed to be meeting in my office this afternoon," she heard him say in his slow, lazy drawl. "We need to talk about your programme for next term."

Programme for what, buddy? I'm outta here in a few weeks and after that I don't give a continental what you do with these kids and how you run this school. You won't be seeing this little chicken again back here next term. No, sir!

Shelley frowned and looked up at the bedraggled man who stood confronting her on the verandah. She didn't care much for him as a person, and she cared even less for his judgement as an educator. Shelley knew damn well that he had been in the outback way too long. He would *never* get a job back in the mainstream of education. She knew that for sure. Still, he could make her last few weeks miserable if he chose to, so she had to tread wearily all the same. Shelley decided not to let on about leaving yet.

But when I go there are a few facts you're going to have to face, my man, and you can rest assured I'll tell you straight to your ugly face what I really think about you and your unrealistic life up here in this little kingdom which you've carved out for yourself. Yeah, you sure are in for one big surprise Mr Power Trip!

Shelley was feeling tetchy now in the man's presence. She wanted him to go. He was spoiling her happiness. Bursting the bubble. She'd decided to get rid of him the easy way this afternoon to avoid unnecessary confrontation.

"Oh, I must have forgotten about the meeting. There was a lot happening at home time and it just slipped my mind. I can't come back to school now as I've promised to meet some of the women over at the store to look at their artwork, and I can't let them down now, can I?" Shelley glanced up at him with a polite smile spread across her face, hoping that he'd buy the lie today. He didn't really have much choice. There was no way Shelley was going back to a meeting with him now, and he sensed that in her tone.

And soon I won't have to go to any of your time wasting meetings at all. I'll be free of you and this place. Yippeee!

Chapter Forty-Two

Archie had been working at the café now for months. It had become second nature to him. He easily fitted into the lifestyle and routines of the weeks working with Nora in the town. His life was somehow easy and uncluttered and back on track.

But Archie knew there was something missing, itching just below the surface of his daily existence. Something that Archie couldn't quite put his finger on. Just *something*.

What is it, Mother, and why am I feeling this way and what should I do about it, eh?

He'd tried talking things over with Nora and Kirra a few times, but they weren't really much help. Archie knew that his restlessness was somehow connected to his dreaming and his music and his people, but he wasn't sure how. And to be honest, most of the time he didn't *want* to know how. It bugged him, but that's how thing were, and Archie tried to push things away that upset his world for now. There was enough to think about without the dreaming and the ancestors and all that stuff. No, it could wait.

But the soft low winds of the mulga were calling and the red dirt shone through the spinifex and the dull pad of corroboree-feet were coming closer, closer all the time.

There was nothing really in his day-to-day existence that Archie was dissatisfied with, but still something lingered at the back of his mind to unnerve him. He wasn't ready to deal with it. He didn't even know how to truly identify it yet. But for Archie, it was the only blot on the landscape of his current existence.

Nora had been true to her word and fulfilled her part of the bargain, providing Archie with a home and work. For that he was grateful, and Archie truly appreciated the effort Nora had gone to for him. But still something was missing from his life, and he needed to find out what it was.

Nora had been generous with Archie. She'd even replaced his smashed guitar with a shiny new one ordered from the city. That meant a lot to Archie, more than he cared to admit. It was his pride and joy. His key to his music and his soul. His one true outlet.

But there are other things that are important too, boy, and you've got to learn them and recognise them and be part of them in time… eh.

Ken had become a regular visitor to the café now, and Archie felt as though they were becoming part of each other's lives. He liked that. It felt good to belong somewhere and with someone again. He knew that Ken could never replace his mum, but still in his own small way he tried. Archie couldn't ask for more than that. And besides, Ken still had some connection with Flynn, and Archie knew in his head that was important.

It seemed to Archie that there were some pieces of the puzzle of his short life that were still missing, but he knew that he couldn't control that. It simply *was*.

"Hey, Arch," called out Nora from the back of the café, "penny fer 'em, love!"

Archie turned and grinned sheepishly. He felt like he'd been caught out somehow. "Yer don' wanna know, Nora," he replied hurriedly, trying to cover his embarrassment a little as he got back to stacking the fridge with fresh drinks. "Trust me, it's nothin'."

Nora smiled proudly at Archie as she appeared behind the counter once more. She'd become fond of him since taking him in, and had to admit that he'd helped fill a gap in her busy life. A big gap, if she was honest; one that her sister and work had so far been unable to fill in her world.

But Nora was no fool, she knew that one day young Archie would move on. In fact, she would encourage him to do just that. Go south, get some more education, settle somewhere away from here. That's what he needed, or so she thought. A chance at a future of his own.

Nora was a practical person, and so far she had filled her entire life with practicalities.

She'd had dreams of course, hadn't everyone? But they'd somehow fizzled early in life and sunk into the mire of her harsh day-to-day existence. Yes, she had to admit that it had been a battle, and there'd been precious little time for indulgence or fancy. Janie was the only one who'd been allowed some latitude when it came to enjoyment, and Nora sometimes resented the way things had panned out. But she kept it to herself and plodded on stoically through each day, making sure that their lives were taken care of.

Nora and Janie were almost exact opposites in every way, a fact that they had both been reminded of often enough in their girlhood.

Look at Janie, doesn't she look so pretty just look at those beautiful curls and that lovely dress doesn't she make the prettiest picture out there on the swing and why can't you be more like your sister Nora, just look at the mess you've made, go and change out of those muddy boots and clean yourself up for dinner will you.

Nora sighed at the memories as she washed another load of dishes there in the cramped kitchen of her outback café. She pushed her hair back from her forehead with an impatient shrug, feeling a little lost and a little forlorn all of a sudden. It wasn't really like her to feel sorry for herself, and Nora quickly shook herself and got on with the task at hand. There was no time for dreaming now. There would be customers relying on her, and she had a business to run after all. And then there was Archie. Maybe that was the problem. Maybe his youth had reminded her of her own lost years. Her dreams. Her goals and aspirations. Nora knew that was part of it. But something else niggled at her as she scoured the last of the pots in the sink, something bigger and more meaningful. It was making her restless and fidgety, but she couldn't put her finger on what it was.

Damn this for happening now just when my life was running so smoothly and me and Janie had our system of living all sorted into days and weeks and months and years and the only things that upset our routine were the occasional local disasters round here that tipped over the apple cart every now and then.

"Hey, Nora, there's a man out here wants ter see yer, gotta minute?" called out Archie from the front of the shop, suddenly interrupting Nora's thoughts.

What, what, what... who is that? Archie... Archie.

Nora flushed as she wiped her hands hurriedly on the damp tea towel and went through to the shop. She was annoyed with herself for being distracted. She felt caught out, as though her wistfulness was uncharacteristic, and therefore unworthy. She wanted to get back into her reality: the shop, the customers, orders, meals, cooking, cleaning, discussing local events with her regulars, going home, making tea, chatting to Janie, going to bed. That was the pattern of her life, and it had kept her going all these years. It would all be just fine, Nora decided. But *something* was shifting slightly, and she felt the balance of her life move just a little as she looked up to meet the gaze of the stranger who waited in her café.

Who is that he looks familiar like someone I once knew a long long time ago. He's not from around here but from another place and he once knew... once knew... who?

Nora stopped in her tracks for a brief moment as the man advanced towards her with his hand outstretched in greeting. She looked up at his tall lean frame trying to recall something. Trying to gain some insight, some reminder. But it wasn't until her hand touched his and his voice reached hers that she suddenly remembered who he was. It all came flooding back. Yes, Nora knew alright.

But how did he find me and what is he doing here and when did he get out of prison and what will I do now that he is here and why did this have to happen to me now when my whole life is running so smoothly… why? Why? Why?

"Hi, Nora, how are you? It's a nice café you've got here; this young lad was just telling me all about you. Looks like you sure have landed on your feet, eh?" Nora heard him say as he took hold of her hand in a tight grip. Ownership. Possession. It reminded Nora of a part of her past that she desperately wanted to forget. Why had he turned up now and what did he want with her?

"Jim! What are you doing here?" Nora asked roughly, withdrawing her hand from his. "I thought you were still down south. When did you get out?"

There were too many painful memories and too many unanswered questions and too much sorrow at what had been and what might have been. Nora didn't want to relive that part of her life. No, she sure as hell did not. It was gone. Dead and buried. Leave well enough alone, Nora thought as she turned back towards the counter.

She needed a physical barrier between her and this man who'd almost ruined her life for good. Nora was not going to be caught out twice, and she knew what he was capable of.

Get out, get out, leave me alone. I don't want you here and whatever is it you've come here for I'm no longer part of it, so just go and leave me alone once more to get on with my life, will you?

"It's good to see you again, Nora, after all these years. Spent a lot of time inside thinking about you I did. Yeah a *lot* of time. And it wasn't all that bad either, I've learned a trade and studied and mended my ways, I sure have. Found God, too," drawled the tall man, advancing now towards Nora once more.

"What do you want from me, Jim? Why are you here?" Nora asked warily. She knew that he would not have come here for nothing. There had to be a catch. Nora had good reason to mistrust this man, after all, she'd once been his wife. If anyone knew about old Jim, it was Nora, and she sure wasn't about to let him hoodwink her again. No damn way! He could go to hell in a handcart as far as she was concerned, and the sooner the better!

Jim eyed her from across the counter and broke into a grin. "Aw now, Nora, don't be like that, my dear, I've only come to pay you a short visit. I promise I'll only be here a day or two and then I'll be gone. You'll see. I thought you'd be pleased to see me after all these years," said Jim from behind his moustache, fixing her with a steely gaze.

But Nora had regained her composure and would have none of his rubbish. She remembered the pain and loss he'd caused her all those years ago down south when he'd abandoned her and the new baby and run off with that floozy from the corner store. Oh yes, she remembered all right!

And now he turns up bold as brass expecting me to speak to him and believe that he's changed, and what the hell does he want with me? It's all long gone between us, dead and buried like that poor child of ours in the cemetery and I don't need him back in my life, oh no!

Nora stood her ground and measured her words carefully before she replied. She knew that he had a terrible temper, and she didn't want a scene in the shop. She just wanted him to go and never come back, and she was worried that he would hang around town a while and try to sponge off her again. No, Nora would have to convince him somehow to leave. To leave for good this time.

And let's face it, Jim, after all these years what good can come of it when all's said and done; there's been too much history between us and too much sadness and far too much tragedy and loss to ever think that you could just walk back into my life and pick up the pieces. I don't even want to think about it, Jim. It's over.

Archie glanced up from the counter and stared straight into the eyes of the stranger who'd come into the café and asked to see Nora. There was something hard and steely about him, as though he'd been worn down by time and years of frustration and anger. Archie sensed rage hiding in those eyes; he'd seen it before in his mob. Still, he'd asked for Nora, so Archie had called out to her.

Now he wasn't sure that he had done the right thing by Nora. He'd seen the reaction she gave when she saw the man waiting in the café, and Archie knew that something wasn't right. Yeah, he'd been around the mob enough to sense hostility.

But for now there was little he could do but wait it out here in the café, and hang around in case of trouble. Not that he figured he was big enough to take on a complete stranger, but at least he could protect Nora if needs be. Archie hoped so anyway. There was something else about the man that Archie didn't like. He couldn't quite put his finger on what it was, but he knew it was there all the same. Something about his manner. His sly smile. His air of possessiveness with Nora, almost as though she should jump to his command. No, Archie didn't like this guy one bit.

"Well then, I'll be seeing you," the man said softly as he turned to leave. It was as though he hissed out the words between clenched teeth with piston precision, menacing with unspent force. A hint of menace and arrogance born of long-forgotten familiarity. A past unspoken until now.

Archie watched him leave and turned back to Nora as the door banged shut. She was pale and clearly shaken, but was trying to quickly compose herself and get on with the day. Typical Nora, he thought.

"You OK, Nora?" he asked, full of concern about this visit from a stranger. "Here, sit down fer a minute an' I'll get yer a cuppa. Won't be long."

Archie went through to the kitchen and put the jug on to boil. He glanced through to check on Nora while he got two mugs out and put the sugar and milk in, listening for customers at the same time. He didn't want Nora to have to deal with anything yet. She was still pretty shaken, he could tell.

He wondered who this guy was and what his connection to Nora was. She'd never talked much about her past, and this man had obviously upset her. Upset her a *lot*. There was a lot more to Nora than met the eye, and Archie realised that he didn't really know much about her. He knew that she was kind and generous and extremely hard-working, and he had grown very fond of her. She'd taken him in and given him a job and a chance of a future of sorts, and he would always be grateful for that. But she never really talked much about herself, and Archie wondered now what her life had been like when she was his age. When she'd had dreams.

Were they like my dreams and did she often feel sad and wish that better things would happen and did she ever feel like she didn't belong where she was but wasn't too sure of where she really should be, like me... did she?

"Here you go then, Nora, here's a nice hot cuppa to sort yer out. That'll do the trick," said Archie as he brought the two steaming cups through to the café. "Have a good sip of this, eh?"

Nora reached out vacantly for the tea that Archie had made for her and smiled at him thinly. She was regaining some colour in her cheeks, and Archie felt a little better about things now that Jim had gone and they were alone in the café once more. He knew that the afternoon rush of customers would soon be here, and he wanted Nora to settle down a bit first. He could see that Jim had really rattled her. A visit from the past, and obviously one that Nora had not expected or wanted. Yeah, he knew what that was like. Better give her some time to get over it, he decided.

Chapter Forty-Three

Archie was getting bored. He'd been here in town working at the café with Nora for six months, and the novelty of town life had well and truly worn off. From time to time he felt truly happy, but more and more he was beginning to feel restless again.

Occasionally Archie visited Ken over at town camp. Spending time there was OK, but often it only served as a reminder of his other self, his dreaming and his ancestors. And in truth, there was something about Ken that felt a bit spooky. Too close, like he was family.

How could that be?

Archie didn't want to be reminded of that stuff, and he sure didn't want to deal with it now. He had other plans. He still thought of Flynn often, and wondered if they'd meet over at the camp, but it just didn't seem to happen. So Archie shoved it aside and put his emotions on hold for now.

His guitar and his music and his on-going friendship with Kirra were the strengths that kept Archie going, although lately it seemed to him that Kirra's life was getting constantly more difficult back at half way camp. He wanted to try to help her more, but Archie knew it was way too big for him to deal with. Besides, he wasn't allowed near the camp, and that made it even more frustrating.

Kirra seemed to have lost her freshness and her laughter, and Archie puzzled about how to get it back. He knew that her mum had got back on the grog, and that made Kirra's life even more difficult. Kirra had truly believed that this time her mum would stay off the booze, and to have her trust shattered once more was soul- destroying. It made Archie angry just to think about it.

Geez, Beryl, couldn't yer have stayed off the grog fer once and tried ter help yer kids an' be a good mum jez for now, couldn't yer, eh? Yer breakin' their poor hearts again!

It was hopeless he knew, but still Archie worried about the effect it was having on Kirra. He knew she was far too young to be saddled with the burden of taking care of her mum and the little kids and the household, but what could he do?

Maybe we could both go away and get out of here and head over to the coast and try to work our way down south to the city and see all the sights ... maybe.

The plan just popped into his head. Once there, it seemed to take hold. And grow.

I've still got some of mum's money and with what I've saved from working in the café we should have enough ter get to the coast an' find somewhere ter stay, shouldn't we?

Archie sat in the sun and smiled to himself. He was suddenly feeling invigorated for the first time in weeks. He felt alive again, with renewed hope for the future. A sense of adventure overtook him as the shadows of late afternoon stretched across his face. The dreams and hopes and images of other lives began stirring within. The reality of change kicked in briefly, offering a world beyond the window of the café. Archie jumped up and let out a loud whoop of excitement, and his feet began dancing the steps of his ancestors without him even knowing.

But the elders are calling and reaching out to you with splayed fingers and beckoning you to take the first steps of the journey.

It was almost dark, and Archie still hadn't moved. He wanted to talk to Kirra, to invite her along. He wanted to tell Nora about his half-formed plans, but now was not the right time. The red-orange rays of the sun cast their final glow across his outstretched legs, and Archie watched as the shadows advanced and turned the light to blue-grey. He stretched out his hands and rubbed his tired brow, feeling drained and cautious and a little frayed now.

It was getting late, and he had to get back to Nora's ready for tea, or she would wonder where he was. His plans could wait for now. Archie hurried back to town feeling unusually prickly. His mind was buzzing in all directions. He found it hard to settle.

What will Kirra think of my plans and what on earth will Nora say when I tell her that I'm thinking of heading off and going to the coast then down south to the city?

Archie didn't have time now to stop and ponder the consequences, he only knew that the possibility of another fresh start was tantalisingly close. If only the others would agree to it. See it his way. Let him go through with it. Of course, he didn't really need their permission or approval, he could go anyway despite any possible objections. But that would only have upset Nora and Kirra, and he didn't want to do that.

For all his youthfulness and inexperience, Archie had developed a fairly complex understanding of human nature, and at times he startled Nora and Kirra with his insights. It just seemed to come naturally to Archie, and he didn't really stop to think about why. It just *was*.

Is that a gift you gave to me, Mother, before you left this world and is that what you were trying to tell me when you were dying and is that one of the reasons I hear the voices of the ancestors and the dreamtime stories echo in my head, is it, Mother?

Archie grappled briefly with a sudden overpowering sense of sadness, then dismissed it quickly and hurried back to town. Back to the warmth and safety of Nora's. Back to tea and a chat and some company once more. Back to his world.

For now.

It didn't matter that the other thoughts and plans were still spinning in his head. Archie needed some normality. And besides, he was hungry. As he bounded up the last few steps of the front verandah, Nora's familiar voice called out from the kitchen. "Is that you, Archie? I was just wondering where you'd got to. Tea's ready, mate!"

How does she do that? How did she know that it was me?

"Be right there, Aunty Nora," Archie replied as he hurried in through the door and headed towards the bathroom to wash his hands before tea. He was feeling more settled now that he was back home, and decided to put any talk of his half-formed plans on hold for the time being. It wasn't fair to upset Nora just yet, not till he'd talked things through with Kirra to gauge her reaction. No, it could definitely wait.

"How did things go at the café this arvo, Nora? Did yer have lots of customers? What time did yer close today?" Archie asked in an interested sort of tone as he took his place at the table opposite Nora. Jane wasn't in tonight, so it was just the two of them.

"Yeah it was alright this afternoon, got busy though around five. A bus load came in from the coast. All weary and dusty they was, those tourists. Just lookin' for a nice cuppa and something to eat and a quiet place to rest their weary bones, if yer ask me. I was wishing I'd kept you on ter help this arvo, but I managed alright by meself anyways, so not to worry."

Nora dished up the tea as she spoke, then shoved their plates on the table and sank wearily into her chair. It was the end of the week, and she was bone-tired. She glanced across at Archie casually, then lifted her fork silently and began eating. She was oblivious to external issues as she munched her way through the rissoles and mashed potatoes, hoping that Archie would stay silent too for a bit. Nora was too tired for conversation right now. Yeah, just too tired.

"Nice meal, Aunty," Archie said between mouthfuls, "yer a great cook, yer know."

Nora raised her eyes and gave Archie a tired smile. She was glad that he was home safe tonight, and hoped that he wouldn't be going over to the camp to meet Ken. She didn't know why, but she didn't trust the man. There was just something about him that disquieted her. Something that she couldn't quite put her finger on, but it was there nonetheless. She cut through the last of her rissole and gave it a liberal squirt of tomato sauce before popping it into her mouth with a scraping of mashed spud. Ah, that tasted good. Plain, simple food, that's what she liked at home.

At the café it was different, and Nora made a real effort to vary the menu and keep up some wholesome and hearty meals for the locals. (Though sometimes she wondered why she bothered.)

Still, after all these years in the café, Nora kept trying to interest the local population in a healthy diet, and refused to serve only junk food at the café. Sure, she still stocked sweets and smokes and ice creams and packets of chips, which some would say was ironic. But at least she balanced it with fruit and salads and casseroles and rice dishes. Yes, Nora did her best, and that was all you could ask of anyone, wasn't it?

"Hey, Nora, are you OK?" asked Archie suddenly, noticing how pale and washed out she seemed at the table. "Is everything alright?"

Secretly Archie worried about the visit by the stranger, Jim. He'd seen the instant shock on Nora's face when the guy had walked in the other day, and although he would not press her about it, Archie had been concerned and a bit worried by it ever since. What if Jim had come back to harm Nora, or lay claim to something that wasn't rightfully his? What if he was waiting in town right now to pay a visit? He must surely have found out by now where Nora lived, it wouldn't take a brain surgeon to figure that out in a small backwater town like this. Archie had been surprised at Nora's reaction, and sensed a story there that Nora had long ago buried and sure as hell didn't want resurrected. No, the jerk was up to no good, that's for sure, and Archie intended to keep an eye out for Nora while Jim was in town. She'd taken him in and looked after him, after all, and it seemed only fair that Archie would repay the favour. Besides, he was genuinely fond of Nora, and cared about her welfare.

If that's the case, Arch, my man, then why are you thinking of moving on and going south and abandoning all that she has given you here in this small town, huh?

Archie wrestled briefly with his conscience there at the kitchen table as he finished his tea and looked across at Nora. He cleared his throat and mumbled something under his breath about friends and families and fortunes, but it wasn't enough to save him from guilt.

What should I do, Mum, and why is it sometimes so hard to make choices and when is the right time to stay or to go or to speak or stay silent? Why didn't you teach me these things, Mother? Why?

Archie knew in his heart that he had not been ready for life lessons when his mother had been alive. He accepted that she had tried, but he'd ignored her and run from her and hidden behind the wall of his innocence for far too long. He should have listened and tried to accommodate his mother more, but he knew that he had still too much growing to do. Even now, Archie recognised that his journey was hardly under way. But at least he knew that it had begun finally, and it was up to him to take it further, to leave this place. He had to find out for himself what it was that the ancestors wanted him to do, and where he fitted in. Archie knew it was almost time, just as his mum had recognised her time.

But his mum's time had been for the final journey back to the dreaming, and for Archie it was only the beginning. His map was a life-map, and not the journey of death.

Chapter Forty-Four

Shelley scratched at the tiredness in the corners of her eyes, trying to fend off sleep for a while yet. The night was still and oppressive, and even the sight of her favourite grey gum standing guard at the end of the verandah did nothing to alleviate her despondence tonight.

She sipped slowly at the mug of coffee and called the dog over to sit on her lap, despite the heat. The moon was low in the sky, outlining the distant hills. Shelley sat and sighed and listened to the night sounds. She could hear the bush noises at the edge of the camp mingling with the sounds of humans: coughs, shouts, cries, howls, grunts, laughter, TV, voices, music, snuffles. Strange that she should have developed such an intense ear for individual sounds out here in such a short time. Perhaps it was the isolation and the vastness of the Kimberley plains that formed the basis of her temporary world that gave her the newfound skill.

Bugger it, what do I care we're leaving in a couple of weeks anyway, back to the real world. And people who actually give meaning and structure and support to my life. People who actually care.

Shelley recognised that she had become bitter about the way things had turned out here for her, and she hated herself for that. Hated what the place had become. Hated the intrusion of whitefella values and white systems and white jobs and money and dependence. It shouldn't have been this way, but it was. And Shelley knew that there wasn't a damned thing she could do about it. *That* was the most frustrating part.

Everything out here revolved around handouts from the government, and had for a long time. Shelley knew it, her partner knew it, the school knew it, the shopkeeper knew it, and the locals knew it. They were all in the same boat really, paid directly or indirectly from the same big money trough. Whitefella, blackfella; all the same. It was hard to accept the system but it was incredibly simple to understand. Guilt money. Fix-it-up money. Work for the dole money. Wages, salaries, handouts. All the same out here really, and you didn't even get to *see* what you were paid in hard cash, it just went on your tab. Easy, book it up at the store. Simple, eh?

Shelley smiled bitterly to herself, trying not to let the anger at the injustice take over. She should have known it would be like this, but no one had warned her. No one had given her the slightest hint about how people lived and survived up here in the remote communities. No, they sure had not!

And would you have come if you'd known? And would you have believed them? And would you have buried your pride and scoffed at the suggestion that things were really this bad and come up here anyway?

The night sky seemed to be falling, pressing in on her senses as she sipped at the last of the cold coffee. Shelley waited and watched, wanting an external sign of some sort to calm her fuddled brain. She could hear the air conditioner chugging away inside, and she knew that she should get to bed soon and try to get some sleep, tomorrow was the last day of the working week, and they would throw their camping gear in the land cruiser and head off to town for the weekend. Away from the camp. Away from the other unfriendly staff. Away from the bastard of a principal, who thought that he could control their lives and their every waking moment. And away from the kids.

She was supposed to be teaching them, but it meant nothing to them. The whole damn thing was meaningless, and had nothing to do with their needs or wants or aspirations for the future, did it? It was really all about numbers and funding and grants and lost dreams.

There'd been a time when she first came up here that Shelley had truly believed she would fit in and make some sort of difference to the lives of these kids. But it had lasted only fleetingly, and by the end of the first week in the classroom

Shelley knew that it was an impossible task to achieve anything up here. At least at the school anyway.

Still, she persevered for a while, changing strategies almost daily to try to deal with the constant anger and defiance and discord amongst her students. She thought that if she continued to display an interest in their world they would eventually come round and try to complete some work tasks, but it hadn't happened. Not yet, anyway. And Shelley wasn't prepared to wait it out up here on the slim chance that it might.

She'd worked in schools long enough to recognise defeat, and when it was her own that stared her in the face one day she'd decided the time had come to get out. Leave this mess for someone else to deal with. Let them try to sort it out if they could, it would no longer be *her* problem.

The trouble was that her ego was slightly dented in the process, and now that she had made the decision to go, there was, of course, a touch of regret mingled in with the relief she also felt. But still, she didn't dwell on the negatives for too long. It simply didn't matter to Shelley in the big scheme of things. It was far more important to get her life back on track and find her feet once more and re-establish herself back home. There were doubts of course, but at this stage of her working life Shelley figured that she'd given it her best shot up here and it just hadn't worked out. It was time to go, end of story.

But part of her felt cheated; as though she was quitting and letting go the dreams she'd brought up here. Part of her rebelled and shouted out that she was not fulfilling her promises and leaving to soon, too soon... wasn't she?

Ah, what the hell! Nothing she could do would change all this. Shelley recognised right from the start that what really mattered was not what she thought could be done but what simply could not be done, and there was a huge chasm in between the two.

She asked herself for the umpteenth time why she had come, and discovered yet again that she was still no closer to the truth. Still no nearer to any real discovery. And still not really accepting that the dream was finally shattered.

The disillusionment, however, was very real, and Shelley knew that it would change her value system forever.

But it had been with her for so long and she recognised that even as a child she'd felt the sting of social injustice and seen the barriers created by the empowered over the disenfranchised.

A tear rolled down her face as she felt the slow cascading of sliding dreams collapsing in on each other. Shelley tried to hold them back, but they crashed and fell within. She gazed up vacantly at the darkening sky, surprised by the all-consuming strength of her emotions. She hadn't intended to journey into the minefield of her belief systems tonight; it had simply happened. Perhaps it was because she was leaving this place. Perhaps it was time.

Or perhaps it's another part of your own journey and your own reconciliation and your own dreaming. Could it be the voices of your ancestors calling out to you and beckoning you and stirring in the cold dark fog of other lands and other times and other places far, far away from here... could it be?

Shelley shrugged off her despair and forced herself to focus on the here and the now. She stood up and stretched her weary limbs, then crossed to the back door and went in. She felt tired and leaden and overwrought. She needed to sleep, yes, she sure did.

In her dreams the night birds came, and Shelley cried out silently there in the outback room and pulled at the rumpled sheets as the long line of strangers from her past filed slowly and methodically through the space inside her skull. Echoes of shrill calls and tramping feet called out to her from somewhere within, and she tossed and turned and suddenly sat bolt upright as the line between dreaming and reality fused in her head. Where am I, where am I and who were all those people that I saw?

Shelley shuddered slightly and got up. She needed desperately to shake off the dread of the vision. She had to get outside and dance under the stars and howl at the moon. She needed escape and release from the torment.

Don't go there, Shelley, you know, yes you know that it's just in your head. Get a grip! Get over it.

She could feel the oppressiveness of the heat bearing down on her now as she padded softly through to the kitchen to put the kettle on. She needed a cup of tea to calm her nerves. Shelley went through the ritual of the late night cuppa, just as she had so many times before in her life.

And what does that tell you, Shelley, dear?

She took her mug out to the back verandah and sat in the now familiar cane chair. The ghost gum was silhouetted by the moon, and gave Shelley some much needed reassurance tonight. She loved that tree. It reminded her of all that was natural and pure and untouched in this world. It was her rock in times of need.

Why had the dreams returned now and what should she do to alleviate the messages?

It had to have something to do with the journey. With the decision to leave. But for now Shelley didn't want to contemplate the next stage. She simply wanted to acknowledge the step forward, not the outcomes. Time would take care of the rest, and Shelley knew from past experience that there would always be something better ahead. Yes, let tomorrow take care of itself, it was today that mattered most.

Chapter Forty-Five

Archie was feeling testy. He'd wanted to talk to Nora about his plans to leave, but the right time hadn't presented itself yet, so he'd had to put things on hold. He hadn't seen much of Kirra lately either, and he missed her company more than he cared to admit. He'd spoken to her a few times on the phone this week, but it wasn't the same as spending time together. Archie wasn't fooled by Kirra's show of independence and pleasantries one bit. He knew that things weren't going so well for her back at home, but she denied any problems when he asked.

It wasn't like Kirra to hide things from Archie, so naturally he worried about her. And that only added to his current dilemma. He decided that he would have to convince her to come into town again soon and meet him at the café after work. Archie knew that she could get in to town after school most nights providing that things weren't too bad at home. He really needed to see her and discuss his plans, and besides, he was genuinely worried about Kirra.

"Hey, Archie, have you finished loading the drink fridge yet?" called out Nora from the kitchen. "I need yer out here to give me a hand with the lunch orders soon."

Archie frowned and swore under his breath. It wasn't like Nora to hurry him along at work. And it sure wasn't like Archie to get annoyed with her. But today they were probably both a bit out of sorts and that was a recipe for conflict.

Archie shoved the last of the drinks into the fridge and slammed the door. He gathered up the empty cartons and stacked them under his arm. He went out the front door of the café and took the cartons round the back to the incinerator, then stood there for a while chucking them in one by one. He didn't want to go back inside and confront Nora just yet, so he stayed out the back and lit the old drum of rubbish. Archie smiled as he watched the flames kick into life then dance upwards, crackling and soaring around him.

And the fires of the old people were coming towards him. And their feet were coming closer. And the smell of the roasting goanna meat was in his nostrils. And the old people's dreams were back in his skull.

"Gawd, Archie, what the hell are yer doin' lighting the fire now in the middle of the day? Doncha know we're not s'posed ter light it till after dark, eh? What do yer think yer doin', Archie?" bawled out Nora, as she rushed out the back door of the café and grabbed the hose near the tap. "Geez, Arch, we'd better put it out now, orright?"

Archie turned towards the fire and stood stock still while Nora splattered the water onto the offending flames. He felt flattened and foolish. He knew that he shouldn't have lit the fire, but it had been something to get him out of going back inside with Nora. He felt a bit guilty that he'd upset her even more, but it wasn't entirely his fault that she was in her current mood. No, it wasn't his fault at all.

Blame that bastard Jim who'd turned up like a bad smell the other day and walked back into her life as bold as brass and reminded Nora of something that she obviously wanted to forget. Yeah, blame him, not me!

Archie dropped the last of the cardboard boxes he'd been holding and turned slowly towards the remaining flames leaping in the drum. It looked sad and forlorn now, and he peered into the ruined and soggy mess that had been a roaring fire just seconds ago. All that was left was a jumbled mass of twisted black and grey embers and a strong stench of smoke and chemical residue. It reminded him suddenly of death.

And the faces of the ancestors were fading in the fires of his dreams. He could see the embers of their fires too. And the smells of their food were still before him. Dying.

Archie turned away from the drum and scrambled back inside, not wanting to further antagonise Nora now. He hated being alienated from anyone, much less Nora, and he knew that she was already upset as it was. He decided it would be best to let things blow over and get on with helping her now in the café.

"Sorry about that, Nora, I just thought it'd be a good idea ter get rid of them boxes fer ya. I didn't mean ter upset ya, orright?" he asked sheepishly, knowing that it was only a half-truth. He'd been angry and churlish, and really it wasn't Nora's fault. Archie wanted to bridge their distance now before things got worse.

"S'orright, Arch," Nora grinned at him, "I'm real sorry that I yelled at yer before. I've just had a lot on me mind lately; not your fault though. Come here an' give yer ol', Aunty Nora a big hug, eh?"

She reached out and folded him in a generous embrace. Archie could smell her body warmth, a mixture of cheap talc and cooking smells. He didn't mind, it was the closest he came to feeling like he truly belonged since his mum had died. Yeah, he didn't mind at all.

The two of them laughed together and their friendship was renewed once more.

"Now can we get on with the rolls and sandwich orders, mate? Time's running out you know. Them customers will soon be on their lunch breaks and you know where they'll be headed fer a bite to eat," Nora chided Archie playfully, tousling his hair like a small child.

Archie grinned back at her and began to spread the rolls from the large tub of margarine. It felt good to be back to normal now here in the café with Nora. Archie felt like he belonged once more. He put the other plans right out of his head, knowing that now was not the time to bring up any talk of leaving. Besides, Nora had enough on her plate at the moment what with this Jim-thing and running the café, and he knew that she was far more rattled and upset than she let on.

I wonder who he is and what he wants and why he's come all the way out here to see Nora when clearly she doesn't want anything at all to do with him?

"What are we using for filling today, Nora?" Archie asked as he finished spreading the last roll. "The usual?"

"Nah, I cooked up some chicken this morning and got in some of them avocados. Thought we needed a bit of a change, and it'll do the locals good to have a different menu today," Nora replied, as she stooped down to get the ingredients she needed from the kitchen fridge. "I've been thinking about making a few changes round here too, Arch, might have a chat about them later today, eh, after the lunch rush had died down. What d'yer think?"

Arch was a bit nonplussed. He wasn't sure whether she was talking about food changes or shop alterations or maybe even hiring more staff. It was a bit unnerving, and unlike Nora to talk about change.

But perhaps it could be to my advantage and it might give me an opportunity to talk about my plans after all. Yeah, it just might.

"OK, Nora, that's fine by me. How about I make us a cuppa and fix us some late lunch when the customers have gone? Then we can sit and have a chat if you like," Archie responded, feeling a bit more confident now about broaching the subject of him leaving. He knew that Nora would be really sorry to see him go, but she'd said right from the start that she knew one day he'd be off to the city, hadn't she? In fact, he remembered that she'd been the one to encourage him to think that way. To get an education. To better himself sometime. Yeah, he didn't think she'd be too surprised by his plans at all.

It was mid-afternoon in the café and things had slowed to a trickle. Nora and Archie sat at the table near the window and watched the last customers amble along the pavement under the hot afternoon sun. The fan above them whirled slowly, stirring up the fuggy mix of heat and cooking smells and food scraps and body sweat that hung in the air like a shadow of other peoples' lives.

Nora sighed and propped on her elbows as she surveyed the mess. Normally she would have cleaned it all away and tidied the place up before she stopped for a rest, but today she had things on her mind. Distractions. Plans. Thoughts.

"Hey, Archie, d'yer mind makin' yer ol' aunty a cuppa an' a sandwich, lovie? I could really do with a break," Nora said to Archie, yawning and sighing with the weight of issues that she had to deal with today.

Archie looked across at the tables strewn with the detritus of human contact, knowing that he should clear them up first before they had their own lunch. But he realised that Nora had something on her mind. The dishes and cleaning could wait for once. Archie got up from the table and made his way past the mess to the kitchen.

"S'alright, Aunty, I'll get the kettle on then make us some salad rolls. I'll clear up some of this stuff now and stack it all in the sink till later. Don't you worry about a thing, you just rest yerself fer a bit while I get our cuppas," Archie said gently to the figure now slumped at the front table. "Won't be a jiff."

He put the kettle on then went back through to the tables and started stacking plates and cups hurriedly onto a large tray. In no time at all he'd cleared all the tables, and then Archie went through and quickly wiped them all down. He knew Nora hated the café to be messy, so he wanted to get things in order, at least out the front of the place anyway. The dishes could wait till after they'd had their lunch, and besides, Archie figured that Nora wanted to have that chat she'd referred to this morning. He was a bit curious, but guessed that it was about Jim, the stranger from her past who'd suddenly turned up.

And what the hell is that all about anyway, Nora?

Archie gathered their tea and rolls onto a tray and went back through to the table where Nora sat. "Here you go then, Aunty. Come on, have a cuppa and something ter eat. You'll feel much better then," he encouraged. "I've stacked up in the kitchen so's I can finish off after, orright?"

Nora looked around at the clean tables and smiled at Archie thankfully. He was a good boy, and she knew how lucky she was to have him in her life. But she knew that he wouldn't stay here in town forever. She knew he'd go sometime soon.

Just like my own little boy, the one I had with Jim, God bless his poor little soul.

"Thanks, Arch," sighed Nora wearily, "yer a real gem you are."

"That's OK, Aunty, are you alright? What's bothering yer today?" Archie replied with concern.

Nora munched slowly on the roll Archie had brought her and gazed up at the ceiling. She felt heavy and leaden, weighed down by the burdens of the past that she'd tucked away and hidden oh so long ago.

But not forgotten completely, oh no, never forgotten.

She sipped her cup of hot sweet tea and gazed across the table at Archie.

So young and innocent with so much life ahead of him. Should I tell him? Should I?

Archie began to feel the pressure of the silence. Something hung in the air, oppressive and threatening. Something to do with Jim and Nora and the past. Something he could sense and almost feel, and he didn't like it. No, not one bit.

He supposed that it really wasn't any of his business and it had nothing to do with him, after all, but a part of him wanted to protect Nora at all costs, so he began to suffer a little on her behalf.

"What's the matter, Nora? Yer not yerself today an' I'm worried about yer. Is it something to do that that Jim character who came in here the other day? Is there anything I can do ter help yer?" he asked, full of concern now that the two of them were alone here in the heat and silence of the afternoon lull. He wanted to get it over with so that he could talk about his own plans to leave here, but Archie knew deep down that he couldn't go yet with Nora like this. He would have to wait till this thing with Jim was sorted. It wouldn't be fair on the old girl to leave now.

Nora finished her cup of tea and looked directly at Archie. She opened her mouth to speak, and then closed it again, hesitating.

What should I tell the boy and does he really need to know? Gawd sakes I've kept it to meself all these years and Janie is the only one that really knows the truth except for me an' Jim, of course, the bastard! Still, I guess it won't hurt him ter know about me past mistakes an' maybe it'll teach him a little bit about how yer can't really can't trust people all the time an' how sometimes people take advantage of yer, specially those yer love!

"That Jim, he's a right bastard, Arch. Fair dinkum, I swore long ago that if he ever so much as come near me again I'd knock his bloomin' head off, struth I would!" blurted out Nora.

Archie could see that she was trembling now and patted her hand. He was embarrassed for Nora, but also concerned. He'd never seen her upset like this. She was usually so calm and in control of things. To be honest, Archie had never really thought about Nora's private world. He only dealt with the day-to-day stuff, and that was about it.

"What'd he do to yer, Nora? It must have been somethin' pretty bad ter get yer so upset." Archie asked full of curiosity now about Jim. "I don't mean to pry or nothin', it's just that you aren't yer usual self at the moment, and I don't know what to do to help yer."

Might as well tell the kid a bit about me past, after all, he's become a bit like a son ter me has Arch, and it won't hurt him ter know. He doesn't need ter know everything, just the basics. Heaven knows it was all so long ago, and what harm can come of it now? That lazy bastard Jim will be gone in a day or two, mark my words. And Arch might just be able to help speed up his departure.

"We was married once, me an' Jim, two young lovebirds we was in them days, couldn't separate us yer couldn't. He was such a dandy, got all the young girls' hearts racin' did Jim in them days. But I was the one he picked, least I thought he did for a while," blurted out Nora at the table, ready now to share her story with Archie.

"In them days we didn't have much, an' what we did have wouldn't amount to anything these days. But we were in love, and that was all that mattered," Nora went on, pouring herself another cup of tea from the pot Archie had brought through. "I thought I'd found my one true love, fair dinkum I did, an' I was that proud of him, you wouldn't believe it!"

Nora stopped and drew in her breath, a vacant look spreading across her face. It was as though she had gone back now, and was stuck in the past with Jim.

"What happened, Nora? Why did it change?"

Nora was silent for a while, as though she hadn't heard.

The bastard got me pregnant and denied he was the father and swore the baby wasn't his responsibility, then run off with that floozy before out poor child saw the light of day, didn't he?

"He told me that he loved me and there was no one else but me for him and I believed him, honest to God I did."

Bloody lying mongrel bastard!

"But then as soon as I told him I was pregnant things changed and they were never the same again," whispered Nora, trying now to keep from crying. She could feel the rawness at the back of her throat. She felt hot around her eyes, and her skin prickled at the memories of those times with Jim.

How could I have been so wrong about him?

A single tear trickled down her cheek, Nora felt a bit foolish in front of Archie, but she couldn't help it now. Besides, she knew Archie well enough to know that he wouldn't say anything. She could tell that he was concerned about her.

"It' alright, it's over now. Dead and buried in the past," she added, trying to bring the subject to a close now for both their sakes.

"But what happened to the baby, and where did you go after he left you? Did your parents look after you?" Archie asked, wanting to hear the end of the story now.

"Nah, they wouldn't have nothing to do with me after that. Said that I'd made me own bed and I could damn well lie in it. Told me that I should never have taken up with the likes of that dandy anyways, and I only had meself to blame. It was Janie who took me in and took care of me while I had the bub, and I'll owe her that debt as long as we both live. Without her I woulda been out on the street and that's fer sure!" Nora uttered, a touch of anger still at the memory slipping into her voice.

"An' then when the baby died from the colic, it was Janie who nursed me through it an' held me hand and fed me and listened to me talk and held me all those nights when I cried meself ter sleep. She never let me down, not once, yer understand?"

Archie reached across the table and took Nora's hand in his for reassurance. He wanted to ease her burden at the memories, but he was too young to fully understand. Still, it pained him to see her reduced to this, so he comforted her as best he could.

"Don't worry, Nora, I'll go and see Ken tomorrow. We'll make sure that bastard Jim leaves town before the end of the week. Don't you worry about a thing, you'll be rid of him sooner than you think. And good riddance ter the mongrel!" Archie spat out between clenched teeth, hoping to sound convincing enough to comfort Nora a little. He didn't want to know any more. Archie had heard Nora mention that Jim had been in prison, but for now he'd heard enough. He needed to get things back on an even keel so that Nora was no longer focusing on her past sadness. Archie desperately wanted to cheer her up.

Maybe I'll call Kirra and see if she can come up into town and we'll take Nora out for a walk ter the river and wander over and get some fish and chips for tea later on. Maybe that'll take her mind off things fer a while?

Archie released Nora's hand and stood up. He pulled back her chair and guided her through to the kitchen.

"Come on, Aunty, take yer apron off for a while and let's just shut the shop for half an hour and go shopping together. You never know, there might be some new clothes in over at the store you can look at. It'll do yer good ter buy something new, cheer yer up a bit. Come on, what do yer say, Nora?" Archie urged, hoping that he could convince her to get out of the café for a while and do something different. "Come on!" Archie steered her towards the door and they went out into the sunshine.

Chapter Forty-Six

Shelley and her partner had been in Broome for a while now enjoying the change of lifestyle. They'd emptied their house and packed up the old land cruiser after Shelley had finished at the school, and driven out of Pantura along the dusty red road for the last time. Shelley had few regrets. She'd given it her best shot and it simply hadn't worked.

They'd arrived in Broome one hot sultry afternoon and booked into an old van at the town beach caravan park. Shelley had kicked back and started to unwind over the next few days, relishing the freedom and diversity and laid back lifestyle. She'd forgotten how much they had enjoyed the place for a brief time when they'd first flown up here. It seemed like so long ago, but now that they were back time just drifted along for them. Each day they awoke refreshed.

It was market day, and Shelley wandered round amongst the stalls happily. She breathed in the heady aromas of tropical flowers and timbers and incense. There was so much to see and so many stalls to scan, and Shelley smiled at her partner as they roamed amongst the tourists and locals scattered around them. The place was buzzing, and Shelley felt truly alive for the first time since leaving the remote community out west.

Ah, just look at all these things we could buy and just breathe in the smells of the place and just look at all these interesting people wandering around, doesn't it make you feel great to be alive?

"Hey, Donna, do you think this tie-dye wrap suits me?" Shelley called out above the din of the crowd at the colourful stall. "Should I buy it?"

She held the multi-coloured garment in front of her and twirled round to show her partner, laughing like a kid there under the large palm leaves. Her face was glowing and happy. The memories of Pantura were fading already, and the battles she'd faced there each day were sliding away into oblivion. She was a different person already.

"Yeah, it looks good on you. Why don't you buy it? You could use it round the beach anyway, Shell," Donna replied with a smile. It was good to see Shelley happy and smiling and laughing once more after the rough time she'd had at the school. Yeah, she'd had it tough alright, and that bastard principal hadn't helped one bit, just expected her to get on with things regardless of the incredible problems the students and staff faced. Bloody old fart, he made sure that *he* never had to actually teach the kids, didn't he?

Shelley paid for the bright wrap and tossed it in her woven bag, then grabbed Donna and dragged her over to the Astrology stall to get their fortunes read. It was an interest that she'd half-pursued over the years, and Shelley was constantly fascinated by the predictions of the daily stars. It was just a bit of fun really, but she always read aloud her stars in the paper and laughed at their daily forecasts. She didn't take it too seriously, but enjoyed it nonetheless.

"Come on, Donna, let's go and get our tarot cards done, what do you think?" she asked her partner excitedly. "Wanna give it a go?"

They pushed their way through the crowd to the astrology stall where a large woman dressed in gypsy red sat before them at a small card table, seemingly ignoring their presence.

"How much to get our cards read?" enquired Shelley, impatiently. "Do you have time to do it now?"

The old woman looked up from the table and scorched Shelley with a withering stare. She shifted her weight onto her elbows and remained silent, her eyes fixed on Shelley for the while. It was almost as though she was looking right into her soul.

Shelley felt uncomfortable. She was almost ready to give up the idea, when the woman slowly reached out and grabbed her hand. She spoke for the first time.

"You must sit down here now and I will read your cards. Tell your future. Come. This thing I will do for you," she whispered dramatically, pulling Shelley down onto a stool at the small table where she sat. "You, I will do later," she added, glancing briefly at Donna, her eyes averted now towards the cards that lay on the table spread before her. "Come, sit down here, you must be first," she added softly, beckoning back to Shelley as she patted the table in front of her. "I will tell you what lies in store for you, eh?"

Shelley sat at the small space opposite the fortune teller, wondering now if this was such a good idea after all. She had really only wanted a bit of fun, but the woman who sat hunched over the cards on the other side of the table seemed suddenly far too serious and intense for her liking.

Maybe I should just say that I've changed my mind about the reading and that it's all been a bit of a mistake, thank you very much.

"Hold out your hands like this," the gypsy woman instructed Shelley, spreading her broad hands palm upwards on the soft batik cloth. "Here, you see?" She pointed to Shelley's hands. "Lots of lines there, pathways to your soul."

Shelley was embarrassed and a bit put out by the old woman. She felt uncomfortable, as though she was somehow a fraud. She wanted to end the session right now, but something kept her here to discover more. To find out what the old woman had to say. Shelley was overcome by curiosity now, and despite her misgivings, was keen to hear more.

"What does it mean? What do the lines on my hands say about me?" she asked the woman nervously, pulling away briefly. "Is it good news or not?"

There was a pause and a long dramatic sigh from across the table, before the woman answered. Then she smiled at Shelley and spoke haltingly to her. "Yes, is good, very good. You have a long life here; I see it in your hands. And strength too. And strong love and compassion. You are a good person, and you give much of yourself to others. You will have much happiness ahead. Some sadness too, but most is gone. That is good, you know," she concluded with a toothy grin, releasing Shelley's hand now from her steely grip. "You want I should do your cards now?"

Shelley let out a long breath of relief. She felt a lot better now that the old woman had been so positive. She laughed and tuned back to Donna. "Do you want your palm read too?" she asked her, not wanting to waste any more time with the cards this morning.

"No, I must still finish with you!" the fortune teller blurted out suddenly, startling Shelley. "Is no good doing only half, must finish all for you. Sit down and I tell your cards, OK?"

Shelley sat obediently as the old woman began to shuffle through the tarot cards. She felt a bit uneasy once more, not sure whether she should go ahead with this or not. But still, the old woman had been fairly insistent, and it was just a bit of simple fun, after all. Shelley watched as the cards flicked before her, catching occasional glimpses of images and colours and symbols.

The woman glanced up at her as she laid down the first three cards on the bright material before her. She paused and frowned and tugged at her large hoop earrings that spun and glinted in the filtered sunlight. She stared at the cards then she stared at Shelley, clicking her tongue and sucking in her breath all the while.

It seemed that time had lost all meaning as Shelley sat opposite and waited for the old woman to speak. She seemed oblivious to their presence, lost in another world. Shelley sat quietly and let it all sink in, staring beyond the woman into the vibrant market scene. She felt a bit detached, as though she was about to hear something which she didn't want to hear.

Don't be so silly, you are a grown woman and you have lived half your life and achieved so much already, and how can you now be scared of something that this stranger sitting opposite is going to tell you?

"Ah, I see your pathway, is crooked for a bit, then straightens up again. You have mountains to climb to reach your final destination near the sea, where you will find lasting peace and happiness and all your dreams will be fulfilled," murmured the fortune teller as she gazed at the cards before her.

Shelley felt instant relief. She had been secretly dreading the death card, Lord knows there'd been enough of that already in her life. She sure as hell didn't need to go there again!

The old woman turned over some new cards and smiled. She looked up at Shelley. "Ah, I see a resolving of something that has been troubling you for long time. Is good. Someone special is coming back into your life, someone very dear to you. Things get smoother between you both. Life is getting better for you, yes?" she asked encouragingly.

Shelley shifted uncomfortably on the tiny stool. She knew who that was! She felt better instantly.

"Does it say anything else in the cards?" Shelley asked, wanting to finish up the session now and get back to normality. She had heard enough for now.

"You are a little bit gypsy like me I'm thinking," the old woman laughed. "You will be moving many times to make you happy. This not such a bad thing, no?"

Shelley looked across to where Donna was watching and they both laughed aloud. It was true what the old woman had said. They *had* moved a lot in the past few years. Maybe the fortune teller really did have some true insight into her life after all!

"Your turn now," she smiled at Donna, dragging her across to the table. "I've heard enough to keep me going for a long time!"

They were both getting a bit impatient now to continue shopping at the market, but Shelley knew that Donna was keen to have her fortune told too.

"You go on and I'll catch up with you soon," Donna told her. "No use both of us hanging round here."

Shelley wandered off gratefully. She'd been a bit rattled by the closeness of the fortune teller, and some of her predictions were pretty accurate. Shelley didn't want to dwell on it now, she just wanted to lighten up and enjoy the rest of the morning in town. Life was far too short to get so serious for the time being, so she dismissed what the old woman had said and got on with browsing through the wonderful range of goods on offer at the market. There would be enough time later to discuss their fortunes over coffee and lunch at their favourite café in the arcade.

Chapter Forty-Seven

Kirra had had enough. She was tired and fractious and wanted to get away from everything. It was all too much, and she resented having to be the one who cared for the others all the time. It was as though no one understood her needs, except maybe Archie. She sighed and stared vacantly at the overhead fan as it whirred and jerked to a sudden halt.

God struth that's all I need now with this heat and the mess I still have to clean up after breakfast and the beds to make and the washing to do and the dishes all piled up in the kitchen! Aaaagh!

She slumped onto the floor and covered her eyes with her arms as she lay silently on her back by the grotty sofa. It was the final straw for Kirra this morning. She was feeling bereft and abandoned and totally exhausted. She lay there on the dusty floor with her eyes shut tight and abandoned all thoughts of movement for the moment, not wanting to move even the slightest muscle. The dreams were returning and she felt the darkness closing in on her. Kirra was scared.

It's the nightmares coming back to me and the sweat-drenched bodies of the old men clamouring for me and I can smell their beer breath so close to me and I can feel the weight of their bodies pressing at me pressing at me no, no, no, no, nooo!

She let out a harsh guttural cry of protest and sat bolt upright there on the lounge room floor. Kirra stood up and ran outside. Away through the fence. Across the bush boundary. Through the scrub. Away, away, away.

And the old men chased her in her dreams as she ran.

Finally she stopped, exhausted. She slumped to the ground by an old river gum tree, clawing at the rough bark in protest.

Her body felt numb. She felt cheated out of everything that should have been hers. Her life had become a treadmill of daily chores and lost dreams. She was too young to bear this burden anymore.

Kirra decided that it was time she did something about her life. Time she got away. Time she did something for *her* for a change.

Hadn't Archie mentioned something about leaving? What was it that he said yesterday at the café? Did he really say that he was going to head over to the coast then try to work his way down south to the city? Maybe… maybe… I could go, too!

Kirra sat up now, feeling slightly better about things. A plan was starting to form in her mind. Ideas had begun to leap into her head. It was what she'd always dreamed of, after all.

And I just can't stay here anymore and waste my life with mum and the littlies and all of the problems at half way camp. There's no future for me here and I need more than this in my life, don't I deserve that much? Why shouldn't I have a chance at something better than this, too?

The sound of the slow flowing river came into her ears now, and Kirra was aware for the first time of a real future. A chance to get away. She knew that Archie was pretty keen to leave soon, and she had decided that she would go with him. She felt free for the first time in ages, and Kirra let out a whoop of joy and excitement as she danced around the large tree, waving her arms round and round with glee.

There would be plans to be made and things she would have to sort through, but Kirra was determined now to go through with it. To get away from here. To do something for herself for a change.

And you must have known, Mum, that I couldn't stay and look after you forever. You'll have to make some effort of your own now, for your sake and my sisters'. It's not always going to be up to me, Mum, you must have known that all along.

Kirra followed the river along towards the town, hoping to catch up with Archie before he finished his morning shift at the café. She wanted to talk to him and discuss her plans. Not that she had completely made up her mind to leave, she needed his support and encouragement. Kirra knew that she had been secretly coming to this realisation since Archie had broached the subject days ago, but at first she had dismissed the idea as simply too unattainable. But the more she thought about it, the more it seemed to draw her in.

Yeah, it's time I looked after myself, isn't it?

It was a way out of the mess that her life had become. Had always been, if she was honest. And could continue to be if she stayed here in this town with these people. Kirra had known for a long time that there was no future here for her with her people; it just wasn't going to happen for her. She needed more than what was on offer round here, and nothing she could do would change that for now.

She wasn't like Archie. She didn't feel the pulse of the elders or have visions of the ancestors and the dreaming. For her, life was bitter and demanding and abjectly depressing. If it hadn't been for Archie's friendship and the occasional success at school, Kirra didn't know how she would have coped lately. It had all just started to cave in on her as her world had begun to crumble.

But really it's been coming for a long time and I just kept on going for the sake of my sisters' and I kept on hoping that Beryl would come off the benders for long enough to look after herself and I kept on giving and giving till I was too scared to stop and I almost had nothing left, did I?

Kirra paused at the edge of town and ran her fingers through the thick tangled mass of her hair. She straightened her long shorts and T-shirt and scuffed at the dusty roadside with her bare toes. She contemplated how she would approach the subject of leaving with Archie, knowing that he would welcome her along anyway. Still, she didn't want him to think that she was using him in any way.

A group of older kids from the town camp wandered past and whistled at Kirra. One of them jeered at her and waved some lewd hand signs her way, while the others looked on and laughed. Kirra hated them for being so crass and so demeaning. She knew that it was always this way round here with these guys, but that didn't make it right. She resented their boldness and invasiveness and their crudeness. It was as though they just saw girls as sex targets, and Kirra loathed them for that. She wished that the pervasive attitudes and values of the townies could somehow be improved, but she knew it was hopeless. They had been this way all her short life, and she knew they would continue along the path of alcohol abuse and sniffing and unemployment and dysfuntionalism as long as they remained in the area. But *she* had a choice now, and she was damn well going to take her chance and get the hell out of the place.

Kirra had seen too many of her friends ruin their lives; too many succumb to boredom and self-abuse. And way too many end up on skid row and hide behind the bottle like Beryl. She was determined not to be one of them. No way!

I've got too much pride and too many dreams and my goals and aspirations are implanted firmly within me and I won't let go of them just yet, I won't, I won't.

She crossed the street to the café and went in, hoping that Archie was still here. Kirra needed his reassurance now that she had decided she might leave with him. She called out to him as she banged the door and went past the laminex tables at the front of the shop.

"Kirra's great ter see ya! Waddya doin' in town?" exclaimed Archie as he came through from the kitchen, wiping his hands on a grubby apron. "Do yer want some cakes, we've got some left over?"

"Nah, she's right, I jez came in ter talk ter you. C'n you get some time off soon?" replied Kirra, a bit nervous now that she was here with Archie. She was beginning to have doubts, to worry that he might reject her decision and try to talk her out of going with him. She needed to discuss the whole thing with him before she changed her mind and chickened out of her plan.

"Yeah sure, Nora's out the back here and it's pretty quiet right now anyways. She won't need me till we have ter get ready fer the lunch rush, which means I c'n have an hour off now. Hang on, I'll jez go tell her, orright?" Archie muttered all in a rush, wanting to spend some time with someone of his own age for a short while.

Archie had missed spending carefree time with Kirra in town since he'd started working at the café, and he didn't want to waste time here at work now that she had turned up unexpectedly. Besides, there was something urgent in her manner today, and he sensed that she wanted to discuss something pretty important with him.

"Hi yer, Kirra, lovie, what are you up to today then? Nice ter see yer in town. How's that mum of yours these day, is she getting any better, eh? Would yer like a milkshake while yer waitin' fer Archie, dear?" Nora asked as she came through to the shop and gave Kirra a brief motherly hug. She didn't like to press Kirra too much about her family. She knew that things weren't the best for the poor girl back at half way camp, so she tried in her own small way to help Kirra whenever she came into town. Tried to give her a bit of acknowledgement and recognition and acceptance, to make up for what she obviously missed out on at home.

Kirra was really quite fond of Nora and would miss her a lot if they left. But it wasn't enough to keep her here, and she knew that Nora would want what was best for the both of them when it came right down to it. She was nobody's fool old Nora, and both of them knew it. Still it would be hard to say goodbye when the time came, and Kirra knew that Nora would miss them both. More than she cared to admit.

"Come on then," said Archie as he burst back into the café. "Let's go, Kirra. See yer jez before lunch, Aunty."

"Bye for now then, don't you two be late, yer can have some lunch with me before we feed the customers today," Nora said, as they went out the front door. "Enjoy yerselves, now."

Archie glanced across at Kira as they walked quickly across the supermarket car park. Rubbish was strewn everywhere as usual, and the pack dogs were fighting over the remains of some takeaway hamburgers carelessly left behind. Little kids raced up and down the pavement in the heat, ignored for the most part by the adults who sat around in large groups, drinking and smoking and arguing. It was the same every weekday, worse on pension days. Archie and Kirra were immune to it all; it was as though they didn't even see what lay before them. They were toughened and hardened to this aspect of their world, and they both knew there was nothing that either of them could do to change it. It simply was.

"D'yer wanna go down the river or over to the park or up to the roadhouse fer a change, Kirra?" asked Archie. "Let's go somewhere to get out of this heat."

"Orright, let's go to the roadhouse today. At least we'll be out of the sun there and they'll have the air-con on anyways. Yeah, let's walk over there then, Arch, good idea. I wanna talk ter yer about something important, an' I don't want ter run into any of mum's cronies hangin' round here like a bad smell, that's fer sure," spluttered Kirra.

She knew that the likelihood of seeing some of the half way mob at the roadhouse wasn't likely at this time of day. It was still too early for many of them to be out of bed yet, and Kirra knew that most of them would be waking up nursing sore heads and hangovers from the night before. They'd get up mid-morning and have a smoke and put the frying pan on for the usual cooked breakfast of fatty eggs and bacon and sausages. Then they'd wander outside and see who was around and start up a card game or a drinking session or another fight with a neighbour about nothing much in particular. Yeah. She knew there wasn't much chance of them being downtown yet, it was way too early in the day for that.

Archie grabbed Kirra's hand and gave it a quick squeeze for reassurance as they neared the roadhouse at the other end of town. She seemed preoccupied with something big; something that Archie sensed involved him somehow.

What has happened to change her mood and is it something I could have helped her with? Has Beryl upset her again? Has she been having the same old nightmare and got herself all worked up?

Archie shoved open the door to the roadhouse café and led Kirra inside.

They were immediately assailed with the sounds and sights and smells of the place. Country music blared out from the small CD player balanced on the counter, while the smell of fried and fatty food seemed to cling to them instantly in the heavy atmosphere of the place.

Beside them near the door stood two shelves of tourist goods; kangaroos, koalas, keyrings, road signs, place mats, tea towels, T-shirts, caps, etc. There were maps and drink flasks and spades and buckets and jerry cans and mosquito nets and fishing gear and camping stuff set back further into the shop on shelves that ran round the walls of the dining area.

Archie and Kirra wandered across and browsed while they decided what to eat and drink. They didn't have much time, as Archie had to get back to help Nora before lunch.

"Check out some of this camping stuff, Kirra," Archie said as they scanned the shelves. "Yer sure could set yerself up for a while with all of this, couldn't yer?"

"Let's go and grab some drinks and sit over in the dining section fer a while, Archie, I want to talk ter yer about something," Kirra replied impatiently, wanting to get her plans off her chest now that they were alone this morning. She had come this far, and now she wanted to share her decision with Archie to see what he felt about it. There would be enough time later to have a browse through the camping gear and other goods that they sold here at the roadhouse.

"Alright, d'yer want a coke then and some chips? Let's share a bag, OK, Kirra?" Archie asked, not wanting to upset her at all. "You go through and get us a table, and I'll order."

Kirra wandered through to the dining area and sat at a table near the front windows. She liked to gaze out and watch the travellers arriving in their different vehicles. Some vehicles towed vans and some had boats and bikes and trailers attached. There were all sorts of people who stopped for petrol and diesel and refreshments, and Kirra liked to guess where they were from and what their real lives were like away from here and who they might be back in another world.

It helped occupy the time and provided Kirra with some excitement while she waited for Archie to join her. She smiled to herself as she pictured in her mind the imaginary spaces these people occupied: other worlds, other lives, other dreams. Places that were outside her experience so far. Lives that she could only dream of. Events that one day maybe she could touch and see and feel and *live* for herself.

"Here yer go than, Kirra, chips an' coke fer us." Archie cut into her thoughts at the table. "Now, what was it yer wanted ter talk ter me about this mornin'?"

Kirra took a deep breath then opened her mouth to speak. But before she could get a word out a car outside screeched its brakes as it pulled in and they both heard the loud insistent bark of a horn sounding from just beyond the window.

Archie and Kirra both turned towards the noise, wondering what was going on.

Who could be making all this fuss, and why was the car so noisy? Just when I was about to tell Archie my plans about going with him when he leaves here – Bugger!

As they watched, a small boy and girl emerged from the back seat of the offending vehicle and ran across the asphalt and into the roadhouse. The two adults in the front stayed where they were, as though there was nothing unusual at all about arriving in such an unceremonious fashion. It was almost comical, and Kirra and Archie began to laugh aloud there by the window as they watched the drama unfold.

The front passenger's door opened, and a seedy-looking man half-fell out of the car, picking himself up as the door was slammed shut behind him. He spun round as the engine revved, a look of total disbelief on his face as the driver gunned the motor and sped out of the place, leaving a strong smell of burning rubber and a lingering sound of squealing tyres behind.

"Gawd sakes, would yer jez look at that!" exclaimed Archie. "Waddya reckon got up those two?"

"Dunno, but geez I reckon he's for it," Kirra giggled in response. The tension she'd been feeling this morning had now totally dissipated as she watched the latest arrival slink in through the door of the roadhouse to join the two kids. She forgot about her conversation with Archie and amused herself with speculation about these troubled travellers.

"Wonder where they've come from and what they're up to?" she said to Archie. "Geez I feel sorry fer them kids!"

"Yeah, gawd knows when the missus'll be back!" put in Archie, a smile still spread across his face. "Wouldn't like to be in that man's shoes right now, would you?"

They both gazed across to the counter where the man and the two kids were now pushing and shoving at each other to get a look at the food on offer in the diner. The kids were jostling and shoving and kicking, while the man tried his best to ignore them completely. But it was a lost cause; they were far too insistent and demanding to be overlooked for any length of time.

Archie turned back to Kirra and whispered in a low voice, "Geez them kids are rough with the ol' man, would yer jez have a look at them, eh?"

But Kirra was wondering by now about what had caused them to be suddenly all abandoned here at the roadhouse, and why the woman, presumably their mum, had driven off in such a tearing hurry and left them behind.

I think I know how she feels and maybe she'd just had enough of the kids and the ol' man and trying to keep everything going smoothly and it all just caved in on her suddenly.

Kirra averted her eyes from the scene at the counter now and tapped Archie gently on the arm. She wanted to get her plans out in the open now, and ask Archie about his trip. She wanted to know if it would be alright if she came along too. She had to know now whether she had a chance to get away from here and maybe start afresh somewhere new. Somewhere she could make something of her life.

I deserve that much... don't I?

"Archie, there's something I need ter ask you," she began, "a big favour."

Chapter Forty-Eight

Ken was half way into town when he suddenly remembered that he'd forgotten to pick up the parcels he had to post today.

Bugger, I've been doing that a lot lately.

Forgetting little things. Damn it was annoying!

He braked to a halt and spun the wheels in the loose gravel, sending up a cloud of dust that enveloped the car as it stopped. He scratched at his forehead and got out. Feeling the need to pee.

Shouldn't have had so much ter drink with me mates over at the card night.

He slapped his fly shut and stamped his boots hard against the bitumen at the edge of the road, feeling the frustration of time wasted this morning. Ken knew that it didn't really matter, he had all day, after all. But the mail left in an hour, and now he had to turn around and get back home once more to collect the missing parcels. He liked promptness despite everything, and it annoyed him that he had forgotten something so simple.

Geez, I must be getting old or something!

Ken had had lots on his mind lately, and a lot of it was to do with Archie. He'd been worried about the kid ever since his mum had died and Archie had been sent over to the other camp in his aunty's care. Ken hadn't liked the decision to move the kid in the first place, and he'd tried to help out in whatever way he could. But he felt like he hadn't really done enough, and he wished that there'd been some way he could be more involved in Archie's life.

And there's something stronger that Archie's mum used to talk about, something about me an' Archie, a bond of sorts, but I'm not sure what it is.

Archie's mum had been so secretive all these years. She'd kept her past to herself, and even though Ken had known her all his life, there was so much she'd never told to anyone, let alone him.

But something had always niggled at him... something important... something about... about... who?

Ken spat at the ground and jerked open the rusty car door, before shoving himself back in the driver's seat. He started the motor and turned his car back along the road to the camp, wanting to hurry now and get the parcels for the post. It didn't really matter if they went today, but Ken had promised himself that he'd pop in at the café and see how Archie was going. The post office was next door, so it was a convenient excuse.

Gawd, Ken, as if yer need an excuse ter check up on the young fella!

But Ken knew that Archie had his pride, and he wouldn't want to think that he was being watched over by one of the elders. No, Ken had to keep things at arm's length; he'd promised Archie's mum that's how it would be.

But sometimes I wish that things were different and that I could see more of the boy and maybe take him hunting and fishing and teach him more of the ways of our culture. Yeah, sometimes I wish that I could!

As he pulled up outside his house, Ken noticed that the place was looking pretty neglected right now, and decided that as soon as the weather cooled off a bit he'd try to fix things up. Give the old place a coat of paint. Get the garden sorted out. Do some weeding. Tidy up the rubbish. Maybe plant some veggies to supplement his diet and give him something to do other than spending his time drinking and smoking down the road every day. Yeah, maybe he'd get things sorted out around here after the rainy season.

Ken went into the house to retrieve the forgotten parcels. They were sitting on the kitchen table, exactly where he'd left them when he left for town this morning. He walked over and bundled them carefully under his arm, before returning to the car. He slammed the front door behind him, and felt the shudder of the old door as it creaked in protest on its worn rusty hinges.

One of these days, Kennie, my boy, that ol' door is gonna give up on you an' jez fall off completely if yer don' do somethin' soon ter fix it, you mark my words!

The motor was still idling as Ken eased his bulky frame into the driver's seat once more. He let the handbrake out and eased the old car into first gear before squeezing on the accelerator. The car jerked forwards then shot down the road as Ken cranked it up a notch, hurrying now to get to the post office before they cleared the mail.

Geez the ol' girl is purring this morning, almost knows her way ter town without me this car.

Ken chuckled to himself as he remembered some of the exploits he'd got up to in this old car of his. Yeah, he'd sure done heaps with this old girl, hadn't he?

An' I took Archie's mum fer a few spins in 'er too when we was both young an' carefree, remember? Cor, she sure was a looker in them days, weren't she, eh?

Ken pulled into the car park and braked to a halt outside the store. He grabbed the parcels and went into the post office, noticing that the queue was long again today, as usual on mail days. He walked impatiently to the end of the line, fidgeting with the parcels, distracted. He glanced at the others ahead of him and nodded as a sign of recognition, but he turned away from them this morning. He wasn't in a social mood, and he didn't feel like passing pleasantries this morning. Ken had other things on his mind, and they had nothing to do with these people.

Gawd we had lots of fun didn't we, eh? Me and Archie's mum. Before she met that mad cattleman from over the hills and I had ter go off drovin'.

"Watcha got for me this morning, Kennie?" a voice from directly in front interrupted his reverie. "Got some parcels there, have we?"

Ken looks up, startled out of his dreaming. "Yeah, two for the city. Sending me little nephews some birthday presents," he replied with a grin, suddenly remembering why he was here.

"That's nice," replied the post lady as she took the parcels to weigh them. "They're lucky kids to have such a caring uncle."

Yeah, I guess they are, but I wish I'd taken the time ter have kids of me own, I sure do!

Ken paid for the parcels and mumbled goodbye to the lady behind the counter as he hurried out of the post office. He looked at his watch to see whether it was too early to go on and have a cuppa at the café. He didn't want to upset Archie's routine at work, but he didn't really have much else to do in town this morning either. It was still pretty early, and he decided that it wasn't time yet for morning tea.

There were other shops he could visit, and maybe he'd look for some new fishing gear to replace the old stuff he had that was almost worn out. Yeah, that'd do, a trip up to the general store.

Ken crossed the pavement and ambled across the car park and up the gravel road that led to the store. As he approached the main door he spotted a group of town kids running along the road yelling and yahooing and tossing something away into the bushes. Ken recognised instantly that they were up to no good, but decided against chasing them himself.

Nah, leave that to the powers that be, he was getting too old for that sort of stuff now. Besides, it wasn't really his problem these days. Damn kids didn't respect their elders no more, that's for sure!

Ken watched the kids as they headed off into the scrub at the end of the track. He saw the door of the store fling open and heard the loud despairing voice of the owner holler after the kids. Curses and threats hung in the air, but it was too late. The kids had cleared out, and were likely to be well on their way to one of their hideouts by now to lay low for a while. In their eyes, it was just a bit of harmless fun, but to the shopkeeper the constant stealing was another matter. Yeah, another matter entirely!

As he pushed past the by- now simmering and disgruntled owner, Ken smiled at him sympathetically.

The man acknowledged his loss with a grunt and a shake of his weary head, feeling that at least in Ken he had an ally of sorts. He'd run this store for long enough in this god-forsaken outpost to know what to expect, but still it pissed him off when his efforts to make an honest living were constantly eroded by the local youths. Yeah, he just hated it when they stole from him and took it pretty hard. It was a personal attack, or that's how he saw it at any rate.

God damned kids, why can't they stay in school and get an education and try to earn some of their own money to buy things instead of stealing from me, eh?

He'd been up here for long enough to figure out the system and how things worked in the white world and the black world, but still he questioned the disparity between the two. Yeah, he knew it was something that he couldn't control, but that didn't make him feel any damn better about a lot of things up here. No way, it sure didn't.

Guess I can't really blame them; they're only taking things they can't afford to buy.

But still it made him angry and caused him a lot of grief. He wanted to express some of that now, and Ken was the only other person in the store, so he copped an earful whether he wanted to hear it or not.

Which I don't yer silly old fart, especially not this morning. I only came in here ter kill some time an' maybe look at yer fishin' gear fer a bit.

"Yer reckon them kids would have something better to do with their time than come in here every day causing me trouble, wouldn't yer?" he asked Ken, still irritated by the recent theft from the shop. "It's not like I haven't tried ter help them out over the years yer know, and what do I get for my troubles?" added the shop owner, still smarting from the altercation.

Ken tried to disengage himself from the conversation, but he knew it was a lost cause. "Yeah, them kids sure to know how ter push yer buttons sometimes, don't they?" he replied, turning away and heading towards the camping section of the store. He was hoping to put a bit of space between the two of them, but the man followed him as he walked.

Damn! I know the kids were up to no good, but they're good kids at heart and I've known most of them since they were little tackers. It's not their fault that things have turned out this way for them.

Ken decided that he would get out of the store and head over to the café to meet Archie. He'd heard enough rambling from the store owner for now, and he wasn't about to get drawn into further discussion this morning.

"I have ter go now," he said as he hurried towards the door, "see yer."

Gawd it's always the same with them, isn't it? Everything's about them and their world and profit and loss and material stuff and who pays. We've paid too, haven't we? But what would they know about our price?

Chapter Forty-Nine

Archie looked up from the café tables he was wiping as the door swung open. He recognised the large frame of Ken in the doorway, and a smile of welcome spread across his face.

"Hi yer, Ken, what are you doin' in town this mornin'?" Archie asked, wondering whether Ken had somehow got wind of his plans to leave.

Don't be stupid, Archie, yer haven't told anyone yet except Kirra.

He was glad to see Ken. It did him good to be with some adult male company from time to time, and besides, it was a link with his mum. He knew that they'd been friends when they were younger, and it made him aware of her afresh.

But he didn't know exactly how *close they'd been. Only Ken knew that, and even he didn't know the full story at this stage.*

"I came into town to catch the mail with some presents fer me brother's kids down south. Thought I'd call in and see if yer have any time off today, Arch," said Ken as he sat at the nearest table to where Archie was cleaning. "Thought we might get a spot of fishing in up at the waterhole if yer interested. Reckon Nora would give yer the arvo off, mate?"

Archie grinned down at Ken and answered in a nonchalant tone, "Yeah, I reckon she'd give me that OK. Things are pretty quiet here today anyways, Ken. That'd be great."

Just then Nora came through to the café and spotted Ken seated at the table. She still had some misgivings about him, but she knew that Archie was fond of him, so she encouraged their friendship whenever she could. Yeah, poor Archie, he needed that.

"How are you, Ken? What brings you to town today, a spot of shopping?" Nora asked in her cordial, polite voice, trying to remain onside with the man. "The kettle's on if you'd like a cuppa," she offered.

"Gee thanks, Nora, wouldn't mind a cuppa, I sure wouldn't," answered Ken as he accepted Nora's kind offer. He was a bit intimidated by Nora most of the time. She had a reputation round town as being a tough cookie, and people like him often came out with a tongue-lashing if they strayed onto the wrong subject in Nora's company. Still, they all knew that she had a heart of gold, and over the years she'd proved it time and time again with her generosity here in the outback. She'd gone out of her way on countless occasions to help his people find work and housing and food. Yes, she was a good stick that Nora.

"Aunty, do you think I could have the afternoon off to go fishing with Ken?" asked Archie boldly, seizing the moment now that Ken and Nora seemed comfortable with pleasantries here in the café. "It's pretty quiet today, and Ken's not in town much anymore. I'd really like some time off if that's alright," he finished in a rush, sucking in his breath and hoping that Nora would be OK with his proposal.

There was a moment's pause before Nora smiled and answered Archie. She knew that he was a good kid, and he'd worked really hard this week. It wouldn't hurt the lad to have the afternoon off, and God knows he needed some company apart from hers. He was growing up fast, and she realised that living with her and Janie wasn't exactly the stimulation that a teenager needed. But she tried her best, and she'd taken him in after things had gone downhill at the last camp, hadn't she? She'd done the best that she could under the circumstances, and tried to give him a sense of belonging once more and somewhere he could call home. Yes, she'd tried her best.

But maybe it's not enough, Nora. You tried your best so long ago with your own flesh and blood and that hadn't been enough to save the poor wee thing... had it?

Kirra had had a bad start to the day. Beryl had been up early and tried to fix breakfast for the girls in a rare show of domesticity, but things had soon gone awry. She'd lit the stove under the fry pan then gone out the back to have her first ciggie for the day. Before long she'd forgotten all about breakfast and the stove and cooking and the girls, and had wandered off into the spinifex to have a pee. Her mind was unusually sharp for this hour of the morning, but it was focused on other messages, and not the family duties back in the house.

Beryl wandered around the bush silently, her feet padding softly in circles of ever-diminishing circumference. She was chanting something under her breath. A soft moaning whisper was on her lips, but it wasn't the death-song that she echoed here in the empty landscape. It was the call of her ancestors, the old ones. It was something that she only half-recognised as she stopped and squatted by the river gum and buried her head in her hands, trying to shut out the external world and focus on her inner self.

Beryl wasn't familiar with much of her past. She'd spent too many years drowning her world with the bottle, and to have this vision now of what she might have been was nothing short of extraordinary. Or at least, that's how Beryl saw it.

There was something that she couldn't quite put her finger on. A message that she should have been familiar with but wasn't. She looked down at the red dirt beneath her and let out a long frustrated sigh. There was *something* that she should know. It was, it was… what?

I can almost hear you, Mama. I can almost feel your touch. I remember how you sang to me and crooned and told me all the dreamtime stories and cradled me and carried me and taught me all the bush tucker ways. Yes, I remember, Mama.

But it was too late for all that. It was no good. Those ways had long gone. She should have known that, shouldn't she? *Help me, Mama. Help me!*

Beryl kicked at the dirt with anger and stood up. She had a headache from the night before, and her mood was fragile now. She could feel the old shame and torment creeping back to take hold of her, and she wanted another drink desperately. She started to shake a little, and her balance was wobbly as she started the walk back to the house. Damn!

I can still see you and feel you here within me, Mama. Let me be, eh?

But it was no good. Beryl knew that she was not alone out here this morning. Somehow the spirits from the past had come back to lay claim to her, and she recognised the message by degrees.

It's got something to do with Kirra. But what?

Beryl was almost at the house when the feeling came upon her once ore. She sank to the ground and lay prone under the large branches of the gums, closing her eyes to find some sort of peace. Her breathing was laboured as she held herself together, hoping that whatever the spirits wanted with her would soon pass.

I know I should have tried harder and not got on the grog so much, Mama. I'll try and be a better mum to my own kids and I promise to you here and now that I'll give up the boozing once and for all. Mama?

"Jesus bloody hell!" she heard coming from the house. "Christ, Mum, where are you? You left the stove on and the pan's burnt and the kitchen's full of smoke! Shit, can't you do anything right fer gawd sakes!"

It's Kirra. That's who it is. I have ter get home and fix things up and start being a good mum and stop drinkin' so much. I will, Mama, I will!

Beryl scrambled up and raced back to the house. She pushed her way through the back door and was met by a thick wall of acrid smoke. She shielded her eyes and grabbed a tea towel to fend off the smell, trying to open some windows as well. At the same time she heard Kirra let out another tirade of admonishment.

"Christ, Mum, where've yer been? We could have all been killed by your stupidity yer old bag! What on earth were yer thinking of leaving the stove on and going outside? How many times have I told yer not to try cooking unless yer stay inside and keep an eye on the stove?"

I'm sorry, I'm sorry, I'm sorry!

Something in Beryl finally snapped. She knew that she'd done the wrong thing, but she wasn't going to put up with Kirra's disapproval for one more minute here in the smoky and messy kitchen. She'd had enough.

"Alright, Kirra, you've said yer bit, now leave it. I'll sort things out in here, you go and check on the littlies, OK?" Beryl said firmly, waving Kirra away and dismissing her attempts to further admonish her. She felt like her time of responsibility was back. Beryl was regaining some dignity and self-empowerment once more. Despite the present mess that surrounded her in the kitchen, the mess of her own life was ebbing away. She was beginning to feel the first seeds of strength and self-belief emerge, and she was determined not to let Kirra take that away from her.

It's alright, Mama, it's going to be alright.

Kirra was shocked and dumbfounded into silence by the change in Beryl as she stood opposite her in the smoke-filled kitchen. She had expected her to collapse in helpless tears and beg forgiveness as she usually did. She hadn't expected to see this change in her mother, and she wasn't sure what to do. But there was something in Beryl's voice now that told her she should do as she was asked, so Kirra backed out of the kitchen and ran down the hallway to the bedroom her two sisters shared.

She pushed open the door to see if they were awake. Her mind was racing with so many thoughts, but first and foremost was the welfare of her two siblings. They were both just waking, and Kirra was pleased to see that the kitchen disaster hadn't even caused them to stir.

"Hi yers, you two, do yer want me ter get yer brekkie, eh?" she asked them, relieved that they were none the wiser as to what had recently happened in the house. "There's a bit of a mess in the kitchen, so we might have cereal out on the back verandah this morning. Would yer like that?" she asked, trying to sound cheerful as the girls kicked back the covers of their beds and got up. She ruffled their hair and gave them an affectionate peck on the cheek as she led them across the hall to the bathroom. "Clean yer teeth and I'll get things ready for yers, orright?" Kirra added as she left them in the bathroom and wandered back up to the messy kitchen. She wondered what Beryl would be doing now.

Probably hitting the bottle again and getting in her first drink for the day if I know the old girl!

Kirra entered the kitchen and came to an abrupt halt. Her eyes could hardly believe what they were seeing. She gasped and slapped her hands to her mouth.

Gawd I don't believe it, mum's actually tidied the place up and put on a clean apron and she's cooking some eggs and bacon in the new pan we got last Christmas. Wonders will never cease!

Beryl turned and beamed at her daughter. It felt good to be back in control of things. She was proud to be busy once more and providing something for her kids. Beryl was a different person. She felt strong and the world seemed full of promise.

See, Mama, I told you I could do it, didn't I?

Chapter Fifty

"Yeah, that'll be fine, Archie. An afternoon fishing with Ken should do yer the world of good. Bring us back some fish and we'll cook them up here for supper. You can stay and share them with us too if yer like, Ken," Nora muttered all in one long breath. She was less than optimistic about their chances of actually catching anything down at the old waterhole, but still, you never know. And she wanted to make Ken feel welcome in Archie's life, after all. Nora knew that it would have been important to Archie's mum, so she went along with it regardless of any of her own doubts. It was not up to her, after all, to dictate whether Archie's mum had made the right choice in Ken. That had been for others to decide.

Nora greeted the idea of supper with the enthusiasm that she shared each day with those who came into her path. Her out of town customers and her regulars were all treated the same. Nora was not one to make distinctions with people. As long as they treated her fair, she would do the same to them. It didn't matter to her who they were or had been or pretended to be, she made no bones about being friendly and approachable to all on an equal footing.

Except that bastard Jim, who'd reappeared suddenly like a ghost from the past that I'd rather never see again in this life so help me, God.

She stood up to take off her apron in readiness to pour them all a cuppa. Then Nora prepared a tray back in the kitchen with mugs and milk and sugar and some of her best orange slice. She knew it was one of Archie's favourites, and she felt sure that Ken would enjoy a piece or two as well.

Nora smiled to herself as she returned to their table in the café and sat down opposite Ken and Archie. "Here you are then, boys," she said, "tuck in."

Archie and Ken helped themselves to a steaming hot mug of tea and a couple of slices of cake each.

"Gee thanks, Nora, me favourite slice," spluttered Archie with his mouth full.

"Thanks, Nora, yer a good sport," muttered Ken. "I sure hope we get a few fish this arvo. We'll try out best, won't we, Archie? Might go over to the store before we head out to the waterhole, there's a couple of bits and pieces I need, orright, Arch?"

Ken and Archie finished their tea and orange slice in silence while Nora sipped her tea contentedly. Now that she knew Archie would be in safe hands for the afternoon, she started making her own plans.

I might just close the café for a few hours before the afternoon rush and do something for myself for a change. Spend some time browsing the shops, or get my hair done, or get a video out to watch at home by myself. Yeah, just might do that! Have some time for me for once, that'd be a real treat.

"Off you go then, you two, and have a good time. I might close up for a bit and do a few things before the afternoon rush. See yer around five then?" Nora urged, wanting to get on her way now that she had decided to have some free time.

"Orright, Nora, we'll get going then. Don't do anything we wouldn't do," Ken added cheekily with a grin spread across his face. "See yer later!"

Archie and Ken left the café and headed across the car park to Ken's old car.

"Might as well drive over to the store, mate," said Ken. "Never know who we might run into round here today, they might hold us up too long."

And I don't want to get involved in another argument with that stupid bastard who runs the joint about the local kids pilfering his stuff again either, stupid mongrel.

By the time Ken and Archie had finished at the store Ken had built up a bit of a thirst, so he headed back to the liquor store to get a few stubbies to take fishing. He reckoned that it'd be alright if he and Archie had a couple of drinks while they fished, and he supposed that it'd be OK with Nora. Besides, Archie was independent enough by now to decide these things for himself.

Ken steered the old jalopy along the track towards the fishing spot gingerly, not wanting to fishtail it in the rutted ground. They drove along in silence for a bit, then Ken began humming some old tune that he'd learned way back when. He tapped the steering wheel unconsciously with his fingers as he drove, beating out the rhythm as he sang.

Archie was impressed. He hadn't remembered that Ken had such a good voice, and he wondered aloud about the songs he sang.

"Where'd yer learn all them songs, Ken?" he asked as the car lurched a bit on the rough terrain. "Yer sing mighty nice yer know."

Ken turned to him and smiled as he yanked the wheel sharply to avoid a steer that had suddenly darted out onto the road ahead. He stared straight ahead before he replied. "Dunno where I got the songs from, mate, they've been with me for years an' years. Used ter sing an' play me guitar in pubs and clubs around the traps yer know. Yeah, those were the days," he mused as he changed beat and broke into a different tune.

Archie glanced across at Ken and started to say something in reply, but his words were lost as the car accelerated up a steep incline then bumped down into the dry river bed ahead. Like most of the tracks round here, the road was unmade and pretty rough; dusty and just passable in the dry season, and boggy as hell in the wet.

Archie thought about Ken as he sang. There was so much really that he didn't know. His mum had often talked about Ken, but Archie hadn't been that interested then. Besides, the only dad he'd known briefly in his life had been a right bastard, and cleared off when Archie was just a little tacker.

But not before he'd taught me all about fear and the meaning of uselessness and getting a good belting often enough when the grog got ter him. The bastard.

"Nearly there, mate," said Ken as they rounded another bend and headed straight towards a large stand of river gums. "She's jez up here a bit, the ol' waterhole. Reckon we might just be in luck today an' catch us a barra, eh?"

Archie smiled up at Ken, remembering the time when he and Jess and Jacko had caught the big barramundi down the river. He remembered the swimming race and the feeling of brief victory over the others when he'd won. He was suddenly lost in the past as the car pulled to a halt and sent a cloud of red dust rising all round them.

"C'arn, Arch, mate, we haven't got all day," called out Ken as he clambered out of the driver's seat. "Let's get started, eh."

Archie looked up with surprise as Ken leaned in his window and tousled his hair.

What, what, what? Where am I?

He laughed back at Ken as he got out and joined him at the back of the car. They got the fishing gear and supplies out and headed down the track to the water. By now it was pretty hot, so Archie dropped the stuff he was carrying and ran the short distance to the edge of the waterhole. He let out a shrill whistle and leapt into the cool clear water, splashing and hollering with delight as he swam out to the middle.

"It's great in here, Ken, are yer comin' in fer a bit before we start fishin'?" Archie called out across the rippled surface of the river. "Come on!"

"Nah, I'll jez sit here for a bit and have a drink while you have yer swim. Don't want ter upset them fish too much now, do we?" Ken replied, smiling over at the splashing figure of Archie as he ripped the top of his first drink. It was quite hot now even in the shade of the river gums, but Ken was used to the heat. He squatted down in the warm sand and made himself a hollow to sit in, then propped himself against the trunk of a tree. He sipped at the beer slowly as he watched young Archie emerge from the river, musing about his own younger days.

Ah they'd had so much fun, hadn't they? Down the river. At the dances. Droving and fencing. Entertaining. Fighting and brawling. Courting the ladies. Getting drunk on Saturday nights. Yeah, it'd been fun, hadn't it?

Ken remembered the time he'd been with Archie's mum, and a fresh wave of sadness at her passing washed over him. He reminisced about what their lives might have been if he'd stayed around. If that other bastard she'd got with hadn't turned up and captured her heart with his cheating and lying ways. Yeah, things sure might have been different then!

And when I heard a bit late that she'd had a kid me heart fair broke in two, knowing that bastard would be treating them both bad, the mongrel. But what could I do?

"Hey, Arch, d'yer wanna beer, mate?" Ken called out. "There's plenty here if yer feel like a coldie!"

Archie swam the few strokes it took him to get to the edge slowly, savouring the coolness of the moment. He was in no hurry to start fishing, and he reckoned that a drink with Ken would be pretty good right now.

"Yeah, OK, Ken. A beer'd be jez fine," he replied as he got out of the water and shook himself half-dry. "Thanks, mate."

They sat in silence as they slowly drank the refreshing beer at the edge of the river. Time had become irrelevant, and Archie reckoned that it wouldn't really matter to Nora when they got back to town, as long as it was before dark.

Just like we used ter have ter get back when mum was still alive!

Flies buzzed around them as they leaned against the old gum and stared at the water, each lost in their own thoughts. It was Archie who finally stirred and turned to Ken.

"Reckon we should get them lines in soon, eh, Ken. We might jez get lucky and catch us a barra this arvo, waddya think?" he asked, nudging Ken as he spoke.

"Yeah, yer might just be right, Arch, a barra fer tea would be pretty good, eh? They're not that easy to catch though, mate, and there's not too many of the buggers left round these parts yer know. Still, who knows?"

They both grabbed fishing gear and cast a line into the water then resumed drinking.

Kent watched idly as the line snaked out across the water, pulled this way and that occasionally by unseen forces. His mind was elsewhere, drifting of its own accord back through the waters of his life. The beer left a dribble on his chin as he emptied the last of his stubbie and tossed the glass on the ground beside him. He kicked at the remains of an old campfire with his tough old feet, remembering all the fires he'd sat around over the years.

And he remembered the faces of some of the others who'd shared the fires with him. Some of his old mates. His working buddies. His drinking buddies. Most of them gone now, in prison or dead.

Ken sat up suddenly with a jolt as his line went taut. A buzz went through him as he yelled out to Archie. "Yeeha! Might have me something here. Waddya reckon, Arch?" Ken scrambled upright and grabbed the line with both hands, not wanting to lose whatever was on the other end of his line at this early stage. It might just be a barra!

Chapter Fifty-One

Beryl wad glad that Kirra and the girls had finished their breakfast and were now outside mucking round on the back verandah for a while. She sat back on her cheap vinyl chair at the kitchen table and crooned to herself. Beryl lit a cigarette and drew in the sharp taste that had become so familiar to her over the years, surveying the kitchen but not really taking it in. She was stuck back in her own childhood, reflecting on the stored images she held within.

She had had a happy if migratory childhood. She grew up in the remote part of the Kimberley where the bush met the homesteads, surrounded by friends and family and belonging to her mob. She had felt secure and cared for till they shut down the station and kicked her mob off the property and out of their meagre dwellings.

It was then that things had started to come unhinged, and Beryl had suffered her first sexual indignity, compliments of that bastard uncle.

Bloody mongrel he was. I was glad when the old bugger fell off his horse and broke his bloody neck a few years later. Served the mongrel right! He had no right molesting me and me cousins, shoulda kept his dirty hands to himself he should.

But by then the fabric of her world was fast unravelling, and Beryl's mum was hitting the grog fairly regularly.

And dad weren't much better after he got the sack. Just went downhill like a bag of spuds, didn't he? Lost his pride and his dignity and his self-respect. Went on benders with those no-hopers from the town mob, and weren't ever the same again. It was left to me and me brother to take care of everything after that, no more schoolin' fer us, eh! Yeah, no time for that, we had chores to do, didn't we?

335

Beryl's eyes glazed over as she recalled the day her dad had died. He'd only been in his late forties, but he'd seemed like an old and broken man; worn down by hopelessness and despair.

And the cheap grog, of course.

Her mum had tried to stay off the grog long enough to bury the old man and go through the rituals, but it hadn't lasted long. Beryl remembered so many times when she'd had to pick her mum up off the road or the floor or the verandah and cart her home with her brother's help. Yeah, she remembered all right!

Then why the hell did you end up doing the same to your own kids Beryl, answer me that!

Enough! She didn't need further admonishment. She'd had enough from Kirra over the years, and it was time to stop. Time to take stock. Time to make changes round here and get things back into perspective. Yes, Beryl realised that things would have to improve dramatically if she was to get her life back on track.

You can do it, I know yer can!

The smoke had almost burned down to a stubble between her calloused fingers, so she took a last pull on the tiny morsel that remained then crunched it into her saucer. She sipped the cold remains of her tea and surveyed the mess at the table. Beryl would not leave it for Kirra this morning, she would clean up the kitchen herself. Give Kirra a break. Let the kid just relax and enjoy the day for once. Yeah, surely that's what mothers did, didn't they?

But she couldn't remember her own mother doing it too often for her, could she? Nah she was usually too out of it with the grog to do much of anything, wasn't she?

Beryl sighed and heaved herself up from the table. She began to collect the dishes and pile them up at the sink. She sang softly to herself as she cleaned. She felt renewed.

She knew that it wasn't really much, but it was a start, and Beryl smiled to herself as she stood at the sink washing the dishes.

One step at a time, eh. You can do it, Beryl.

Through the window she could see the smaller girls playing hopscotch on the concrete as Kirra stood by counting for them. It did Beryl's heart good to watch her daughters play this morning, and she clapped her hands together at the sink quietly in acknowledgement of something precious that she couldn't quite define. It made her feel proud for the first time in so very long; proud to be alive, proud to be their mum, proud to be *doing* something finally instead of hitting the bottle this morning.

And do you think you can keep this up, dearie, do yer?

Beryl hunkered down at the sink and splashed her way through the pile of dirty dishes until they were all done. Next she spread the tea towel over them then turned to sweep the dusty and dirty floor. She had ignored the housework for such a long time, and felt guilty now about the load that she had left to her eldest daughter all this time. Beryl knew that it would take a lot of forgiveness on Kirra's part, but she hoped that at least time would perhaps help to make up for her parental omissions.

But will it mend broken hearts and shattered trust and wasted years?

It was way too early to tell, and Beryl couldn't predict how things would turn out in the household. But she knew one thing for certain; *her drinking days were over.*

Lordy Lordy, you certain of that, Beryl? How many times've you said that before?

The kitchen was finally in order when Beryl went out the back door to join her daughters.

"You kids want to come into town with me this morning? I thought we'd go to the store and maybe get you some new clothes. Would you like that? We could have lunch at the café too if yer want, jez fer a treat," Beryl told the stunned trio. "Waddya say?"

The two small girls jumped about excitedly with squeals of delight. They didn't see their mum smile too often, and treats were usually saved for birthdays. But Kirra was more reserved. She'd heard it all before, and was a lot more wary than her trusting sisters.

Yeah sure, Mum, no guesses where you'll end up when we get to town, and I'll have to look after the littlies again, won't I?

Still, Beryl did look different this morning, and she *had* cooked their breakfast and stayed inside to clean up the kitchen. Perhaps the trip to town was a sign of better things to come.

Yeah right, like she's gonna change just like that? I don't think so!

"Maybe, dunno," replied Kirra half-heartedly, not sure whether to commit to the trip to town or not. Still, the offer of new clothes was tempting! "As long as I don't have to look after the girls for ya," she added, eyeballing her mother as she spoke.

"Nah, of course not, love, it's a day out fer all of us, orright?" Beryl replied casually. "I promise I'll stay away from the grog, if that's what yer worried about, Kirra."

Geez, Mum, pigs'll fly!

But her sisters weren't so questioning. A trip to town to go shopping with their mum was a pretty rare event. "Mum, Mum, Mum!" they shouted enthusiastically. "Can we buy some toys too if we're real good, can we, can we?"

Beryl laughed aloud at their antics as they hopped up and down on the back verandah. They were so young and so innocent. It brought tears to her eyes to realise how much of their lives she had already missed out on. She was determined more than anything to make up for lost time and rebuild her world for her kids' sake. Yeah. She owed it to them, didn't she?

Kirra stomped across the verandah and went in the back door. She was still uncertain about Beryl's motives and this sudden change of heart, but her sisters were so full of enthusiasm and excitement now, that she decided to go in and help them dress for town.

Not that they have much choice when it came right down to it. Their wardrobe consisted of precious few garments anyway. There wasn't much call for too much variety up here in the Kimberley.

She found them in their bedroom jumping up and down on the beds, squealing with delight.

"Come over here, Kirra, come and help me get dressed," shouted both of them in unison. "No, me first! Me first!" they giggled.

Kirra laughed and crossed to their small wardrobe painted in flaky pink paint and covered with old peeling stickers they'd collected from food packets and footy games and school. There were horses and flowers and rainbows and butterflies and dolphins and trees in almost every imaginable colour. The girls thought they looked terrific, but to Kirra the whole thing just looked cheap and tatty.

Gawd it's depressing this room and this old furniture that used to be mine when I was at primary school before the girls moved into this room. Still looks the same, nothing's changed, has it?

"Come down from the bed both of you, and we'll decide what you want to wear into town, alright? Come on, quick. Mum wants to get going soon, and we don't want to miss out on the trip, do we?" she called out to them as she reached up to drag them off the bed, not wanting to burst their bubble of enjoyment for now. "Here you go then," Kirra added as she helped them off the bed and grabbed some clothes for the two of them. "Now, you two get dressed while I go and change, OK?"

Kirra bounced out of the room and along the hallway to her own bedroom. She went in and slammed the door behind her, hoping that Beryl would hear her and be reminded about their excursion to town. She knew that her mum often forgot stuff like that, and Kirra had to remind her what went on from time to time.

"Hey, Mum," Kirra called out across the hall as she finished dressing, "do you want me to bring the shopping trolley or not?"

"Nah, let's get a taxi home today," replied Beryl. Kirra wasn't sure if she'd heard right. A taxi! They *never* got taxis anywhere. Beryl must have lost the plot, she decided.

"Gawd, Mum, are ya sure?" Kirra asked with her jaw wide open. "Can we afford it?"

"Yeah, I've saved up a bit and me last welfare cheque jez came in, she's right lovie, don't you worry. We're gonna have a right good time in town today, jez see if we don't. Yer ready then, all of yers?" Beryl asked, pacing the hallway now in her best cotton print dress.

Gawd she's even ironed a clean dress fer once, strike me pink. Wonders will never cease! The old girl looks pretty damn smart fer once.

They all came together suddenly there in the hallway, laughing aloud and sharing a common bond as a family. It was a pretty rare event in the household, and Kirra couldn't help but be impressed momentarily by their togetherness. She looked over at Beryl and met her gaze, amazed for once to see strength and pride and resilience in her worn features.

Maybe I should stay and help her see things through this time. Perhaps I don't have to run off, after all. But I just don't know whether this will last or she'll be back on the grog and all over the place like so many times before. Dunno what to do now. Should I tell Arch I'm going with him or not?

Chapter Fifty-Two

"Hold onto him, Ken, play the thing a bit, that's right!" yelled Archie excitedly as he watched Ken's line zing across the water. He could see the fish just below the surface, and it seemed to be a decent size. "Watch 'im mate, he'll do a runner on yer if yer not careful."

Ken ignored Archie's pleas for the moment, he was too busy struggling with the heavy fish at the end of his line. Besides, he'd caught enough fish in his life to know what to do, used to fishing, was Ken.

"Look, there he is!" screamed Archie. "Hold onto 'im, Ken."

The two of them were up on their feet now, watching the drama play out on the water as the fish leaped and twisted at the end of the line. Then just as suddenly, the line went dead. Flat. Nothing.

"Bugger, I think he's gone," said Ken despondently, "He was a nice fish too."

"Nah, look! He's still there, jez playin' with yer a bit," called out Archie, running along the bank a bit to get a better view of the fish. "He's a crafty old bugger that one, Ken,"

Ken gave a gentle but firm pull on his rod, and sure enough the fish surfaced once more. He was tiring, and Ken drew him closer to the river bank, reeling him in slowly. He didn't want to lose this one. He'd bragged to Nora that they'd catch a barra for tea, and he reckoned this one would impress her no end. Yeah, Ken was mighty pleased. But he knew it wasn't over yet. These burra were mighty stubborn, so Ken watched carefully as he slowly turned his reel.

"Easy does it boy," he muttered at the fish, "come on in now, just a little bit more."

Archie ran back to be near the spot where the fish would reach the sandy edge. He wanted to be ready to help Ken grab the thing and bring it up onto the shore. Yeah, it would need the both of them to land this fish, he knew that much.

"Nearly there, Ken, here he comes," Archie shouted with glee. "Yeehah!"

With one final jerk of his rod Ken dragged the large fish onto the sand, as Archie leapt on it and grabbed it round its girth. He'd seen them flip over and slip back into the water and swim away, and he sure didn't want this one to be lost. It was a decent enough size, and both Ken and Archie felt proud of the catch.

"Will yer jez look at that, Ken? What a beauty! Yer did a great job, mate," Archie jabbered in his excitement. "I reckon Aunty Nora will be impressed!"

Ken smiled across at Archie and sat down on the sand to have a good look at the fish. He removed the hook and picked up the barra to inspect it. Then he killed it quickly with a blow to its head and washed it carefully in the river.

"Should make fine eating this one," he said to Archie. "We'll wrap it in some wet sack cloth and put it in the shade for a bit before we head back to town. Might as well have another go with your rod, Arch. See if you can do any good, eh?"

Ken leaned back against the tree once more and pulled out his smokes. He lit one up and closed his eyes as he savoured the taste of the smoke drawing down this throat. He knew that it was probably doing him some damage, but Ken reckoned it wasn't much. Besides, he'd always been a smoker, hadn't he? What was the point of trying to give up now? Yeah, what'd be the point?

"Pass us a stubbie, Arch, will yer, mate?" he called across to Archie. "You gonna have anothery, too?"

"Nah, I'm gonna fish fer a bit before we have to get back. Reckon I might just get a barra, too," Archie replied cheekily as he passed Ken a warm stubbie. "You never know yer luck!"

Ken grinned back at Archie as he flipped open the bottle of beer, watching the boy now as he cast his line out over the still water. He was growing fast, and Ken realised that he was almost a man. Ken knew that Archie had had a pretty rough start in life, and he hoped that things were getting easier now that Nora had taken him in. Still, he figured that a lot lay ahead for him, and Ken knew that Archie wouldn't stay with Nora working at the café for long. Nah, Archie had other ambitions, he knew that much. He was a talented kid when it came to music and songs.

"Hey, Archie, yer had any bites yet, mate?" Ken called across to the figure hunched down in the sand by the edge of the waterhole.

There was silence for a while before Archie replied. "Nah, nothin' much happening down here, Ken, reckon I might give it away soon and join yer in a drink."

"Orright then, Arch, I'll get one ready for ya," Ken replied, as he reached into the plastic bag he carried their things in. "Here yer go."

Archie flopped down next to Ken and the two of them sat side by side drinking beer and quietly thinking their own thoughts. There was an uncanny resemblance between them sometimes if they had only realised, but it was more to do with mannerisms than anything physical, so it had slipped by them unnoticed all this time.

Ken broke the silence first as they sat there under the large river gum.

"How's that music of yours going these days, Arch? Yer still playin' and practicing a bit, eh?"

"Yeah, I get in a bit of a session most days after tea, Ken. I've started writing songs too, and trying to set them to music. Just a few chords here and there," Archie replied hesitantly, not wanting to give too much away yet. He had only told Kirra about his song writing so far, and he hoped that Ken wouldn't laugh at his admission.

But Ken was impressed. "That's great, mate, do yer reckon you could play one for me sometime? I'd love ter hear one of yer songs, and I might be able to give you some help with the music if yer like," he said.

"Really? That'd be great, Ken," replied Archie, feeling encouraged by Ken's support. "Maybe later after tea I can show you a couple of my songs and play you a tune or two back at home."

Ken smiled knowingly and winked back at Archie. "That'd be my pleasure, Archie, it sure would, mate. I'd love ter hear yer play."

The heat of the afternoon was building now as the sun climbed higher in the sky above them. Archie finished his beer and threw the bottle lazily down at his feet. He looked across at Ken, who had fallen asleep where he sat, propped up by the old gnarled tree.

Archie smiled and stood up. He wandered down to the water and splashed in up to his knees. Ah that felt cool! The afternoon sun caught him as he dived into the water and pushed out for the far side, swimming strong and smooth. He felt free and uncluttered and connected to his environment as the cool water washed over him.

I am frog, I am fish, I am crocodile, I am bird, I am lizard, I am water spirit, I am sun.

Archie reached the middle and rolled over onto his back to float there under the clear blue sky of the Kimberley. He closed his eyes and was suffused with the world around him. He felt light and dreamy and detached.

And the images of the ancestors' were re-forming in his skull. And their feet were making the patterns once more. And their hands were skimming the water. And their voices were echoing out over the ranges and calling out to him from

somewhere way beyond his world. Archie... Archie... Aaar...
ch... ieee!

***

Nora was lying full stretch on the massage table. She was face-down with her arms hanging loosely over the edge and almost touching the floor. Her bum was covered with a towel, but apart from that she was naked. She sighed with contentment as the masseuse, who also worked at the local pub as a barmaid, rubbed and kneaded and prodded Nora's tired body. Ah, it was bliss!

Why haven't I done this before?

Nora didn't know why she had suddenly decided to have a massage today. She just *had*. Call it a sudden whim. But she was glad that she'd come in to the massage shop today. It just felt right somehow. She'd never had a massage before, and wondered now why she hadn't taken the time more often over the years to indulge herself and spoil herself a little more.

But you do know really don't you, dear? You've simply been too busy and too practical and too concerned with the day-to-day worries of running the business and looking after the house and taking care of Janie, haven't you?

She gazed at the ground beneath the table where she lay prone while her back muscles groaned under the heavy pressure of strong hands. She was being kneaded and pummelled and stretched. Her skin felt taut but her body relaxed more by the minute. Nora felt as though she could easily drift off to sleep as her worries and day- thoughts subsided on the massage table. She let go her conscious world and slid into the abyss half way between sleep and wakefulness. She felt fuzzy and warm as her senses blurred. She was almost into the darkness when something small crept into her sub-consciousness. Something that niggled at her. Tiny. Questioning.

What, what, what?

It was *someone*. A person from her past. It was… it was… who?

You know, you know who it is, don't you, Nora?

Nora's eyes shot wide open now and the floor below her came fully into focus. She could see the dust curled in balls on the scuffed green lino as she lay there trying to remain calm and still. She breathed in and out rhythmically, holding her breath from time to time to shake off the fear she felt.

Why did he come back at all?

Nora shook herself free from the masseuse's hands now and sat up straight. She swung her legs down onto the floor and hitched up the towel to cover her torso there on the couch. She faced the masseuse and apologised for interrupting the session, mumbling something about an appointment she'd suddenly remembered. She got down and crossed to the changing cubicle where she's left her clothes. Nora scurried inside and pulled the curtain across behind her, wanting to get dressed quickly now and get the whole thing finished.

What whole thing, Nora, the message or the memory? It's too late, too late, you know that don't you?

Nora fumbled with her purse and paid for the massage. She stood in the doorway for a brief moment, and then stepped back outside into the heat of the outback afternoon. She was trying to settle down and deal with that bastard Jim again.

Gawd have I taken leave of me senses?

She hurried up the street and round to the back of the café, where she let herself in to the kitchen. The fan whirred slowly above her and she plonked herself down on a stool at the bench, providing some relief from the stifling heat. Nora kicked off her scuffs and leaned her head on the cool laminex bench top. She closed her eyes and forced herself to look at things rationally. She knew that Jim had gone, Archie and Ken had seen to that, but somehow he still had a hold on her. Nora didn't like it, not one bit.

Don't be so stupid, Nora, he's gone for good. You know he won't be back again, don't you? Ken and his mates put the curse on him and kicked him outta town. Nah, he'll stay away from yer now, Nora, he will. You won't see him round these parts again!

Nora got up and put the kettle on. A nice hot cuppa would fix her up in no time. She shoved the bad thoughts from her past back into the deepest recesses of her mind, determined to leave well enough alone for now. Let the past stay there, she didn't want any part of it now. It was all long gone. Dead and buried for good.

And let it stay that way from now on, as far as I'm concerned that bastard Jim never existed at all.

But Nora knew that seeing Jim again recently had rattled her more than she cared to admit. It had brought all the unresolved anger and sadness to the surface. And it wasn't just the cruddy stuff that he'd left her as a legacy, there were good times too. And that was part of the trouble, Nora decided. She remembered those times too.

Ah he used ter be so loving when we first got together and he told me such sweet things and held me close and whispered in my ear that he'd always be mine and always take care of me and... and... I believed in him, didn't I?

The sharp whistle of the kettle interrupted Nora's dreams as she stood at the sink looking out across the fence towards the pub. She shook herself out of her reminiscing and poured herself a strong cup of tea. She sighed as she reached for a biscuit from the jar on the top shelf, and then went through to her favourite table near the door in the café. Nora sat down and gazed through the lace curtains out at the street scene. She could see that there were not many people about now, so she was pleased that she'd closed the café for a while. Still, she knew people would begin to reappear as the afternoon wore on, so she planned to open up once things were sorted out here and she was ready for the afternoon crowd. It would get her mind off things, she decided.

Yes, but will it work forever?

Nora decided that she was being too hard on herself. She needed to get out a bit more and make some new friends. She needed to stop working so hard; after all, they didn't need the money so much now. They were well-established here in town. Nora had no debts and very few overheads running the café. Maybe it was time she and Janie got away for a holiday. Took a trip or a cruise somewhere. Had some fun for once. Yeah, perhaps that was the answer!

And what about Archie? Where does he fit into all this? How would you explain it to him if you decided to go away for a while?

Nora had reached another brick wall in her life, but she wasn't sure if this one was insurmountable. In fact, the more she thought about a holiday, the more plausible it seemed. She knew that she'd have to talk to Archie about it, but somehow she figured that he'd be only too happy to stay with Ken at the town camp for a while. After all, they'd always both understood that the arrangement at her place had never been forever. She'd known all along that Archie would want to leave and branch out and be on his own at some time in the future, hadn't she? It had simply not been necessary to state it in obvious terms when she'd taken Archie in. Neither of them had discussed the future too much, it was the present that had mattered most.

Archie's a good lad and a good worker and he's done me proud, but he has bigger and better and brighter things ahead. I can't hold him here forever, and I know that soon he'll want to stretch his wings and make his own way in the world and see what lies out there for him. He needs to be with his own people and to learn more about his own world and to play his music and write his songs and be free.

Chapter Fifty-Three

Ken broke the silence of the hot afternoon as they sat by the waterhole. "Reckon we should head back ter town soon, eh, Archie," he drawled in the stillness, watching the water flow slowly past. "Want another stubbie before we go?"

Archie stared straight ahead at the water. He was feeling lazy and content and happy to stay right where he was for now. He was in no rush to get back to town. It was peaceful and relaxed out here, and besides, he was enjoying being with Ken.

"Yeah, let's have another drink before we go back to town. Nora won't mind if we're a bit late, really she won't, Ken," he replied, turning towards the bag of beer. "Besides, we might jez catch another fish yet, mate."

Ken laughed at Archie as he responded. "Not bloody likely, Arch, yer haven't even got yer rod in, mate."

They opened their bottles and sipped the warm beer, each lost in their own thoughts.

"Penny fer 'em," muttered Ken, turning his head towards where Archie sat drinking. "What's yer thinkin' about, Archie?"

Archie had been caught out. He was thinking about his music and living with Nora and leaving town soon, but he didn't want to let Ken know it yet in case he disapproved. Besides, he figured that Nora should be the first to know before Ken. It was only fair.

Gawd I hope she understands that it's not about her but about me.

"Aw, nothin' much, Ken, jez me music mainly," Archie replied quickly, hoping to steer the conversation that way. "D'yer wanna hear me play somethin' when we get back to town?"

"Yeah, that'd be terrific, Arch. Yer know Flynn was askin' about yer the other day? He came into town fer a bit, and I told him you was over workin' at the café, but he had ter get back out bush. Said ter say hi, and he'd see yer round sometime. Asked me how yer music was goin' he did," put in Ken, taking a long pull on his stubbie.

Archie blushed. He was a bit taken aback at the mention of Flynn. "Yeah, I'd heard he was in town, but I didn't see him this trip," Archie replied as he looked down at the sand, not knowing anything else to say. He felt a bit prickly and uncomfortable talking about Flynn, and he hoped that Ken would drop the subject and talk about something else. "Let's finish off these beers and head back, eh, Ken?"

"There's no rush, mate, we'll get goin' in a little while. I'm jez enjoyin' it out here fer now," Ken replied. "What's yer hurry?"

The silence consumed them once more as the time dragged by. Neither spoke for a while as they drained their stubbies and watched the flow and ebb of the river. Ken lit another smoke and closed his eyes again briefly. He was thinking about Archie's future, his music. How he could help him, maybe.

"Hey, Arch, I could come into town a bit more regular if yer like and give yer some help with yer guitar playin'. I'd enjoy that," Ken offered, looking over at Archie. "Waddya reckon, mate?"

And maybe I could teach you some more of the ways of the ancestors too.

Archie frowned and scratched at the ground. He wanted to talk to Ken about his plans. *Really* talk to him. But it was too soon. Yeah, too soon.

Maybe later at Nora's when we are all together and having tea if the time is right I can tell them both together. Yeah, maybe tonight.

Archie smiled across at Ken. He wasn't quite so nervous now that he'd reached a decision. He felt as though it would all work out just fine.

Ken and Archie drove back towards town in silence. Ken felt as though he'd missed an opportunity to have a good talk with Archie. He should have told him more about the ways of their people, their mob, their culture. He should be educating him, that's what Archie's mum would have expected. But it wasn't that simple, and he felt the time had to be right.

Archie was a good kid, but he needed his own space. His own time and place. He needed to stretch and grow at his own pace. Yeah, Ken would watch and wait. He would be there to help Archie for now with his music. That was enough.

"D'yer reckon Nora will be impressed with the barra, mate?" Ken asked Archie as they rattled their way into town across the parched paddocks of the old stock route. "Waddya think she'll say when she sees our prize catch, eh?"

Archie grinned at Ken as he thought ahead of the surprised look that would be on Nora's face when she saw the fish. He knew that she hadn't really expected them to catch anything this afternoon. She'd probably already prepared a casserole for tea, thinking they would return empty-handed. She was pretty predictable, ol' Nora. She'd been really kind and helpful. Archie thought the world of her for that.

Then why are you thinking of leaving?

But it wasn't enough to hold him here. There were other things in life besides working here in town at the café, and Archie knew that he had to pursue them. His music for one.

Yah, but is that enough of a reason to go?

Archie was lost in his thoughts as they neared the outskirts of the town. He hadn't noticed it was late afternoon by now, and the heat was still stifling.

"We'd better get this fish over to the café and into the fridge first, Arch. Don't want it ter go off in the heat, do we?" Ken interrupted Archie's daydreams. "D'yer reckon Nora will have room in the kitchen fer this whopper?" he added laughing.

"Yeah, she'll be right, Ken," Archie mumbled. "No worries."

They drove the remaining distance up the road towards the shops in silence, each wondering what the other was thinking. Ken glanced across at Archie as he turned the car into the main square outside the shops.

This is no place for you now, Archie, it's time to move on.

He shut the motor down as the car came to a halt outside the supermarket. "Jez goin' in ter get another packet of smokes. Meet yer over at the café in a tick, Archie. D'yer wanna take the barra in fer us?" Ken nodded towards the back seat where the fish still lay wrapped in the wet sacking. "I'll be over in a minute, orright?"

Archie nodded in reply and reached over into the back seat for the fish. He grabbed hold of it with both hands and got out of the car. It was then that he saw Kirra crossing the road towards the general store.

I didn't know she was coming in to town today.

Archie was about to run over and see what Kirra was up to when he remembered that Nora would be waiting for him in the café, so he slammed the car door and walked along the footpath with the fish. He'd put the thing in the fridge first, then go over to the store and see what Kirra was doing. He didn't want to make a fuss in front of Ken, and Archie knew that if Kirra was with her sisters she'd probably come over to the café for ice cream anyway.

We won't be able to spend any time together today what with Ken and Nora here and the fish to cook for tea, I'll just have to tell Kirra we'll try to meet some other time. I wonder how her mum's going? I hope she's not still giving Kirra a hard time.

Chapter Fifty-Four

Beryl watched proudly as her daughters shopped at the store. Kirra roamed the aisles of the clothing section, while the two little ones ran through the toys. They squealed with delight at the bright colours and shiny plastic gadgets that were on display. Her heart was full. Beryl was content.

I knew I could do it, I knew I could.

Kirra was trying to decide whether to ask her mum if she could buy some sandals and a top. She'd seen a nice pair of shorts as well, but she didn't think that Beryl would be able to spend too much today. Besides, her sisters would love some new toys, so Kirra decided to just go for the top. She went over to try it on.

"What do you think, Mum?" she asked as she emerged from the change room. "Do you like this colour?" Kirra was trying to get her mum involved for once, to interest her in things.

"Yeah, love, it looks good on you. Do you want to buy that one then?" Beryl replied.

They paid for the top, and then wandered over together to the toy section. Beryl bought the younger girls a Barbie doll each and some Playdough, then took them by the hand and led them towards the door.

"Come on, let's go and have some ice cream. Kirra, d'yer want to come over to the café with us?" she called to her older daughter. "We're going to have ice cream at the café."

Kirra followed them out of the store and up the dusty road that led to the main shops. She wasn't too sure about running into Archie today. It was different being in town with her family, and Kirra hoped in a way that it was Archie's afternoon off.

That's not like you, Kirra.

Just then she noticed Ken's car pull into the car park over by the supermarket. Archie got out and walked over towards the café. Kirra wasn't sure if he had seen her, so instead of continuing she turned back towards the store.

What are you doing, Kirra? Why don't you want to see Archie now?

"Hey, Kirra, yer coming with us to the café?" called out Beryl from the car park. "We'll meet yer inside."

But now Archie had gone into the café, and Kirra realised that she couldn't stall for time much longer. She knew that she normally enjoyed meeting Archie in town, but that was without her family. Today it was different, and Kirra didn't want Beryl to think that she and Archie were friends. She'd get things all wrong, and assume it was more than that. Kirra wasn't too good at pretending.

And I really wanted to talk to Archie about his plans to leave. I can't do that now with Beryl in town, can I?

Kirra felt frustrated. She kicked at the dirt as she slowly walked across to the café to join her mum and sisters. She'd just have to play it cool and stay offhand with Ken and Archie and Nora today. She didn't want them to ruin things in front of Beryl, and she didn't want to have to explain things to Beryl either.

Damn, I wish I was in town by myself as usual. Then Archie and I could go down the river for a bit and I could talk to him about things that matter.

Kirra went into to the café to join the others. She hoped that Archie would be out the back in the kitchen. She might be able to talk to him briefly out there if her mum and sisters were busy choosing their ice creams. Kirra looked up as she entered the café and heard Nora greet her warmly.

"Hi yer, Kirra, what brings you lot into town today? We haven't seen yer round much lately. Are you all in town shopping then?" Nora greeted them warmly.

"I was just telling Archie how I'd missed yer lately round here. He's out the back in the kitchen if yer want to see him, lovie. Just go through."

Don't be so friendly in front of me mum, Nora, she'll start asking all sorts of questions and I don't want to answer them today.

"This's my mum, Beryl," replied Kirra, ignoring Nora's comments about Archie for the time being. "I don't think you've met before."

"I… er, pleased ter meet ya," said Beryl, smiling shyly at Nora. "Kirra's talked a bit about you, she has."

Gawd, Mum, please don't start!

"Hope it'll all good then," laughed Nora. "She's a nice girl that Kirra. Bet yer proud of her, eh?"

Beryl was embarrassed. She shuffled from one foot to the other and looked away, not sure of what to say next.

Yeah, I'm proud of the kid but I'm ashamed of what I've put her through all this time when I've been drinkin' instead of being a good mum. Gawd help me though, I'll try me best ter make it up to Kirra, see if I don't.

But Nora was oblivious to Beryl's discomfort. She was just happy to have finally met the woman, to put a face to a name at last. She could see the resemblance between Kirra and her mum, both in their looks and their mannerisms. Beryl seemed far more coherent and sociable now than Nora would have imagined, and she guessed that the woman hadn't had a drink for at least a few days.

Well, that's a good sign, isn't it?

Nora suddenly remembered her manners and stopped musing. "Sit down, Beryl, would you like a cuppa? What about something to eat? We've got some nice scones in the kitchen, I could rustle up a few if yer like. What about the girls, would they like a milkshake and ice cream each?" she asked, quickly tying her apron on as she hurried towards the kitchen. "I'll tell Archie you're here too, Kirra."

With that, Nora disappeared behind the counter before any of them could even reply.

Kirra knew that she would soon be back with a tray full of food and drinks for them, so she sat down next to her mum and chatted to her sisters at the table. She showed them some pictures of animals in the magazines, and they laughed together as she slowly turned the pages.

Beryl was so glad to be here and to see the girls happy. It made her heart swell with pride. She had made the first step on the journey back to reclaim her life, and she felt powerful and strong.

But yer have to keep it up this time, Beryl, and stay off the grog fer good and stay away from them drunken friends and the card games and the late nights and the brawls. Yer have to keep going now and not give in to the grog again, Beryl, yer know that, don't yer? For their sake as well as yours.

Kirra had decided not to go out the back to see Archie. It would be too obvious. Her mum would start asking questions that Kirra didn't want to answer. Beryl wouldn't understand their friendship, she'd read more into it. The last thing Kirra needed right now when she had a lot at stake was to be teased by Beryl, even in jest.

But she seriously wanted to see Archie and discuss her plans with him soon.

"Hi yer, Kirra, it's great to see ya in town. What have you been up to lately?" Archie asked as he approached their table. He stopped short of any physical greeting, sensing that Kirra was trying to lay low.

Gawd this must be Beryl, Kirra's mum.

Kirra turned round with a start and glared at Archie, trying to give him a signal to keep his distance today. She hesitated before replying curtly, "Not much, you?"

Chapter Fifty-Five

It was getting late and Ken and Archie had enjoyed a fine meal of fish and some rice salad that Nora had made for tea. Janie had contributed a trifle which reminded Archie of the ones his mum used to make sometimes. They were all out on the back verandah now having coffee. Janie and Ken were smoking and the conversation was slowing. It had been a great night, one which they'd all enjoyed.

Archie?" asked Nora suddenly. "I'm sure Ken'd love ter hear you play, wouldn't you, Ken?"

"Too right, Arch, that'd be terrific. Might even play one of me old tunes too. We could all have a bit of a sing-along, waddya think?" he grinned, turning to Nora and Jane.

Archie was feeling relaxed and comfortable. He wasn't sure if he was ready to perform tonight, but decided that he might as well give it a go.

Geez, I hope they like the stuff I've written though.

He went inside and pulled his guitar from the top of the wardrobe where he kept it, then returned back through the house. On his way through the kitchen, Archie grabbed a glass of water to take with him. Singing made him thirsty, and he'd had enough beer today at the river. Nora wouldn't like it if he had any more, and besides, he wanted to stay focused on his playing.

"Here you go then," said Archie nervously. "This is a song I wrote a while ago after mum died. *Blackfella Dreamin'*."

The others all stopped talking and turned towards Archie as he began playing. He strummed a few chords, and then began the song. Softly. Haltingly at first. Voice rising and falling and filled with tears and loss. Pain in the words. Haunting melody.

Sadness and love and loss. Memories of something beautiful that had been and was no more.

Archie sang the last few words and then there was silence. Words and music hung in the trees around them, echoing still in their heads. His voice still seemed to be calling them away to another place. They felt stunned and blessed to have heard such a powerful song, their silence broken only by the night sounds as they sat and absorbed what Archie had just done.

There were tears rolling down Nora's cheeks when she finally spoke. She didn't dare to look at the others. Nora was lost in her own memories. Her own dreams. And losses.

"God, Archie, that was beautiful. I had no idea you could sing and play so well, truly I didn't," she sighed. "You have a natural talent, Arch, a fair dinkum gift."

Archie looked down at his guitar, embarrassed. He knew that things he sang sounded OK to him, but he had only played in his room or on the verandah when no one was home, so he hadn't had a chance before to entertain. He felt awkward but pleased. He wondered what Ken had thought of the song. Archie didn't have long to wait.

"That was bloody fantastic, mate," said Ken quietly as he gazed in awe at Archie. "Nora's right, you *have* got a talent, mate. Would yer play us anothery, Arch?"

They actually like my music and my songs! They do, they do!

Archie began another ballad that he'd written about the trip to his new camp after his mum's death. It was about his sadness and his fear of the unknown and his loss and the changes he was going through at the time. It was poetry put to music.

It was about anger and shame and humiliation and loneliness and feeling betrayed. It was trying to come to terms with life issues. It was about saying goodbye to friends and people from his mob and his special places and feelings and adventures. It was holding on to some things too: river, sky rocks, dirt, Mo… th… er!

There was a hushed silence out on Nora's verandah. No one spoke for a while. They were all too intent on reflection. They were absorbing the music and the words and the images created by Archie. In short, they were spellbound.

Archie began another song, one that he'd written about friendship. It was about Kirra, but he wasn't going to tell his audience that. Not tonight.

Not ever.

When he had finished he cleared his throat and put the guitar down. It was getting late and Archie was beginning to feel tired. It had been a long day, and he'd been busier than he had in a while. Despite his youth, Archie still felt the pressures and demands of others on his life. He needed some space now and some time alone with his thoughts. Still, there was one more thing he had to do tonight. He'd promised himself that he'd raise the issue of leaving here with Ken and Nora, and he knew that it was now or never.

Maybe the music will be a way out!

"That was lovely, Arch, really it was. You should chase a career in singing and playing music, mate. I might be able to help yer, I've still got a few contacts yer know," Ken said thoughtfully, trying to sound encouraging. He knew how hard it must have been for Archie to play his personal songs for them, and to his credit he'd done a great job. He had an amazing voice, and he also had the talent to harmonise and find the right chords to evoke emotion and empathy with the lyrics. The lad was a born muso, he could see that for sure.

And he sure didn't get it from that mongrel his mum had been with when the kid was born, no good lousy bastard! Must have been someone else.

Archie seized the moment to raise the topic of leaving. He hoped that Nora and Ken weren't too surprised. He wanted both of them to support his plans so that he could leave on a good note. Archie wasn't a quitter, and he desperately needed them to understand his motives for going.

Even if he didn't fully understand them himself.

"I'm glad yer liked me songs, Ken. There's something I've been meaning to talk to you and Nora about lately. I've really loved it being here in town an' all, but I reckon it's almost time I moved away and tried to learn a bit more about music. I can't do it here, there's not enough opportunities," Archie poured out, all in a rush of words. "It's not that I don't appreciate everything yer've both done for me. I do, truly. It's just that I need more than this place has to offer, d'yer understand?"

He looked across at Ken, trying to avoid Nora's gaze for as long as he could. Archie knew she'd be devastated, but there was nothing he could do about that for now.

Besides, I never said I'd stay forever, did I? We both knew that one day I'd clear out of here, and I think right from the start there was an unspoken understanding between us... wasn't there?

Still, Archie felt pretty miserable now that it was finally out in the open. He didn't want to hurt anyone, least of all Nora. She'd had faith in him and taken him in when he was at risk of losing his way. He would always be indebted to her for that, and Archie tried to assuage his guilt just a little with the thoughts that at least Nora had a sister to share her life with. It was more than he had in the family way, much more.

There's only me now and it's hard sometimes to believe that I ever had a family at all. I'm not like Kirra or Nora or Ken, they still have other brothers and sisters, but since mum died I have no one. Not close family anyways. That's why Kirra has become so special, she's like a sister to me, and I'm gonna miss her, I sure am!

Ken was speechless at first, but not totally surprised at Archie's announcement. It had sort of come out of left field, but the more Ken thought about it, the more sense it made. Archie really *did* have musical talent, and there wasn't much on offer to assist him round here.

He needed more than the occasional gig at the local watering hole with a bunch of local boozers for God's sake. No, that was no way to help the lad, was it?

Then it hit him, like a flash!

He could go and live with me cousin in Broome fer a bit. He's a muso with regular work in the industry and he'd be able ter teach him lots about music and song writing and how to get started in the entertainment world. Yeah, what an idea, eh! And maybe Nora wouldn't feel too bad if she knew that Archie had somewhere to live and some place safe to find his feet away from here.

Nora was in tears as she continued looking at Archie after he'd finished making his announcement. She knew deep down in her heart that she had no right to hold him here, but she also knew that it would tear her apart when he left. He'd become like a son to her, and she tried not to admit how much she cared about him.

Gawd, Nora, yer silly old cow, how can he be yer son when he's black and you're white? Have yer taken leave of yer senses? Besides, the only son you ever had is long gone, isn't he? Lyin' stone cold in that ol' cemetery way down south.

She wiped at her face with the edge of her apron, feeling a hot prickly heat take hold at the back of her throat. Nora didn't quite trust herself to speak yet. She knew that her words would let her down, and could never express what was in her heart. It was simply too difficult right now. She felt like she'd turned to stone.

Ken sensed how bad Nora was feeling right now, and tried to say something to ease her pain slightly. He felt sorry for her, and he knew that Archie had become very special in Nora's daily life. Still, nothing in life ever stayed still for long, and he realised that underneath it all, Nora must have known that Archie wouldn't stay here forever.

"It mightn't be so bad if we could find yer somewhere to live, Arch, I've got a cousin in Broome who's a muso, and I reckon he'd love to take yer in and show you the ropes. Waddya say, Arch, d'yer want me ter get in touch with him?" Ken asked kindly, trying to get eye contact with Nora at the same time. What do you think, Nora?" he added softly, hoping that she would get involved now in Archie's plans.

I knew that he had to go some time but it's too soon, too soon, too soon.

Archie felt as though things were suddenly proceeding without him, but he didn't like to say so. He was glad that so far Ken seemed to be taking his plans alright, but it was Nora who worried him.

Archie waited for a brief spell before addressing her. "Aunty, it won't be forever you know. I can always come back from time to time, and maybe you and Jane could come over to Broome for a holiday yourselves sometime. What do yer think, Aunty?"

I'm going anyway, but I really don't want to hurt you and I'll always care about you!

Finally Nora spoke in a hushed and gravelly voice. She knew that she had to let Archie go, and she knew that he was too talented to waste his life here in the remote outback. But still, it was hard. Nora felt defeated and alone.

I know that I've got Janie and the café and I should be truly grateful for that, but it won't be quite the same without Archie around when he goes, will it?

"I guess I'd feel better if I knew you were going with Ken's family, Archie. Waddya reckon? Would yer like to give it a try in Broome, mate? Maybe me an' Janie could come down for a spell at Christmas if yer like, what do yer think?" she spluttered.

But gawd I'll miss yer round here, Arch, I really will!

Chapter Fifty-Six

Kirra was hurrying the girls along this morning. She wanted them to finish their breakfast so she could plonk them in front of the telly and get things cleaned up around the house. Beryl was still in bed having a sleep-in after their trip to town yesterday.

And for once it's not after a night on the slops, thank God. I'm so proud of her stayin' away from the grog.

There were a few dishes still lying around the lounge room from last night, so Kirra gathered them up as she switched on the TV for her sisters. She was in a hurry this morning. She wanted to get into town to meet Archie. She'd called from the phone box down the road last night and arranged to meet him in town at the café.

"Come on you two, I'm washing up now and I need you to finish yer cereal, orright?" she bawled at the kids as she rushed around finishing the cleaning. "Hurry up fer gawd's sake!"

I need to leave soon and get into town to see Archie.

Kirra had really wanted to have a good talk to Archie yesterday, but it had been hopeless even thinking of talking about anything much in from of her mum and sisters when they'd been at the café. She'd had to play it cool and act like she didn't really know Archie at all.

Maybe Beryl had picked up on Nora's cues and figured out that it was more than that, but she sure hadn't let on. Suits me fine. No good worrying about it now.

Kirra put the last of the dishes away and hurried through to check on the girls. They were both lying on the couch covered with a thick blue blanket watching the morning kids' show. They looked so young and innocent and fresh.

Yeah, I can't leave them now, can I? Not yet.

She went into her bedroom and donned a pair of shorts and her new T-shirt. Kirra slicked her hair and glanced in the mirror.

Yer look jez fine, girl, get out of here.

Back in the lounge, she told the girls that she was going over to see some friends for a while. She checked in on Beryl, and then went quietly out the front door. The morning was clear and crisp and warming already. Kirra was nervous. She still hadn't quite decided what she would do about her plans. Should she stay or go?

I'd love to go with Archie and see what its' like in Broome and try to finish school there and get away from this dump, but then there's me mum and the littlies ter think of. What should I do?

Kirra argued in her head all the way to town. She talked herself into exhaustion. She was puzzled and troubled by conflicting emotions as she trotted the last bit of the road that led to the shops. By the time she reached the café, she'd reached a decision.

And I sure as hell hope that I don't regret it later on.

Archie was waiting for her outside the café. The shops weren't open yet, so no one was around. He greeted Kirra fondly and gave her a brotherly hug.

"Hi yer, Kirra, I'm glad yer got away orright. D'yer want to go down the river?" Archie asked as he tried to gauge Kirra's mood this morning. "Remember when we first met and we went swimming down the river that real hot day?"

"Yeah, that'd be great, Arch, let's go," replied Kirra. "I need ter talk to ya."

They linked hands and ran down towards the river. Kirra felt less apprehensive now that she was with Archie. She'd been worrying since yesterday about what to do, but now it all seemed to be falling into place. She'd decided to stay till the end of the year and make sure that Beryl stayed off the grog and got herself sorted out properly.

Maybe I can go to Broome when I've finished school at the end of the year.

They arrived at the river and flopped down on the bank by the old river gum. Archie wanted to tell Kirra about Ken's offer last night, but he let her talk first.

"What d'yer wan ter talk about, Kirra? It sounded important on the phone last night. It's not about yer mum again, is it?" he asked cautiously, hoping that things were OK at home.

"Nah, me mum's doing well. She's still off the grog, and I'm real proud of her. It's about you going away, Archie. I was gonna ask yer if I could go too, but then I did some thinking and I've decided that I really shouldn't go just yet. I need ter stay and make sure things are alright at home. And I really need ter finish this year at school. But I'm gonna miss yer, Archie, yer me best friend yer know." Kirra trailed off. She had a lump in her throat. It was difficult to look at Archie. She wanted to cry just thinking about him not being here. They'd been through so much in such a short time really, and it would be difficult not to have his support. Yes, she'd miss him alright.

I'll miss you too, Kirra, yer've been there for me too, yer me best friend.

Archie didn't know what to say. He'd thought about asking Kirra if she wanted to go with him, but at the time he hadn't been quite sure enough. Besides, he knew it would have been impossible for her to leave her two sisters. He was stuck for words.

Should I tell her about Ken's offer?

They sat in silence for a long time just gazing at the river. Flies droned around them as the water slowly ebbed past. The heat was building once more.

"Ken came over last night fer tea, and I played some of me songs for him. He really liked the music, and so did Nora," Archie splurted out, breaking the silence finally. "Ken's offered to let me stay with his cousin in Broome, Kirra. You could come down there too from time ter time for a visit, I'm sure they wouldn't mind. Ken's gonna drive me there in a couple of weeks if it's OK with his cousin, and I'm sure he'd bring you over too sometime," he added all in a rush, trying to offer some small hope to Kirra. He smiled over at her and gave her an affectionate hug. Archie didn't want to leave Kirra behind. She was a true and trusted friend to him, and he valued everything she'd done for him. But he'd been offered a golden opportunity, and it was one that he was pretty excited about. Besides, Kirra knew how much Archie's music and songs meant to him. He knew that she'd understand why he had to go.

But I hope it's not going to be too hard to say goodbye.

It seemed to Archie suddenly that his whole life had been about departures of one sort of another. Places, people; everything. Nothing seemed to stay with him for too long.

It's all since my mum died. That's when my world started changing, didn't it?

And now here he was, preparing to leave yet again.

Is it meant to be this way?

"That's great news, Archie, and it means that Nora won't mind as much about yer going if you've got some place ter stay. What'd she say when you told her your plans? I'll bet she was upset, if I know Nora. She dotes on you, Archie, treats yer like a long lost son, she does. Gawd she'll miss yer. We both will," Kirra said sadly, tears trickling out of her eyes. "When are you gowin', Arch?"

Don't cry, don't cry... there, there, there!

"Probably in a week or two, Kirra. Don't worry, we'll still have time to spend together before I go, and we'll come down to the river again too. Soon. And I promise I'll call yer every week and I'll write some songs fer ya too, would you like that, Kirra?" Archie replied as he held her hand. *Don't cry, don't cry!* It was hard for him too, and he didn't know how he would let Kirra go. But he knew they'd be friends forever.

Chapter Fifty-Seven

Nora was dealing with the demons of denial as she lay in her old rumpled bed. The sun was climbing, and she knew already that she would be late getting started today, but she made no effort to get up just yet. She lay on her back and stared straight up at the ceiling. Thoughts of last night ran round and round in her head like a race car speeding around a track. She felt flat and deflated.

Gawd, Nora, get over it. It's not as if you couldn't see it coming. You knew Archie was not here forever.

She tried to be realistic and practical and pull herself together, but this morning Nora was definitely out of sorts with the world. She sighed and stretched and felt the burden of sadness overtake her once more.

It feels like the last time when I lost me darling baby boy. What am I going to do?

Nora felt lost and abandoned. She didn't know where to start this morning. It felt as though there was nothing to get up for now, as though her world had crumbled.

Gawd, Nora, just have a look at yourself willya? Get a grip on things!

She heard Janie fussing round in the kitchen, it sounded like she was preparing breakfast out there.

That's odd, Janie never gets the breakfast. I'm the one who always does that.

There was a tentative tap at the door, and Nora could hear Janie's voice come through. "You awake in there, Nora? I've made you some breakfast and a nice hot cuppa. Do you want to come out or will I bring it through for you on a tray?"

Well I never! Being waited on by Janie for once, that's a turnaround if ever there was one!

Nora sat up and rubbed at her tired and puffy eyes. She felt ashamed of her selfish behaviour, but decided defiantly to stay in bed just for once.

"Come in, Janie," she called out through the bedroom door. "Thanks for getting the breakfast. Yeah, I'd love to have mine in bed this morning if yer don't mind. That sure would be a nice treat fer me."

She heard Jane retreat to the kitchen and shuffle a few bits and pieces around to prepare the tray. Nora lay back on the pillows and closed her eyes once more, trying to pull herself together before Jane came in. She'd always seen herself as the strong one. The reliable one. The practical one of the two.

But it doesn't have to stay that way forever, does it?

Nora looked up and smiled as Janie brought the tray in. she was glad that she had Janie in her life. It wouldn't be so hard after Archie left with Janie around. And maybe she'd take more of an interest in Kirra too, and make sure that she came into the café on a regular basis.

Perhaps I could offer her some work now that Archie's going. I'm sure that she could use the money. And maybe I could make friends with Beryl too now that she's trying so hard to be a good mum once more. It can't be easy for her, I'm sure.

Nora's mind began racing and planning even before the tray had settled on her knee. She smiled up at Janie and gave her a hug. It felt good to be looked after for a change, and she thanked Janie for her support.

She's probably going to miss Archie round here too.

Nora realised suddenly that things were going to be quite different round here now, but she felt sure that everything was going to be just fine. It was time for her to start relaxing and enjoying life a bit more, and sharing things with Janie.

Yeah, it's all going to work out between us, I feel it in me bones.

Chapter Fifty-Eight

Archie had been in Broome now for a few weeks. He loved it here. Everything seemed to be going his way. Ken's cousin Rick was great, and they got on really well together. Archie reckoned that Rick's music was awesome, and he respected him for that. In his turn, Rick believed in Archie's talent, and encouraged him to practice playing regularly and continue with his song-writing. He knew that the lad had enormous potential, and wanted to make sure that Archie reached his goal.

Archie should be ready soon to start some busking and playing occasionally for the public. We might see if we can set up at the market at the end of the month.

Archie was becoming more confident around people, and he had Rick to thank for that. And Ken, who'd introduced him to his new life. Archie would always be grateful to Ken for that.

He missed Nora and Kirra and his life back at the café, but it was so much more interesting here in Broome living with Rick. He spoke to Kirra by phone a couple of times a week and talked to Nora every Monday night when she phoned from town. He knew that they both missed him, and he missed them too, but things were working out for him here.

Archie's favourite spot so far was town beach. He'd take his guitar there some nights and sit by the water with the sun going down behind him and strum away and dream of his future. His thoughts were often interrupted by other people walking along the beach and sharing his space, but Archie had grown accustomed to that in a short time. He thrived on the difference and the opportunities this place offered him. Broome was such a world away from the small outback places where he'd spent all of his life up till now, it was like being reborn somehow, and Archie finally felt that he was where he should be. Where he mattered. Where he could truly be himself at last.

The sea was glassy smooth and opaque here on this side of the town, and he noticed how refreshed and clean and energised he always felt after swimming here. He liked it better than Table Beach where all the tourists went to spend their money and be seen. Archie felt hemmed in over there. There were too many people trying too hard to have a good time, and he hated the falseness and crassness and mindlessness of the place. No, give him town beach any day. It was far more relaxing and far less crowded most of the time.

He loved wandering through the caravan park beside the beach on his way back to Rick's place. The trees and palms and flowers always looked bright and cheerful and tropical. He loved the sights and the sounds and the smells of the place. It cheered him up and lifted his spirits. He always came here for inspiration, and his new songs reflected the bustle of other lives and the beauty of the place.

And the moods and the natural scenery. I am rock, I am sand, I am tree, I am sky.

Ken would be leaving tomorrow and heading back to his home once more.

Back to where Kirra and Nora still are. I miss them, I miss them, but...

They were going to the market in the morning before Ken left. Archie wanted to buy Ken something as a gift in appreciation of all that he had done. He loved the market with its range of colourful stalls spread under the cool trees. He loved the people and the variety and the aromas and the pleasure he got each time he strolled around the place.

Maybe one day I'll take my guitar down there and see if I can make some money busking. I'll have to talk to Rick about it and see what he thinks about the idea. I reckon I could do that now that I know a few songs.

Sometimes Archie went exploring round the back streets of Broome, just wandering where his feet took him. He found places that were just as interesting as the main shopping area.

Places where there were hidden corners of people's lives: overgrown gardens and rundown homes. Sheds full of car wrecks and motor parts and rusty ruins. He loved to clamber through the out of the way spots and comb for treasures.

And he stored them in his head as words for his songs.

At first he'd enjoyed the air-conditioned shopping centre and the arcades and the incredible variety of goods on display in the town centre. Archie had been overwhelmed when he first came to Broome by the differences to his former life. He'd been amazed by the brightness and dazzled by the shops and the cafés and the fast food outlets and neon lights and crowds and cars and buildings. To Archie, this place was heaven.

But it hadn't taken him long to feel familiar here and find out where the places of most interest were. He loved spending time at the mall, but he began to move away from the brightness of the commercial centre and out into the back streets a bit more. Archie wasn't sure what he was searching for, but he knew that it wasn't to be found in the manmade structures of Broome.

Ah, it's not the songs of the ancestors' calling you back again, it is Archie?

It was more than that. Archie knew he was still a bit restless. He knew there was so much that lay ahead, and he knew it would take time for his journey. But it was more than that, much more.

It was something about, something about... who?

There seemed to be one big obstacle that confronted him now that he was here. Archie felt it getting stronger day by day. He couldn't pinpoint what it was or why it had come to him now. He just knew there was something important that he was meant to learn, and it would come to him here. *Soon.*

It had something to do with, something to do with... who?

Perhaps it was his mother who was sitting in his subconscious and sending him messages. Archie wondered if she would have approved of him now. If she would still recognise him as her baby son. If she would be proud of the man he was fast growing into.

Is it you, Mother, is it you?

He picked up his guitar as the sun sank below the horizon and silhouetted the tops of the trees behind him. The sand was still warm under his feet as he walked slowly back along the beach. Archie was still puzzled by his inner feelings as he made his way back to Rick's place, but he put them aside for now. He wanted to enjoy his last night with Ken before he left tomorrow. Other things could wait for now.

But he knew they would not wait for long. They were pressing in on him now, weren't they? Something important in his life was a lot closer than he'd realised. Something that would open a door for him finally. What?

***

Ken and Archie were up early. It was the day Ken was leaving, and they were going to the market together. They had a cup of tea out under the palm tree in Rick's yard, and then headed off on the short walk to town. It was a beautiful clear day with a sky so bright that it almost pierced through your eyeballs. Archie decided that he'd have to buy a cheap pair of sunglasses today at the market. And he still hadn't decided what to buy for Ken, just that it had to be special and significant.

I'll know what it is when I get there. I'm sure it'll be something that seems just right when I see it.

They chatted away about this and that as they approached the market. Ken wanted to get some presents for his mates back in town, and he knew that Archie wanted to get something for him to take back for Kirra and Nora.

But there was something else that he had to find here today too. Something important. Something... what was it?

"I'll head off over this way and meet yer in half an hour or so over at the wood stall, orright?" Ken said to Archie, as he turned and headed off along the first row of stalls. "See yer soon." He figured that Archie would rather spend time alone looking for things too, but without Ken tagging along, and in truth he wanted to be by himself to get something for Archie as well.

Archie grinned and began wandering slowly among the stalls. He had to get something for Kirra first, so he stopped at a stall where they sold bright jewellery. He picked out some nice bracelets which he knew she'd like and paid for them with money he'd earned at the café. Archie knew that he'd have to find a job soon, but for now he had enough money to tide him over. Rick hadn't asked him yet for anything towards food or rent, but he knew that if he stayed for any length of time he'd want to earn his keep. He'd have a talk to Rick about it once Ken had gone. He stopped and bought a colourful scarf for Nora, and then ambled over to the stall where he was to meet Ken.

He was almost there when he noticed a fortune teller. It was the same stall that Shelley and Donna visited before they headed back on their long drive home, but Archie didn't know that. He'd long since forgotten his teacher from Pantura.

And about Rett and that lousy principal and the big fight and his smashed up guitar and the fire and running, running, running... away!

As he approached the fortune teller, a strange thing happened to Archie. The hairs on the back of his neck stood up. It was as though an invisible current jolted through his body. It felt *weird*.

This is it, this is it!

She looked up at him from her seat at the covered card table. Her eyes were strong and piercing. Archie felt like she was seeing right through him, boring holes in his skin. He felt as though he was *meant* to be here.

Is this why the ancestors have been calling to me lately?

"Come, come, sit down here. I must read your cards for you. Something important. Now. Now!" the old lady motioned Archie forwards and half-pushed him with strong hands onto the stool opposite where she sat. She looked long and hard at him, and then began shuffling the cards. The first card was flipped over in front of Archie, followed quickly by another two. The old woman scanned them before looking up at Archie with a serious expression on her face. Her brows were furrowed with concentration, then sudden understanding. "Is here! Is here!" she exclaimed suddenly, waving her arms around Archie in a wide circle. "Someone special, your father I think. Is here! You look, is here, right behind you!"

Archie was dumbfounded. His father? Here?

What does the old cow mean? No way. My dad couldn't be here! But... could he?"

Then Archie had a *feeling*. A connection. A bond with someone special.

Who could it be?

He turned round and saw who it was.

Ken! It's Ken! I knew there was something special between us, I knew all along. Dad, dad. We're finally home!